WALK IN TH
& TWENTY-TH

Walk in the Light
& Twenty-three Tales

LEO TOLSTOY

Translated from the Russian by
Louise and Aylmer Maude

THE PLOUGH PUBLISHING HOUSE

Walk in the Light While There is Light and *Twenty-Three Tales*
were translated from the Russian by Louise and Aylmer Maude.

This edition reprinted 1998 by The Plough Publishing House
of The Bruderhof Foundation, Inc., Farmington, PA 15437 USA and by Bruderhof
Communities in the UK, Robertsbridge, East Sussex TN32 5DR UK
by arrangement with Oxford University Press.

First published by Oxford University Press in 1928 and 1934.

Cover art (woodcut of Tolstoy) by Karl Mahr, 1923
for *Gemeinschafts-Verlag Eberhard Arnold,* Sannerz/Leipzig.

09 08 07 06 05 04 03 02   14 13 12 11 10 9 8 7 6

A catalog record for this book is available from the British Library.

Library of Congress Cataloging-in-Publication Data
Tolstoy, Leo, graf, 1828–1910.
       [Short stories. English. Selections]
       Walk in the light & twenty-three tales / Leo Tolstoy ; translated
from the Russian by Louise and Aylmer Maude.
       p.cm.
       ISBN 0-87486-967-6 (pbk.)
       1. Tolstoy, Leo, graf, 1828–1910--Translations into English.
2. Christian fiction, Russian--Translations into English.
I. Maude, Louise Shanks, 1855–1939. II. Maude, Aylmer, 1858–1938.
III. Title. IV. Title: Walk in the light and twenty-three tales.
PG3366.A1M3 1999
891.73'3--dc21   98-47656
                                                          CIP

Printed in the USA

Contents

WALK IN THE LIGHT
WHILE THERE IS LIGHT

A Talk among Leisured People

An Introduction to the Story that Follows

SOME GUESTS ASSEMBLED at a wealthy house one day happened to start a serious conversation about life. They spoke of people present and absent, but failed to find anyone who was satisfied with his life. Not only could no one boast of happiness, but not a single person considered that he was living as a Christian should do. All confessed that they were living worldly lives concerned only for themselves and their families, none of them thinking of their neighbors, still less of God.

So said all the guests, and all agreed in blaming themselves for living godless and unchristian lives. "Then why do we live so?" exclaimed a youth. "Why do we do what we ourselves disapprove of? Have we no power to change our way of life? We ourselves admit that we are ruined by our luxury, our effeminacy, our riches, and above all by our pride – our separation from our fellow men. To be noble and rich we have to deprive ourselves of all that gives man joy. We crowd into towns, become effeminate, ruin our health, and in spite of all our amusements we die of ennui, and of regrets that our life is not what it should be.

"Why do we live so? Why do we spoil our lives and all the good that God gives us? I don't want to live in that old way! I will abandon the studies I have begun – they would only bring me to the same tormenting life of which we are all now complaining. I will renounce my property and go to the country and live among the poor. I will work with them, will learn to labor with my hands, and if my education is of any use to the poor I will share it with them, not through institutions and books but directly by living with them in a brotherly way.

"Yes, I have made up my mind," he added, looking inquiringly at his father, who was also present.

"Your wish is a worthy one," said his father, "but thoughtless and ill-considered. It seems so easy to you only because you do not know life. There are many things that seem to us good, but the execution of what is good is complicated and difficult. It is hard enough to walk well on a beaten track, but it is harder still to lay out a new one. New paths are made only by men who are thoroughly mature and have mastered all that is attainable by man. It seems to you easy to make new paths of life only because you do not yet understand life. It is an outcome of thoughtlessness and youthful pride. We old folk are needed to moderate your impulsiveness and guide you by our experience, and you young folk should obey us in order to profit by that experience. Your active life lies before you. You are now growing up and developing. Finish your education, make yourself thoroughly conversant with things, get on to your own feet, have firm convictions of your own, and then start a new life if you feel you have strength to do so. But for the present you should obey those who are guiding you for your own good, and not try to open up new paths of life."

The youth was silent and the older guests agreed with what the father had said.

"You are right," said a middle-aged married man, turning to the youth's father. "It is true that the lad, lacking experience of life, may blunder when seeking new paths of life and his decision cannot be a firm one. But you know we all agreed that our life is contrary to our conscience and does not give us happiness. So we cannot but recognize the justice of wishing to escape from it.

"The lad may mistake his fancy for a reasonable deduction, but I, who am no longer young, tell you for myself that as I listened to the talk this evening the same thought occurred to me. It is plain to me that the life I now live cannot give me peace of mind or happiness. Experience and reason alike show me that. Then what am I waiting for? We struggle from morning to night for our families, but it turns out that we and our families live ungodly lives and get more and more sunk in sins. We work for our families, but our families are no better off, because we are not doing the right thing for them. And so I often think that it would be better if I changed my whole way of life and did just what that young man proposed to do: ceased to bother about my wife and children and began to think about my soul. Not for nothing did Paul say: 'He that is married careth how he may please his wife, but he that is unmarried careth how he may please the Lord.'"

But before he had finished speaking his wife and all the women present began to attack him.

"You ought to have thought about that before," said an elderly woman. "You have put on the yoke, so you must draw your load. Like that, everyone will say he wishes to go off and save his soul when it seems hard to him to support and feed his family. That is false and cowardly. No! A man should be able to live in godly fashion with his family. Of course it would be easy enough to save your own soul all by yourself. But to behave like that would be to run contrary to Christ's teaching. God bade us love others; but in that way you would in His name offend others. No. A married man has his definite obligations and he must not shirk them. It's different when your family are already on their own feet. But no one has a right to force his family."

But the man who had spoken did not agree. "I don't want to abandon my family," he said. "All I say is that my family should not be brought up in a worldly fashion, nor brought up to live for their own pleasure, as we have just been saying, but should be brought up from their early days to become accustomed to privation, to labor, to the service to others, and above all to live a brotherly life with all men. And for that we must relinquish our riches and distinctions."

"There is no need to upset others while you yourself do not live a godly life," exclaimed his wife irritably. "You yourself lived for your own pleasure when you were young, then why do you want to torment your children and your family? Let them grow up quietly, and later on let them do as they please without coercion from you!"

Her husband was silent, but an elderly man, who was there spoke up for him.

"Let us admit," he said, "that a married man, having accustomed his family to a certain comfort, cannot suddenly deprive them of it. It is true that when you have begun to educate your children it is better to finish it than to break up everything – especially as the children when they grow up will choose the path they consider best for themselves. I agree that for a family man it is difficult and even impossible to change his way of life without sinning. But for us old men it is what God commands. Let me say for myself: I am now living without any obligations, and to tell the truth, simply for my belly. I eat, drink, rest, and am disgusting and revolting even to myself. So it is time for me to give up such a life, to give away my property, and at least before I die to live a while as God bids a Christian live."

But the others did not agree with the old man. His niece and godchild was present, to all of whose children he had stood sponsor and gave presents on holidays. His son was also there. They both protested.

"No," said the son, "You worked in your time, and it is time for you to rest and not trouble yourself. You have lived for sixty years with certain habits and must not change them now. You would only torment yourself in vain."

"Yes, yes," confirmed his niece. "You would be in want and out of sorts, and would grumble and sin more than ever. God is merciful and will forgive all sinners – to say nothing of such a kind old uncle as you!"

"Yes, and why should you?" added another old man of the same age. "You and I have perhaps only a couple of days to live, so why should we start new ways?"

"What a strange thing!" exclaimed one of the visitors who had hitherto been silent. "What a strange thing! We all say that it would be good to live as God bids us and that we are living badly and suffer in body and soul, but as soon as it comes to practice it turns out that the children must not be upset and must be brought up not in godly fashion but in the old way. A married man must not upset his wife and children and must live not in a godly way but as of old. And there is no need for old men to begin anything: they are not accustomed to it and have only a couple of days left to live. So it seems that none of us may live rightly: we may only talk about it."

1893

WALK IN THE LIGHT
WHILE THERE IS LIGHT

A Story of Early Christian Times

IT HAPPENED in the reign of the Roman Emperor Trajan a hundred years after the birth of Christ, at a time when disciples of Christ's disciples were still living and Christians held firmly to the Teacher's law, as is told in the Acts:

> And the multitude of them that believed were of one heart and of one soul: neither said any of them that aught of the things which he possessed was his own; but they had all things in common. And with great power gave the apostles witness of the resurrection of the Lord Jesus: and great grace was upon them all. Neither was there any among them that lacked; for as many as were possessors of lands or houses sold them and brought the prices of the things that were sold, and laid them down at the apostles' feet: and distribution was made unto every man according as he had need   *—Acts iv. 32—35*

I

In those early times there lived in the province of Cilicia, in the city of Tarsus, a rich Syrian merchant, Juvenal by name, who dealt in precious stones. He was of poor and humble origin, but by industry and skill in his business had earned wealth and the respect of his fellow citizens. He had traveled much in foreign countries, and though uneducated he had come to know and understand much, and the townsfolk respected him for his ability and probity. He professed the pagan Roman faith that was held by all respectable citizens of the Roman Empire, the ritual of which had been strictly enforced since the time of the

Emperor Augustus and was still adhered to by the present Emperor Trajan. Cilicia was far from Rome, but was ruled by Roman governors, and all that was done in Rome was reflected in Cilicia, whose governors imitated their Emperor.

Juvenal remembered the stories he had heard in childhood of what Nero had done in Rome, and later on he saw how the emperors perished one after another, and being a clever man he understood that there was nothing sacred in the Roman religion but that it was all the work of human hands. But being a clearheaded man he understood that it would not be advantageous to struggle against the existing order of things, and that for his own tranquillity it was better to submit to it. The senselessness of the life all around him, and especially of what went on in Rome, where he repeatedly went on business, often however perplexed him. He had his doubts, he could not grasp it all, and he attributed this to his lack of learning.

He was married and had had four children, but three of them had died young and only one son, Julius, was left.

To him Juvenal devoted all his love and care. He particularly wished to educate his son so that the latter might not be tormented by such doubts about life as perplexed himself. When Julius had passed his fifteenth year his father entrusted him to a philosopher who had settled in their town and who received youths for their instruction. His father gave his son to this philosopher, together with his comrade Pamphilius, the son of a former slave whom Juvenal had freed.

The lads were friends, of the same age, and both handsome fellows. Both studied diligently and both were well conducted. Julius distinguished himself more in the study of the poets and in mathematics, but Pamphilius in the study of philosophy. A year before the completion of their studies, Pamphilius at school one day informed his teacher that his widowed mother was moving to the town of Daphne, and that he would have to abandon his studies.

The teacher was sorry to lose a pupil who was doing him credit, Juvenal too was sorry, but sorriest of all was Julius. But nothing would induce Pamphilius to remain, and after thanking his friends for their love and care, he took his leave.

Two years passed. Julius had finished his studies and during all that time had not once seen his friend.

One day however he met him in the street, invited him to his home, and began asking him how and where he was living. Pamphilius told him that he and his mother were still living in the same place.

"We are not living alone," said he, "but among many friends with whom we have everything in common."

"How 'in common'?" inquired Julius.

"So that none of us considers anything his own."

"Why do you do that?"

"We are Christians," said Pamphilius.

"Is it possible?" exclaimed Julius. "Why, I have heard that the Christians kill children and eat them! Is it possible that you take part in that?"

For to be a Christian in those days was the same thing as in our days to be an anarchist. As soon as a man was convicted of being a Christian he was immediately thrown into prison, and if he did not renounce his faith, was executed.

"Come and see," replied Pamphilius. "We do not do anything strange. We live simply, trying to do nothing bad."

"But how can you live if you do not consider anything your own?"

"We manage to live. If we work for our brethren they do the same for us."

"But if your brethren take your labor and do not give you theirs – how then?"

"There are none of that sort," said Pamphilius. "Such people like to live in luxury and will not come to us. Our life is simple and not luxurious."

"But there are plenty of lazy people who would be glad to be fed for nothing."

"There are such, and we receive them gladly. Lately a man of that kind came to us, a runaway slave. At first, it is true, he was lazy and led a bad life, but he soon changed his habits, and has now become a good brother."

"But suppose he had not improved?"

"There are such, too, and our Elder, Cyril, says that we should treat these as our most valued brethren, and love them even more."

"How can one love a good-for-nothing fellow?"

"One cannot help but love a man!"

"But how can you give to all whatever they ask?" queried Julius. "If my father gave to all who ask he would very soon have nothing left."

"I don't know about that," replied Pamphilius. "We have enough left for our needs, and if it happens that we have nothing to eat or to wear, we ask of others and they give to us. But that happens rarely. It only once happened to me to go to bed supperless, and then only because I was very tired and did not wish to go to ask for anything."

"I don't know how you manage," said Julius, "but my father says that if you don't save what you have, and if you give to all who ask, you will yourself die of hunger."

"We don't! Come and see. We live, and not only do not suffer want, but even have plenty to spare."

"How is that?"

"Why, this way. We all profess one and the same faith, but the strength to fulfill it differs in each of us. One has more and another less of it. One has advanced much in the true path of life, while another is only just beginning it. In front of us all stands Christ with his life, and we all try to emulate him and see our welfare in that alone. Some of us, like the Elder Cyril and his wife Pelagia, are leaders, others stand behind them, others again are still farther behind, but we are all following the same path. Those in front already approach a fulfillment of Christ's law – self renunciation and readiness to lose their life to save it. These desire nothing. They do not spare themselves, and in accord with Christ's law are ready to give the last of their possessions to those who ask. Others are feebler, they weaken and are sorry for themselves when they lack their customary clothing and food, and they do not give away everything. There are others who are still weaker – such as have only recently started on the path. These still live in the old way, keeping much for themselves, and only giving away their superfluities. And it is these hindmost people who give the largest material assistance to those in the van. Besides this, we are all of us entangled by our relationships with the pagans. One man's father is a pagan who has property and gives to his son. The son gives to those who ask, but then the father again gives to him. Another has a pagan mother who is sorry for her son and helps him. A third is the mother of pagan children, who take care of her and give her things, begging her not to give them away, and she takes what they give her out of love for them, but still gives to others. A fourth has a pagan wife and a fifth a pagan husband. So we are all entangled, and the foremost, who would gladly give away their all, are not able to do so. That is why our life does not prove too hard for those weak in the faith, and why it happens that we have much that is superfluous."

To this Julius said:

"But if that is so, then you fail to observe Christ's teaching and only pretend to do so. If you do not give up everything there is no difference between you and us. To my mind if a man is a Christian he ought to fulfill Christ's whole law – give up everything and become a pauper."

"That would be best of all," said Pamphilius. "Why do you not do it?"

"Yes, I will when I see you do it."

"We don't want to do anything for show. And I don't advise

you to come to us and renounce your present way of life for the sake of appearances. We act as we do not for appearances, but according to our faith."

"What does 'according to our faith' mean?"

"'According to our faith' means that salvation from the evils of the world, from death, is only to be found in a life according to the teaching of Christ. We are indifferent to what people may say of us. We act as we do not for men's approval, but because in this alone do we see life and welfare."

"It is impossible not to live for oneself," said Julius. "The gods themselves have implanted it in us that we love ourselves more than others and seek pleasure for ourselves. And you do the same. You yourself say that some among you have pity on themselves. They will seek pleasures for themselves more and more, and will more and more abandon your faith and behave just as we do."

"No," said Pamphilius, "our brethren are traveling another path and will not weaken but will grow ever stronger, just as a fire will never go out when more wood is laid on it. That is our faith."

"I don't understand what this faith of yours is!"

"Our faith consists in this, that we understand life as Christ has explained it to us."

"How is that?"

"Christ once told this parable. Certain men kept a vineyard and had to pay rent to its owner. That is, we men who live in the world must pay rent to God by doing His will. But these men, in accord with their worldly belief, considered that the vineyard was theirs and that they need pay no rent for it, but had only to enjoy its fruits. The owner sent a messenger to them to collect the rent, but they drove him away. Then the owner sent his son, but him they killed, thinking that after that no one would disturb them. That is the faith of the world by which all worldly people live who do not acknowledge that life is only given us that we may serve God. But Christ has taught us that this worldly belief – that it is better for man if he drives the messenger and the owner's son out of the vineyard and avoids paying the rent – is a false one, for there is no avoiding the fact that we must either pay the rent or be driven out of the garden. He has taught us that all the things we call pleasures – eating, drinking, and merrymaking – cannot be pleasures if we devote our lives to them, but are pleasures only when we are seeking something else – to live a life in conformity with the will of God. Only then do these pleasures follow as a natural reward of the fulfillment of His will. To wish to take the pleasures without the labor of fulfilling God's will – to tear the pleasures away from duty – is the same as to tear up a flower and replant it without its roots. We believe this, and so we cannot follow error when we see the truth. Our faith is that the good of life is not in its pleasures but in the fulfillment of God's will, without any thought of present or future pleasures. And the longer we live the more we see that the pleasures and the good come in the wake of a fulfillment of God's will, as a wheel follows the shafts. Our Teacher said: 'Come unto me, all ye that labor and are heavy laden, and I will give you rest. Take my yoke upon you, and learn of me, for I am meek and lowly in heart, and ye shall find rest unto your souls. For my yoke is easy and my burden is light.'"

So spoke Pamphilius. Julius listened and his heart was touched, but what Pamphilius had said was not clear to him. At first it seemed to him that Pamphilius was deceiving him; but then he looked into his friend's kindly eyes and remembered his goodness, and it seemed to him that Pamphilius was deceiving himself.

Pamphilius invited Julius to come to see their way of life and, if it pleased him, to remain to live with them.

And Julius promised, but he did not go to see Pamphilius, and being absorbed by his own affairs he forgot about him.

II

Julius's father was wealthy, and as he loved his only son and was proud of him, he did not grudge him money. Julius lived the usual life of a rich young man, in idleness, luxury, and dissipated amusements, which have always been and still remain the same: wine, gambling, and loose women.

But the pleasures to which Julius abandoned himself demanded more and more money, and he began to find that he had not enough. On one occasion he asked his father for more than he usually gave him. His father gave what he asked, but reproved his son. Julius, feeling himself to blame, but unwilling to admit it, became angry and was rude to his father, as those who know they are to blame and do not wish to acknowledge it, always do.

The money Julius got from his father was very soon all spent. And just at that time it happened that he and a drunken companion became involved in a brawl and killed a man. The city prefect heard of this and would have had him arrested, but his father intervened and obtained his pardon. Julius now needed still more money for dissipation, and this time he borrowed it from a companion, promising to repay it. Moreover his mistress demanded a present: she had taken a fancy to a pearl necklace, and Julius knew that if he did not gratify her wish she would abandon him and attach herself to a rich man who had long been trying to entice her away.

Julius went to his mother and told her that he must have some money, and that he would kill himself if he could not get what he needed. He placed the blame for his being in such a position not on himself but on his father. He said: "My father accustomed me to a life of luxury and then began to grudge me money. Had he given me at first and without reproaches what he gave me later, I should have arranged my life properly and should not have been in such difficulties, but as he never gave me enough I had to go to the moneylenders and they squeezed everything out of me, and I had nothing left on which to live the life natural to me as a rich young man, and was made to feel ashamed among my companions. But my father does not wish to understand anything of all this. He forgets that he was young once himself. He has brought me to this state, and now if he will not give me what I ask I shall kill myself."

The mother, who spoilt her son, went to his father, and Juvenal called his son and began to upbraid both him and his mother. Julius answered his father rudely and Juvenal struck him. Julius seized his father's arm, at which Juvenal shouted to his slaves and bade them bind his son and lock him up.

Julius was left alone, and he cursed his father and his own life.

It seemed to him that the only way of escape from his present position was either by his own or his father's death.

Julius's mother suffered even more than he did. She did not try to understand who was to blame for all this. She only pitied her adored son. She went again to her husband to implore him to forgive the youth, but he would not listen to her, and reproached her for having spoilt their son. She in turn reproached him, and it ended by Juvenal beating his wife. Disregarding this, however, she went to her son and persuaded him to beg his father's pardon and yield to his wishes, in return for which she promised to take the money he needed from her husband by stealth, and give it him. Julius agreed, and then his mother again went to Juvenal and urged him to forgive his son. Juvenal scolded his wife and son for a long time, but at last decided that he would forgive Julius, on condition that he should abandon his dissolute life and marry the daughter of a rich merchant – a match Juvenal was very anxious to arrange.

"He will get money from me and also have his wife's dowry," said Juvenal, "and then let him settle down to a decent life. If he promises to obey my wishes, I will forgive him; but I will not give him anything at present, and the first time he transgresses I will hand him over to the prefect."

Julius submitted to his father's conditions and was released. He promised to marry and to abandon his bad life, but he had no intention of doing so.

Life at home now became a hell for him. His father did not speak to him and quarreled with his mother on his account, and his mother wept.

One day she called him into her apartments and secretly handed him a precious stone which she had taken from her husband's room.

"Go and sell it," she said, "not here but in another town, and then do what you have to do. I shall be able to conceal its loss for the present, and if it is discovered I will lay the blame on one of the slaves."

Julius's heart was pierced by his mother's words. He was horrified at what she had done, and without taking the precious stone he left the house.

He did not himself know where he was going or with what aim. He walked on and on out of the town, feeling that he needed to be alone, and thinking over all that had happened to him and that awaited him. Going farther and farther away at last he reached the sacred grove of the goddess Diana. Coming to a secluded spot he began to think, and the first thought that occurred to him was to seek the goddess's aid. But he no longer believed in the gods, and knew that he could not expect aid from them. And if not from them, then from whom?

To think out his position for himself seemed to him too strange. All was darkness and confusion in his soul. But there was nothing else to be done. He had to listen to his conscience, and began to consider his life and his actions in the light of it. And both appeared to him bad, and above all stupid. Why had he tormented himself like this? Why had he ruined his young life in such a way? It had brought him little happiness and much sorrow and unhappiness. But chiefly he felt himself alone. Formerly he had had a mother whom he loved, a father, and friends. Now there was no one. Nobody loved him! He was a burden to them all. He had been a cause of suffering to all who knew him. For his mother he was the cause of discord with his father. For his father he was the dissipater of the wealth collected by a lifetime of labor. For his friends he was a dangerous and disagreeable rival. They must all desire his death.

Passing his life in review he remembered Pamphilius and his last meeting with him, and how Pamphilius had invited him to go there, to the Christians. And it occurred to him not to return home, but to go straight to the Christians and remain with them.

But could his position be so desperate, he wondered. Again he recalled all that had happened to him, and again he was horrified at the idea that nobody loved him and that he loved no one. His mother, father, and friends did not care for him and must wish for his death. But did he himself love anyone? His friends? He felt that he loved none of them: they were all his rivals and would be pitiless to him now that he was in distress. His father? He was seized with horror when he put himself that question. He looked into his heart and found that not only did he not love his father, he even hated him for the restraint and insult he had put upon him. He hated him, and more than that he saw clearly that his father's death was necessary for his own happiness.

"Yes," he said to himself. "If I knew that no one would see it or ever know of it, what should I do if I could immediately, at one stroke, deprive him of life and free myself?"

And he answered his own question: "I should kill him!" And he was horrified at that reply.

"My mother? I am sorry for her but I do not love her: it is all the same to me what becomes of her. All I need is her help... I am a beast, and a wretched, hunted one at that. I only differ from a beast in that I can by my own will quit this false and evil life. I can do what a beast cannot do – I can kill myself. I hate my father. There is no one I love...neither my mother nor my friends...unless, perhaps, Pamphilius alone?"

And he again thought of him. He recalled their last meeting, their conversation, and Pamphilius's words that, according to their teaching, Christ had said: "Come unto me all ye that labor and are heavy laden, and I will give you rest." Could that be true?

He went on thinking, and remembering Pamphilius's gentle, fearless, and happy face, he wished to believe what Pamphilius had said.

"What indeed am I?" he said to himself. "Who am I? A man seeking happiness. I sought it in my lusts and did not find it. And all who live as I did fail to find it. They are all evil and suffer. But there is a man who is always full of joy because he demands nothing. He says that there are many like him and that all men will be such if they follow their Master's teaching. What if this be true? True or not it attracts me and I will go there."

So said Julius to himself, and he left the grove, having decided not to return home but to go to the village where the Christians lived.

III

Julius went along briskly and joyously, and the farther he went the more vividly did he imagine to himself the life of the Christians, recalling all that Pamphilius had said, and the happier he felt. The sun was already declining towards evening and he wished to rest, when he came upon a man seated by the roadside having a meal. He was a man of middle age with an intelligent face, and was sitting there eating olives and a flat cake. On seeing Julius he smiled and said:

"Greeting to you, young man! The way is still long. Sit down and rest."

Julius thanked him and sat down.

"Where are you going?" asked the stranger.

"To the Christians," said Julius, and by degrees he recounted to the unknown his whole life and his decision.

The stranger listened attentively and asked about some details without himself expressing an opinion, but when Julius had ended he packed the remaining food in his wallet, adjusted his dress, and said:

"Young man, do not pursue your intention. You would be making a mistake. I know life; you do not. I know the Christians; you do not. Listen! I will review your life and your thoughts, and when you have heard them from me, you will take what decision seems to you wisest. You are young, rich, handsome, strong, and the passions boil in your veins. You wish to find a quiet refuge where they will not agitate you and you would not suffer from their consequences. And you think that you can find such a shelter among the Christians.

"There is no such refuge, dear young man, because what troubles you does not dwell in Cilicia or in Rome but in yourself. In the quiet solitude of a village the same passions will torment you, only a hundred times more strongly. The deception of the Christians, or their delusion – for I do not wish to judge them – consists in not wishing to recognize human nature. Only an old man who has outlived all his passions could fully carry out their teaching. But a man in the vigor of life, or a youth like you who has not yet tested life and tried himself, cannot submit to their law, because it is based not on human nature but on idle speculations. If you go to them you will suffer from what makes you suffer now, only to a much greater extent. Now your passions lead you into wrong paths, but having once mistaken your road you can correct it. Now at any rate you have the satisfaction of desires fulfilled – that is life. But among the Christians, forcibly restraining your passions, you will err yet more and in a similar way, and besides that suffering you will have the incessant suffering of unsatisfied desires. Release the water from a dam and it will irrigate the earth and the meadows and supply drink for the animals, but confine it and it will burst its banks and flow away as mud. So it is with the passions. The teaching of the Christians (besides the belief in another life with which they console themselves and of which I will not speak) – their practical teaching is this: They do not approve of violence, do not recognize wars, or tribunals, or property, or the sciences and arts, or anything that makes life easy and pleasant.

"That might be well enough if all men were such as they describe their Teacher as having been. But that is not and cannot be so. Men are evil and subject to passions. That play of passions and the conflicts caused by them are what keep men in the social condition in which they live. The barbarians know no restraint, and for the satisfaction of his desires one such man would destroy the whole world if all men submitted as these Christians do. If the gods implanted in men the sentiments of anger, revenge, and even of vindictiveness against the wicked, they did so because these sentiments are necessary for human life. The Christians teach that these feelings are bad, and that without them men would be happy, and there would be no murders, executions, and wars. That is true, but it is like supposing that people would be happy if they did not eat food. There would then indeed be no greed or hunger, or any of the calamities that result from them. But that supposition would not change human nature. And if some two or three dozen people believed in it, and did actually refrain from food and die of hunger, it would still not alter human nature. The same is true of man's other passions: indignation, anger, revenge, even the love of women, of luxury, or of the pomp and grandeur characteristic of the gods and therefore unalterable characteristics of man too. Abolish man's nutrition and man will be destroyed. And similarly abolish the passions natural to man and mankind will be unable to exist. It is the same with ownership, which the Christians are supposed to reject. Look around you: every vineyard, every enclosure, every house, every ass, has been produced by man under conditions of ownership. Abandon the rights of property and not one vineyard will be tilled or one animal raised and tended. The Christians say that they have no property, but they enjoy the fruits of it. They say that they have all things in common and that everything is brought together into a common pool. But what they bring together they have received from people who owned property. They merely deceive others, or at best deceive themselves. You say that they themselves work to support themselves, but what they get by work would not support them if they did not avail themselves of what men who recognize ownership have produced. Even if they could support themselves it would be a bare subsistence, and there would be no place among them for the sciences or arts. They do not even recognize the use of our sciences and arts. Nor can it be otherwise. Their whole teaching tends to reduce them to a primitive condition of savagery – to an animal existence.

"They cannot serve humanity by our arts and sciences, and being ignorant of them they condemn them. Nor can they serve humanity in any of the ways which constitute man's peculiar prerogative and ally him to the gods. They have neither temples nor statues nor theaters nor museums. They say they do not need these things. The easiest way to avoid being ashamed of one's degradation is to scorn what is lofty, and that is what they do. They are atheists. They do not acknowledge the gods or their participation in human affairs. They believe only in the Father of their Teacher, whom they also call their Father, and the Teacher himself, who they think has revealed to them all the mysteries of life. Their teaching is a pitiful fraud! Consider just this. Our religion says: The world depends on the gods, the gods protect men, and in order to live well men must respect the gods, and must themselves search and think. In this way our life is guided on the one hand by the will of the gods, and on the other by the collective wisdom of mankind. We live, think, search, and thus advance towards the truth.

"But these Christians have neither the gods, nor their own will, nor the wisdom of humanity. They have only a blind faith in their crucified Teacher and in all that he said to them. Now consider which is the more trustworthy guide – the will of the gods and the free activity of collective human wisdom, or the compulsory, blind belief in the words of one man?"

Julius was struck by what the stranger said and particularly by his last words. Not only was his intention of going to the Christians shaken, but it now appeared to him strange that, under the influence of his misfortunes, he could ever have decided on such an insanity. But the question still remained of what he was to do now, and what exit to find from the difficult circumstances in which he was placed, and so, having explained his position, he asked the stranger's advice.

"It was just of that matter I now wished to speak to you," replied the stranger. "What are you to do? Your path – in as far as human wisdom is accessible to me – is clear. All your misfortunes have resulted from the passions natural to mankind. Passion has seduced you and led you so far that you have suffered. Such are the ordinary lessons of life. We should avail ourselves of them. You have learned much and know what is bitter and what is sweet, you cannot now repeat those mistakes. Profit by your experience. What distresses you most is your enmity towards your father. That enmity is due to your position. Choose another and it will cease, or at least will not manifest itself so painfully. All your misfortunes are the result of the irregularity of your situation. You gave yourself up to youthful pleasures: that was natural and therefore good. But it was good only as long as it corresponded to your age. That time passed, but though you had grown to manhood you still devoted yourself to the frivolities of youth, and this was bad. You have reached an age when you should recognize that you are a man, a citizen, and should serve the State and work on its behalf. Your father wishes you to marry. His advice is wise. You have outlived one phase of life – your youth – and have reached another. All your troubles are indications of a period of transition. Recognize that youth has passed, boldly throw aside all that was natural to it but not natural for a man, and enter upon a new path. Marry, give up the amusements of youth, apply yourself to commerce, public affairs, the sciences and arts, and you will not only be reconciled to your father and friends, but will yourself find peace and happiness. You have reached manhood, and should marry and be a husband. So my chief advice is: accede to your father's wish and marry. If you are attracted by the seclusion you thought to find among the Christians, if you are inclined to philosophy and not towards an active life, you can with advantage devote yourself to it only after you have experienced the real meaning of life. But you will know that only as an independent citizen and the head of a family. If afterwards you still feel drawn to solitude, yield to that feeling. It will then be a true desire and not a mere flash of vexation such as it is now. Then go!"

These last words persuaded Julius more than anything else. He thanked the stranger and returned home.

His mother welcomed him with joy. His father too, on hearing of his intention to submit to his will and marry the girl he had chosen for him, was reconciled to his son.

IV

Three months later the marriage of Julius with the beautiful Eulampia was celebrated. The young couple lived in a separate house belonging to Julius, and he took over a branch of his father's business which was transferred to him. He had now changed his way of life entirely.

One day he went on business to a neighboring town, and there, while sitting in a shop, he saw Pamphilius passing by with a girl whom Julius did not know. They both carried heavy baskets of grapes which they were selling. On seeing his friend, Julius went out to him and asked him into the shop to have a talk.

The girl, seeing that Pamphilius wished to go with his friend but hesitated to leave her alone, hastened to assure him that she did not need his help, but would sit down with the grapes and wait for customers. Pamphilius thanked her, and he and Julius went into the shop.

Julius asked the shopkeeper, whom he knew, to let him take his friend into a private room at the back of the shop, and having received permission they went there.

The two friends questioned each other about their lives. Pamphilius was still living as before in the Christian community and had not married, and he assured his friend that his life had been growing happier and happier each year, each day, and each hour.

Julius told his friend what had happened to himself, and how he had actually been on his way to join the Christians when an encounter with a stranger cleared up for him the mistakes of the Christians and showed him what he ought to do, and how he had followed that advice and had married.

"Well, and are you happy now?" inquired Pamphilius. "Have you found in marriage what the stranger promised you?"

"Happy?" said Julius. "What is happiness? If you mean the complete satisfaction of my desires, then of course I am not happy. I am at present managing my business successfully, people begin to respect me, and in both these things I find some satisfaction. Though I see many men richer and more highly regarded than myself, I foresee the possibility of equaling or even surpassing them. That side of my life is full, but marriage, I will say frankly, does not satisfy me. More than that, I feel that it is just my marriage – which should have given me happiness – that has failed. The joy I at first experienced gradually diminished and at last vanished, and instead of happiness came sorrow. My wife is beautiful, clever, well-educated, and kind. At first I was perfectly happy. But now – not having a wife you will not have experienced this – differences arise, sometimes because she desires my attentions when I am indifferent to her, and sometimes for the contrary reason. Besides this, for passion novelty is essential. A woman less fascinating than my wife attracts me more when I first know her, but afterwards becomes still less attractive than my wife: I have experienced that. No, I have not found satisfaction in marriage. Yes, my friend," Julius concluded, "the philosophers are right. Life does not afford us what the soul desires. I have now experienced that in marriage. But the fact that life does not give the happiness that the soul desires does not prove that your deception can give it," he added with a smile.

"In what do you see our 'deception'?" asked Pamphilius.

"Your deception consists in this: that to deliver man from the evils connected with life, you reject all life – repudiate life itself. To avoid disenchantment you reject enchantment. You reject marriage itself."

"We do not reject marriage," said Pamphilius.

"Well, if you don't reject marriage, at any rate you reject love."

"On the contrary, we reject everything except love. For us it is the basis of everything."

"I do not understand you," said Julius. "As far as I have heard from others and from yourself, and judging by the fact that you are not yet married though you are the same age as myself, I conclude that your people do not marry. Those who are already married continue to be so, but the others do not form fresh marriages. You do not concern yourself about continuing the human race. And if you were the only people the human race would long ago have died out," he concluded, repeating what he had often heard said.

"That is unjust," replied Pamphilius. "It is true that we do not set ourselves the aim of continuing the human race, and do not

make it our concern in the way I have often heard your philosophers speak of it. We suppose that our Father has already provided for that. Our aim is simply to live in accord with His will.
If it is His will that the human race should continue, it will do
so, if not it will end. That is not our affair, nor our care. Our care
is to live in accord with His will. And His will is expressed both
in our teaching and in our revelation, in which it is said that a
husband shall cleave unto his wife and they twain shall be one
flesh.

"Marriage among us is not only not forbidden, but it is en-
couraged by our elders and teachers. The difference between
marriage among us and marriage among you consists only in the
fact that our law reveals to us that every lustful look at a woman
is a sin, and so we and our women, instead of adorning ourselves
to stimulate desire, try so to avoid it that the feeling of love between us as between brothers and sisters, may be stronger than
the feeling of desire for a woman which you call love."

"But all the same you cannot suppress admiration for beauty,"
said Julius. "I feel sure, for instance, that the beautiful girl with
whom you were bringing the grapes evokes in you the feeling of
desire – in spite of the dress which hides her charms."

"I do not yet know," said Pamphilius, blushing. "I have not
thought about her beauty. You are the first to speak to me of it.
To me she is as a sister. But to continue what I was saying about
the difference between our marriages and yours, that difference
arises from the fact that among you lust, under the name of
beauty and love, and the worship of the goddess Venus, is evoked
and developed in people. With us on the contrary lust is considered, not as an evil – for God did not create evil – but as a good
which begets evil when it is out of place: a temptation as we call
it. And we try by all means to avoid it. And that is why I am not
yet married, though very possibly I may marry tomorrow."

"But what will decide that?"

"The will of God."

"How will you know it?"

"If you never seek its indications you will never discern it, but if you constantly seek them they become clear, as divinations from sacrifices and birds are for you. And as you have your wise men who interpret for you the will of the gods by their wisdom and from the entrails of their sacrificed animals and by the flight of birds, so we too have our wise men who explain to us the will of the Father according to Christ's revelation and the promptings of their hearts and the thoughts of others, and chiefly by their love of men."

"But all this is very indefinite," retorted Julius. "Who will indicate to you, for instance, when and whom to marry? When I was about to marry I had the choice of three girls. Those three were chosen from among others because they were beautiful and rich, and my father was agreeable to my marrying any one of them. Of the three I chose Eulampia because she was the most beautiful, and more attractive to me than the others. That is easily understood. But what will guide you in your choice?"

"To answer you," said Pamphilius, "I must first tell you that as by our teaching all men are equal in our Father's eyes, therefore they are also equal in our eyes both in their station and in their spiritual and bodily qualities, and consequently our choice (to use a word we consider meaningless) cannot in any way be limited. Anyone in the whole world may be the husband or wife of a Christian."

"That makes it still more impossible to decide." said Julius.

"I will tell you what our Elder said to me about the difference between the marriage of a Christian and a pagan. A pagan, such as yourself, chooses the wife who in his opinion will give him the greatest amount of personal enjoyment. In such circumstances the eye wanders and it is difficult to decide, especially as the enjoyment is to be in the future. But a Christian has no such choice to make, or rather, when choosing, his personal enjoyment occupies not the first but a secondary place. For a Christian the question is how not to infringe the will of God by his marriage."

"But in what way can there be an infringement of God's will by marriage?"

"I might have forgotten the Iliad which we used to read and study together, but you who live among sages and poets cannot have forgotten it. What is the whole Iliad? It is a story of the infringement of God's will in relation to marriage. Menelaus and Paris and Helen; Achilles and Agamemnon and Chryseis – it is all a description of the terrible ills that flowed and still flow from such infringements."

"But in what does the infringement consist?"

"In this: that a man loves a woman for the enjoyment he can get by connection with her and not because she is a human being like himself. He marries her solely for his own enjoyment. Christian marriage is possible only when a man loves his fellow men, and when the object of his carnal love is first of all an object of this brotherly love. As a house can only be built rationally and durably when there is a foundation, and a picture can be painted only when something has been prepared on which to paint it, so carnal love is only legitimate, reasonable, and permanent when it is based on the respect and love of one human being for another. Only on that foundation can a reasonable Christian family life be established."

"But still," said Julius, "I do not see why such a Christian marriage, as you call it, excludes the kind of love for a woman that Paris experienced..."

"I do not say that Christian marriage does not admit of any exclusive feeling for one woman: on the contrary, only then is it reasonable and holy. But an exclusive love for one woman can arise only when the previously existent love for all men is not infringed.

"The exclusive love for one woman which the poets sing, considering it as good in itself without being based on the general love of man, has no right to be called love. It is animal lust and very often changes into hatred. The best examples of how such so-called love (eros) becomes bestial when it is not based on brotherly love for all men are cases like this: the very woman the man is supposed to love is violated by him; he causes her to suffer and ruins her. In such violence there is evidently no brotherly love, for the man torments the one he loves. In unchristian marriage there is often a concealed violence – as when a man who marries a girl who does not love him, or who loves another, compels her to suffer, and has no compassion for her, using her merely to satisfy his 'love.'"

"Granted that that is so," said Julius, "but if the maiden loves him there is no injustice and I don't see the difference between Christian and pagan marriage."

"I do not know the details of your marriage," replied Pamphilius, "but I know that every marriage based on nothing but personal happiness cannot but result in discord, just as among animals, or men differing little from animals, the simple act of taking food cannot occur without quarreling and strife. Each wants a nice morsel, and as there are not enough choice morsels for all, discord results. Even if it is not expressed openly it is still there secretly. The weak man desires a dainty morsel but knows that the strong man will not give it to him, and though he knows it is impossible to take it away directly from the strong man, he watches him with secret and envious malice and avails himself of the first opportunity to take it from him by guile. The same is true of pagan marriage, but there it is twice as bad because the object of desire is a human being, so that the enmity arises between husband and wife."

"But how can married couples possibly love no one but each other? There will always be some man or woman who loves the one or the other, and then, in your opinion, marriage is impossible. So I see the justice of what is said of you – that you deny marriage. That is why you are not married and probably will not marry. It is not possible for a man to marry a woman without ever having aroused the feeling of love in some other woman, or for a girl to reach maturity without having aroused any man's feeling for herself. What ought Helen to have done?"

"Our Elder Cyril speaks thus about it: In the pagan world men, without thinking of loving their brethren – without cultivating that sentiment – think only of arousing in themselves passionate love for a woman, and they foster that passion in themselves. And so in their world Helen, and every woman like her, arouses the love of many men. Rivals fight one another and strive to surpass one another, as animals do to possess a female. And to a greater or lesser extent their marriage is an act of violence. In our community we not only do not think about the personal enjoyment a woman's beauty may afford, but we avoid all temptations which lead to this – which in the pagan world is regarded as a merit and an object of worship. We, on the contrary, think of those obligations of respect and love of our neighbor which we feel for all men, for the greatest beauty and the greatest deformity. We cultivate them with all our might, and so the feeling of brotherly love supplants the seduction of beauty, vanquishes it, and eliminates the discords arising from sexual intercourse. A Christian marries only when he knows that his union with the woman will not cause pain to anyone."

"But is that possible?" rejoined Julius. "Can men control their passions?"

"It is impossible if they are allowed free play, but we can prevent their awakening and being aroused. Take, for example, the relations of a father and his daughter, a mother and her son, or of brothers and sisters. However beautiful she may be, the mother is for her son an object of pure love and not of personal enjoyment. And it is the same with a daughter and her father, and a sister and her brother. Feelings of desire are not awakened. They would awaken only if the father learned that she whom he considered to be his daughter was not his daughter, and similarly in the relation of a mother and son, and a brother and sister. But even then the sensation would be very feeble and easily suppressed, and it would be in the man's power to restrain it. The feeling of desire would be feeble because at its base would lie the sentiment of maternal, paternal, or fraternal love. Why do you not wish to believe that such a feeling towards all women – as mothers, sisters, and daughters – may be cultivated and confirmed in men, and that the feeling of conjugal love could grow up on the basis of that feeling? As the brother will only allow a feeling of love for her as a woman to arise in himself after he has learned that she is not his sister, so also a Christian will only allow that feeling to arise in his soul when he feels that his love will cause pain to no one."

"But suppose two men love the same girl?"

"Then one will sacrifice his happiness for that of the other."

"But how if she loves one of them?"

"Then the one whom she loves less will sacrifice his feeling for her happiness."

"And if she loves both of them and they both sacrifice themselves, she will not marry at all?"

"No, in that case the elders will look into the matter and advise so that there may be the greatest good for all with the greatest amount of love."

"But you know that is not done! It is not done because it would be contrary to human nature."

"Contrary to human nature? What human nature? A man is a human being besides being an animal, and while it is true that such a relation to a woman is not consonant with man's animal nature, it is consonant with his rational nature. When man uses his reason to serve his animal nature he becomes worse than an animal, and descends to violence and incest and to things no animal would do. But when he uses his reason to restrain his animal nature, then that animal nature serves his reason, and only then does he attain a happiness that satisfies him."

V

"But tell me about yourself," said Julius. "I see you with that lovely girl, it seems that you live near her and help her. Is it possible that you do not wish to become her husband?"

"I do not think about it," said Pamphilius. "She is the daughter of a Christian widow. I serve them as others do. You ask whether I love her so that I wish to unite my life with hers? That question is hard for me to answer, but I will do so frankly. That thought has occurred to me but I dare not as yet entertain it, for there is another young man who loves her. That young man is a Christian and loves us both, and so I cannot do anything that would cause him pain. I live without thinking of it. I seek only one thing: to fulfill the law of love of man. That is the one thing needful. I shall marry when I see that it is necessary."

"But it cannot be a matter of indifference to her mother to get a good industrious son-in-law. She will want you and not someone else."

"No, it is a matter of indifference to her, because she knows that we are all ready to serve her, as we would anyone else, and that I should serve her neither more nor less whether I became her son-in-law or not. If it comes about that I marry her daughter, I shall accept it gladly, as I should do her marriage with someone else."

"That is impossible!" exclaimed Julius. "What is so terrible about you is that you deceive yourselves and so deceive others. What that stranger told me about you was correct. When I listen to you I involuntarily yield to the beauty of the life you describe, but when I reflect I see that it is all a deception leading to savagery, to a coarseness of life resembling that of the animals."

"In what do you see this savagery?"

"In this, that supporting yourselves by labor, you can have neither leisure nor opportunity to occupy yourselves with the sciences and arts. Here you are in ragged garments, with coarsened hands and feet; and your companion, who could be a goddess of beauty, resembles a slave. You have neither songs to Apollo, nor temples, nor poetry, nor games – none of the things the gods have given for the adornment of man's life. To work, to work like slaves or like oxen, merely to feed coarsely – is not this a voluntary and impious renunciation of man's will and of human nature?"

"Again 'human nature'!" said Pamphilius. "But in what does this nature consist? In tormenting slaves to work beyond their strength, in killing one's brother-men and enslaving them, and making women into instruments of pleasure? All this is needed for that beauty of life which you consider natural for human beings. Is that man's nature? Or is it to live in love and concord with all men, feeling oneself a member of one universal brotherhood?

"You are much mistaken, too, if you think that we do not recognize the arts and sciences. We value highly all the capacities with which human nature is endowed, but we regard all man's inherent capacities as means for the attainment of one and the same end, to which we consecrate our lives, namely the fulfillment of God's will. We do not regard art and science as an amusement, of use only to while away the time of idle people. We demand of science and art, as of all human occupations, that in them should be realized that activity of love of God and of our neighbors which should be the aim of all Christian activities. We regard as true science only such knowledge as helps us to live a better life, and we esteem as art only what purifies our thoughts, elevates our souls, and strengthens the powers we need for a life of labor and love. Such knowledge we do not fail to develop in ourselves and in our children as far as we can, and to such art we willingly devote our leisure time. We read and study the works bequeathed to us by the wisdom of those who lived before us. We sing songs and paint pictures, and our poems and pictures brace our spirit and console us in moments of grief. That is why we cannot approve of the applications you make of the arts and sciences. Your learned men employ their mental capacities to devise new means of injuring men. They perfect methods of warfare, that is of murder. They contrive new methods of gain, by getting rich at the expense of others. Your art serves for the erection and adornment of temples in honor of gods in whom the more educated among you have long ceased to believe, but whom you encourage others to believe in, in order by such deception the better to keep them in your power. You erect statues in honor of the most powerful and cruel of your tyrants, whom none respect but all fear. In your theaters performances are given extolling guilty love. Music serves for the delectation of your rich, who glut themselves with food and drink at their luxurious feasts. Painting is employed in houses of debauchery to depict scenes such as no sober man, or man not stupefied by animal passion, could look at without blushing. No, not for such ends have those higher capacities which distinguish him from the animals been given to man. They must not be employed for bodily gratification. Devoting our whole lives to the fulfillment of God's will, we employ our highest faculties especially in that service."

"Yes," said Julius. "All that would be excellent if life were possible under such conditions, but one cannot live so. You deceive yourselves. You condemn our laws, our institutions, and our armies. You do not recognize the protection we afford. If it were not for the Roman legions could you live at peace? You profit by the protection of the State without acknowledging it. Some of your people, as you told me yourself, have even defended themselves. You do not recognize the right of private property, but you make use of it. Our people have it and give to you. You yourself do not give away your grapes, but sell them and buy other things. It is all a deception! If you did what you say that would be all right, but as it is you deceive yourselves and others!"

He spoke heatedly and said all that he had in his mind. Pamphilius waited in silence, and when Julius had finished, he said:

"You are wrong in thinking that we avail ourselves of your protection without acknowledging it. Our welfare consists in not requiring defense, and this no one can take from us. Even if material things which in your eyes constitute property pass through our hands, we do not regard them as our own, and we give them to anyone who needs them for their sustenance. We sell the grapes to those who wish to buy them, not for the sake of personal gain, but solely to acquire necessities for those who need them. If someone wished to take those grapes from us we should give them up without resistance. For the same reason we are not afraid of an incursion of the barbarians. If they began to take from us the product of our toil we should let them have it, and if they demanded that we should work for them, we should also do that gladly; and they would not merely have no reason to kill or ill-treat us, but it would conflict with their own interests to do so. They would soon understand and learn to love us, and we should have less to suffer from them than from the civilized people who now surround us and persecute us.

"You say that the things necessary for existence can only be produced under a system of private property. But consider who really produces the necessaries of life. To whose labor do we owe all these riches of which you are so proud? Were they produced by those who issued orders to their slaves and workmen without themselves moving a finger, and who now possess all the property; or were they produced by the poor slaves who carried out their masters' orders for their daily bread, and who now possess no property and have barely enough to supply their daily needs? And do you suppose that these slaves, who expend all their strength in executing orders often quite incomprehensible to them, would not work for themselves and for those they love and care for if they were allowed to do so – that is to say, if they might work for aims they clearly understood and approved of?

"You accuse us of not completely achieving what we strive for, and for taking advantage of violence and property even while we do not recognize them. If we are cheats, it is no use talking to us and we are worthy neither of anger nor of exposure, but only of contempt. And we willingly accept your contempt, for one of our precepts is the recognition of our insignificance. But if we sincerely strive towards what we profess, then your accusation of fraud is unjust. If we strive, as I and my brethren do, to fulfill our Master's law and to live without violence and without private property – which is the result of violence – we do so not for external ends, riches or honors – we account these as nothing – but for something else. We seek happiness just as you do, only we have a different conception of what it is. You believe that happiness is to be found in wealth and honors, but we believe it is found in something else. Our belief shows us that happiness lies not in violence, but in submissiveness; not in wealth, but in giving everything up. And we, like plants striving towards the light, cannot help but press forward in the direction of our happiness. We do not accomplish all that we desire for our own welfare. That is true. But can it be otherwise? You strive to have the most beautiful wife and the largest fortune. But have you, or has anyone else, ever attained them? If an archer does not hit the mark will he cease to aim at it because he often fails? So it is with us. Our happiness, according to Christ's teaching, lies in love. We seek our happiness, but attain it far from fully and each in his own way."

"Yes, but why do you disbelieve all human wisdom? Why have you turned away from it? Why do you believe only in your crucified Master? Your slavish submission to him – that is what repels me."

"There again you are mistaken, and so is anyone who thinks that we hold our faith because we were bidden to do so by the man in whom we believe. On the contrary, those who with their whole soul seek a knowledge of the truth and communion with the Father – all those who seek for the good – involuntarily come to the path which Christ followed, and so cannot but see him before them, and follow him! All who love God will meet on that path, and you will, too! Our master is the son of God and a mediator between God and men, not because someone has said so and we blindly believe it, but because all who seek God find His son before them on the path, and involuntarily come to understand, to see, and to know God, only through him."

Julius did not reply, and they sat in silence for a long time.

"Are you happy?" he asked.

"I wish for nothing better. More than that, I generally experience a feeling of perplexity and am conscious of a kind of injustice that I am so tremendously happy," said Pamphilius with a smile.

"Yes," said Julius, "perhaps I should be happier if I had not met that stranger and had come to you."

"If you think so, what keeps you back?"

"How about my wife?"

"You say that she is inclined towards Christianity – so she might come with you."

"Yes, but we have already begun a different kind of life. How can we break it up? As it has been begun we must live it out," said Julius, picturing to himself the dissatisfaction of his father, his mother, his friends, and above all the effort that would have to be made to effect the change.

Just then the maiden, Pamphilius's companion, came to the door accompanied by a young man. Pamphilius went out to them, and in Julius's presence the young man explained that he had been sent by Cyril to buy some hides. The grapes were already sold and some wheat purchased. Pamphilius proposed that the young man should go with Magdalene and take the wheat home, while he would himself buy and bring home the hides. "It will be better for you," he said.

"No, Magdalene had better go with you," said the young man, and went away.

Julius took Pamphilius into the shop of a tradesman he knew, and Pamphilius poured the wheat into bags, and having given

Magdalene a small share to carry, took up his own heavy load, bid farewell to Julius, and left the town with the maiden. At the turning of the street he looked round and nodded to Julius with a smile. Then, with a still more joyous smile, he said something to Magdalene and they disappeared from view.

"Yes, I should have done better had I then gone to them," thought Julius. And in his imagination two pictures alternated: the kindly bright faces of the lusty Pamphilius and the tall strong maiden as they carried the baskets on their heads; and then the domestic hearth from which he had come that morning and to which he must soon return, where his beautiful, but pampered and wearisome wife, who had become repulsive to him, would be lying on rugs and cushions, wearing bracelets and rich attire.

But Julius had no time to think of this. Some merchant companions of his came up to him, and they began their usual occupations, finishing up with dinner and drinking, and spending the night with women.

VI

Ten years passed. Julius had not met Pamphilius again, and the meeting with him had slowly passed from his memory, and the impression of him and of the Christian life wore off.

Julius's life ran its usual course. During these ten years his father had died and he had taken over the management of his whole business, which was a complicated one. There were the regular customers, salesmen in Africa, clerks, and debts to be collected and paid. Julius found himself involuntarily absorbed in it all and gave his whole time to it. Besides this, new cares presented themselves. He was elected to a public office, and this new occupation, which flattered his vanity, attracted him. In addition to his business affairs he now attended to public matters also, and being capable and a good speaker he began to distinguish himself among his fellows, and appeared likely to reach high public office. In his family life a considerable and unpleasant change had occurred during these ten years. Three children had been born to him, and this had separated him from his wife. In the first place she had lost much of her beauty and freshness, and in the second place she paid less attention to her husband. All her tenderness and endearments were devoted to her children. Though according to the pagan custom the children were handed over to wet-nurses and attendants, Julius often found them with their mother, or found her with them instead of in her own apartments. For the most part Julius found the children a burden, affording him more annoyance than pleasure.

Occupied with business and public affairs he had abandoned his former dissipated life, but considered that he needed some refined recreation after his labors. This, however, he did not find with his wife, the more so as during this time she had cultivated an acquaintance with her Christian slave girl, had become more and more attracted by the new teaching, and had discarded from her life all the external, pagan things that had attracted Julius. Not finding what he wanted in his wife, Julius formed an intimacy with a woman of light conduct, and passed with her the leisure that remained after his business.

Had he been asked whether he was happy or unhappy during those years he would have been unable to answer.

He was so busy! From one affair or pleasure he passed to another affair or pleasure, but not one of them was such as fully to satisfy him or make him wish it to continue. Everything he did was of such a nature that the quicker he could free himself from it the better he was pleased, and his pleasures were all poisoned in some way, or the tedium of satiety mingled with them.

In this way he was living when something happened that came near to altering his whole manner of life. He took part in the races at the Olympic Games, and was driving his chariot successfully to the end of the course when he suddenly collided with another which was overtaking him. His wheel broke, and he was thrown out and broke his arm and two ribs. His injuries were serious, though they did not endanger his life, and he was taken home and had to keep to his bed for three months.

During these three months of severe physical suffering his mind worked, and he had leisure to think about his life as if it were someone else's. And his life presented itself to him in a gloomy light, the more so as during that time three unpleasant events occurred which much distressed him.

The first was that a slave, who had been his father's trusted servant, decamped with some precious jewels he had received in Africa, thus causing a heavy loss and a disorganization of Julius's affairs.

The second was that his mistress deserted him and found herself another protector.

The third and most unpleasant event for him, was that during his illness there was an election, and his opponent secured the position he had hoped to obtain.

All this, it seemed to Julius, came about because his chariot wheel had swerved a finger-breadth to the left.

Lying alone on his couch he began involuntarily to reflect on the fact that his happiness depended on such insignificant happenings, and these thoughts led him on to others, and to the recollection of his former misfortunes, of his attempt to go to the Christians, and of Pamphilius, whom he had now not seen for ten years. These recollections were strengthened by conversations with his wife, who was often with him during his illness and told him everything she had learned about Christianity from her slave girl.

This slave girl had at one time been in the same community with Pamphilius, and knew him. Julius wished to see her, and when she came to his couch questioned her about everything in detail, and especially about Pamphilius.

Pamphilius, the slave girl said, was one of the best of the brethren, and was loved and esteemed by them all. He had married that same Magdalene whom Julius had seen ten years ago, and they already had several children.

"Yes, any man who does not believe that God has created men for happiness should go to see their life," concluded the slave girl.

Julius let the slave girl go, and remained alone, thinking of what he had heard. It made him envious to compare Pamphilius's life with his own, and he did not wish to think about it.

To distract himself he took up a Greek manuscript which his wife had left by his couch, and began to read as follows:[1]

There are two ways: one of life and the other of death. The way of life is this: First, thou shalt love God who has created thee, secondly, thou shalt love thy neighbor as thyself; and thou shalt do to no one what thou wouldst not have him do to thee.

Now this is the meaning of these words: Bless them that curse you, pray for your enemies and for those that persecute you. For what merit have you if you love only those who love you? Do not the heathen so? Love them that hate you, and you shall have no enemies. Put away from you all carnal and worldly desires. If a man smites you on the right cheek, turn to him the other also, and you shall be perfect. If a man compelleth thee to walk a mile with him, go with him two. If he taketh what belongeth to thee, demand it not again, for this thou shalt not do; if he taketh thy outer garment, give him thy shirt also. Give to everyone that asketh of thee, and demand nothing back, for the Father wishes that His abundant gifts should be received by all. Blessed is he who giveth according to the commandment!

The second commandment of the teaching is this: Do not kill, do not commit adultery, do not be wanton, do not steal, do not employ sorcery, do not poison, do not covet thy neigh-

---

[1] The following text reproduces, in substance, the first part of *The Teaching of the Twelve Apostles* (The Didache), a very early Christian manuscript discovered at Constantinople in 1875, which greatly interested Tolstoy. – A. M.

bor's goods. Take no oath, do not bear false witness, speak no evil, do not remember injuries. Shun duplicity in thy thoughts and be not double-tongued. Let not thy words be false nor empty, but in accord with thy deeds. Be not covetous, nor rapacious, nor hypocritical, nor ill-tempered, nor proud. Have no evil intention against thy neighbor. Cherish no hatred of any man, but rebuke some, pray for others, and love some more than thine own soul.

My child! Shun evil and all appearance of evil. Be not angry, for anger leadeth to murder. Be not jealous, nor quarrelsome, nor passionate, for of all these things cometh murder.

My child! Be not lustful, for lust leadeth to wantonness, and be not foul-mouthed, for of this cometh adultery.

My child! Be not untruthful, for lying leadeth to theft; neither be fond of money, nor vain, for of all these cometh theft also.

My child! Do not repine, for that leadeth to blasphemy; neither be arrogant, nor a thinker of evil, for of all these things cometh blasphemy also. Be humble, for the meek shall inherit the earth. Be long-suffering, merciful, forgiving, humble, and kind, and take heed of the words that ye hear. Do not exalt thyself, and yield not thy soul to arrogance nor let thy soul cleave to the proud, but have converse with the humble and just. Accept as a blessing all that befalleth thee, knowing that nothing happens without God's will…

My child! Do not sow dissensions, but reconcile those that are at strife. Stretch not out thy hand to receive, nor hold it back from giving. Be not slow in giving, nor repine when giving, for thou shalt know the good Giver of rewards. Turn not away from the needy, but in everything have communion with thy brother, and call not anything thy own, for if ye are partakers in that which is incorruptible, how much more so in that which is corruptible. Teach thy children the fear of God from their youth. Deal not with thy slave in anger, lest he

cease to fear God who is above you both, for He is no respec-
ter of persons but calleth those whom the Spirit hath prepared.

But this is the way of death: First of all it is wrathful and
full of curses; here are murder, adultery, lust, wantonness,
theft, idolatry, sorcery, poisoning, plundering, false witness,
hypocrisy, deceitfulness, insidiousness, pride, malice, arrogance, avarice, obscenity, envy, insolence, presumption, and
vanity. Here are the persecutors of the righteous, haters of the
truth, lovers of falsehood, who do not acknowledge the reward
for righteousness nor cleave to what is good or to righteous
judgments, who are vigilant not for what is good but for evil,
from whom meekness and patience are far removed. Here are
those that love vanity, who follow after rewards, who have no
pity for their neighbors and do not labor for the oppressed or
know their Creator. Here are the murderers of children, de-
stroyers of God's image, who turn away from the needy. Here
are the oppressors of the oppressed, defenders of the rich, unjust judges of the poor, sinners in all things. Beware, children,
of all these!

Long before he had read the manuscript to the end, Julius had
entered with his whole soul into communion with those who
had inspired it – as often happens to men who read a book (that
is, another person's thoughts) with a sincere desire to discern the
truth. He read on, guessing in advance what was coming, and
not only agreed with the thoughts expressed in the book but
seemed to be expressing them himself.

He experienced that ordinary, but mysterious and significant
phenomenon, unnoticed by many people: of a man, supposed to
be alive, becoming really alive on entering into communion with
those accounted dead, and uniting and living one life with them.

Julius's soul united with him who had written and inspired
those thoughts, and in the light of this communion he contem-
plated himself and his life. And it appeared to him to be all a terrible mistake. He had not lived, but had only destroyed in himself
the possibility of living by all the cares and temptations of life.

"I do not wish to ruin my life. I want to live and to follow the path of life !" he said to himself.

He remembered all that Pamphilius had said to him in their former conversations, and it all now seemed so clear and unquestionable that he was surprised that he could have listened to the stranger and not have held to his intention of going to the Christians. He remembered also that the stranger had said to him: "Go when you have had experience of life!"

"I have now had experience of life, and have found nothing in it!" thought Julius.

He also recalled the words of Pamphilius: that whenever he might go to the Christians, they would be glad to receive him.

"No, I have erred and suffered enough!" he said to himself. "I will give up everything and go to them and live as it says here!"

He told his wife of his plan, and she was delighted with it. She was ready for everything. The only difficulty was to decide how to put the plan into execution. What was to be done with the children? Were they to be taken with them or left with their grandmother? How could they be taken? How, after the delicacy of their upbringing, could they be subjected to all the difficulties of a rough life? The slave girl proposed to go with them, but the mother was afraid for the children, and said that it would be better to leave them with their grandmother and to go alone. And to this they agreed.

All was decided. Only Julius's illness delayed the execution of their plans.

VII

In that state of mind Julius fell asleep. In the morning he was told that a skillful physician was visiting the town and wished to see him, promising him speedy relief. Julius willingly consented to see him, and the physician proved to be none other than the stranger whom he had met when he started to join the

Christians. Having examined his injuries the physician pre-
scribed certain potions of herbs to strengthen him.

"Shall I be able to work with my hands?" inquired Julius.

"Oh yes! You will be able to write and to drive a chariot."

"But hard work – digging?"

"I was not thinking of that," said the physician, "because it
cannot be necessary for a man in your position."

"On the contrary, it is just what is wanted," said Julius, and
he told the physician that since he had last seen him he had followed his advice and had experienced life; and that life had not
given him what it promised, but on the contrary had disillu-
sioned him, and that he now wished to carry out the intention
he had then spoken of.

"They have evidently employed all their deceptions and have
enchanted you so that in spite of your position and the responsibilities that rest upon you – especially in regard to your children – you still do not see their error."

"Read that!" was all Julius said in reply, handing him the
manuscript he had been reading.

The physician took the manuscript and looked at it.

"I know this," he said. "I know this deception, and am surprised that such a man as you should be caught by such a snare."

"I don't understand you. Where is the snare?"

"It is all tested by life! These sophists and rebels against men
and gods propose a way of life in which all men will be happy,
and there will be no wars or executions, no poverty or depravity,
no strife or anger. And they insist that this condition will come
about when all men fulfill the law of Christ – not to quarrel, nor
yield to lust, nor take oaths, nor do violence, nor take arms
against another nation. But they deceive themselves and others
by taking the end for the means.

"Their aim is not to quarrel, not to bind themselves by oaths,
not to be wanton, and so forth, and this aim can only be attained
by means of public life. But what they say is as if a teacher of ar-

chery should say: 'You will hit the target when your arrow flies to it in a straight line.' The problem is how to make it fly straight. And that result is attained in archery by having a taut bowstring, a flexible bow, and a straight arrow. It is the same in life. The best life, in which men have no need to quarrel, to be wanton, or to commit murder, is attained by having a taut bowstring (the rulers), a flexible bow (the power of government), and a straight arrow (the justice of the law). But they, under pretext of living a better life, destroy all that has improved or does improve it. They recognize neither government, nor the authorities, nor the laws."

"But they say that if men fulfill the law of Christ, life will be better without rulers, authorities, and laws."

"Yes, but what guarantee is there that men will fulfill it? None! They say: 'You have experienced life under rulers and laws, and life has not been perfected. Try it now without rulers and laws and it will become perfect. You cannot deny this, for you have not tried it.' But this is the obvious sophistry of these impious people. In saying that, is it not in effect as though a man should say to a farmer: 'You sow your seed in the ground and cover it up, and yet the harvest is not what you would wish. I advise you to sow in the sea. It will be better like that – and you cannot deny my proposition, for you have not tried it'?"

"Yes, that is true," said Julius, who was beginning to waver.

"But that is not all," continued the physician. "Let us assume the absurd and impossible. Let us assume that the principles of the Christian teaching can be poured into men like medicine, and that suddenly all men will begin to fulfill Christ's teaching, to love God and their fellows, and to fulfill his commandments. Even assuming all that, the path of life inculcated by them would still not stand examination. Life would come to an end and the race would die out. Their Teacher was a young vagabond, and such will his followers be, and according to our supposition such would the whole world become if it followed his teaching. Those living would last their time, but their children would not survive, or hardly one in ten would do so. According to their teaching all children should be alike to every mother and to every father, whether they are their own children or not. How will these children be looked after, when we see that all the devotion and all the love implanted in mothers hardly preserves their own children from perishing? What will happen when this devotion is replaced by a compassion shared by all children alike? Which child is to be taken and preserved? Who will sit up at night with a sick (and malodorous) child except its own mother? Nature has provided a protection for the child in its mother's love, but the Christians want to deprive it of that protection, and offer nothing in exchange! Who will train a son, who will penetrate into his soul like his father? Who will defend him from dangers? All this they reject! All life – that is, the continuation of the human race – is made away with."

"That also is true," said Julius, carried away by the physician's eloquence.

"Yes, my friend, have nothing to do with these ravings. Live rationally, especially now that you have such great and serious and pressing responsibilities. It is a matter of honor for you to fulfill them. You have reached the second period of your doubts, but go on and your doubts will vanish. Your first and evident duty is the education of your children, which you have neglected. You must train them to be worthy servants of their country. The existing political structure has given you everything you have, and you must serve it yourself and give it worthy servants in the persons of your children, on whom you will thereby also confer a benefit. Another obligation you have is the service of the community. You are mortified and discouraged by your accidental and temporary failure. But nothing is achieved without effort and struggle, and the joy of triumph is great only when the victory has been hardly won. Leave it to your wife to amuse herself with the babble of the Christian writers. You should be a man, and bring up your children to be men. Begin to live with the consciousness of duty, and all your doubts will fall away of themselves. They were caused by your illness. Fulfill your duty to the State by serving it and by preparing your children for its service. Set them on their feet, so that they may be able to take your place, and then peacefully abandon yourself to the life which attracts you. Till then you have no right to do so, and were you to do so you would encounter nothing but suffering."

VIII

Whether it was the effect of the medicinal herbs or the advice given him by the wise physician, Julius speedily recovered, and his plans of adopting a Christian life now appeared to him like raving.

After staying a few days the physician left the city. Soon afterwards Julius left his sick bed and began a new life in accord with the advice he had received. He engaged teachers for his children and supervised their studies himself. He spent his own time on public affairs and soon acquired great influence in the city.

So a year passed, and during that time Julius did not even think about the Christians. But at the end of the year a legate from the Roman Emperor arrived in Cilicia to suppress the Christian movement, and a trial was arranged to take place in Tarsus. Julius heard of the measures that were being undertaken against the Christians, but he paid no attention to them, not thinking that they related to the commune in which Pamphilius was living. But one day as he was walking in the forum to attend to his duties, a poorly dressed elderly man approached him whom he did not at first recognize. It was Pamphilius. He came up to Julius leading a child by the hand, and said:

"Greetings, friend! I have a great favor to ask of you, but now that the Christians are being persecuted I do not know whether you will wish to acknowledge me as your friend, or whether you will not be afraid of losing your post if you have anything to do with me."

"I am not afraid of anyone," replied Julius, "and as a proof of it I ask you to come with me to my house. I will even neglect my business in the forum to have a talk with you and help you. Come with me. Whose child is that?"

"He is my son."

"I need not have asked. I recognize your features in him, and I also recognize those light blue eyes, and need not ask who your wife is. She is the lovely girl I saw you with several years ago."

"You have guessed right," replied Pamphilius. "She became my wife soon after you saw us."

On reaching the house, Julius called his wife and handed the boy over to her, and then led Pamphilius to his luxurious private room.

"You can speak freely here," he said. "No one will hear us."

"I am not afraid of being heard," replied Pamphilius. "My request is not that the Christians who have been arrested should not be judged and executed, but only that they should be allowed to announce their faith in public."

And Pamphilius told how the Christians who had been seized by the authorities had succeeded in sending word from their prison to the community telling of their condition. Cyril the Elder, knowing of Pamphilius's relations with Julius, had sent him to intercede for the Christians. They did not ask for mercy. They looked upon it as their vocation to testify to the truth of Christ's teaching, and they could do this equally well by suffering martyrdom as by a life of eighty years. They would accept either fate with equal indifference, and physical death, which must inevitably overtake them, was as welcome and void of terror now as it would be fifty years hence. But they wished by their death to serve their fellowmen, and therefore Pamphilius had been sent to ask that their trial and execution should be public.

Julius was surprised at Pamphilius's request, but promised to do all in his power to aid him.

"I have promised to help you," he said, "out of friendship, and because of the particular feeling of tenderness you have always aroused in me, but I must say that I consider your teaching most senseless and harmful. I can judge of this because some time ago, when I was ill, disappointed, and low spirited, I myself once again shared your views and came very near to abandoning everything and joining your community. I know now on what your error is based, for I have myself experienced it. It is based on love of self, weakness of spirit, and sickly enervation. It is a creed for women, not for men."

"But why?"

"Because, while you recognize the fact that discord lies in man's nature and that strife results therefrom, you do not wish to take part in that strife or to teach others to do so; and without taking your share of the burden you avail yourselves of the organization of the world, which is based on violence. Is that fair? Our world owes its existence to the fact that there have always been rulers. Those rulers took on themselves the trouble and all the responsibility of defending us from foreign and domestic foes, and in return for that we subjects submitted to them and rendered them honor, or helped them by serving the State. But you, out of pride, instead of taking your part in the affairs of the State and rising higher and higher in men's regard by your labors and to the extent of your deserts – you in your pride at once declare all men to be equal, in order that you may consider no one higher than yourself, but may reckon yourself equal to Caesar. That is what you yourself think and teach others to think. And for weak and idle people that is a great temptation! Every slave, instead of laboring, at once considers himself Caesar's equal. But you do more than this: you deny taxes, and slavery, and the courts, and executions, and war – everything that holds people together. If people listened to you, society would fall to pieces and we should return to primitive savagery."

"Living under a government you preach the destruction of government. But your very existence is dependent on that government. Without it you would not exist. You would all be slaves of the Scythians or the barbarians – the first people who happened to hear of your existence. You are like a tumor which destroys the body but can only nourish itself on the body. And a living body resists that tumor and overcomes it! We do the same with you, and cannot but do so. And in spite of my promise to help you obtain your wish, I look upon your teaching as most harmful and despicable: despicable because I consider it dishonorable and unjust to gnaw the breast that feeds you – to avail yourselves of the advantages of governmental order, and to destroy that order by which the State is maintained, without taking part in it!"

"If we really lived as you suppose there would be much justice in what you say," replied Pamphilius. "But you do not know our life, and have formed a false conception of it. The means of subsistence which we employ are obtainable without the aid of violence. It is difficult for you, with your luxurious habits, to realize on how little a man can live without privation. A healthy man is so constituted that he can produce with his hands far more than he needs for his subsistence. Living together in a community we are able by our common work to feed without difficulty our children, our old people, and the sick and weak. You say of the rulers that they protect people from external and internal enemies – but we love our enemies, and so we have none. You assert that we Christians stir up in the slave a desire to be Caesar, but on the contrary, both by word and deed we profess one thing: patient humility and labor, the humblest of labor, that of a working man. We neither know nor understand anything about political matters. We only know one thing, and we know that with certainty, that our welfare lies solely in the good of others, and we seek that welfare. The welfare of all men lies in their union with one another, and union is attained not by violence but by love. The violence of a brigand inflicted on a traveler is as atrocious to us as the violence of an army to its prisoners, or of a judge to those who are executed, and we cannot intentionally participate in the one or the other. Nor can we profit by the labor of others enforced by violence. Violence is reflected on us, but our participation in violence consists not in inflicting it but in submissively enduring its infliction on ourselves."

"Yes," said Julius, "you preach about love, but when one looks at the results it turns out to be quite another thing. It leads to barbarism and a reversion to savagery, murder, robbery, and violence, which according to your doctrine must not be repressed in any way."

"No, that is not so," said Pamphilius, "and if you really examine the results of our teaching and of our lives carefully and impartially, you will see that not only do they not lead to murder, robbery, and violence, but on the contrary those crimes can only be opposed by the means we practice. Murder, robbery, and all evils, existed long before Christianity, and men have always contended with them, but unsuccessfully, because they employed means that we deplore, meeting violence by violence; and this never checks crime, but on the contrary provokes it by sowing hatred and exasperation.

"Look at the mighty Roman Empire. Nowhere else is such trouble taken about the laws as in Rome. Studying and perfecting the laws constitutes a special science. The laws are taught in the schools, discussed in the Senate, and reformed and administered by the most educated citizens. Legal justice is considered the highest virtue, and the office of Judge is held in peculiar respect. Yet in spite of this it is known that there is now no city in the world so steeped in crime and corruption as Rome. Remember Roman history: in olden times when the laws were very primitive the Roman people possessed many virtues, but in our days, despite the elaboration and administration of law, the morals of the citizens are becoming worse and worse. The number of crimes constantly increases, and they become more varied and more elaborate every day.

"Nor can it be otherwise. Crime and evil can be successfully opposed only by the Christian method of love, and not by the heathen methods of revenge, punishment, and violence. I am sure you would like men to abstain from evil voluntarily and not from fear of punishment. You would not wish men to be like prisoners who only refrain from crime because they are watched by their jailers. But no laws or restrictions or punishments make men averse to doing evil or desirous of doing good. That can only be attained by destroying evil at its root, which is in the heart of man. That is what we aim at, while you only try to repress the outward manifestations of evil. You do not look for its source and do not know where it is, and so you can never find it.

"The commonest crimes – murder, robbery, and fraud – are the result of men's desire to increase their possessions, or even to obtain the necessaries of life which they have been unable to procure in any other way. Some of these crimes are punished by the law, but the most important and far-reaching in their consequences are perpetrated under the wing of the law, as, for instance, the huge commercial frauds and the innumerable ways in which the rich rob the poor. Those crimes which are punished by law may indeed to a certain extent be repressed – or rendered more difficult of execution – and the criminals for fear of punishment become more prudent and cunning and invent new forms of crime which the law does not punish. But by leading a Christian life a man preserves himself from all these crimes, which result on the one hand from the struggle for money and possessions, and on the other from the unequal concentration of riches in the hands of the few. Our one way of checking theft and murder is to keep for ourselves only as much as is indispensable for life, and to give to others all the superfluous products of our toil. We Christians do not lead men into temptation by the sight of accumulated wealth, for we rarely possess more than enough for our daily bread. A hungry man, driven to despair and ready to commit a crime for a piece of bread, if he comes to us will find all he wants without committing any crime, because that is what we live for – to share all we have with those who are cold and hungry. And the result is that one sort of evildoer avoids us, while others turn to us, give up their criminal life, and are saved, and gradually become workers laboring for the good of all.

"Other crimes are prompted by the passions of jealousy, revenge, carnal love, anger and hatred. Such crimes cannot be suppressed by law. A man who commits them is in a brutal state of unbridled passion; he is incapable of reflecting on the consequences of his actions, opposition only exasperates him, so the law is powerless to restrain these crimes. We however believe that man can find satisfaction and the meaning of life only in the spirit, and that as long as he serves his passions he can never find happiness. We curb our passions by a life of love and labor, and develop in ourselves the power of the spirit, and the more deeply and widely our faith spreads the rarer will crime inevitably become.

"A third class of crime," Pamphilius continued, "arises from the desire to help men. Some men – revolutionary conspirators – are anxious to alleviate the people's lot, and kill tyrants, imagining that they are thereby doing good to the majority of the people. The origin of such crimes is the belief that one can do good by committing evil. Such crimes, prompted by an idea, are not crushed out by legal punishments: on the contrary they are inflamed and evoked by them. In spite of their errors the men who commit them do so from a noble motive – a desire to serve mankind. They are sincere, they readily sacrifice themselves and do not shrink from danger. And so the fear of punishment does not stop them. On the contrary, danger stimulates them, and sufferings and executions exalt them to the dignity of heroes, gain sympathy for them, and incite others to follow their example. We see this in the history of all nations. But we Christians believe that evil will only pass away when men understand the misery that results from it both for themselves and for others. We know that brotherhood can only be attained when we are all brothers – that brotherhood without brothers is impossible.

"And though we see the errors of the revolutionary conspirators, yet we appreciate their sincerity and unselfishness, and are attracted by the good that is in them.

"Which of us then is more successful in the struggle with crime and does more to suppress evil – we Christians, who prove by our life the happiness of a spiritual existence from which no evil results and whose means of influence are example and love; or you, whose rulers and judges pass sentences in accord with the dead letter of the law, ruin their victims, and drive them to the last extremity of exasperation?"

"When one listens to you," said Julius, "one almost begins to think that you may be right. But tell me, Pamphilius, why are people hostile to you? Why do they persecute you, hunt you down, and kill you? Why does your teaching of love lead to discord?"

"The reason of that lies not in us but outside us. Till now I have been speaking of crimes which are regarded as such both by the State and by us. These crimes constitute a form of violence which infringes the temporary laws of any State. But besides these there are other laws implanted in man – laws that are eternal, common to all men, and written in their hearts. We Christians obey these divine, universal laws, and find their fullest, clearest, and most perfect realization in the words and life of our Master, and we regard as a crime any violence that transgresses the commands of Christ, because they express God's law. We consider that to avoid discord we must also obey the State laws of the country we live in, but we regard the law of God, which governs our conscience and reason, as supreme, and we can only obey those human laws which do not conflict with the divine Law. 'Render unto Caesar the things that are Caesar's, and unto

God the things that are God's.' Our struggle against crime is therefore both deeper and wider than the State's, for while we avoid transgressing the laws of the particular country we happen to live in, we seek above all not to infringe the will of God – the law common to all human nature. And because we regard the law of God as the highest law, men hate and fear us, for they consider some particular laws as supreme – the legislation of their own country, for instance, or even very often some custom of their own class. They are incapable of becoming, or unwilling to become, real human beings, in the sense of Christ's saying that 'The truth shall make you free.' They are content with their position as subjects of this or that State or as members of society, and so they naturally feel enmity towards those who see and proclaim the higher destiny of man. Incapable of understanding, or unwilling to understand, this higher destiny for themselves, they are unwilling to admit it for others. It was of such that Christ said: 'Woe unto you, Pharisees! for ye take away the key of knowledge: ye enter not in yourselves, and them that are entering in ye hinder.' They are the authors of those persecutions which raise doubts in your mind.

"We have no enmity towards any man, not even towards those who persecute us, and our life brings harm and injury to no one. If men are irritated against us and even hate us, the reason can only be that our life is a thorn in their side, a constant condemnation of their own life which is founded on violence. We are unable to prevent this enmity against us, which does not proceed from us, for we cannot forget the truth we have understood, and cannot begin to live contrary to our conscience and our reason. Of this hostility which our belief provokes against us in others our Teacher said: 'Think not that I come to bring peace upon earth. I come not to bring peace, but a sword!' Christ himself experienced this hostility, and he warned us, his pupils, of it more than once. He said: 'The world hateth me, because its deeds are evil. If ye were of the world, the world would love you, but because ye are not of the world and I have delivered you from the world, therefore the world hateth you. The time cometh that whosoever killeth you will think that he doeth God service.'

"But we, like Christ, fear not them that kill the body and then can do nothing more to us. Sufferings and the death of the flesh will not pass any man by, but we live in the light and therefore our life does not depend on the body. It is not we who suffer from the attacks upon us, but our persecutors and enemies, who suffer from the feeling of enmity and hatred they nurse like a serpent in their breasts. 'And this is the condemnation, that light is come into the world, and men loved darkness rather than light, because their deeds were evil.' There is no need to be disconcerted about this, for the truth will prevail. The sheep hear the voice of the shepherd and follow him, because they know his voice. And Christ's flock will not perish, but increase, drawing new sheep to itself from all the countries of the earth, for the Spirit bloweth where it listeth, and thou hearest the sound thereof but canst not tell whence it cometh nor whither it goeth."

"Yes," Julius interrupted him, "but are there many among you who are sincere? You are often accused of only pretending to be martyrs and glad to die for the truth, but the truth is not on your side. You are proud madmen, destroying all the foundations of social life!"

Pamphilius made no reply, and looked sorrowfully at Julius.

IX

Just then Pamphilius's little son ran into the room and pressed close to his father's side.

Despite the caresses Julius's wife had bestowed upon him, he had run away from her to find his father. Pamphilius sighed, caressed the child, and got up to go, but Julius detained him, asking him to stay to dinner and have a further talk.

"It surprises me," he said, "to see that you are married and have children. I cannot understand how you Christians can bring up a family while having no property. How can the mothers among you live at peace, knowing that their children are not provided for?"

"Why are our children less provided for than yours?"

"Because you have neither slaves nor property. My wife is much inclined to Christianity. She even at one time wished to give up our way of life, and I intended to go away with her. But she feared the insecurity and poverty she foresaw for the children, and I could not but agree with her. That was at the time of my illness. My whole way of life was repulsive to me just then and I wished to abandon it. But my wife's fears, and the explanation given me by the physician who was treating me, convinced me that though a Christian life as you live it may be right and possible for people who have no family, it is impossible for family people, or for mothers with children: that with your outlook life itself – the human race – would cease to exist. And it seems to me that that is quite correct. So your appearance with a son greatly surprised me."

"Not only a son – there is also one at the breast and a three-year-old girl, who have remained at home."

"But I don't understand it! Not so long ago I was ready to give up everything and become one of you. But I had children, and it was clear to me that, however good your life might be for myself, I had no right to sacrifice my children. So for their sake I remained here, living as before, that they might be brought up in the conditions in which I myself grew up and have lived."

"It is strange how differently we look at things," said Pamphilius. "We say that if adults live in the worldly way it may be excused, for they are already spoiled, but for children it is terrible. To bring them up in worldly fashion and expose them to temptation! 'Woe unto the world because of occasions of stumbling; for it must needs be that the occasions come; but woe to that man through whom the occasion cometh!' So says our Teacher, and I repeat it to you not as a retort, but because it is really true. The chief necessity for us to live as we do comes from the fact that there are children among us; those children of whom it is said: 'Except ye become as little children ye shall not enter the kingdom of heaven.'"

"But how can a Christian family manage to live without definite means of livelihood?"

"According to our belief there is only one means – that of loving work for men. Your method is violence. But that method may fail and be destroyed, as riches are destroyed, and then only work and the love of men is left. We consider that love is the basis of all, and should be firmly held to and increased. And when that is so, families live and prosper. No," continued Pamphilius, "if I doubted the truth of Christ's teaching, or hesitated to follow it, my doubts and hesitations would vanish when I thought of the fate of children brought up among the pagans in the conditions in which you and your children have been and are being brought up. Whatever arrangement of life some people may make, with palaces, slaves, and the imported produce of other lands, the life of the majority of men will remain as it should be. And the security for that life will always be the same – brotherly love and labor. We wish to exempt ourselves and our children from these conditions, and make men work for us by means of violence and not by love, and strange to say the more we apparently secure ourselves thereby, the more do we actually deprive ourselves of the true, natural, and reliable security – that of love. The greater a ruler's power the less he is loved. It is the same with the other security – labor. The more a man frees himself from labor and accustoms himself to luxury, the less capable of work he becomes and the more he deprives himself of true and reliable security. And yet when people have placed their children in these conditions they say they have 'provided for them!' Take your son and mine and send the two of them to find their way anywhere, to transmit instructions, or to do some necessary thing, and you will see which of the two will do it better. Or offer them for education, and you will see which of the two would be accepted the more readily. No! Do not make that terrible statement that a Christian life is only possible for the childless. On the contrary it might be said that a pagan life may be pardonable only for those who have no children. 'But woe unto him that shall cause one of these little ones to stumble.'"

Julius was silent for some time.

"Yes," he said at last. "Perhaps you are right. But my children's education has been begun, they have the best teachers. Let them learn all we know – there can be no harm in that. There is time enough both for me and for them. They can come to you when they are grown up if they find it necessary. And I can do the same when I have set them on their feet and am left free."

"Know the truth, and the truth shall make you free," said Pamphilius. "Christ gives perfect freedom at once: the world's teaching will never give it. Farewell!" And Pamphilius called his son and went away.

The Christians were condemned and executed publicly, and Julius saw Pamphilius with other Christians clearing away the bodies of the martyrs.

He saw him, but from fear of the higher authorities did not approach him or invite him to his house.

X

Another twenty years passed. Julius's wife died. His life flowed on in public activity and in efforts to obtain power, which sometimes seemed within his reach and sometimes eluded him. His wealth was great and continued to increase.

His sons had grown up; and the second, especially, began to lead an extravagant life. He made holes in the bottom of the bucket which held his father's wealth, and in proportion as that wealth increased so did the rapidity of the outflow through those holes. And here began for Julius a conflict with his sons such as he had had with his father – anger, hatred, and jealousy.

About this time a new Prefect was appointed and deprived Julius of favor. His former flatterers abandoned him, and he was in danger of banishment. He went to Rome to explain matters but was not received, and was ordered to return.

On reaching home he found his son carousing with dissolute companions. A report had spread in Cilicia that Julius was dead, and the son was celebrating his father's death! Julius lost control of himself and felled his son to the ground. He then retired to his wife's rooms. There he found a copy of the Gospels, and read:

"Come unto me, all ye that labor and are heavy laden, and I will give you rest. Take my yoke upon you, and learn of me; for I am meek and lowly in heart; and ye shall find rest unto your souls. For my yoke is easy, and my burden is light."

"Yes," thought Julius, "he has long been calling me. I did not believe him but was refractory and wicked, and my yoke was heavy and my burden grievous."

He sat there for a long time with the open Gospel on his knee, thinking over his whole past life and remembering all that Pamphilius had said to him at different times. At last he rose and went to his son. To his surprise he found him on his feet, and was inexpressibly glad to find that he had sustained no injury.

Without saying a word to his son Julius went out into the street and set off towards the Christian settlement. He walked all day, and in the evening stopped at a villager's for the night. In the room which he entered lay a man, who got up at the sound of footsteps. It was his acquaintance the physician.

"No, this time you shall not dissuade me!" cried Julius. "This is the third time I have started to go thither, and now I know that only there shall I find peace of mind."

"Where?" asked the physician.

"Among the Christians."

"Yes, perhaps you may find peace of mind, but you will not have fulfilled your duty. You lack manliness: misfortunes crush your spirit. Not so do true philosophers behave! Misfortunes are only the fire in which gold is tried. You have passed through a test. And now that you are wanted you run away! Now is the time to try people and yourself. You have acquired true wisdom and should employ it for the good of your country. What would happen to the people if all who have learned to know men, their passions, and the conditions of life, were to bury their knowledge and experience in their search for peace of mind, instead of sharing them for the benefit of society? Your experience of life was gained among men and you ought to use it for their benefit."

"But I have no wisdom at all! I am altogether sunk in error! My errors have not become wisdom because they are ancient, any more than water becomes wine because it is stale and foul."

And seizing his cloak Julius hastily left the house and set out to walk farther, without staying to rest. By the close of another day he reached the Christian settlement.

They received him gladly, though they did not know that he was a friend of Pamphilius, whom they all loved and respected. At the refectory Pamphilius, seeing his friend, ran to him gladly and embraced him.

"At last I have come," said Julius. "Tell me what I am to do and I will obey you."

"Don't trouble about that," said Pamphilius. "Come with me." And he led Julius into the guest house, and showing him a bed, said:

"When you have had time to observe our life you will see for yourself how you can best be of use to men. But I will show you something to do tomorrow to occupy your time for the present. We are gathering grapes in our vineyards. Go there and help. You will see yourself what you can do."

Next morning Julius went into the vineyards. The first was of young vines which were loaded with clusters. Young people were plucking and gathering them. The places were all occupied and Julius, having walked about for some time, found no place for himself. He went on farther and came to an older vineyard where there was less fruit. But here also there was nothing for him to do; the gatherers were all working in pairs and there was no place for him. He went still farther and entered a very old, deserted vineyard. The vine-stocks were gnarled and crooked and Julius could see no grapes.

"There, that is like my life," he said to himself. "Had I come the first time, it would have been like the fruit in the first vineyard. Had I come when I started the second time, it would have been like the fruit in the second vineyard. But now here is my life – like these useless superannuated vines, only fit for fuel!" And Julius was terrified at what he had done, terrified at the punishment awaiting him for having uselessly wasted his life. And he became sad and said aloud:

"I am no longer good for anything and can now do nothing!" And he sat down and wept because he had wasted what he could never recover. Suddenly he heard the voice of an old man calling him:

"Work, brother!" said the voice.

Julius looked round and saw an old man, gray and bowed by age and scarcely able to move his feet. He was standing by the vines and gathering the few sweet bunches that still remained here and there. Julius went up to him.

"Work, dear brother! Work is joyous!" And the old man showed him where to look for bunches of the grapes that still remained. Julius began to look for them, and finding some, brought them and laid them in the old man's basket. And the old man said to him:

"Look, in what way are these bunches any worse than those they are gathering in the other vineyards? 'Walk while ye have the light!' said our Teacher. 'The will of Him that sent me is that every one who seeth the son, and believeth on him, may have everlasting life: and I will raise him up at the last day. For God sent not His son into the world to condemn the world; but that the world through him might be saved. He that believeth on him is not condemned, but he that believeth not is condemned already, because he hath not believed in the son, who is of one nature with God. And this is the condemnation, that light is come into the world, and men loved darkness rather than light, because their deeds were evil. For every one that doeth evil hateth the light, neither cometh to the light, lest his deeds should be reproved. But he that doeth truth cometh to the light, that his deeds may be made manifest, that they are wrought in God.' My son, be not unhappy! We are all sons of God and His servants! We are all one army! Do you think that He has no servants besides you, and that if you had devoted yourself to His service with your whole strength you could have done all that He needs – all that is needful for the establishment of His kingdom? You say you would do twice, ten times, a hundred times, more than you did. But if you did ten thousand times ten thousand more than all men have done, what would that have been in the work of God? A mere nothing! God's work, like Himself, is infinite. God's work is you. Come to Him, and be not a laborer but a son, and you will become a partner of the infinite God and of His world. In God's sight there is neither small nor great, there is only what is straight and what is crooked. Enter into the straight path of life and you will be with God and your work will be neither small nor great, it will be God's work. Remember that in heaven there is more joy over one sinner than over a hundred just persons. The world's work – all that you have neglected to do – has only shown you your sin, and you have repented. And when you repented you found the straight path. Go forward and follow it, and do not think of the past nor of what is great or small. All men are equal in God's sight! There is one God and one life!"

And Julius was comforted, and from that day he lived and worked for the brethren according to his strength. And so he lived joyfully for another twenty years, and did not notice how death took his body.

1893

Twenty-three Tales

PART I

Tales for Children

God Sees the Truth, but Waits

In the town of Vladimir lived a young merchant named Ivan Dmitritch Aksyonof. He had two shops and a house of his own.

Aksyonof was a handsome, fair-haired, curly-headed fellow, full of fun, and very fond of singing. When quite a young man he had been given to drink, and was riotous when he had had too much, but after he married he gave up drinking, except now and then.

One summer Aksyonof was going to the Nizhny Fair, and as he bade good-bye to his family his wife said to him, "Ivan Dmitritch, do not start today; I have had a bad dream about you."

Aksyonof laughed, and said, "You are afraid that when I get to the fair I shall go on the spree."

His wife replied: "I do not know what I am afraid of; all I know is that I had a bad dream. I dreamt you returned from the town, and when you took off your cap I saw that your hair was quite gray."

Aksyonof laughed. "That's a lucky sign," said he. "See if I don't sell out all my goods, and bring you some presents from the fair."

So he said good-bye to his family, and drove away.

When he had traveled halfway, he met a merchant whom he knew, and they put up at the same inn for the night. They had some tea together, and then went to bed in adjoining rooms.

It was not Aksyonof's habit to sleep late, and, wishing to travel while it was still cool, he aroused his driver before dawn, and told him to put in the horses.

Then he made his way across to the landlord of the inn (who lived in a cottage at the back), paid his bill, and continued his journey.

When he had gone about twenty-five miles, he stopped for the horses to be fed. Aksyonof rested awhile in the passage of the inn, then he stepped out into the porch and, ordering a samovar to be heated got out his guitar and began to play.

Suddenly a troyka drove up with tinkling bells, and an official alighted, followed by two soldiers. He came to Aksyonof and began to question him, asking him who he was and whence he came. Aksyonof answered him fully, and said, "Won't you have some tea with me?" But the official went on cross questioning him and asking him, "Where did you spend last night? Were you alone, or with a fellow merchant? Did you see the other merchant this morning? Why did you leave the inn before dawn?"

Aksyonof wondered why he was asked all these questions, but he described all that had happened, and then added, "Why do you cross question me as if I were a thief or a robber? I am travelling on business of my own, and there is no need to question me."

Then the official, calling the soldiers, said, "I am the police officer of this district, and I question you because the merchant with whom you spent last night has been found with his throat cut. We must search your things."

They entered the house. The soldiers and the police officer unstrapped Aksyonof's luggage and searched it. Suddenly the officer drew a knife out of a bag, crying, "Whose knife is this?"

Aksyonof looked, and seeing a bloodstained knife taken from his bag, he was frightened.

"How is it there is blood on this knife?"

Aksyonof tried to answer, but could hardly utter a word, and only stammered: "I – I don't know – not mine."

Then the police officer said, "This morning the merchant was found in bed with his throat cut. You are the only person who could have done it. The house was locked from inside, and no one else was there. Here is this bloodstained knife in your bag, and your face and manner betray you! Tell me how you killed him, and how much money you stole."

Aksyonof swore he had not done it; that he had not seen the merchant after they had had tea together; that he had no money except eight thousand roubles of his own, and that the knife was not his. But his voice was broken, his face pale, and he trembled with fear as though he were guilty.

The police officer ordered the soldiers to bind Aksyonof and to put him in the cart. As they tied his feet together and flung him into the cart, Aksyonof crossed himself and wept. His money and goods were taken from him, and he was sent to the nearest town and imprisoned there. Enquiries as to his character were made in Vladimir. The merchants and other inhabitants of that town said that in former days he used to drink and waste his time, but that he was a good man. Then the trial came on: he was charged with murdering a merchant from Ryazan, and robbing him of twenty thousand roubles.

His wife was in despair, and did not know what to believe. Her children were all quite small; one was a baby at her breast. Taking them all with her, she went to the town where her husband was in gaol. At first she was not allowed to see him; but, after much begging, she obtained permission from the officials, and was taken to him. When she saw her husband in prison dress and in chains, shut up with thieves and criminals, she fell down, and did not come to her senses for a long time. Then she drew her children to her, and sat down near him. She told him of things at home, and asked about what had happened to him. He told her all, and she asked, "What can we do now?"

"We must petition the Tsar not to let an innocent man perish."

His wife told him that she had sent a petition to the Tsar, but that it had not been accepted.

Aksyonof did not reply, but only looked downcast.

Then his wife said, "It was not for nothing I dreamt your hair had turned gray. You remember? You should not have started that day." And passing her fingers through his hair, she said: "Vanya dearest, tell your wife the truth; was it not you who did it?"

"So you, too, suspect me!" said Aksyonof, and hiding his face in his hands, he began to weep. Then a soldier came to say that the wife and children must go away; and Aksyonof said good-bye to his family for the last time.

When they were gone, Aksyonof recalled what had been said, and when he remembered that his wife also had suspected him, he said to himself, "It seems that only God can know the truth, it is to Him alone we must appeal, and from Him alone expect mercy."

And Aksyonof wrote no more petitions; gave up all hope, and only prayed to God.

Aksyonof was condemned to be flogged and sent to the mines. So he was flogged with a knout, and when the wounds made by the knout healed, he was driven to Siberia with other convicts.

For twenty-six years Aksyonof lived as a convict in Siberia. His hair turned white as snow and his beard grew long, thin, and gray. All his mirth went; he stooped; he walked slowly, spoke little, and never laughed, but he often prayed.

In prison Aksyonof learnt to make boots, and earned a little money, with which he bought *The Lives of the Saints*. He read this book when there was light enough in the prison; and on Sundays in the prison-church he read the lessons and sang in the choir; for his voice was still good.

The prison authorities liked Aksyonof for his meekness, and his fellow prisoners respected him: they called him "Grandfather," and "The Saint." When they wanted to petition the prison authorities about anything, they always made Aksyonof their spokesman, and when there were quarrels among the prisoners they came to him to put things right, and to judge the matter.

No news reached Aksyonof from his home, and he did not even know if his wife and children were still alive.

One day a fresh gang of convicts came to the prison. In the evening the old prisoners collected round the new ones and asked them what towns or villages they came from, and what they were sentenced for. Among the rest Aksyonof sat down near the newcomers, and listened with downcast air to what was said.

One of the new convicts, a tall, strong man of sixty, with a closely cropped gray beard, was telling the others what he had been arrested for.

"Well, friends," he said, "I only took a horse that was tied to a sledge, and I was arrested and accused of stealing. I said I had only taken it to get home quicker, and had then let it go; besides, the driver was a personal friend of mine. So I said, 'It's all right.' 'No,' said they, 'you stole it.' But how or where I stole it they could not say. I once really did something wrong, and ought by rights to have come here long ago, but that time I was not found out. Now I have been sent here for nothing at all…Eh, but it's lies I'm telling you; I've been to Siberia before, but I did not stay long."

"Where are you from?" asked some one.

"From Vladimir. My family are of that town. My name is Makar, and they also call me Semyonitch."

Aksyonof raised his head and said: "Tell me, Semyonitch, do you know anything of the merchants Aksyonof, of Vladimir? Are they still alive?"

"Know them? Of course I do. The Aksyonofs are rich, though their father is in Siberia: a sinner like ourselves, it seems! As for you, Gran'dad, how did you come here?"

Aksyonof did not like to speak of his misfortune. He only sighed, and said, "For my sins I have been in prison these twenty-six years."

"What sins?" asked Makar Semyonitch.

But Aksyonof only said, "Well, well – I must have deserved it!" He would have said no more, but his companions told the newcomer how Aksyonof came to be in Siberia: how some one had killed a merchant and had put a knife among Aksyonof's things, and Aksyonof had been unjustly condemned.

When Makar Semyonitch heard this, he looked at Aksyonof, slapped his own knee, and exclaimed, "Well this is wonderful! Really wonderful! But how old you've grown, Gran'dad!"

The others asked him why he was so surprised, and where he had seen Aksyonof before; but Makar Semyonitch did not reply. He only said: "It's wonderful that we should meet here, lads!"

These words made Aksyonof wonder whether this man knew who had killed the merchant; so he said, "Perhaps, Semyonitch, you have heard of that affair or maybe you've seen me before?"

"How could I help hearing? The world's full of rumors. But it's long ago, and I've forgotten what I heard."

"Perhaps you heard who killed the merchant?" asked Aksyonof.

Makar Semyonitch laughed, and replied, "It must have been him in whose bag the knife was found! If some one else hid the knife there, 'he's not a thief till he's caught,' as the saying is. How could any one put a knife into your bag while it was under your head? It would surely have woke you up?"

When Aksyonof heard these words, he felt sure this was the man who had killed the merchant. He rose and went away. All that night Aksyonof lay awake. He felt terribly unhappy, and all sorts of images rose in his mind. There was the image of his wife as she was when he parted from her to go to the fair. He saw her as if she were present; her face and her eyes rose before him; he heard her speak and laugh. Then he saw his children, quite little, as they were at that time: one with a little cloak on, another at his mother's breast. And then he remembered himself as he used to be – young and merry. He remembered how he sat playing the guitar in the porch of the inn where he was arrested, and how free from care he had been. He saw, in his mind, the place where he was flogged, the executioner, and the people standing around; the chains, the convicts, all the twenty-six years of his prison life, and his premature old age. The thought of it all made him so wretched that he was ready to kill himself.

"And it's all that villain's doing!" thought Aksyonof. And his anger was so great against Makar Semyonitch that he longed for vengeance, even if he himself should perish for it. He kept repeating prayers all night, but could get no peace. During the day he did not go near Makar Semyonitch, nor even look at him.

A fortnight passed in this way. Aksyonof could not sleep at nights, and was so miserable that he did not know what to do.

One night as he was walking about the prison he noticed some earth that came rolling out from under one of the shelves on which the prisoners slept. He stopped to see what it was. Suddenly Makar Semyonitch crept out from under the shelf, and looked up at Aksyonof with frightened face. Aksyonof tried to pass without looking at him, but Makar seized his hand and told him that he had dug a hole under the wall, getting rid of the earth by putting it into his high-boots, and emptying it out every day on the road when the prisoners were driven to their work.

"Just you keep quiet, old man, and you shall get out too. If you blab they'll flog the life out of me, but I will kill you first."

Aksyonof trembled with anger as he looked at his enemy. He drew his hand away, saying, "I have no wish to escape, and you have no need to kill me; you killed me long ago! As to telling of you – I may do so or not, as God shall direct."

Next day, when the convicts were led out to work, the convoy soldiers noticed that one or other of the prisoners emptied some earth out of his boots. The prison was searched, and the tunnel found. The Governor came and questioned all the prisoners to find out who had dug the hole. They all denied any knowledge of it. Those who knew, would not betray Makar Semyonitch, knowing he would be flogged almost to death. At last the Governor turned to Aksyonof, whom he knew to be a just man, and said:

"You are a truthful old man; tell me, before God, who dug the hole?"

Makar Semyonitch stood as if he were quite unconcerned, looking at the Governor and not so much as glancing at Aksyonof. Aksyonof's lips and hands trembled, and for a long time he could not utter a word. He thought, "Why should I screen him who ruined my life? Let him pay for what I have suffered. But if I tell, they will probably flog the life out of him and maybe I suspect him wrongly. And, after all, what good would it be to me?"

"Well, old man," repeated the Governor, "tell us the truth: who has been digging under the wall?"

Aksyonof glanced at Makar Semyonitch, and said "I cannot say, your honour. It is not God's will that I should tell! Do what you like with me; I am in your hands."

However much the Governor tried, Aksyonof would say no more, and so the matter had to be left.

That night, when Aksyonof was lying on his bed and just beginning to doze, some one came quietly and sat down on his bed. He peered through the darkness and recognized Makar.

"What more do you want of me?" asked Aksyonof. "Why have you come here?"

Makar Semyonitch was silent. So Aksyonof sat up and said, "What do you want? Go away, or I will call the guard!"

Makar Semyonitch bent close over Aksyonof, and whispered, "Ivan Dmitritch, forgive me!"

"What for?" asked Aksyonof.

"It was I who killed the merchant and hid the knife among your things. I meant to kill you too, but I heard a noise outside; so I hid the knife in your bag and escaped out of the window."

Aksyonof was silent, and did not know what to say. Makar Semyonitch slid off the bed-shelf and knelt upon the ground. "Ivan Dmitritch," said he, "forgive me! For the love of God, forgive me! I will confess that it was I who killed the merchant, and you will be released and can go to your home."

"It is easy for you to talk," said Aksyonof, "but I have suffered for you these twenty-six years. Where could I go to now?...My wife is dead, and my children have forgotten me. I have nowhere to go..."

Makar Semyonitch did not rise, but beat his head on the floor. "Ivan Dmitritch, forgive me!" he cried. "When they flogged me with the knout it was not so hard to bear as it is to see you now...yet you had pity on me, and did not tell. For Christ's sake forgive me, wretch that I am!" And he began to sob.

When Aksyonof heard him sobbing he, too, began to weep. "God will forgive you!" said he. "Maybe I am a hundred times worse than you." And at these words his heart grew light, and the longing for home left him. He no longer had any desire to leave the prison, but only hoped for his last hour to come.

In spite of what Aksyonof had said, Maker Semyonitch confessed his guilt. But when the order for his release came, Aksyonof was already dead.

1872

2

A Prisoner in the Caucasus

I

AN OFFICER NAMED ZHILIN was serving in the army in the Caucasus.

One day he received a letter from home. It was from his mother, who wrote: "I am getting old, and should like to see my dear son once more before I die. Come and say good-bye to me and bury me, and then, if God pleases, return to service again with my blessing. But I have found a girl for you, who is sensible and good and has some property. If you can love her, you might marry her and remain at home."

Zhilin thought it over. It was quite true, the old lady was failing fast and he might not have another chance to see her alive. He had better go, and, if the girl was nice, why not marry her?

So he went to his Colonel, obtained leave of absence, said good-bye to his comrades, stood the soldiers four pailfuls of vodka as a farewell treat, and got ready to go.

It was a time of war in the Caucasus. The roads were not safe by night or day. If ever a Russian ventured to ride or walk any distance away from his fort, the Tartars killed him or carried him off to the hills. So it had been arranged that twice every week a body of soldiers should march from one fortress to the next to convoy travellers from point to point.

It was summer. At daybreak the baggage train got ready under shelter of the fortress; the soldiers marched out; and all started along the road. Zhilin was on horseback, and a cart with his things went with the baggage train. They had sixteen miles to go. The baggage train moved slowly; sometimes the soldiers stopped, or perhaps a wheel would come off one of the carts, or a horse refuse to go on, and then everybody had to wait.

When by the sun it was already past noon, they had not gone half the way. It was dusty and hot, the sun was scorching and there was no shelter anywhere: a bare plain all round – not a tree, not a bush, by the road.

Zhilin rode on in front, and stopped, waiting for the baggage to overtake him. Then he heard the signal horn sounded behind him: the company had again stopped. So he began to think: "Hadn't I better ride on by myself? My horse is a good one: if the Tartars do attack me, I can gallop away. Perhaps, however, it would be wiser to wait."

As he sat considering, Kostilin, an officer carrying a gun, rode up to him and said:

"Come along, Zhilin, let's go on by ourselves. It's dreadful; I am famished, and the heat is terrible. My shirt is wringing wet."

Kostilin was a stout, heavy man, and the perspiration was running down his red face. Zhilin thought awhile, and then asked: "Is your gun loaded?"

"Yes it is."

"Well, then, let's go, but on condition that we keep together."

So they rode forward along the road across the plain, talking, but keeping a lookout on both sides. They could see afar all round. But after crossing the plain the road ran through a valley between two hills, and Zhilin said: "We had better climb that hill and have a look round, or the Tartars may be on us before we know it."

But Kostilin answered: "What's the use? Let us go on."

Zhilin, however, would not agree.

"No," he said; "you can wait here if you like, but I'll go and look round." And he turned his horse to the left, up the hill. Zhilin's horse was a hunter, and carried him up the hillside as if it had wings. (He had bought it for a hundred roubles as a colt out of a herd, and had broken it in himself.) Hardly had he reached the top of the hill, when he saw some thirty Tartars not much more than a hundred yards ahead of him. As soon as he caught sight of them he turned round but the Tartars had also seen him, and rushed after him at full gallop, getting their guns out as they went. Down galloped Zhilin as fast as the horse's legs could go, shouting to Kostilin: "Get your gun ready!"

And, in thought, he said to his horse: "Get me well out of this, my pet; don't stumble, for if you do it's all up. Once I reach the gun, they shan't take me prisoner."

But, instead of waiting, Kostilin, as soon as he caught sight of the Tartars, turned back towards the fortress at full speed, whipping his horse now on one side now on the other, and its switching tail was all that could be seen of him in the dust.

Zhilin saw it was a bad lookout; the gun was gone, and what could he do with nothing but his sword? He turned his horse towards the escort, thinking to escape, but there were six Tartars rushing to cut him off. His horse was a good one, but theirs were still better; and besides, they were across his path. He tried to rein in his horse and to turn another way, but it was going so fast it could not stop, and dashed on straight towards the Tartars. He saw a red-bearded Tartar on a gray horse, with his gun raised, come at him, yelling and showing his teeth.

"Ah," thought Zhilin, "I know you, devils that you are. If you take me alive, you'll put me in a pit and flog me. I will not be taken alive!"

Zhilin, though not a big fellow, was brave. He drew his sword and dashed at the red-bearded Tartar thinking: "Either I'll ride him down, or disable him with my sword."

He was still a horse's length away from him, when he was fired at from behind, and his horse was hit. It fell to the ground with all its weight, pinning Zhilin to the earth.

He tried to rise, but two ill-savored Tartars were already sitting on him and binding his hands behind his back. He made an effort and flung them off, but three others jumped from their horses and began beating his head with the butts of their guns. His eyes grew dim, and he fell back. The Tartars seized him, and, taking spare girths from their saddles, twisted his hands behind him and tied them with a Tartar knot. They knocked his cap off, pulled off his boots, searched him all over, tore his clothes, and took his money and his watch.

Zhilin looked round at his horse. There it lay on its side, poor thing, just as it had fallen; struggling, its legs in the air, unable to touch the ground. There was a hole in its head, and black blood was pouring out, turning the dust to mud for a couple of feet around.

One of the Tartars went up to the horse and began taking the saddle off, it still kicked, so he drew a dagger and cut its windpipe. A whistling sound came from its throat, the horse gave one plunge, and all was over.

The Tartars took the saddle and trappings. The red-bearded Tartar mounted his horse, and the others lifted Zhilin into the saddle behind him. To prevent his falling off, they strapped him to the Tartar's girdle; and then they all rode away to the hills.

So there sat Zhilin, swaying from side to side, his head striking against the Tartar's stinking back. He could see nothing but that muscular back and sinewy neck, with its closely shaven, bluish nape. Zhilin's head was wounded: the blood had dried over his eyes, and he could neither shift his position on the saddle nor wipe the blood off. His arms were bound so tightly that his collarbones ached.

They rode up and down hills for a long way. Then they reached a river which they forded, and came to a hard road leading across a valley.

Zhilin tried to see where they were going, but his eyelids were stuck together with blood, and he could not turn.

Twilight began to fall; they crossed another river and rode up a stony hillside. There was a smell of smoke here, and dogs were barking. They had reached an Aoul (a Tartar village). The Tartars got off their horses; Tartar children came and stood round Zhilin, shrieking with pleasure and throwing stones at him.

The Tartar drove the children away, took Zhilin off the horse, and called his man. A Nogay with high cheekbones, and nothing on but a shirt (and that so torn that his breast was all bare), answered the call. The Tartar gave him an order. He went and fetched shackles: two blocks of oak with iron rings attached, and a clasp and lock fixed to one of the rings.

They untied Zhilin's arms, fastened the shackles on his leg, and dragged him to a barn, where they pushed him in and locked the door.

Zhilin fell on a heap of manure. He lay still awhile then groped about to find a soft place, and settled down.

II

That night Zhilin hardly slept at all. It was the time of year when the nights are short, and daylight soon showed itself through a chink in the wall. He rose, scratched to make the chink bigger, and peeped out.

Through the hole he saw a road leading downhill; to the right was a Tartar hut with two trees near it, a black dog lay on the threshold, and a goat and kids were moving about wagging their tails. Then he saw a young Tartar woman in a long, loose, bright-colored gown, with trousers and high boots showing from under it. She had a coat thrown over her head, on which she carried a large metal jug filled with water. She was leading by the hand a small, closely-shaven Tartar boy, who wore nothing but a shirt; and as she went along balancing herself, the muscles of her back quivered. This woman carried the water into the hut, and, soon after, the red-bearded Tartar of yesterday came out dressed in a silk tunic, with a silver-hilted dagger hanging by his side, shoes on his bare feet, and a tall black sheepskin cap set far back on his head. He came out, stretched himself, and stroked his red beard. He stood awhile, gave an order to his servant, and went away.

Then two lads rode past from watering their horses. The horses' noses were wet. Some other closely-shaven boys ran out, without any trousers, and wearing nothing but their shirts. They crowded together, came to the barn, picked up a twig, and began pushing it in at the chink. Zhilin gave a shout, and the boys shrieked and scampered off, their little bare knees gleaming as they ran.

Zhilin was very thirsty: his throat was parched, and he thought: "If only they would come and so much as look at me!"

Then he heard some one unlocking the barn. The red-bearded Tartar entered, and with him was another smaller man, dark, with bright black eyes, red cheeks and a short beard. He had a merry face, and was always laughing. This man was even more richly dressed than the other. He wore a blue silk tunic trimmed with gold, a large silver dagger in his belt, red morocco slippers worked with silver, and over these a pair of thick shoes, and he had a white sheepskin cap on his head.

The red-bearded Tartar entered, muttered something as if he were annoyed, and stood leaning against the doorpost, playing with his dagger, and glaring askance at Zhilin, like a wolf. The dark one, quick and lively and moving as if on springs, came straight up to Zhilin, squatted down in front of him, slapped him on the shoulder, and began to talk very fast in his own language. His teeth showed, and he kept winking, clicking his tongue, and repeating, "Good Russ, good Russ."

Zhilin could not understand a word, but said, "Drink! give me water to drink!"

The dark man only laughed. "Good Russ," he said, and went on talking in his own tongue.

Zhilin made signs with lips and hands that he wanted something to drink.

The dark man understood, and laughed. Then he looked out of the door, and called to some one: "Dina!"

A little girl came running in: she was about thirteen, slight, thin, and like the dark Tartar in face. Evidently she was his daughter. She, too, had clear black eyes, and her face was good-looking. She had on a long blue gown with wide sleeves, and no girdle. The hem of her gown, the front, and the sleeves, were trimmed with red. She wore trousers and slippers, and over the slippers stouter shoes with high heels. Round her neck she had a necklace made of Russian silver coins. She was bareheaded, and her black hair was plaited with a ribbon and ornamented with gilt braid and silver coins.

Her father gave an order, and she ran away and returned with a metal jug. She handed the water to Zhilin and sat down, crouching so that her knees were as high as her head, and there she sat with wide open eyes watching Zhilin drink, as though he were a wild animal.

When Zhilin handed the empty jug back to her, she gave such a sudden jump back, like a wild goat, that it made her father laugh. He sent her away for something else. She took the jug, ran out, and brought back some unleavened bread on a round board, and once more sat down, crouching, and looking on with staring eyes.

Then the Tartars went away and again locked the door.

After a while the Nogay came and said: "Ayda, the master, Ayda!"

He, too, knew no Russian. All Zhilin could make out was that he was told to go somewhere.

Zhilin followed the Nogay, but limped, because the shackles dragged his feet so that he could hardly step at all. On getting out of the barn he saw a Tartar village of about ten houses, and a Tartar church with a small tower. Three horses stood saddled before one of the houses; little boys were holding them by the reins. The dark Tartar came out of this house, beckoning with his hand for Zhilin to follow him. Then he laughed, said something in his own language, and returned into the house.

Zhilin entered. The room was a good one: the walls smoothly plastered with clay. Near the front wall lay a pile of bright colored feather beds; the side walls were covered with rich carpets used as hangings, and on these were fastened guns, pistols and swords, all inlaid with silver. Close to one of the walls was a small stove on a level with the earthen floor. The floor itself was as clean as a thrashing-ground. A large space in one corner was spread over with felt, on which were rugs, and on these rugs were cushions stuffed with down. And on these cushions sat five Tartars, the dark one, the red-haired one, and three guests. They were wearing their indoor slippers, and each had a cushion behind his back. Before them were standing millet cakes on a round board, melted butter in a bowl and a jug of buza, or Tartar beer. They ate both cakes and butter with their hands.

The dark man jumped up and ordered Zhilin to be placed on one side, not on the carpet but on the bare ground, then he sat down on the carpet again, and offered millet cakes and buza to his guests. The servant made Zhilin sit down, after which he took off his own overshoes, put them by the door where the other shoes were standing, and sat down nearer to his masters on the felt, watching them as they ate, and licking his lips.

The Tartars ate as much as they wanted, and a woman dressed in the same way as the girl – in a long gown and trousers, with a kerchief on her head – came and took away what was left, and brought a handsome basin, and an ewer with a narrow spout. The Tartars washed their hands, folded them, went down on their knees, blew to the four quarters, and said their prayers. After they had talked for a while, one of the guests turned to Zhilin and began to speak in Russian.

"You were captured by Kazi-Mohammed," he said, and pointed at the red-bearded Tartar. "And Kazi-Mohammed has given you to Abdul Murat," pointing at the dark one. "Abdul Murat is now your master."

Zhilin was silent. Then Abdul Murat began to talk, laughing, pointing to Zhilin, and repeating, "Soldier Russ, good Russ."

The interpreter said, "He orders you to write home and tell them to send a ransom, and as soon as the money comes he will set you free."

Zhilin thought for a moment, and said, "How much ransom does he want?"

The Tartars talked awhile, and then the interpreter said, "Three thousand roubles."

"No," said Zhilin, "I can't pay so much."

Abdul jumped up and, waving his arms, talked to Zhilin, thinking, as before, that he would understand. The interpreter translated: "How much will you give?"

Zhilin considered, and said, "Five hundred roubles." At this the Tartars began speaking very quickly, all together. Abdul began to shout at the red-bearded one, and jabbered so fast that the spittle spurted out of his mouth. The red-bearded one only screwed up his eyes and clicked his tongue.

They quietened down after a while, and the interpreter said, "Five hundred roubles is not enough for the master. He paid two hundred for you himself. Kazi-Mohammed was in debt to him, and he took you in payment. Three thousand roubles! Less than that won't do. If you refuse to write, you will be put into a pit and flogged with a whip!"

"Eh!" thought Zhilin, "the more one fears them the worse it will be."

So he sprang to his feet, and said, "You tell that dog that if he tries to frighten me I will not write at all, and he will get nothing. I never was afraid of you dogs, and never will be!"

The interpreter translated, and again they all began to talk at once.

They jabbered for a long time, and then the dark man jumped up, came to Zhilin, and said: "Dzhigit Russ, dzhigit Russ!"

(Dzhigit in their language means "brave.") And he laughed, and said something to the interpreter, who translated: "One thousand roubles will satisfy him."

Zhilin stuck to it: "I will not give more than five hundred. And if you kill me you'll get nothing at all."

The Tartars talked awhile, then sent the servant out to fetch something, and kept looking, now at Zhilin, now at the door. The servant returned, followed by a stout, barefooted, tattered man, who also had his leg shackled.

Zhilin gasped with surprise: it was Kostilin. He, too, had been taken. They were put side by side, and began to tell each other what had occurred. While they talked, the Tartars looked on in silence. Zhilin related what had happened to him; and Kostilin told how his horse had stopped, his gun missed fire, and this same Abdul had overtaken and captured him.

Abdul jumped up, pointed to Kostilin, and said something. The interpreter translated that they both now belonged to one master, and the one who first paid the ransom would be set free first.

"There now," he said to Zhilin, "you get angry, but your comrade here is gentle; he has written home, and they will send five thousand roubles. So he will be well fed and well treated."

Zhilin replied: "My comrade can do as he likes; maybe he is rich, I am not. It must be as I said. Kill me, if you like – you will gain nothing by it; but I will not write for more than five hundred roubles."

They were silent. Suddenly up sprang Abdul, brought a little box, took out a pen, ink, and a bit of paper, gave them to Zhilin, slapped him on the shoulder, and made a sign that he should write. He had agreed to take five hundred roubles.

"Wait a bit!" said Zhilin to the interpreter; "tell him that he must feed us properly, give us proper clothes and boots, and let us be together. It will be more cheerful for us. And he must have these shackles taken off our feet," and Zhilin looked at his master and laughed.

The master also laughed, heard the interpreter, and said: "I will give them the best of clothes: a cloak and boots fit to be married in. I will feed them like princes; and if they like they can live together in the barn. But I can't take off the shackles, or they will run away. They shall be taken off, however, at night." And he jumped up and slapped Zhilin on the shoulder, exclaiming: "You good, I good!"

Zhilin wrote the letter, but addressed it wrongly, so that it should not reach its destination, thinking to himself: "I'll run away!"

Zhilin and Kostilin were taken back to the barn and given some maize straw, a jug of water, some bread, two old cloaks, and some worn out military boots – evidently taken from the corpses of Russian soldiers, At night their shackles were taken off their feet, and they were locked up in the barn.

III

Zhilin and his friend lived in this way for a whole month. The master always laughed and said: "You, Ivan, good! I, Abdul, good!" But he fed them badly giving them nothing but unleavened bread of millet flour baked into flat cakes, or sometimes only unbaked dough.

Kostilin wrote home a second time, and did nothing but mope and wait for the money to arrive. He would sit for days together in the barn sleeping, or counting the days till a letter could come.

Zhilin knew his letter would reach no one, and he did not write another. He thought: "Where could my mother get enough money to ransom me? As it is she lived chiefly on what I sent her. If she had to raise five hundred roubles, she would be quite ruined. With God's help I'll manage to escape!"

So he kept on the lookout, planning how to run away.

He would walk about the Aoul whistling; or would sit working, modelling dolls of clay, or weaving baskets out of twigs: for Zhilin was clever with his hands.

Once he modelled a doll with a nose and hands and feet and with a Tartar gown on, and put it up on the roof. When the Tartar women came out to fetch water, the master's daughter, Dina, saw the doll and called the women, who put down their jugs and stood looking and laughing. Zhilin took down the doll and held it out to them. They laughed, but dared not take it. He put down the doll and went into the barn, waiting to see what would happen.

Dina ran up to the doll, looked round, seized it, and ran away.

In the morning, at daybreak, he looked out. Dina came out of the house and sat down on the threshold with the doll, which she had dressed up in bits of red stuff, and she rocked it like a baby, singing a Tartar lullaby. An old woman came out and scolded her, and snatching the doll away she broke it to bits, and sent Dina about her business.

But Zhilin made another doll, better than the first, and gave it to Dina. Once Dina brought a little jug, put it on the ground, sat down gazing at him, and laughed, pointing to the jug.

"What pleases her so?" wondered Zhilin. He took the jug thinking it was water, but it turned out to be milk. He drank the milk and said: "That's good!"

How pleased Dina was! "Good, Ivan, good!" said she, and she jumped up and clapped her hands. Then, seizing the jug, she ran away. After that, she stealthily brought him some milk every day.

The Tartars make a kind of cheese out of goat's milk, which they dry on the roofs of their houses; and sometimes, on the sly, she brought him some of this cheese. And once, when Abdul had killed a sheep she brought Zhilin a bit of mutton in her sleeve. She would just throw the things down and run away.

One day there was a heavy storm, and the rain fell in torrents for a whole hour. All the streams became turbid. At the ford, the water rose till it was seven feet high, and the current was so strong that it rolled the stones about. Rivulets flowed everywhere, and the rumbling in the hills never ceased. When the storm was over, the water ran in streams down the village street. Zhilin got his master to lend him a knife, and with it he shaped a small cylinder, and cutting some little boards, he made a wheel to which he fixed two dolls, one on each side. The little girls brought him some bits of stuff, and he dressed the dolls, one as a peasant, the other as a peasant woman. Then he fastened them in their places, and set the wheel so that the stream should work it. The wheel began to turn and the dolls danced.

The whole village collected round. Little boys and girls, Tartar men and women, all came and clicked their tongues.

"Ah, Russ! Ah, Ivan!"

Abdul had a Russian clock, which was broken. He called Zhilin and showed it to him, clicking his tongue.

"Give it me, I'll mend it for you," said Zhilin.

He took it to pieces with the knife, sorted the pieces, and put them together again, so that the clock went all right.

The master was delighted, and made him a present of one of his old tunics which was all in holes. Zhilin had to accept it. He could, at any rate, use it as a coverlet at night.

After that Zhilin's fame spread; and Tartars came from distant villages, bringing him now the lock of a gun or of a pistol, now a watch, to mend. His master gave him some tools – pincers, gimlets, and a file.

One day a Tartar fell ill, and they came to Zhilin saying, "Come and heal him!" Zhilin knew nothing about doctoring, but he went to look, and thought to himself, "Perhaps he will get well anyway."

He returned to the barn, mixed some water with sand, and then in the presence of the Tartars whispered some words over it and gave it to the sick man to drink. Luckily for him, the Tartar recovered.

Zhilin began to pick up their language a little, and some of the Tartars grew familiar with him. When they wanted him, they would call: "Ivan! Ivan!" Others, however, still looked at him askance, as at a wild beast.

The red-bearded Tartar disliked Zhilin. Whenever he saw him he frowned and turned away, or swore at him. There was also an old man there who did not live in the Aoul, but used to come up from the foot of the hill. Zhilin only saw him when he passed on his way to the Mosque. He was short, and had a white cloth wound round his hat. His beard and moustaches were clipped, and white as snow; and his face was wrinkled and brick red. His nose was hooked like a hawk's, his gray eyes looked cruel, and he had no teeth except two tusks. He would pass, with his turban on his head, leaning on his staff, and glaring round him like a wolf. If he saw Zhilin he would snort with anger and turn away.

Once Zhilin descended the hill to see where the old man lived. He went down along the pathway and came to a little garden surrounded by a stone wall; and behind the wall he saw cherry and apricot trees, and a hut with a flat roof. He came closer, and saw hives made of plaited straw, and bees flying about and humming. The old man was kneeling, busy doing something with a hive. Zhilin stretched to look, and his shackles rattled. The old man turned round, and, giving a yell, snatched a pistol from his belt and shot at Zhilin, who just managed to shelter himself behind the stone wall.

The old man went to Zhilin's master to complain. The master called Zhilin, and said with a laugh, "Why did you go to the old man's house?"

"I did him no harm," replied Zhilin. "I only wanted to see how he lived."

The master repeated what Zhilin said.

But the old man was in a rage; he hissed and jabbered, showing his tusks, and shaking his fists at Zhilin.

Zhilin could not understand all, but he gathered that the old man was telling Abdul he ought not to keep Russians in the Aoul, but ought to kill them. At last the old man went away.

Zhilin asked the master who the old man was.

"He is a great man!" said the master. "He was the bravest of our fellows; he killed many Russians and was at one time very rich. He had three wives and eight sons, and they all lived in one village. Then the Russians came and destroyed the village, and killed seven of his sons. Only one son was left, and he gave himself up to the Russians. The old man also went and gave himself up, and lived among the Russians for three months. At the end of that time he found his son, killed him with his own hands, and then escaped. After that he left off fighting, and went to Mecca to pray to God; that is why he wears a turban. One who has been to Mecca is called 'Hadji,' and wears a turban. He does not like you fellows. He tells me to kill you. But I can't kill you. I have paid money for you and, besides, I have grown fond of you, Ivan. Far from killing you, I would not even let you go if I had not promised." And he laughed, saying in Russian, "You, Ivan, good; I, Abdul, good!"

IV

Zhilin lived in this way for a month. During the day he sauntered about the Aoul or busied himself with some handicraft, but at night, when all was silent in the Aoul, he dug at the floor of the barn. It was no easy task digging, because of the stones; but he worked away at them with his file, and at last had made a hole under the wall large enough to get through.

"If only I could get to know the lay of the land," thought he, "and which way to go! But none of the Tartars will tell me."

So he chose a day when the master was away from home, and set off after dinner to climb the hill beyond the village, and to look around. But before leaving home the master always gave orders to his son to watch Zhilin, and not to lose sight of him. So the lad ran after Zhilin, shouting: "Don't go! Father does not allow it. I'll call the neighbors if you won't come back."

Zhilin tried to persuade him, and said: "I'm not going far; I only want to climb that hill. I want to find a herb – to cure sick people with. You come with me if you like. How can I run away with these shackles on? Tomorrow I'll make a bow and arrows for you."

So he persuaded the lad, and they went. To look at the hill, it did not seem far to the top; but it was hard walking with shackles on his leg. Zhilin went on and on, but it was all he could do to reach the top. There he sat down and noted how the land lay. To the south, beyond the barn, was a valley in which a herd of horses was pasturing and at the bottom of the valley one could see another Aoul. Beyond that was a still steeper hill, and another hill beyond that. Between the hills, in the blue distance, were forests, and still further off were mountains, rising higher and higher. The highest of them were covered with snow, white as sugar; and one snowy peak towered above all the rest. To the east and to the west were other such hills, and here and there smoke rose from Aouls in the ravines. "Ah," thought he, "all that is Tartar country." And he turned towards the Russian side. At his feet he saw a river, and the Aoul he lived in, surrounded by little gardens. He could see women, like tiny dolls, sitting by the river rinsing clothes. Beyond the Aoul was a hill, lower than the one to the south, and beyond it two other hills well wooded; and between these, a smooth bluish plain, and far, far across the plain something that looked like a cloud of smoke. Zhilin tried to remember where the sun used to rise and set when he was living in the fort, and he saw that there was no mistake: the Russian fort must be in that plain. Between those two hills he would have to make his way when he escaped.

The sun was beginning to set. The white, snowy mountains turned red, and the dark hills turned darker; mists rose from the ravine, and the valley, where he supposed the Russian fort to be, seemed on fire with the sunset glow. Zhilin looked carefully. Something seemed to be quivering in the valley like smoke from a chimney, and he felt sure the Russian fortress was there.

It had grown late. The Mullah's cry was heard. The herds were being driven home, the cows were lowing, and the lad kept saying, "Come home!" But Zhilin did not feel inclined to go away.

At last, however, they went back. "Well," thought Zhilin, "now that I know the way, it is time to escape." He thought of running away that night. The nights were dark – the moon had waned. But as ill luck would have it, the Tartars returned home that evening. They generally came back driving cattle before them and in good spirits. But this time they had no cattle. All they brought home was the dead body of a Tartar – the red one's brother – who had been killed. They came back looking sullen, and they all gathered together for the burial. Zhilin also came out to see it.

They wrapped the body in a piece of linen, without any coffin, and carried it out of the village, and laid it on the grass under some plane-trees. The Mullah and the old men came. They wound clothes round their caps, took off their shoes, and squatted on their heels, side by side, near the corpse.

The Mullah was in front: behind him in a row were three old men in turbans, and behind them again the other Tartars. All cast down their eyes and sat in silence. This continued a long time, until the Mullah raised his head and said: "Allah!" (which means God). He said that one word, and they all cast down their eyes again, and were again silent for a long time. They sat quite still, not moving or making any sound.

Again the Mullah lifted his head and said, "Allah!" and they all repeated: "Allah! Allah!" and were again silent.

The dead body lay immovable on the grass, and they sat as still as if they too were dead. Not one of them moved. There was no sound but that of the leaves of the plane-trees stirring in the breeze. Then the Mullah repeated a prayer, and they all rose. They lifted the body and carried it in their arms to a hole in the ground. It was not an ordinary hole, but was hollowed out under the ground like a vault. They took the body under the arms and by the legs, bent it, and let it gently down, pushing it under the earth in a sitting posture, with the hands folded in front.

The Nogay brought some green rushes, which they stuffed into the hole, and, quickly covering it with earth, they smoothed the ground, and set an upright stone at the head of the grave. Then they trod the earth down, and again sat in a row before the grave, keeping silence for a long time.

At last they rose, said "Allah! Allah! Allah!" and sighed.

The red-bearded Tartar gave money to the old men; then he too rose, took a whip, struck himself with it three times on the forehead, and went home.

The next morning Zhilin saw the red Tartar, followed by three others, leading a mare out of the village. When they were beyond the village, the red-bearded Tartar took off his tunic and turned up his sleeves, showing his stout arms. Then he drew a dagger and sharpened it on a whetstone. The other Tartars raised the mare's head, and he cut her throat, threw her down and began skinning her, loosening the hide with his big hands. Women and girls came and began to wash the entrails and the innards. The mare was cut up, the pieces taken into the hut, and the whole village collected at the red Tartar's hut for a funeral feast.

For three days they went on eating the flesh of the mare, drinking buza, and praying for the dead man. All the Tartars were at home. On the fourth day at dinner time Zhilin saw them preparing to go away. Horses were brought out, they got ready, and some ten of them (the red one among them) rode away; but Abdul stayed at home. It was new moon, and the nights were still dark.

"Ah!" thought Zhilin, "tonight is the time to escape." And he told Kostilin; but Kostilin's heart failed him.

"How can we escape?" he said. "We don't even know the way."

"I know the way," said Zhilin.

"Even if you do," said Kostilin, "we can't reach the fort in one night."

"If we can't," said Zhilin, "we'll sleep in the forest. See here, I have saved some cheeses. What's the good of sitting and moping here? If they send your ransom – well and good; but suppose they don't manage to collect it? The Tartars are angry now, because the Russians have killed one of their men. They are talking of killing us."

Kostilin thought it over.

"Well, let's go," said he.

V

Zhilin crept into the hole, widened it so that Kostilin might also get through, and then they both sat waiting till all should be quiet in the Aoul.

As soon as all was quiet, Zhilin crept under the wall, got out, and whispered to Kostilin, "Come!" Kostilin crept out, but in so doing he caught a stone with his foot and made a noise. The master had a very vicious watchdog, a spotted one called Oulyashin. Zhilin had been careful to feed him for some time before. Oulyashin heard the noise and began to bark and jump, and the other dogs did the same. Zhilin gave a slight whistle, and threw him a bit of cheese. Oulyashin knew Zhilin, wagged his tail, and stopped barking.

But the master had heard the dog, and shouted to him from his hut, "Hayt, hayt, Oulyashin!"

Zhilin, however, scratched Oulyashin behind the ears, and the dog was quiet, and rubbed against his legs, wagging his tail.

They sat hidden behind a corner for awhile. All became silent again, only a sheep coughed inside a shed, and the water rippled over the stones in the hollow. It was dark, the stars were high overhead, and the new moon showed red as it set, horns upward, behind the hill. In the valleys the fog was white as milk.

Zhilin rose and said to his companion. "Well, friend, come along!"

They started; but they had only gone a few steps when they heard the Mullah crying from the roof, "Allah. Beshmillah! Ilrahman!" That meant that the people would be going to the Mosque. So they sat down again, hiding behind a wall, and waited a long time till the people had passed. At last all was quiet again.

"Now then! May God be with us!" They crossed themselves, and started once more. They passed through a yard and went down the hillside to the river, crossed the river, and went along the valley.

The mist was thick, but only near the ground; overhead the stars shone quite brightly. Zhilin directed their course by the stars. It was cool in the mist, and easy walking, only their boots were uncomfortable, being worn out and trodden down. Zhilin took his off, threw them away, and went barefoot, jumping from stone to stone, and guiding his course by the stars. Kostilin began to lag behind.

"Walk slower," he said, "these confounded boots have quite blistered my feet."

"Take them off!" said Zhilin. "It will be easier walking without them."

Kostilin went barefoot, but got on still worse. The stones cut his feet and he kept lagging behind. Zhilin said: "If your feet get cut, they'll heal again; but if the Tartars catch us and kill us, it will be worse!"

Kostilin did not reply, but went on, groaning all the time.

Their way lay through the valley for a long time. Then, to the right, they heard dogs barking. Zhilin stopped, looked about, and began climbing the hill feeling with his hands.

"Ah!" said he, "we have gone wrong, and have come too far to the right. Here is another Aoul, one I saw from the hill. We must turn back and go up that hill to the left. There must be a wood there."

But Kostilin said: "Wait a minute! Let me get breath. My feet are all cut and bleeding."

"Never mind, friend! They'll heal again. You should spring more lightly. Like this!"

And Zhilin ran back and turned to the left up the hill towards the wood.

Kostilin still lagged behind, and groaned. Zhilin only said "Hush!" and went on and on.

They went up the hill and found a wood as Zhilin had said. They entered the wood and forced their way through the brambles, which tore their clothes. At last they came to a path and followed it.

"Stop!" They heard the tramp of hoofs on the path, and waited, listening. It sounded like the tramping of a horse's feet, but then ceased. They moved on, and again they heard the tramping. When they paused, it also stopped. Zhilin crept nearer to it, and saw something standing on the path where it was not quite so dark. It looked like a horse, and yet not quite like one, and on it was something queer, not like a man. He heard it snorting. "What can it be?" Zhilin gave a low whistle, and off it dashed from the path into the thicket, and the woods were filled with the noise of crackling, as if a hurricane were sweeping through, breaking the branches.

Kostilin was so frightened that he sank to the ground. But Zhilin laughed and said: "It's a stag. Don't you hear him breaking the branches with his antlers? We were afraid of him, and he is afraid of us."

They went on. The Great Bear was already setting. It was near morning, and they did not know whether they were going the right way or not. Zhilin thought it was the way he had been brought by the Tartars, and that they were still some seven miles from the Russian fort; but he had nothing certain to go by, and at night one easily mistakes the way. After a time they came to a clearing. Kostilin sat down and said: "Do as you like, I can go no farther! My feet won't carry me."

Zhilin tried to persuade him.

"No I shall never get there, I can't!"

Zhilin grew angry, and spoke roughly to him.

"Well, then, I shall go on alone. Good-bye!"

Kostilin jumped up and followed. They went another three miles. The mist in the wood had settled down still more densely; they could not see a yard before them, and the stars had grown dim.

Suddenly they heard the sound of a horse's hoofs in front of them. They heard its shoes strike the stones. Zhilin lay down flat, and listened with his ear to the ground.

"Yes, so it is! A horseman is coming towards us."

They ran off the path, crouched among the bushes and waited. Zhilin crept to the road, looked, and saw a Tartar on horseback driving a cow and humming to himself. The Tartar rode past. Zhilin returned to Kostilin.

"God has led him past us; get up and let's go on!"

Kostilin tried to rise, but fell back again.

"I can't; on my word I can't! I have no strength left."

He was heavy and stout, and had been perspiring freely. Chilled by the mist, and with his feet all bleeding, he had grown quite limp.

Zhilin tried to lift him, when suddenly Kostilin screamed out: "Oh, how it hurts!"

Zhilin's heart sank.

"What are you shouting for? The Tartar is still near; he'll have heard you!" And he thought to himself, "He is really quite done up. What am I to do with him? It won't do to desert a comrade."

"Well, then, get up, and climb up on my back. I'll carry you if you really can't walk."

He helped Kostilin up, and put his arms under his thighs. Then he went out onto the path, carrying him.

"Only, for the love of heaven," said Zhilin, "don't throttle me with your hands! Hold on to my shoulders."

Zhilin found his load heavy; his feet, too, were bleeding, and he was tired out. Now and then he stooped to balance Kostilin better, jerking him up so that he should sit higher, and then went on again.

The Tartar must, however, really have heard Kostilin scream. Zhilin suddenly heard some one galloping behind and shouting in the Tartar tongue. He darted in among the bushes. The Tartar seized his gun and fired, but did not hit them, shouted in his own language, and galloped off along the road.

"Well, now we are lost, friend!" said Zhilin. "That dog will gather the Tartars together to hunt us down. Unless we can get a couple of miles away from here we are lost!" And he thought to himself, "Why the devil did I saddle myself with this block? I should have got away long ago had I been alone."

"Go on alone," said Kostilin. "Why should you perish because of me?"

"No I won't go. It won't do to desert a comrade."

Again he took Kostilin on his shoulders and staggered on. They went on in that way for another half mile or more. They were still in the forest, and could not see the end of it. But the mist was already dispersing, and clouds seemed to be gathering, the stars were no longer to be seen. Zhilin was quite done up. They came to a spring walled in with stones by the side of the path. Zhilin stopped and set Kostilin down.

"Let me have a rest and a drink," said he, "and let us eat some of the cheese. It can't be much farther now."

But hardly had he lain down to get a drink, when he heard the sound of horses' feet behind him. Again they darted to the right among the bushes, and lay down under a steep slope.

They heard Tartar voices. The Tartars stopped at the very spot where they had turned off the path. The Tartars talked a bit, and then seemed to be setting a dog on the scent. There was a sound of crackling twigs, and a strange dog appeared from behind the bushes. It stopped, and began to bark.

Then the Tartars, also strangers, came climbing down, seized Zhilin and Kostilin, bound them, put them on horses, and rode away with them.

When they had ridden about two miles, they met Abdul, their owner, with two other Tartars following him. After talking with the strangers, he put Zhilin and Kostilin on two of his own horses and took them back to the Aoul.

Abdul did not laugh now, and did not say a word to them.

They were back at the Aoul by daybreak, and were set down in the street. The children came crowding round, throwing stones, shrieking, and beating them with whips.

The Tartars gathered together in a circle, and the old man from the foot of the hill was also there. They began discussing, and Zhilin heard them considering what should be done with him and Kostilin. Some said they ought to be sent farther into the mountains; but the old man said: "They must be killed!"

Abdul disputed with him, saying: "I gave money for them, and I must get ransom for them." But the old man said: "They will pay you nothing, but will only bring misfortune. It is a sin to feed Russians. Kill them, and have done with it!"

They dispersed. When they had gone, the master came up to Zhilin and said: "If the money for your ransom is not sent within a fortnight, I will flog you; and if you try to run away again, I'll kill you like a dog! Write a letter, and write properly!"

Paper was brought to them, and they wrote the letters. Shackles were put on their feet, and they were taken behind the Mosque to a deep pit about twelve feet square, into which they were let down.

VI

Life was now very hard for them. Their shackles were never taken off, and they were not let out into the fresh air. Unbaked dough was thrown to them as if they were dogs, and water was let down in a can.

It was wet and close in the pit, and there was a horrible stench. Kostilin grew quite ill, his body became swollen and he ached all over, and moaned or slept all the time. Zhilin, too, grew downcast; he saw it was a bad lookout, and could think of no way of escape.

He tried to make a tunnel, but there was nowhere to put the earth. His master noticed it, and threatened to kill him.

He was sitting on the floor of the pit one day, thinking of freedom and feeling very downhearted, when suddenly a cake fell into his lap, then another, and then a shower of cherries. He looked up, and there was Dina. She looked at him, laughed, and ran away. And Zhilin thought: "Might not Dina help me?"

He cleared out a little place in the pit, scraped up some clay, and began modelling toys. He made men, horses, and dogs, thinking, "When Dina comes I'll throw them up to her."

But Dina did not come next day. Zhilin heard the tramp of horses; some men rode past, and the Tartars gathered in council near the Mosque. They shouted and argued; the word "Russians" was repeated several times. He could hear the voice of the old man. Though he could not distinguish what was said, he guessed that Russian troops were somewhere near, and that the Tartars, afraid they might come into the Aoul, did not know what to do with their prisoners.

After talking awhile, they went away. Suddenly he heard a rustling overhead, and saw Dina crouching at the edge of the pit, her knees higher than her head, and bending over so that the coins of her plait dangled above the pit. Her eyes gleamed like stars. She drew two cheeses out of her sleeve and threw them to him. Zhilin took them and said, "Why did you not come before? I have made some toys for you. Here, catch!" And he began throwing the toys up, one by one.

But she shook her head and would not look at them.

"I don't want any," she said. She sat silent for awhile, and then went on, "Ivan, they want to kill you!" And she pointed to her own throat.

"Who wants to kill me?"

"Father; the old men say he must. But I am sorry for you!"

Zhilin answered: "Well, if you are sorry for me, bring me a long pole."

She shook her head, as much as to say, "I can't!"

He clasped his hands and prayed her: "Dina, please do! Dear Dina, I beg of you!"

"I can't!" she said, "they would see me bringing it. They're all at home." And she went away.

So when evening came Zhilin still sat looking up now and then, and wondering what would happen. The stars were there, but the moon had not yet risen. The Mullah's voice was heard; then all was silent. Zhilin was beginning to doze, thinking: "The girl will be afraid to do it!"

Suddenly he felt clay falling on his head. He looked up, and saw a long pole poking into the opposite wall of the pit. It kept poking about for a time, and then it came down, sliding into the pit. Zhilin was glad indeed. He took hold of it and lowered it. It was a strong pole, one that he had seen before on the roof of his master's hut.

He looked up. The stars were shining high in the sky, and just above the pit Dina's eyes gleamed in the dark like a cat's. She stooped with her face close to the edge of the pit, and whispered, "Ivan! Ivan!" waving her hand in front of her face to show that he should speak low.

"What?" said Zhilin.

"All but two have gone away."

Then Zhilin said, "Well, Kostilin, come; let us have one last try; I'll help you up."

But Kostilin would not hear of it.

"No," said he, "It's clear I can't get away from here. How can I go, when I have hardly strength to turn round?"

"Well, good-bye, then! Don't think ill of me!" and they kissed each other. Zhilin seized the pole, told Dina to hold on, and began to climb. He slipped once or twice; the shackles hindered him. Kostilin helped him, and he managed to get to the top. Dina with her little hands, pulled with all her might at his shirt, laughing.

Zhilin drew out the pole and said, "Put it back in its place, Dina, or they'll notice, and you will be beaten."

She dragged the pole away, and Zhilin went down the hill. When he had gone down the steep incline, he took a sharp stone and tried to wrench the lock off the shackles. But it was a strong lock and he could not manage to break it, and besides, it was difficult to get at. Then he heard some one running down the hill, springing lightly. He thought: "Surely, that's Dina again."

Dina came, took a stone and said, "Let me try."

She knelt down and tried to wrench the lock off, but her little hands were as slender as little twigs, and she had not the strength. She threw the stone away and began to cry. Then Zhilin set to work again at the lock, and Dina squatted beside him with her hand on his shoulder.

Zhilin looked round and saw a red light to the left behind the hill. The moon was just rising. "Ah!" he thought, "before the moon has risen I must have passed the valley and be in the forest." So he rose and threw away the stone. Shackles or no, he must go on.

"Good-bye, Dina dear!" he said. "I shall never forget you!"

Dina seized hold of him and felt about with her hands for a place to put some cheeses she had brought. He took them from her.

"Thank you, my little one. Who will make dolls for you when I am gone?" And he stroked her head.

Dina burst into tears hiding her face in her hands. Then she ran up the hill like a young goat, the coins in her plait clinking against her back.

Zhilin crossed himself took the lock of his shackles in his hand to prevent its clattering, and went along the road, dragging his shackled leg, and looking towards the place where the moon was about to rise. He now knew the way. If he went straight he would have to walk nearly six miles. If only he could reach the wood before the moon had quite risen! He crossed the river; the light behind the hill was growing whiter. Still looking at it, he went along the valley. The moon was not yet visible. The light became brighter, and one side of the valley was growing lighter and lighter, and shadows were drawing in towards the foot of the hill, creeping nearer and nearer to him.

Zhilin went on, keeping in the shade. He was hurrying, but the moon was moving still faster; the tops of the hills on the right were already lit up. As he got near the wood the white moon appeared from behind the hills, and it became light as day. One could see all the leaves on the trees. It was light on the hill, but silent, as if nothing were alive; no sound could be heard but the gurgling of the river below.

Zhilin reached the wood without meeting any one, chose a dark spot, and sat down to rest.

He rested and ate one of the cheeses. Then he found a stone and set to work again to knock off the shackles. He knocked his hands sore, but could not break the lock. He rose and went along the road. After walking the greater part of a mile he was quite done up, and his feet were aching. He had to stop every ten steps.

"There is nothing else for it," thought he. "I must drag on as long as I have any strength left. If I sit down, I shan't be able to rise again. I can't reach the fortress; but when day breaks I'll lie down in the forest, remain there all day, and go on again at night."

He went on all night. Two Tartars on horseback passed him; but he heard them a long way off, and hid behind a tree.

The moon began to grow paler, the dew to fall. It was getting near dawn, and Zhilin had not reached the end of the forest. "Well," thought he, "I'll walk another thirty steps, and then turn in among the trees and sit down."

He walked another thirty steps, and saw that he was at the end of the forest. He went to the edge; it was now quite light, and straight before him was the plain and the fortress. To the left, quite close at the foot of the slope, a fire was dying out, and the smoke from it spread round. There were men gathered about the fire.

He looked intently, and saw guns glistening. They were soldiers – Cossacks!

Zhilin was filled with joy. He collected his remaining strength and set off down the hill, saying to himself: "God forbid that any mounted Tartar should see me now, in the open field! Near as I am, I could not get there in time."

Hardly had he said this when, a couple of hundred yards off, on a hillock to the left, he saw three Tartars.

They saw him also and made a rush. His heart sank. He waved his hands, and shouted with all his might, "Brothers, brothers! Help!"

The Cossacks heard him, and a party of them on horseback darted to cut across the Tartars' path. The Cossacks were far and the Tartars were near; but Zhilin, too, made a last effort. Lifting the shackles with his hand, he ran towards the Cossacks, hardly knowing what he was doing, crossing himself and shouting, "Brothers! Brothers! Brothers!"

There were some fifteen Cossacks. The Tartars were frightened, and stopped before reaching him. Zhilin staggered up to the Cossacks.

They surrounded him and began questioning him. "Who are you? What are you? Where from?"

But Zhilin was quite beside himself, and could only weep and repeat, "Brothers! Brothers!"

Then the soldiers came running up and crowded round Zhilin – one giving him bread, another buckwheat, a third vodka: one wrapping a cloak round him, another breaking his shackles.

The officers recognized him, and rode with him to the fortress. The soldiers were glad to see him back, and his comrades all gathered round him.

Zhilin told them all that had happened to him.

"That's the way I went home and got married!" said he. "No. It seems plain that fate was against it!"

So he went on serving in the Caucasus. A month passed before Kostilin was released, after paying five thousand roubles ransom. He was almost dead when they brought him back.

1870

3

The Bear-Hunt

The adventure here narrated is one that happened
to Tolstoy himself in 1858. More than twenty years later
he gave up hunting, on humanitarian grounds.

WE WERE OUT on a bear-hunting expedition. My comrade had
shot at a bear, but only gave him a flesh wound. There were
traces of blood on the snow, but the bear had got away.

We all collected in a group in the forest, to decide whether we
ought to go after the bear at once, or wait two or three days till
he should settle down again. We asked the peasant bear-drivers
whether it would be possible to get round the bear that day.

"No. It's impossible," said an old bear-driver. "You must let
the bear quiet down. In five days' time it will be possible to
surround him; but if you followed him now, you would only
frighten him away, and he would not settle down."

But a young bear-driver began disputing with the old man,
saying that it was quite possible to get round the bear now.

"On such snow as this," said he, "he won't go far, for he is a
fat bear. He will settle down before evening; or, if not, I can overtake him on snowshoes."

The comrade I was with was against following up the bear,
and advised waiting. But I said:

"We need not argue. You do as you like, but I will follow up the
track with Damian. If we get round the bear, all right. If not, we lose
nothing. It is still early, and there is nothing else for us to do today."

So it was arranged.

The others went back to the sledges, and returned to the village. Damian and I took some bread, and remained behind in
the forest.

When they had all left us, Damian and I examined our guns, and after tucking the skirts of our warm coats into our belts, we started off, following the bear's tracks.

The weather was fine, frosty and calm; but it was hard work snowshoeing. The snow was deep and soft: it had not caked together at all in the forest, and fresh snow had fallen the day before, so that our snowshoes sank six inches deep in the snow, and sometimes more.

The bear's tracks were visible from a distance, and we could see how he had been going; sometimes sinking in up to his belly and ploughing up the snow as he went. At first, while under large trees, we kept in sight of his track; but when it turned into a thicket of small firs, Damian stopped.

"We must leave the trail now," said he. "He has probably settled somewhere here. You can see by the snow that he has been squatting down. Let us leave the track and go round; but we must go quietly. Don't shout or cough, or we shall frighten him away."

Leaving the track, therefore, we turned off to the left. But when we had gone about five hundred yards, there were the bear's traces again right before us. We followed them, and they brought us out on to the road. There we stopped, examining the road to see which way the bear had gone. Here and there in the snow were prints of the bear's paw, claws and all, and here and there the marks of a peasant's bark shoes. The bear had evidently gone towards the village.

As we followed the road, Damian said:

"It's no use watching the road now. We shall see where he has turned off, to right or left, by the marks in the soft snow at the side. He must have turned off somewhere; for he won't have gone on to the village."

We went along the road for nearly a mile, and then saw, ahead of us, the bear's track turning off the road. We examined it. How strange! It was a bear's track right enough, only not going from the road into the forest, but from the forest on to the road! The toes were pointing towards the road.

"This must be another bear," I said.

Damian looked at it, and considered a while.

"No," said he. "It's the same one. He's been playing tricks, and walked backwards when he left the road."

We followed the track, and found it really was so! The bear had gone some ten steps backwards, and then, behind a fir tree, had turned round and gone straight ahead. Damian stopped and said:

"Now, we are sure to get round him. There is a marsh ahead of us, and he must have settled down there. Let us go round it."

We began to make our way round, through a fir thicket. I was tired out by this time, and it had become still more difficult to get along. Now I glided on to juniper bushes and caught my snowshoes in them, now a tiny fir tree appeared between my feet, or, from want of practice, my snowshoes slipped off; and now I came upon a stump or a log hidden by the snow. I was getting very tired, and was drenched with perspiration; and I took off my fur cloak. And there was Damian all the time, gliding along as if in a boat, his snowshoes moving as if of their own accord, never catching against anything, nor slipping off. He even took my fur and slung it over his shoulder, and still kept urging me on.

We went on for two more miles, and came out on the other side of the marsh. I was lagging behind. My snowshoes kept slipping off, and my feet stumbled. Suddenly Damian, who was ahead of me, stopped and waved his arm. When I came up to him, he bent down, pointing with his hand, and whispered:

"Do you see the magpie chattering above that undergrowth? It scents the bear from afar. That is where he must be."

We turned off and went on for more than another half mile, and presently we came on to the old track again. We had, therefore, been right round the bear who was now within the track we had left. We stopped, and I took off my cap and loosened all my clothes. I was as hot as in a steam bath, and as wet as a drowned rat. Damian too was flushed, and wiped his face with his sleeve.

"Well, sir," he said, "we have done our job, and now we must have a rest."

The evening glow already showed red through the forest. We took off our snowshoes and sat down on them, and got some bread and salt out of our bags. First I ate some snow, and then some bread; and the bread tasted so good, that I thought I had never in my life had any like it before. We sat there resting until it began to grow dusk, and then I asked Damian if it was far to the village.

"Yes," he said. "It must be about eight miles. We will go on there tonight, but now we must rest. Put on your fur coat, sir, or you'll be catching cold."

Damian flattened down the snow, and breaking off some fir branches made a bed of them. We lay down side by side, resting our heads on our arms. I do not remember how I fell asleep. Two hours later I woke up, hearing something crack.

I had slept so soundly that I did not know where I was. I looked around me. How wonderful! I was in some sort of a hall, all glittering and white with gleaming pillars, and when I looked up I saw, through delicate white tracery, a vault, raven black and studded with colored lights. After a good look, I remembered that we were in the forest, and that what I took for a hall and pillars, were trees covered with snow and hoarfrost, and the coloured lights were stars twinkling between the branches.

Hoarfrost had settled in the night; all the twigs were thick with it, Damian was covered with it, it was on my fur coat, and it dropped down from the trees. I woke Damian, and we put on our snowshoes and started. It was very quiet in the forest. No sound was heard but that of our snowshoes pushing through the soft snow; except when now and then a tree, cracked by the frost, made the forest resound. Only once we heard the sound of a living creature. Something rustled close to us, and then rushed away. I felt sure it was the bear, but when we went to the spot whence the sound had come, we found the footmarks of hares, and saw several young aspen trees with their bark gnawed. We had startled some hares while they were feeding.

We came out on the road, and followed it, dragging our snowshoes behind us. It was easy walking now. Our snowshoes clattered as they slid behind us from side to side of the hard-trodden road. The snow creaked under our boots, and the cold hoarfrost settled on our faces like down. Seen through the branches, the stars seemed to be running to meet us, now twinkling, now vanishing, as if the whole sky were on the move.

I found my comrade sleeping, but woke him up, and related how we had got round the bear. After telling our peasant host to collect beaters for the morning, we had supper and lay down to sleep.

I was so tired that I could have slept on till midday, if my comrade had not roused me. I jumped up, and saw that he was already dressed, and busy doing something to his gun.

"Where is Damian?" said I.

"In the forest, long ago. He has already been over the tracks you made, and been back here, and now he has gone to look after the beaters."

I washed and dressed, and loaded my guns; and then we got into a sledge, and started.

The sharp frost still continued. It was quiet, and the sun could not be seen. There was a thick mist above us, and hoarfrost still covered everything.

After driving about two miles along the road, as we came near the forest, we saw a cloud of smoke rising from a hollow, and presently reached a group of peasants, both men and women, armed with cudgels.

We got out and went up to them. The men sat roasting pota-toes, and laughing and talking with the women.

Damian was there too; and when we arrived the people got up, and Damian led them away to place them in the circle we had made the day before. They went along in single file, men and women, thirty in all. The snow was so deep that we could only see them from their waists upwards. They turned into the forest, and my friend and I followed in their track.

Though they had trodden a path, walking was difficult, but, on the other hand, it was impossible to fall: it was like walking between two walls of snow.

We went on in this way for nearly half a mile, when all at once we saw Damian coming from another direction – running to-wards us on his snowshoes, and beckoning us to join him. We went towards him, and he showed us where to stand. I took my place, and looked round me.

To my left were tall fir trees, between the trunks of which I could see a good way, and, like a black patch just visible behind the trees, I could see a beater. In front of me was a thicket of young firs, about as high as a man, their branches weighed down and stuck together with snow. Through this copse ran a path thickly covered with snow, and leading straight up to where I stood. The thicket stretched away to the right of me, and ended in a small glade, where I could see Damian placing my comrade.

I examined both my guns, and considered where I had better stand. Three steps behind me was a tall fir.

"That's where I'll stand," thought I, "and then I can lean my second gun against the tree;" and I moved towards the tree, sink-ing up to my knees in the snow at each step. I trod the snow down, and made a clearance about a yard square, to stand on. One gun I kept in my hand; the other, ready cocked, I placed leaning up against the tree. Then I unsheathed and replaced my dagger, to make sure that I could draw it easily in case of need.

Just as I had finished these preparations, I heard Damian shouting in the forest:

"He's up! He's up!"

And as soon as Damian shouted, the peasants round the circle all replied in their different voices.

"Up, up, up! Ou! Ou! Ou!" shouted the men.

"Ay! Ay! Ay!" screamed the women in high-pitched tones.

The bear was inside the circle, and as Damian drove him on, the people all round kept shouting. Only my friend and I stood silent and motionless, waiting for the bear to come towards us. As I stood gazing and listening, my heart beat violently. I trembled, holding my gun fast.

"Now now," I thought. "He will come suddenly. I shall aim, fire, and he will drop – "

Suddenly, to my left, but at a distance, I heard something falling on the snow. I looked between the tall fir trees, and, some fifty paces off, behind the trunks, saw something big and black. I took aim and waited, thinking:

"Won't he come any nearer?"

As I waited I saw him move his ears, turn, and go back; and then I caught a glimpse of the whole of him in profile. He was an immense brute. In my excitement, I fired, and heard my bullet go "flop" against a tree. Peering through the smoke, I saw my bear scampering back into the circle, and disappearing among the trees.

"Well," thought I. "My chance is lost. He won't come back to me. Either my comrade will shoot him, or he will escape through the line of beaters. In any case he won't give me another chance."

I reloaded my gun, however, and again stood listening. The peasants were shouting all round; to the right, not far from where my comrade stood, I heard a woman screaming in a frenzied voice:

"Here he is! Here he is! Come here, come here! Oh! Oh! Ay! Ay!"

Evidently she could see the bear. I had given up expecting him, and was looking to the right at my comrade. All at once I saw Damian with a stick in his hand, and without his snowshoes, running along a footpath towards my friend. He crouched down beside him, pointing his stick as if aiming at something, and then I saw my friend raise his gun and aim in the same direction. Crack! He fired.

"There," thought I. "He has killed him."

But I saw that my comrade did not run towards the bear. Evidently he had missed him, or the shot had not taken full effect.

"The bear will get away," I thought. "He will go back, but he won't come a second time towards me. But what is that?"

Something was coming towards me like a whirlwind, snorting as it came; and I saw the snow flying up quite near me. I glanced straight before me, and there was the bear, rushing along the path through the thicket right at me, evidently beside himself with fear. He was hardly half a dozen paces off, and I could see the whole of him – his black chest and enormous head with a reddish patch. There he was, blundering straight at me, and scattering the snow about as he came. I could see by his eyes that he did not see me, but, mad with fear, was rushing blindly along; and his path led him straight at the tree under which I was standing. I raised my gun and fired. He was almost upon me now, and I saw that I had missed. My bullet had gone past him, and he did not even hear me fire, but still came headlong towards me. I lowered my gun, and fired again, almost touching his head. Crack! I had hit, but not killed him!

He raised his head, and laying his ears back, came at me, showing his teeth.

I snatched at my other gun, but almost before I had touched it, he had flown at me and, knocking me over into the snow, had passed right over me.

"Thank goodness, he has left me," thought I.

I tried to rise, but something pressed me down, and prevented my getting up. The bear's rush had carried him past me, but he had turned back, and had fallen on me with the whole weight of his body. I felt something heavy weighing me down, and something warm above my face, and I realized that he was drawing my whole face into his mouth. My nose was already in it, and I felt the heat of it, and smelt his blood. He was pressing my shoulders down with his paws so that I could not move: all I could do was to draw my head down towards my chest away from his mouth, trying to free my nose and eyes, while he tried to get his teeth into them. Then I felt that he had seized my forehead just under the hair with the teeth of his lower jaw, and the flesh below my eyes with his upper jaw, and was closing his teeth. It was as if my face were being cut with knives. I struggled to get away, while he made haste to close his jaws like a dog gnawing. I managed to twist my face away, but he began drawing it again into his mouth.

"Now," thought I, "my end has come!"

Then I felt the weight lifted, and looking up, I saw that he was no longer there. He had jumped off me and run away.

When my comrade and Damian had seen the bear knock me down and begin worrying me, they rushed to the rescue. My comrade, in his haste, blundered, and instead of following the trodden path, ran into the deep snow and fell down. While he was struggling out of the snow, the bear was gnawing at me. But Damian just as he was, without a gun, and with only a stick in his hand, rushed along the path shouting:

"He's eating the master! He's eating the master!"

And as he ran, he called to the bear:

"Oh you idiot! What are you doing? Leave off! Leave off!"

The bear obeyed him, and leaving me ran away. When I rose, there was as much blood on the snow as if a sheep had been killed, and the flesh hung in rags above my eyes, though in my excitement I felt no pain.

My comrade had come up by this time, and the other people collected round: they looked at my wound, and put snow on it. But I, forgetting about my wounds, only asked:

"Where's the bear? Which way has he gone?"

Suddenly I heard:

"Here he is! Here he is!"

And we saw the bear again running at us. We seized our guns, but before any one had time to fire he had run past. He had grown ferocious, and wanted to gnaw me again, but seeing so many people he took fright. We saw by his track that his head was bleeding and we wanted to follow him up; but, as my wounds had become very painful, we went, instead, to the town to find a doctor.

The doctor stitched up my wounds with silk, and they soon began to heal.

A month later we went to hunt that bear again, but I did not get a chance of finishing him. He would not come out of the circle, but went round and round growling in a terrible voice.

Damian killed him. The bear's lower jaw had been broken, and one of his teeth knocked out by my bullet.

He was a huge creature, and had splendid black fur.

I had him stuffed, and he now lies in my room. The wounds on my forehead healed up so that the scars can scarcely be seen.

1872

PART II

POPULAR STORIES

4

WHAT MEN LIVE BY

We know that we have passed out of death into life, because
we love the brethren. He that loveth not abideth in death.

– I Epistle St. John iii. 14

Whoso hath the world's goods, and beholdeth his brother in
need, and shutteth up his compassion from him, how doth the
love of God abide in him? My little children, let us not love in
word, neither with the tongue; but in deed and truth. *– iii. 17–18*

Love is of God; and every one that loveth is begotten of
God, and knoweth God. He that loveth not knoweth not
God; for God is love.   *– iv. 7–8*

No man hath beheld God at any time; if we love one another, God abideth in us.   *– iv. 12*

God is love; and he that abideth in love abideth in God, and
God abideth in him.   *– iv. 16*

If a man say, I love God, and hateth his brother, he is a liar;
for he that loveth not his brother whom he hath seen, how
can he love God whom he hath not seen?   *– iv. 20*

I

A SHOEMAKER named Simon, who had neither house nor land
of his own, lived with his wife and children in a peasant's hut,
and earned his living by his work. Work was cheap but bread was
dear, and what he earned he spent for food. The man and his
wife had but one sheepskin coat between them for winter wear,
and even that was worn to tatters, and this was the second year
he had been wanting to buy sheepskins for a new coat. Before
winter Simon saved up a little money: a three-rouble note lay
hidden in his wife's box, and five roubles and twenty kopeks were
owed him by customers in the village.

So one morning he prepared to go to the village to buy the sheepskins. He put on over his shirt his wife's wadded nankeen jacket, and over that he put his own cloth coat. He took the three-rouble note in his pocket, cut himself a stick to serve as a staff, and started off after breakfast. "I'll collect the five roubles that are due to me," thought he, "add the three I have got, and that will be enough to buy sheepskins for the winter coat."

He came to the village and called at a peasant's hut, but the man was not at home. The peasant's wife promised that the money should be paid next week, but she would not pay it herself. Then Simon called on another peasant, but this one swore he had no money, and would only pay twenty kopeks which he owed for a pair of boots Simon had mended. Simon then tried to buy the sheepskins on credit, but the dealer would not trust him.

"Bring your money," said he, "then you may have your pick of the skins. We know what debt collecting is like."

So all the business the shoemaker did was to get the twenty kopeks for boots he had mended, and to take a pair of felt boots a peasant gave him to sole with leather.

Simon felt downhearted. He spent the twenty kopeks on vodka, and started homewards without having bought any skins. In the morning he had felt the frost; but now, after drinking the vodka, he felt warm even without a sheep-skin coat. He trudged along, striking his stick on the frozen earth with one hand, swinging the felt boots with the other, and talking to himself.

"I'm quite warm," said he, "though I have no sheepskin coat. I've had a drop, and it runs through all my veins. I need no sheepskins. I go along and don't worry about anything. That's the sort of man I am! What do I care? I can live without sheep-skins. I don't need them. My wife will fret, to be sure. And, true enough, it's a shame; one works all day long, and then does not get paid. Stop a bit! If you don't bring that money along, sure enough I'll skin you, blessed if I don't. How's that? He pays twenty kopeks at a time! What can I do with twenty kopeks: Drink it – that's all one can do! Hard up, he says he is! So he may be – but what about me? You have house, and cattle, and everything; I've only what I stand up in! You have corn of your own growing; I have to buy every grain. Do what I will, I must spend three roubles every week for bread alone. I come home and find the bread all used up, and I have to fork out another rouble and a half. So just you pay up what you owe, and no nonsense about it!"

By this time he had nearly reached the shrine at the bend of the road. Looking up, he saw something whitish behind the shrine. The daylight was fading, and the shoemaker peered at the thing without being able to make out what it was. "There was no white stone here before. Can it be an ox? It's not like an ox. It has a head like a man, but it's too white; and what could a man be doing there?"

He came closer, so that it was clearly visible. To his surprise it really was a man, alive or dead, sitting naked, leaning motionless against the shrine. Terror seized the shoemaker, and he thought, "Someone has killed him, stripped him, and left him here. If I meddle I shall surely get into trouble."

So the shoemaker went on. He passed in front of the shrine so that he could not see the man. When he had gone some way, he looked back, and saw that the man was no longer leaning against the shrine, but was moving as if looking towards him. The shoemaker felt more frightened than before, and thought, "Shall I go back to him, or shall I go on? If I go near him something dreadful may happen. Who knows who the fellow is? He has not come here for any good. If I go near him he may jump up and throttle me, and there will be no getting away. Or if not, he'd still be a burden on one's hands. What could I do with a naked man? I couldn't give him my last clothes. Heaven only help me to get away!"

So the shoemaker hurried on, leaving the shrine behind him – when suddenly his conscience smote him and he stopped in the road.

"What are you doing, Simon?" said he to himself. "The man may be dying of want, and you slip past afraid. Have you grown so rich as to be afraid of robbers? Ah, Simon, shame on you!"

So he turned back and went up to the man.

II

Simon approached the stranger, looked at him, and saw that he was a young man, fit, with no bruises on his body, only evidently freezing and frightened, and he sat there leaning back without looking up at Simon, as if too faint to lift his eyes. Simon went close to him, and then the man seemed to wake up. Turning his head, he opened his eyes and looked into Simon's face. That one look was enough to make Simon fond of the man. He threw the felt boots on the ground undid his sash, laid it on the boots, and took off his cloth coat.

"It's not a time for talking," said he. "Come, put this coat on at once!" And Simon took the man by the elbows and helped him to rise. As he stood there, Simon saw that his body was clean and in good condition, his hands and feet shapely, and his face good and kind. He threw his coat over the man's shoulders but the latter could not find the sleeves. Simon guided his arms into them, and drawing the coat well on wrapped it closely about him, tying the sash round the man's waist.

Simon even took off his torn cap to put it on the man's head, but then his own head felt cold, and he thought: "I'm quite bald, while he has long curly hair." So he put his cap on his own head again. "It will be better to give him something for his feet," thought he; and he made the man sit down, and helped him to put on the felt boots, saying, "There, friend, now move about and warm yourself. Other matters can be settled later on. Can you walk?"

The man stood up and looked kindly at Simon, but could not say a word.

"Why don't you speak?" said Simon. "It's too cold to stay here; we must be getting home. There now, take my stick, and if you're feeling weak, lean on that. Now step out!"

The man started walking, and moved easily, not lagging behind.

As they went along, Simon asked him, "And where do you belong to?"

"I'm not from these parts."

"I thought as much. I know the folks hereabouts. But how did you come to be there by the shrine?"

"I cannot tell."

"Has some one been ill-treating you?"

"No one has ill-treated me. God has punished me."

"Of course God rules all. Still, you'll have to find food and shelter somewhere. Where do you want to go to?"

"It is all the same to me."

Simon was amazed. The man did not look like a rogue, and he spoke gently, but yet he gave no account of himself. Still Simon thought, "Who knows what may have happened?" And he said to the stranger: "Well then, come home with me, and at least warm yourself awhile."

So Simon walked towards his home, and the stranger kept up with him, walking at his side. The wind had risen and Simon felt it cold under his shirt. He was getting over his tipsiness by now, and began to feel the frost. He went along sniffling and wrapping his wife's coat round him, and he thought to himself: "There now – talk about sheepskins! I went out for sheepskins and come home without even a coat to my back and what is more, I'm bringing a naked man along with me. Matryona won't be pleased!" And when he thought of his wife he felt sad; but when he looked at the stranger and remembered how he had looked up at him at the shrine, his heart was glad.

III

Simon's wife had everything ready early that day. She had cut wood, brought water, fed the children, eaten her own meal, and now she sat thinking. She wondered when she ought to make bread: now or tomorrow? There was still a large piece left.

"If Simon has had some dinner in town," thought she, "and does not eat much for supper, the bread will last out another day."

She weighed the piece of bread in her hand again and again, and thought: "I won't make any more today. We have only enough flour left to bake one batch. We can manage to make this last out till Friday."

So Matryona put away the bread, and sat down at the table to patch her husband's shirt. While she worked she thought how her husband was buying skins for a winter coat.

"If only the dealer does not cheat him. My good man is much too simple; he cheats nobody, but any child can take him in. Eight roubles is a lot of money – he should get a good coat at that price. Not tanned skins, but still a proper winter coat. How difficult it was last winter to get on without a warm coat. I could neither get down to the river, nor go out anywhere. When he went out he put on all we had, and there was nothing left for me. He did not start very early today, but still it's time he was back. I only hope he has not gone on the spree!"

Hardly had Matryona thought this, when steps were heard on the threshold, and some one entered. Matryona stuck her needle into her work and went out into the passage. There she saw two men: Simon, and with him a man without a hat, and wearing felt boots.

Matryona noticed at once that her husband smelt of spirits. "There now, he has been drinking," thought she. And when she saw that he was coatless, had only her jacket on, brought no parcel, stood there silent, and seemed ashamed, her heart was ready to break with disappointment. "He has drunk the money," thought she, "and has been on the spree with some good-for-nothing fellow whom he has brought home with him."

Matryona let them pass into the hut, followed them in, and saw that the stranger was a young, slight man, wearing her husband's coat. There was no shirt to be seen under it, and he had no hat. Having entered, he stood neither moving, nor raising his eyes, and Matryona thought: "He must be a bad man – he's afraid."

Matryona frowned, and stood beside the oven looking to see what they would do.

Simon took off his cap and sat down on the bench as if things were all right.

"Come, Matryona; if supper is ready, let us have some."

Matryona muttered something to herself and did not move, but stayed where she was, by the oven. She looked first at the one and then at the other of them, and only shook her head. Simon saw that his wife was annoyed, but tried to pass it off. Pretending not to notice anything, he took the stranger by the arm.

"Sit down, friend," said he, "and let us have some supper."

The stranger sat down on the bench.

"Haven't you cooked anything for us?" said Simon.

Matryona's anger boiled over. "I've cooked, but not for you. It seems to me you have drunk your wits away. You went to buy a sheepskin coat, but come home without so much as the coat you had on, and bring a naked vagabond home with you. I have no supper for drunkards like you."

"That's enough, Matryona. Don't wag your tongue without reason! You had better ask what sort of man – "

"And you tell me what you've done with the money?"

Simon found the pocket of the jacket, drew out the three-rouble note, and unfolded it.

"Here is the money. Trifonof did not pay, but promises to pay soon."

Matryona got still more angry; he had bought no sheepskins, but had put his only coat on some naked fellow and had even brought him to their house.

She snatched up the note from the table, took it to put away in safety, and said: "I have no supper for you. We can't feed all the naked drunkards in the world."

"There now, Matryona, hold your tongue a bit. First hear what a man has to say!"

"Much wisdom I shall hear from a drunken fool. I was right in not wanting to marry you – a drunkard. The linen my mother gave me you drank; and now you've been to buy a coat – and have drunk it too!"

Simon tried to explain to his wife that he had only spent twenty kopeks; tried to tell how he had found the man – but Matryona would not let him get a word in. She talked nineteen to the dozen, and dragged in things that had happened ten years before.

Matryona talked and talked, and at last she flew at Simon and seized him by the sleeve.

"Give me my jacket. It is the only one I have and you must needs take it from me and wear it yourself. Give it here, you mangy dog, and may the devil take you."

Simon began to pull off the jacket, and turned a sleeve of it inside out; Matryona seized the jacket and it burst its seams. She snatched it up, threw it over her head and went to the door. She meant to go out, but stopped undecided – she wanted to work off her anger, but she also wanted to learn what sort of a man the stranger was.

IV

Matryona stopped and said: "If he were a good man he would not be naked. Why, he hasn't even a shirt on him. If he were all right, you would say where you came across the fellow."

"That's just what I am trying to tell you," said Simon. "As I came to the shrine I saw him sitting all naked and frozen. It isn't quite the weather to sit about naked! God sent me to him, or he would have perished. What was I to do? How do we know what may have happened to him? So I took him, clothed him, and brought him along. Don't be so angry, Matryona. It is a sin. Remember, we all must die one day."

Angry words rose to Matryona's lips, but she looked at the stranger and was silent. He sat on the edge of the bench, motionless, his hands folded on his knees, his head drooping on his breast, his eyes closed, and his brows knit as if in pain. Matryona was silent, and Simon said: "Matryona, have you no love of God?"

Matryona heard these words, and as she looked at the stranger, suddenly her heart softened towards him. She came back from the door, and going to the oven she got out the supper. Setting a cup on the table, she poured out some kvas. Then she brought out the last piece of bread, and set out a knife and spoons.

"Eat, if you want to," said she.

Simon drew the stranger to the table.

"Take your place, young man," said he.

Simon cut the bread, crumbled it into the broth, and they began to eat. Matryona sat at the corner of the table, resting her head on her hand and looking at the stranger.

And Matryona was touched with pity for the stranger, and began to feel fond of him. And at once the stranger's face lit up; his brows were no longer bent, he raised his eyes and smiled at Matryona.

When they had finished supper, the woman cleared away the things and began questioning the stranger. "Where are you from?" said she.

"I am not from these parts."

"But how did you come to be on the road?"

"I may not tell."

"Did some one rob you?"

"God punished me."

"And you were lying there naked?"

"Yes, naked and freezing. Simon saw me and had pity on me. He took off his coat, put it on me and brought me here. And you have fed me, given me drink, and shown pity on me. God will reward you!"

Matryona rose, took from the window Simon's old shirt she had been patching, and gave it to the stranger. She also brought out a pair of trousers for him.

"There," said she, "I see you have no shirt. Put this on, and lie down where you please, in the loft or on the stove."

The stranger took off the coat, put on the shirt, and lay down in the loft. Matryona put out the candle, took the coat, and climbed to where her husband lay on the stove.

Matryona drew the skirts of the coat over her and lay down, but could not sleep; she could not get the stranger out of her mind.

When she remembered that he had eaten their last piece of bread and that there was none for tomorrow and thought of the shirt and trousers she had given away, she felt grieved; but when she remembered how he had smiled, her heart was glad.

Long did Matryona lie awake, and she noticed that Simon also was awake – he drew the coat towards him.

"Simon!"

"Well?"

"You have had the last of the bread, and I have not put any to rise. I don't know what we shall do tomorrow. Perhaps I can borrow some of neighbor Martha."

"If we're alive we shall find something to eat."

The woman lay still awhile, and then said, "He seems a good man, but why does he not tell us who he is?"

"I suppose he has his reasons."

"Simon!"

"Well?"

"We give; but why does nobody give us anything?"

Simon did not know what to say; so he only said, "Let us stop talking," and turned over and went to sleep.

V

In the morning Simon awoke. The children were still asleep; his wife had gone to the neighbor's to borrow some bread. The stranger alone was sitting on the bench, dressed in the old shirt and trousers, and looking upwards. His face was brighter than it had been the day before.

Simon said to him, "Well, friend; the belly wants bread and the naked body clothes. One has to work for a living. What work do you know?"

"I do not know any."

This surprised Simon, but he said, "Men who want to learn can learn anything."

"Men work, and I will work also."

"What is your name?"

"Michael."

"Well Michael, if you don't wish to talk about yourself that is your own affair; but you'll have to earn a living for yourself. If you will work as I tell you, I will give you food and shelter."

"May God reward you! I will learn. Show me what to do."

Simon took yarn, put it round his thumb and began to twist it.

"It is easy enough – see!"

Michael watched him, put some yarn round his own thumb in the same way, caught the knack, and twisted the yarn also.

Then Simon showed him how to wax the thread. This also Michael mastered. Next Simon showed him how to twist the bristle in, and how to sew, and this, too, Michael learned at once.

Whatever Simon showed him he understood at once, and after three days he worked as if he had sewn boots all his life. He worked without stopping, and ate little. When work was over he sat silently, looking upwards. He hardly went into the street, spoke only when necessary, and neither joked nor laughed. They never saw him smile, except that first evening when Matryona gave them supper.

VI

Day by day and week by week the year went round. Michael lived and worked with Simon. His fame spread till people said that no one sewed boots so neatly and strongly as Simon's workman, Michael; and from all the district round people came to Simon for their boots, and he began to be well off.

One winter day, as Simon and Michael sat working, a carriage on sledge runners with three horses and with bells, drove up to the hut. They looked out of the window; the carriage stopped at their door, a fine servant jumped down from the box and opened the door. A gentleman in a fur coat got out and walked up to Simon's hut. Up jumped Matryona and opened the door wide. The gentleman stooped to enter the hut, and when he drew himself up again his head nearly reached the ceiling, and he seemed quite to fill his end of the room.

Simon rose, bowed, and looked at the gentleman with astonishment. He had never seen anyone like him. Simon himself was lean, Michael was thin, and Matryona was dry as a bone, but this man was like someone from another world: red-faced, burly, with a neck like a bull's, and looking altogether as if he were cast in iron.

The gentleman puffed, threw off his fur coat, sat down on the bench, and said, "Which of you is the master bootmaker?"

"I am, your Excellency," said Simon, coming forward.

Then the gentleman shouted to his lad, "Hey, Fedka, bring the leather!"

The servant ran in, bringing a parcel. The gentleman took the parcel and put it on the table.

"Untie it," said he. The lad untied it.

The gentleman pointed to the leather.

"Look here, shoemaker," said he, "do you see this leather?"

"Yes, your honor."

"But do you know what sort of leather it is?"

Simon felt the leather and said, "It is good leather."

"Good, indeed! Why, you fool, you never saw such leather before in your life. It's German, and cost twenty roubles."

Simon was frightened, and said, "Where should I ever see leather like that?"

"Just so! Now, can you make it into boots for me?"

"Yes, your Excellency, I can."

Then the gentleman shouted at him: "You can, can you? Well, remember whom you are to make them for, and what the leather is. You must make me boots that will wear for a year, neither losing shape nor coming unsewn. If you can do it, take the leather and cut it up; but if you can't, say so. I warn you now, if your boots come unsewn or lose shape within a year, I will have you put in prison. If they don't burst or lose shape for a year, I will pay you ten roubles for your work."

Simon was frightened, and did not know what to say. He glanced at Michael and nudging him with his elbow, whispered: "Shall I take the work?"

Michael nodded his head as if to say, "Yes, take it."

Simon did as Michael advised, and undertook to make boots that would not lose shape or split for a whole year.

Calling his servant, the gentleman told him to pull the boot off his left leg, which he stretched out.

"Take my measure!" said he.

Simon stitched a paper measure seventeen inches long, smoothed it out, knelt down, wiped his hands well on his apron so as not to soil the gentleman's sock, and began to measure. He measured the sole, and round the instep, and began to measure the calf of the leg, but the paper was too short. The calf of the leg was as thick as a beam.

"Mind you don't make it too tight in the leg."

Simon stitched on another strip of paper. The gentleman twitched his toes about in his sock, looking round at those in the hut, and as he did so he noticed Michael.

"Whom have you there?" asked he.

"That is my workman. He will sew the boots."

"Mind," said the gentleman to Michael, "remember to make them so that they will last me a year."

Simon also looked at Michael, and saw that Michael was not looking at the gentleman, but was gazing into the corner behind the gentleman, as if he saw some one there. Michael looked and looked, and suddenly he smiled, and his face became brighter.

"What are you grinning at, you fool?" thundered the gentleman. "You had better look to it that the boots are ready in time."

"They shall be ready in good time," said Michael.

"Mind it is so," said the gentleman, and he put on his boots and his fur coat, wrapped the latter round him, and went to the door. But he forgot to stoop and struck his head against the lintel.

He swore and rubbed his head. Then he took his seat in the carriage and drove away.

When he had gone, Simon said: "There's a figure of a man for you! You could not kill him with a mallet. He almost knocked out the lintel, but little harm it did him."

And Matryona said: "Living as he does, how should he not grow strong? Death itself can't touch such a rock as that."

VII

Then Simon said to Michael: "Well, we have taken the work, but we must see we don't get into trouble over it. The leather is dear, and the gentleman hot-tempered. We must make no mistakes.

Come, your eye is truer and your hands have become nimbler than mine, so you take this measure and cut out the boots. I will finish off the sewing of the vamps."

Michael did as he was told. He took the leather spread it out on the table, folded it in two, took a knife and began to cut out.

Matryona came and watched him cutting, and was surprised to see how he was doing it. Matryona was accustomed to seeing boots made, and she looked and saw that Michael was not cutting the leather for boots, but was cutting it round.

She wished to say something, but she thought to herself: "Perhaps I do not understand how gentlemen's boots should be made. I suppose Michael knows more about it – and I won't interfere."

When Michael had cut up the leather, he took a thread and began to sew not with two ends, as boots are sewn, but with a single end, as for soft slippers.

Again Matryona wondered, but again she did not interfere. Michael sewed on steadily till noon. Then Simon rose for dinner, looked around, and saw that Michael had made slippers out of the gentleman's leather.

"Ah!" groaned Simon, and he thought, "How is it that Michael, who has been with me a whole year and never made a mistake before, should do such a dreadful thing? The gentleman ordered high boots, welted, with whole fronts, and Michael has made soft slippers with single soles, and has wasted the leather. What am I to say to the gentleman? I can never replace leather such as this."

And he said to Michael, "What are you doing friend? You have ruined me! You know the gentleman ordered high boots, but see what you have made!"

Hardly had he begun to rebuke Michael, when "rat-tat" went the iron ring that hung at the door. Someone was knocking. They looked out of the window; a man had come on horseback, and was fastening his horse. They opened the door, and the servant who had been with the gentleman came in.

"Good day," said he.

"Good day," replied Simon. "What can we do for you?"

"My mistress has sent me about the boots."

"What about the boots?"

"Why, my master no longer needs them. He is dead."

"Is it possible?"

"He did not live to get home after leaving you, but died in the carriage. When we reached home and the servants came to help him alight he rolled over like a sack. He was dead already, and so stiff that he could hardly be got out of the carriage. My mistress sent me here, saying: 'Tell the bootmaker that the gentleman who ordered boots from him and left the leather for them no longer needs the boots, but that he must quickly make soft slippers for the corpse. Wait till they are ready, and bring them back with you.' That is why I have come."

Michael gathered up the remnants of the leather; rolled them up, took the soft slippers he had made, slapped them together, wiped them down with his apron, and handed them and the roll of leather to the servant, who took them and said: "Good-bye, masters, and good day to you!"

VIII

Another year passed, and another, and Michael was now living his sixth year with Simon. He lived as before. He went nowhere, only spoke when necessary, and had only smiled twice in all those years – once when Matryona gave him food, and a second time when the gentleman was in their hut. Simon was more than pleased with his workman. He never now asked him where he came from, and only feared lest Michael should go away.

They were all at home one day. Matryona was putting iron pots in the oven, the children were running along the benches and looking out of the window; Simon was sewing at one window, and Michael was fastening on a heel at the other.

One of the boys ran along the bench to Michael, leant on his shoulder, and looked out of the window.

"Look, Uncle Michael! There is a lady with little girls! She seems to be coming here. And one of the girls is lame."

When the boy said that, Michael dropped his work, turned to the window, and looked out into the street.

Simon was surprised. Michael never used to look out into the street, but now he pressed against the window, staring at something. Simon also looked out, and saw that a well-dressed woman was really coming to his hut, leading by the hand two little girls in fur coats and woollen shawls. The girls could hardly be told one from the other, except that one of them was crippled in her left leg and walked with a limp.

The woman stepped into the porch and entered the passage. Feeling about for the entrance she found the latch, which she lifted, and opened the door. She let the two girls go in first, and followed them into the hut.

"Good day, good folk!"

"Pray come in," said Simon. "What can we do for you?"

The woman sat down by the table. The two little girls pressed close to her knees, afraid of the people in the hut.

"I want leather shoes made for these two little girls, for spring."

"We can do that. We never have made such small shoes, but we can make them; either welted or turnover shoes, linen lined. My man, Michael, is a master at the work."

Simon glanced at Michael and saw that he had left his work and was sitting with his eyes fixed on the little girls. Simon was surprised. It was true the girls were pretty, with black eyes, plump, and rosy-cheeked, and they wore nice kerchiefs and fur coats, but still Simon could not understand why Michael should look at them like that – just as if he had known them before. He was puzzled, but went on talking with the woman, and arranging the price. Having fixed it, he prepared the measure. The woman lifted the lame girl on to her lap and said: "Take two measures from this little girl. Make one shoe for the lame foot and three for the sound one. They both have the same sized feet. They are twins."

Simon took the measure and, speaking of the lame girl, said: "How did it happen to her? She is such a pretty girl. Was she born so?"

"No, her mother crushed her leg."

Then Matryona joined in. She wondered who this woman was, and whose the children were, so she said: "Are not you their mother, then?"

"No, my good woman, I am neither their mother nor any relation to them. They were quite strangers to me, but I adopted them."

"They are not your children and yet you are so fond of them?"

"How can I help being fond of them? I fed them both at my own breasts. I had a child of my own, but God took him. I was not so fond of him as I now am of these."

"Then whose children are they?"

IX

The woman, having begun talking, told them the whole story.

"It is about six years since their parents died, both in one week: their father was buried on the Tuesday, and their mother died on the Friday. These orphans were born three days after their father's death, and their mother did not live another day. My husband and I were then living as peasants in the village. We were neighbors of theirs, our yard being next to theirs. Their father was a lonely man; a woodcutter in the forest. When felling trees one day, they let one fall on him. It fell across his body and crushed his bowels out. They hardly got him home before his soul went to God; and that same week his wife gave birth to twins – these little girls. She was poor and alone; she had no one, young or old, with her. Alone she gave them birth, and alone she met her death.

"The next morning I went to see her, but when I entered the hut, she, poor thing, was already stark and cold. In dying she had rolled on to this child and crushed her leg. The village folk came to the hut washed the body, laid her out, made a coffin, and buried her. They were good folk. The babies were left alone. What was to be done with them? I was the only woman there who had a baby at the time. I was nursing my first-born – eight weeks old. So I took them for a time. The peasants came together, and thought and thought what to do with them, and at last they said to me: 'For the present, Mary, you had better keep the girls, and later on we will arrange what to do for them.' So I nursed the sound one at my breast, but at first I did not feed this crippled one. I did not suppose she would live. But then I thought to myself, why should the poor innocent suffer? I pitied her, and began to feed her. And so I fed my own boy and these two – the three of them – at my own breast. I was young and strong, and had good food, and God gave me so much milk that at times it even overflowed. I used sometimes to feed two at a time, while the third was waiting. When one had had enough I nursed the third. And God so ordered it that these grew up, while my own was buried before he was two years old. And I had no more children, though we prospered. Now my husband is working for the corn merchant at the mill. The pay is good and we are well off. But I have no children of my own, and how lonely I should be without these little girls! How can I help loving them! They are the joy of my life!"

She pressed the lame little girl to her with one hand while with the other she wiped the tears from her cheeks.

And Matryona sighed, and said: "The proverb is true that says, 'One may live without father or mother, but one cannot live without God.'"

So they talked together, when suddenly the whole hut was lighted up as though by summer lightning from the corner where

Michael sat. They all looked towards him and saw him sitting, his hands folded on his knees, gazing upwards and smiling.

X

The woman went away with the girls. Michael rose from the bench, put down his work, and took off his apron. Then, bowing low to Simon and his wife, he said: "Farewell, masters. God has forgiven me. I ask your forgiveness, too, for anything done amiss."

And they saw that a light shone from Michael. And Simon rose, bowed down to Michael, and said: "I see, Michael, that you are no common man, and I can neither keep you nor question you. Only tell me this: how is it that when I found you and brought you home, you were gloomy, and when my wife gave you food you smiled at her and became brighter? Then when the gentleman came to order the boots, you smiled again and became brighter still? And now, when this woman brought the little girls, you smiled a third time, and have become as bright as day? Tell me, Michael, why does your face shine so, and why did you smile those three times?"

And Michael answered: "Light shines from me because I have been punished, but now God has pardoned me. And I smiled three times, because God sent me to learn three truths, and I have learnt them. One I learnt when your wife pitied me and that is why I smiled the first time. The second I learnt when the rich man ordered the boots and then I smiled again. And now, when I saw those little girls, I learnt the third and last truth, and I smiled the third time."

And Simon said, "Tell me, Michael, what did God punish you for? and what were the three truths? that I, too, may know them."

And Michael answered: "God punished me for disobeying Him. I was an angel in heaven and disobeyed God. God sent me to fetch a woman's soul. I flew to earth, and saw a sick woman lying alone, who had just given birth to twin girls. They moved feebly at their mother's side, but she could not lift them to her breast. When she saw me, she understood that God had sent me for her soul, and she wept and said: 'Angel of God! My husband has just been buried, killed by a falling tree. I have neither sister, nor aunt, nor mother: no one to care for my orphans. Do not take my soul! Let me nurse my babes, feed them, and set them on their feet before I die. Children cannot live without father or mother.' And I hearkened to her. I placed one child at her breast and gave the other into her arms, and returned to the Lord in heaven. I flew to the Lord, and said: 'I could not take the soul of the mother. Her husband was killed by a tree; the woman has twins, and prays that her soul may not be taken. She says: "Let me nurse and feed my children, and set them on their feet. Children cannot live without father or mother." I have not taken her soul.' And God said: 'Go – take the mother's soul, and learn three truths: Learn What dwells in man, What is not given to man, and What men live by. When thou hast learnt these things, thou shalt return to heaven.' So I flew again to earth and took the mother's soul. The babes dropped from her breasts. Her body rolled over on the bed and crushed one babe, twisting its leg. I rose above the village, wishing to take her soul to God; but a wind seized me, and my wings drooped and dropped off. Her soul rose alone to God, while I fell to earth by the roadside."

XI

And Simon and Matryona understood who it was that had lived with them, and whom they had clothed and fed. And they wept with awe and with joy. And the angel said: "I was alone in the field, naked. I had never known human needs, cold and hunger, till I became a man. I was famished, frozen, and did not know what to do. I saw, near the field I was in, a shrine built for God, and I went to it hoping to find shelter. But the shrine was locked, and I could not enter. So I sat down behind the shrine to shelter myself at least from the wind. Evening drew on. I was hungry, frozen, and in pain. Suddenly I heard a man coming along the road. He carried a pair of boots, and was talking to himself. For the first time since I became a man I saw the mortal face of a man, and his face seemed terrible to me and I turned from it. And I heard the man talking to himself of how to cover his body from the cold in winter, and how to feed wife and children. And I thought: 'I am perishing of cold and hunger, and here is a man thinking only of how to clothe himself and his wife, and how to get bread for themselves. He cannot help me.' When the man saw me he frowned and became still more terrible, and passed me by on the other side. I despaired, but suddenly I heard him coming back. I looked up, and did not recognize the same man: before, I had seen death in his face; but now he was alive, and I recognized in him the presence of God. He came up to me, clothed me, took me with him and brought me to his home. I entered the house a woman came to meet us and began to speak. The woman was still more terrible than the man had been; the spirit of death came from her mouth; I could not breathe for the stench of death that spread around her. She wished to drive me out into the cold, and I knew that if she did so she would die. Suddenly her husband spoke to her of God, and the woman changed at once. And when she brought me food and looked at me, I glanced at her and saw that death no longer dwelt in her; she had become alive, and in her too I saw God.

"Then I remembered the first lesson God had set me: 'Learn what dwells in man.' And I understood that in man dwells Love! I was glad that God had already begun to show me what He had promised, and I smiled for the first time. But I had not yet learnt all. I did not yet know What is not given to man, and What men live by.

"I lived with you, and a year passed. A man came to order boots that should wear for a year without losing shape or cracking. I looked at him, and suddenly, behind his shoulder, I saw my comrade – the angel of death. None but me saw that angel; but I knew him, and knew that before the sun set he would take that rich man's soul. And I thought to myself, 'The man is making preparations for a year, and does not know that he will die before evening.' And I remembered God's second saying, 'Learn what is not given to man.'

"What dwells in man I already knew. Now I learnt what is not given him. It is not given to man to know his own needs. And I smiled for the second time. I was glad to have seen my comrade angel – glad also that God had revealed to me the second saying.

"But I still did not know all. I did not know What men live by. And I lived on, waiting till God should reveal to me the last lesson. In the sixth year came the girl-twins with the woman; and I recognized the girls, and heard how they had been kept alive. Having heard the story, I thought, 'Their mother besought me for the children's sake, and I believed her when she said that children cannot live without father or mother; but a stranger has nursed them, and has brought them up.' And when the woman showed her love for the children that were not her own, and wept over them, I saw in her the living God, and understood What men live by. And I knew that God had revealed to me the last lesson, and had forgiven my sin. And then I smiled for the third time."

XII

And the angel's body was bared, and he was clothed in light so that eye could not look on him; and his voice grew louder, as though it came not from him but from heaven above. And the angel said:

"I have learnt that all men live not by care for themselves, but by love.

"It was not given to the mother to know what her children needed for their life. Nor was it given to the rich man to know what he himself needed. Nor is it given to any man to know whether, when evening comes, he will need boots for his body or slippers for his corpse.

"I remained alive when I was a man, not by care of myself, but because love was present in a passerby, and because he and his wife pitied and loved me. The orphans remained alive, not because of their mother's care, but because there was love in the heart of a woman, a stranger to them, who pitied and loved them. And all men live not by the thought they spend on their own welfare, but because love exists in man.

"I knew before that God gave life to men and desires that they should live; now I understood more than that.

"I understood that God does not wish men to live apart, and therefore he does not reveal to them what each one needs for himself; but he wishes them to live united, and therefore reveals to each of them what is necessary for all.

"I have now understood that though it seems to men that they live by care for themselves, in truth it is love alone by which they live. He who has love, is in God, and God is in him, for God is love."

And the angel sang praise to God, so that the hut trembled at his voice. The roof opened, and a column of fire rose from earth to heaven. Simon and his wife and children fell to the ground. Wings appeared upon the angel's shoulders, and he rose into the heavens.

And when Simon came to himself the hut stood as before, and there was no one in it but his own family.

1881

5

A Spark Neglected
Burns the House

THEN CAME PETER and said to him, "Lord, how oft shall my brother sin against me, and I forgive him? until seven times?" Jesus saith unto him, "I say not unto thee, until seven times; but, until seventy times seven. Therefore is the kingdom of heaven likened unto a certain king, which would make a reckoning with his servants. And when he had begun to reckon, one was brought unto him, which owed him ten thousand talents. But forasmuch as he had not wherewith to pay, his lord commanded him to be sold, and his wife, and children, and all that he had, and payment to be made. The servant therefore fell down and worshipped him, saying, 'Lord, have patience with me, and I will pay thee all.' And the lord of that servant, being moved with compassion, released him, and forgave him the debt. But that servant went out, and found one of his fellow servants, which owed him a hundred pence: and he laid hold on him, and took him by the throat saying, 'Pay what thou owest.' So his fellow servant fell down and besought him, saying, 'Have patience with me, and I will pay thee.' And he would not: but went and cast him into prison, till he should pay that which was due. So when his fellow servants saw what was done, they were exceeding sorry, and came and told unto their lord all that was done. Then his lord called him unto him, and saith to him, 'Thou wicked servant, I forgave thee all that debt, because thou besoughtest me: shouldest not thou also have had mercy on thy fellow servant, even as I had mercy on thee?' And his lord was wroth, and delivered him to the tormentors, till he should pay all that was due. So shall also my heavenly Father do unto you, if ye forgive not every one his brother from your hearts."

– Matt. xviii. 21–35

THERE ONCE LIVED in a village a peasant named Ivan Stcherbakof. He was comfortably off, in the prime of life, the best worker in the village, and had three sons all able to work. The eldest was married, the second about to marry, and the third was a big lad who could mind the horses and was already beginning to plow. Ivan's wife was an able and thrifty woman, and they were fortunate in having a quiet, hardworking daughter-in-law. There was nothing to prevent Ivan and his family from living happily. They had only one idle mouth to feed; that was Ivan's old father, who suffered from asthma and had been lying ill on the top of the brick oven for seven years. Ivan had all he needed: three horses and a colt, a cow with a calf, and fifteen sheep. The women made all the clothing for the family, besides helping in the fields, and the men tilled the land. They always had grain enough of their own to last over beyond the next harvest and sold enough oats to pay the taxes and meet their other needs. So Ivan and his children might have lived quite comfortably had it not been for a feud between him and his next door neighbor, Limping Gabriel, the son of Gordey Ivanof.

As long as old Gordey was alive and Ivan's father was still able to manage the household, the peasants lived as neighbors should. If the women of either house happened to want a sieve or a tub, or the men required a sack, or if a cart-wheel got broken and could not be mended at once, they used to send to the other house, and helped each other in neighborly fashion. When a calf strayed into the neighbor's thrashing-ground they would just drive it out, and only say, "Don't let it get in again; our grain is lying there." And such things as locking up the barns and out-houses, hiding things from one another, or backbiting were never thought of in those days.

That was in the fathers' time. When the sons came to be at the head of the families, everything changed.

It all began about a trifle.

Ivan's daughter-in-law had a hen that began laying rather early in the season, and she started collecting its eggs for Easter. Every day she went to the cart shed, and found an egg in the cart; but one day the hen, probably frightened by the children, flew across the fence into the neighbor's yard and laid its egg there. The woman heard the cackling, but said to herself: "I have no time now; I must tidy up for Sunday. I'll fetch the egg later on." In the evening she went to the cart, but found no egg there. She went and asked her mother-in-law and brother-in-law whether they had taken the egg. "No," they had not; but her youngest brother-in-law, Taras, said: "Your Biddy laid its egg in the neighbor's yard. It was there she was cackling, and she flew back across the fence from there."

The woman went and looked at the hen. There she was on the perch with the other birds, her eyes just closing ready to go to sleep. The woman wished she could have asked the hen and got an answer from her.

Then she went to the neighbor's, and Gabriel's mother came out to meet her.

"What do you want, young woman?"

"Why, Granny, you see, my hen flew across this morning. Did she not lay an egg here?"

"We never saw anything of it. The Lord be thanked, our own hens started laying long ago. We collect our own eggs and have no need of other people's! And we don't go looking for eggs in other people's yards, lass!"

The young woman was offended, and said more than she should have done. Her neighbor answered back with interest, and the women began abusing each other. Ivan's wife, who had been to fetch water, happening to pass just then, joined in too. Gabriel's wife rushed out, and began reproaching the young woman with things that had really happened and with other things that never had happened at all. Then a general uproar commenced, all shouting at once, trying to get out two words at a time, and not choice words either.

"You're this!" and "You're that!" "You're a thief!" and "You're a slut!" and "You're starving your old father-in-law to death!" and "You're a good-for-nothing!" and so on.

"And you've made a hole in the sieve I lent you, you jade! And it's our yoke you're carrying your pails on – you just give back our yoke!"

Then they caught hold of the yoke, and spilt the water, snatched off one another's shawls, and began fighting. Gabriel, returning from the fields, stopped to take his wife's part. Out rushed Ivan and his son and joined in with the rest. Ivan was a strong fellow, he scattered the whole lot of them, and pulled a handful of hair out of Gabriel's beard. People came to see what was the matter, and the fighters were separated with difficulty.

That was how it all began.

Gabriel wrapped the hair torn from his beard in a paper, and went to the District Court to have the law on Ivan. "I didn't grow my beard," said he, "for pockmarked Ivan to pull it out!" And his wife went bragging to the neighbors, saying they'd have Ivan condemned and sent to Siberia. And so the feud grew.

The old man, from where he lay on the top of the oven, tried from the very first to persuade them to make peace, but they would not listen. He told them, "It's a stupid thing you are after, children, picking quarrels about such a paltry matter. Just think! The whole thing began about an egg. The children may have taken it – well, what matter? What's the value of one egg? God sends enough for all! And suppose your neighbor did say an unkind word – put it right; show her how to say a better one! If there has been a fight – well, such things will happen; we're all sinners, but make it up, and let there be an end of it! If you nurse your anger it will be worse for you yourselves."

But the younger folk would not listen to the old man. They thought his words were mere senseless dotage. Ivan would not humble himself before his neighbor.

"I never pulled his beard," he said, "he pulled the hair out himself. But his son has burst all the fastenings on my shirt, and torn it...Look at it!"

And Ivan also went to law. They were tried by the Justice of the Peace and by the District Court. While all this was going on, the coupling-pin of Gabriel's cart disappeared. Gabriel's womenfolk accused Ivan's son of having taken it. They said: "We saw him in the night go past our window, towards the cart; and a neighbor says he saw him at the pub, offering the pin to the landlord."

So they went to law about that. And at home not a day passed without a quarrel or even a fight. The children, too, abused one another, having learnt to do so from their elders; and when the women happened to meet by the riverside, where they went to rinse the clothes, their arms did not do as much wringing as their tongues did nagging, and every word was a bad one.

At first the peasants only slandered one another; but afterwards they began in real earnest to snatch anything that lay handy, and the children followed their example. Life became harder and harder for them. Ivan Stcherbakof and Limping Gabriel kept suing one another at the Village Assembly, and at the District Court, and before the Justice of the Peace until all the judges were tired of them. Now Gabriel got Ivan fined or imprisoned; then Ivan did as much to Gabriel; and the more they spited each other the angrier they grew – like dogs that attack one another and get more and more furious the longer they fight. You strike one dog from behind, and it thinks it's the other dog biting him, and gets still fiercer. So these peasants: they went to law, and one or other of them was fined or locked up, but that only made them more and more angry with each other. "Wait a bit," they said, "and I'll make you pay for it." And so it went on for six years. Only the old man lying on the top of the oven kept telling them again and again: "Children, what are you doing? Stop all this paying back; keep to your work, and don't bear malice – it will be better for you. The more you bear malice, the worse it will be."

But they would not listen to him.

In the seventh year, at a wedding, Ivan's daughter-in-law held Gabriel up to shame, accusing him of having been caught horse stealing. Gabriel was tipsy, and unable to contain his anger, gave the woman such a blow that she was laid up for a week; and she was pregnant at the time. Ivan was delighted. He went to the magistrate to lodge a complaint. "Now I'll get rid of my neighbor! He won't escape imprisonment, or exile to Siberia." But Ivan's wish was not fulfilled. The magistrate dismissed the case. The woman was examined, but she was up and about and showed no sign of any injury. Then Ivan went to the Justice of the Peace, but he referred the business to the District Court. Ivan bestirred himself: treated the clerk and the Elder of the District Court to a gallon of liquor and got Gabriel condemned to be flogged. The sentence was read out to Gabriel by the clerk: "The Court decrees that the peasant Gabriel Gordeyef shall receive twenty lashes with a birch rod at the District Court."

Ivan too heard the sentence read, and looked at Gabriel to see how he would take it. Gabriel grew as pale as a sheet, and turned round and went out into the passage. Ivan followed him, meaning to see to the horse, and he overheard Gabriel say, "Very well! He will have my back flogged: that will make it burn; but something of his may burn worse than that!"

Hearing these words, Ivan at once went back into the Court, and said: "Upright judges! He threatens to set my house on fire! Listen: he said it in the presence of witnesses!"

Gabriel was recalled. "Is it true that you said this?"

"I haven't said anything. Flog me, since you have the power. It seems that I alone am to suffer, and all for being in the right, while he is allowed to do as he likes."

Gabriel wished to say something more, but his lips and his cheeks quivered, and he turned towards the wall. Even the officials were frightened by his looks. "He may do some mischief to himself or to his neighbor," thought they.

Then the old Judge said: "Look here, my men; you'd better be reasonable and make it up. Was it right of you, friend Gabriel, to strike a pregnant woman? It was lucky it passed off so well, but think what might have happened! Was it right? You had better confess and beg his pardon, and he will forgive you, and we will alter the sentence."

The clerk heard these words, and remarked: "That's impossible under Statute 117. An agreement between the parties not having been arrived at, a decision of the Court has been pronounced and must be executed."

But the Judge would not listen to the clerk.

"Keep your tongue still, my friend," said he. "The first of all laws is to obey God, who loves peace." And the Judge began again to persuade the peasants, but could not succeed. Gabriel would not listen to him.

"I shall be fifty next year," said he, "and have a married son, and have never been flogged in my life, and now that pock-marked Ivan has had me condemned to be flogged, and am I to go and ask his forgiveness? No; I've borne enough...Ivan shall have cause to remember me!"

Again Gabriel's voice quivered, and he could say no more, but turned round and went out.

It was seven miles from the Court to the village, and it was getting late when Ivan reached home. He unharnessed his horse, put it up for the night, and entered the cottage. No one was there. The women had already gone to drive the cattle in, and the young fellows were not yet back from the fields. Ivan went in, and sat down, thinking. He remembered how Gabriel had listened to the sentence, and how pale he had become, and how he had turned to the wall; and Ivan's heart grew heavy. He thought how he himself would feel if he were sentenced, and he pitied Gabriel. Then he heard his old father up on the oven cough, and saw him sit up, lower his legs, and scramble down. The old man dragged himself slowly to a seat, and sat down. He was quite tired out with the exertion, and coughed a long time till he had cleared his throat. Then, leaning against the table, he said: "Well, has he been condemned?"

"Yes, to twenty strokes with the rods," answered Ivan.

The old man shook his head.

"A bad business," said he. "You are doing wrong, Ivan! Ah! it's very bad – not for him so much as for yourself!…Well, they'll flog him: but will that do you any good?"

"He'll not do it again," said Ivan.

"What is it he'll not do again? What has he done worse than you?"

"Why, think of the harm he has done me!" said Ivan. "He nearly killed my son's wife, and now he's threatening to burn us up. Am I to thank him for it?"

The old man sighed, and said: "You go about the wide world, Ivan, while I am lying on the oven all these years, so you think you see everything, and that I see nothing…Ah, lad! It's you that don't see; malice blinds you. Others' sins are before your eyes, but your own are behind your back. 'He's acted badly!' What a thing to say! If he were the only one to act badly, how could strife exist? Is strife among men ever bred by one alone? Strife is always between two. His badness you see, but your own you don't. If he were bad, but you were good, there would be no strife. Who pulled the hair out of his beard? Who spoilt his haystack? Who dragged him to the law court? Yet you put it all on him! You live a bad life yourself, that's what is wrong! It's not the way I used to live, lad, and it's not the way I taught you. Is that the way his old father and I used to live? How did we live? Why, as neighbors should! If he happened to run out of flour, one of the women would come across: 'Uncle Trol, we want some flour.' 'Go to the barn, dear,' I'd say: 'take what you need.' If he'd no one to take his horses to pasture, 'Go, Ivan,' I'd say, 'and look after his horses.' And if I was short of anything, I'd go to him. 'Uncle Gordey,' I'd say, 'I want so-and-so!' 'Take it Uncle Trol!' That's how it was between us, and we had an easy time of it. But now?...That soldier the other day was telling us about the fight at Plevna. Why, there's war between you worse than at Plevna! Is that living?...What a sin it is! You are a man and master of the house; it's you who will have to answer. What are you teaching the women and the children? To snarl and snap? Why, the other day your Taraska – that greenhorn – was swearing at neighbor Irena, calling her names; and his mother listened and laughed. Is that right? It is you will have to answer. Think of your soul. Is this all as it should be? You throw a word at me, and I give you two in return; you give me a blow, and I give you two. No, lad! Christ, when He walked on earth, taught us fools something very different...If you get a hard word from any one, keep silent, and his own conscience will accuse him. That is what our Lord taught. If you get a slap, turn the other cheek. 'Here, beat me, if that's what I deserve!' And his own conscience will rebuke him. He will soften, and will listen to you. That's the way He taught us, not to be proud!...Why don't you speak? Isn't it as I say?"

Ivan sat silent and listened.

The old man coughed, and having with difficulty cleared his throat, began again: "You think Christ taught us wrong? Why, it's all for our own good. Just think of your earthly life; are you better off, or worse, since this Plevna began among you? Just reckon up what you've spent on all this law business – what the driving backwards and forwards and your food on the way have cost you! What fine fellows your sons have grown; you might live and get on well; but now your means are lessening. And why? All because of this folly; because of your pride. You ought to be plowing with your lads, and do the sowing yourself; but the fiend carries you off to the judge, or to some pettifogger or other. The plowing is not done in time, nor the sowing, and mother earth can't bear properly. Why did the oats fail this year? When did you sow them? When you came back from town! And what did you gain? A burden for your own shoulders…Eh, lad, think of your own business! Work with your boys in the field and at home, and if someone offends you, forgive him, as God wished you to. Then life will be easy, and your heart will always be light."

Ivan remained silent.

"Ivan, my boy, hear your old father! Go and harness the roan, and go at once to the Government office; put an end to all this affair there; and in the morning go and make it up with Gabriel in God's name, and invite him to your house for tomorrow's holiday (It was the eve of the Virgin's Nativity). Have tea ready, and get a bottle of vodka and put an end to this wicked business, so that there should not be any more of it in future, and tell the women and children to do the same."

Ivan sighed, and thought, "What he says is true," and his heart grew lighter. Only he did not know how to begin to put matters right.

But again the old man began, as if he had guessed what was in Ivan's mind.

"Go, Ivan, don't put it off! Put out the fire before it spreads, or it will be too late."

The old man was going to say more, but before he could do so the women came in, chattering like magpies. The news that Gabriel was sentenced to be flogged, and of his threat to set fire to the house, had already reached them. They had heard all about it and added to it something of their own, and had again had a row, in the pasture, with the women of Gabriel's household. They began telling how Gabriel's daughter-in-law threatened a fresh action: Gabriel had got the right side of the examining magistrate, who would now turn the whole affair upside down; and the schoolmaster was writing out another petition, to the Tsar himself this time, about Ivan; and everything was in the petition – all about the coupling-pin and the kitchen garden – so that half of Ivan's homestead would be theirs soon. Ivan heard what they were saying, and his heart grew cold again, and he gave up the thought of making peace with Gabriel.

In a farmstead there is always plenty for the master to do. Ivan did not stop to talk to the women, but went out to the threshing floor and to the barn. By the time he had tidied up there, the sun had set and the young fellows had returned from the field. They had been plowing the field for the winter crops with two horses. Ivan met them, questioned them about their work, helped to put everything in its place, set a torn horse collar aside to be mended, and was going to put away some stakes under the barn, but it had grown quite dusk, so he decided to leave them where they were till next day. Then he gave the cattle their food, opened the gate, let out the horses Taras was to take to pasture for the night, and again closed the gate and barred it. "Now," thought he, "I'll have my supper, and then to bed." He took the horse collar and entered the hut. By this time he had forgotten about Gabriel and about what his old father had been saying to him. But, just as he took hold of the door handle to enter the passage, he heard his neighbor on the other side of the fence cursing somebody in a hoarse voice: "What the devil is he good for?" Gabriel was saying. "He's only fit to be killed!" At these words all Ivan's former bitterness towards his neighbor re-awoke. He stood listening while Gabriel scolded, and, when he stopped, Ivan went into the hut.

There was a light inside; his daughter-in-law sat spinning, his wife was getting supper ready, his eldest son was making straps for bark shoes, his second sat near the table with a book, and Taras was getting ready to go out to pasture the horses for the night. Everything in the hut would have been pleasant and bright, but for that plague – a bad neighbor!

Ivan entered, sullen and cross; threw the cat down from the bench, and scolded the women for putting the slop pail in the wrong place. He felt despondent, and sat down, frowning, to mend the horse collar. Gabriel's words kept ringing in his ears: his threat at the law court, and what he had just been shouting in a hoarse voice about some one who was "only fit to be killed."

His wife gave Taras his supper, and, having eaten it, Taras put on an old sheepskin and another coat, tied a sash round his waist, took some bread with him, and went out to the horses. His eldest brother was going to see him off, but Ivan himself rose instead, and went out into the porch. It had grown quite dark outside, clouds had gathered, and the wind had risen. Ivan went down the steps, helped his boy to mount, started the foal after him, and stood listening while Taras rode down the village and was there joined by other lads with their horses. Ivan waited until they were all out of hearing. As he stood there by the gate he could not get Gabriel's words out of his head: "Mind that something of yours does not burn worse!"

"He is desperate," thought Ivan. "Everything is dry, and it's windy weather besides. He'll come up at the back somewhere, set fire to something, and be off. He'll burn the place and escape scot free, the villain!…There now, if one could but catch him in the act, he'd not get off then!" And the thought fixed itself so firmly in his mind that he did not go up the steps but went out into the street and round the corner. "I'll just walk round the buildings; who can tell what he's after?" And Ivan, stepping softly, passed out of the gate. As soon as he reached the corner, he looked round along the fence, and seemed to see something suddenly move at the opposite corner, as if some one had come out and disappeared again. Ivan stopped, and stood quietly, listening and looking. Everything was still; only the leaves of the willows fluttered in the wind, and the straws of the thatch rustled. At first it seemed pitch dark, but, when his eyes had grown used to the darkness, he could see the far corner, and a plow that lay there, and the eaves. He looked a while, but saw no one.

"I suppose it was a mistake," thought Ivan; "but still I will go round," and Ivan went stealthily along by the shed. Ivan stepped so softly in his bark shoes that he did not hear his own footsteps. As he reached the far corner, something seemed to flare up for a moment near the plow and to vanish again. Ivan felt as if struck to the heart; and he stopped. Hardly had he stopped, when something flared up more brightly in the same place, and he clearly saw a man with a cap on his head, crouching down, with his back towards him, lighting a bunch of straw he held in his hand. Ivan's heart fluttered within him like a bird. Straining every nerve, he approached with great strides, hardly feeling his legs under him. "Ah," thought Ivan, "now he won't escape! I'll catch him in the act!"

Ivan was still some distance off, when suddenly he saw a bright light, but not in the same place as before, and not a small flame. The thatch had flared up at the eaves, the flames were reaching up to the roof, and, standing beneath it, Gabriel's whole figure was clearly visible.

Like a hawk swooping down on a lark, Ivan rushed at Limping Gabriel. "Now I'll have him; he shan't escape me!" thought Ivan. But Gabriel must have heard his steps, and (however he managed it) glancing round, he scuttled away past the barn like a hare.

"You shan't escape!" shouted Ivan, darting after him.

Just as he was going to seize Gabriel, the latter dodged him; but Ivan managed to catch the skirt of Gabriel's coat. It tore right off, and Ivan fell down. He recovered his feet, and shouting, "Help! Seize him! Thieves! Murder!" ran on again. But meanwhile Gabriel had reached his own gate. There Ivan overtook him and was about to seize him, when something struck Ivan a stunning blow, as though a stone had hit his temple, quite deafening him. It was Gabriel who, seizing an oak wedge that lay near the gate, had struck out with all his might.

Ivan was stunned; sparks flew before his eyes, then all grew dark and he staggered. When he came to his senses Gabriel was no longer there: it was as light as day, and from the side where his homestead was something roared and crackled like an engine at work. Ivan turned round and saw that his back shed was all ablaze, and the side shed had also caught fire, and flames and smoke and bits of burning straw mixed with the smoke, were being driven towards his hut.

"What is this, friends?..." cried Ivan, lifting his arms and striking his thighs. "Why, all I had to do was just to snatch it out from under the eaves and trample on it! What is this, friends?..." he kept repeating. He wished to shout, but his breath failed him; his voice was gone. He wanted to run, but his legs would not obey him, and got in each other's way. He moved slowly, but again staggered and again his breath failed. He stood still till he had regained breath, and then went on. Before he had got round the back shed to reach the fire, the side shed was also all ablaze; and the corner of the hut and the covered gateway had caught fire as well. The flames were leaping out of the hut, and it was impossible to get into the yard. A large crowd had collected, but nothing could be done. The neighbors were carrying their belongings out of their own houses, and driving the cattle out of their own sheds. After Ivan's house, Gabriel's also caught fire, then, the wind rising, the flames spread to the other side of the street and half the village was burnt down.

At Ivan's house they barely managed to save his old father; and the family escaped in what they had on; everything else, except the horses that had been driven out to pasture for the night, was lost; all the cattle, the fowls on their perches, the carts, plows, and harrows, the women's trunks with their clothes, and the grain in the granaries – all were burnt up!

At Gabriel's, the cattle were driven out, and a few things saved from his house.

The fire lasted all night. Ivan stood in front of his homestead and kept repeating, "What is this?…Friends!…One need only have pulled it out and trampled on it!" But when the roof fell in, Ivan rushed into the burning place, and seizing a charred beam, tried to drag it out. The women saw him, and called him back; but he pulled out the beam, and was going in again for another when he lost his footing and fell among the flames. Then his son made his way in after him and dragged him out. Ivan had singed his hair and beard and burnt his clothes and scorched his hands, but he felt nothing. "His grief has stupefied him," said the people. The fire was burning itself out, but Ivan still stood repeating: "Friends!…What is this?…One need only have pulled it out!"

In the morning the village Elder's son came to fetch Ivan.

"Daddy Ivan, your father is dying! He has sent for you to say good-bye."

Ivan had forgotten about his father, and did not understand what was being said to him.

"What father?" he said. "Whom has he sent for?"

"He sent for you, to say good-bye; he is dying in our cottage! Come along, daddy Ivan," said the Elder's son, pulling him by the arm; and Ivan followed the lad.

When he was being carried out of the hut, some burning straw had fallen on to the old man and burnt him, and he had been taken to the village Elder's in the farther part of the village, which the fire did not reach.

When Ivan came to his father, there was only the Elder's wife in the hut, besides some little children on the top of the oven. All the rest were still at the fire. The old man, who was lying on a bench holding a wax candle in his hand, kept turning his eyes towards the door. When his son entered, he moved a little. The old woman went up to him and told him that his son had come. He asked to have him brought nearer. Ivan came closer.

"What did I tell you, Ivan?" began the old man "Who has burnt down the village?"

"It was he, father!" Ivan answered. "I caught him in the act. I saw him shove the firebrand into the thatch. I might have pulled away the burning straw and stamped it out, and then nothing would have happened."

"Ivan," said the old man, "I am dying, and you in your turn will have to face death. Whose is the sin?"

Ivan gazed at his father in silence, unable to utter a word.

"Now, before God, say whose is the sin? What did I tell you?"

Only then Ivan came to his senses and understood it all. He sniffed and said, "Mine, father!" And he fell on his knees before his father, saying, "Forgive me, father; I am guilty before you and before God."

The old man moved his hands, changed the candle from his right hand to his left, and tried to lift his right hand to his forehead to cross himself, but could not do it, and stopped.

"Praise the Lord! Praise the Lord!" said he, and again he turned his eyes towards his son.

"Ivan! I say, Ivan!"

"What, father?"

"What must you do now?"

Ivan was weeping.

"I don't know how we are to live now, father!" he said.

The old man closed his eyes, moved his lips as if to gather strength, and opening his eyes again, said: "You'll manage. If you obey God's will, you'll manage!" He paused, then smiled, and said: "Mind, Ivan! Don't tell who started the fire! Hide another man's sin, and God will forgive two of yours!" And the old man took the candle in both hands and, folding them on his breast, sighed, stretched out, and died.

Ivan did not say anything against Gabriel, and no one knew what had caused the fire.

And Ivan's anger against Gabriel passed away, and Gabriel wondered that Ivan did not tell anybody. At first Gabriel felt afraid, but after awhile he got used to it. The men left off quarrelling, and then their families left off also. While rebuilding their huts, both families lived in one house; and when the village was rebuilt and they might have moved farther apart, Ivan and Gabriel built next to each other, and remained neighbors as before.

They lived as good neighbors should. Ivan Stcherbakof remembered his old father's command to obey God's law, and quench a fire at the first spark; and if any one does him an injury he now tries not to revenge himself, but rather to set matters right again; and if any one gives him a bad word, instead of giving a worse in return, he tries to teach the other not to use evil words; and so he teaches his womenfolk and children. And Ivan Stcherbakof has got on his feet again, and now lives better even than he did before.

1885

6

Two Old Men

The woman saith unto him, Sir, I perceive that thou art a prophet. Our fathers worshipped in this mountain; and ye say, that in Jerusalem is the place where men ought to worship. Jesus saith unto her, Woman, believe me, the hour cometh when neither in this mountain, nor in Jerusalem, shall ye worship the Father…But the hour cometh, and now is, when the true worshippers shall worship the Father in spirit and truth: for such doth the Father seek to be his worshippers.

— *John iv. 19–21, 23*

I

THERE WERE ONCE two old men who decided to go on a pilgrimage to worship God at Jerusalem. One of them was a well-to-do peasant named Efim Tarasitch Shevelef. The other, Elisha Bodrof, was not so well off.

Efim was a staid man, serious and firm. He neither drank nor smoked nor took snuff, and had never used bad language in his life. He had twice served as village Elder, and when he left office his accounts were in good order. He had a large family: two sons and a married grandson, all living with him. He was hale, long-bearded and erect, and it was only when he was past sixty that a little gray began to show itself in his beard.

Elisha was neither rich nor poor. He had formerly gone out carpentering, but now that he was growing old he stayed at home and kept bees. One of his sons had gone away to find work, the other was living at home. Elisha was a kindly and cheerful old man. It is true he drank sometimes, and he took snuff, and was fond of singing, but he was a peaceable man, and lived on good terms with his family and with his neighbors. He was short and dark, with a curly beard, and, like his patron saint Elisha, he was quite bald-headed.

The two old men had taken a vow long since and had arranged to go on a pilgrimage to Jerusalem together: but Efim could never spare the time; he always had so much business on hand; as soon as one thing was finished he started another. First he had to arrange his grandson's marriage; then to wait for his youngest son's return from the army, and after that he began building a new hut.

One holiday the two old men met outside the hut and, sitting down on some timber, began to talk.

"Well," asked Elisha, "when are we to fulfill our vow?"

Efim made a wry face.

"We must wait," he said. "This year has turned out a hard one for me. I started building this hut thinking it would cost me something over a hundred roubles, but now it's getting on for three hundred and it's still not finished. We shall have to wait until the summer. In summer, God willing, we will go without fail."

"It seems to me we ought not to put it off, but should go at once," said Elisha. "Spring is the best time."

"The time's right enough, but what about my building? How can I leave that?"

"As if you had no one to leave in charge! Your son can look after it."

"But how? My eldest son is not trustworthy – he sometimes takes a glass too much."

"Ah, neighbor, when we die they'll get on without us. Let your son begin now to get some experience."

"That's true enough, but somehow when one begins a thing one likes to see it done."

"Eh, friend, we can never get through all we have to do. The other day the womenfolk at home were washing and house cleaning for Easter. Here something needed doing, there something else, and they could not get everything done. So my eldest daughter-in-law, who's a sensible woman, says: 'We may be thankful the holiday comes without waiting for us, for however hard we worked we should never be ready for it.'"

Efim became thoughtful.

"I've spent a lot of money on this building," he said "and one can't start on the journey with empty pockets. We shall want a hundred roubles apiece – and it's no small sum."

Elisha laughed.

"Now, come, come, old friend!" he said, "you have ten times as much as I, and yet you talk about money. Only say when we are to start, and though I have nothing now I shall have enough by then."

Efim also smiled.

"Dear me, I did not know you were so rich!" said he. "Why, where will you get it from?"

"I can scrape some together at home, and if that's not enough, I'll sell half a score of hives to my neighbor. He's long been wanting to buy them."

"If they swarm well this year, you'll regret it."

"Regret it! Not I, neighbor! I never regretted anything in my life, except my sins. There's nothing more precious than the soul."

"That's so; still it's not right to neglect things at home."

"But what if our souls are neglected? That's worse. We took the vow, so let us go! Now, seriously, let us go!"

II

Elisha succeeded in persuading his comrade. In the morning, after thinking it well over, Efim came to Elisha.

"You are right," said he, "let us go. Life and death are in God's hands. We must go now, while we are still alive and have the strength."

A week later the old men were ready to start. Efim had money enough at hand. He took a hundred roubles himself, and left two hundred with his wife.

Elisha, too, got ready. He sold ten hives to his neighbor, with any new swarms that might come from them before the summer. He took seventy roubles for the lot. The rest of the hundred roubles he scraped together from the other members of his household, fairly clearing them all out. His wife gave him all she had been saving up for her funeral; and his daughter-in-law also gave him what she had.

Efim gave his eldest son definite orders about every thing: when and how much grass to mow, where to cart the manure, and how to finish off and roof the cottage. He thought out everything, and gave his orders accordingly. Elisha, on the other hand, only explained to his wife that she was to keep separate the swarms from the hives he had sold, and to be sure to let the neighbor have them all, without any tricks. As to household affairs, he did not even mention them.

"You will see what to do and how to do it, as the needs arise," he said. "You are the masters, and will know how to do what's best for yourselves."

So the old men got ready. Their people baked them cakes, and made bags for them, and cut them linen for leg bands. They put on new leather shoes, and took with them spare shoes of platted bark. Their families went with them to the end of the village and there took leave of them, and the old men started on their pilgrimage.

Elisha left home in a cheerful mood, and as soon as he was out of the village forgot all his home affairs. His only care was how to please his comrade, how to avoid saying a rude word to any one, how to get to his destination and home again in peace and love. Walking along the road, Elisha would either whisper some prayer to himself or go over in his mind such of the lives of the saints as he was able to remember. When he came across any one on the road, or turned in anywhere for the night, he tried to behave as gently as possible and to say a godly word. So he journeyed on, rejoicing. One thing only he could not do, he could not give up taking snuff. Though he had left his snuffbox behind, he hankered after it. Then a man he met on the road gave him some snuff; and every now and then he would lag behind (not to lead his comrade into temptation) and would take a pinch of snuff.

Efim too walked well and firmly; doing no wrong and speaking no vain words, but his heart was not so light. Household cares weighed on his mind. He kept worrying about what was going on at home. Had he not forgotten to give his son this or that order? Would his son do things properly? If he happened to see potatoes being planted or manure carted, as he went along, he wondered if his son was doing as he had been told. And he almost wanted to turn back and show him how to do things, or even do them himself.

III

The old men had been walking for five weeks, they had worn out their homemade bark shoes, and had to begin buying new ones when they reached Little Russia. From the time they left home they had had to pay for their food and for their night's lodging, but when they reached Little Russia the people vied with one another in asking them into their huts. They took them in and fed them, and would accept no payment; and more than that, they put bread or even cakes into their bags for them to eat on the road.

The old men travelled some five hundred miles in this manner free of expense, but after they had crossed the next province, they came to a district where the harvest had failed. The peasants still gave them free lodging at night, but no longer fed them for nothing. Sometimes, even, they could get no bread: they offered to pay for it, but there was none to be had. The people said the harvest had completely failed the year before. Those who had been rich were ruined and had had to sell all they possessed; those of moderate means were left destitute, and those of the poor who had not left those parts, wandered about begging, or starved at home in utter want. In the winter they had had to eat husks and goosefoot.

One night the old men stopped in a small village; they bought fifteen pounds of bread, slept there, and started before sunrise, to get well on their way before the heat of the day. When they had gone some eight miles, on coming to a stream they sat down, and, filling a bowl with water, they steeped some bread in it, and ate it. Then they changed their leg bands, and rested for a while. Elisha took out his snuffbox. Efim shook his head at him.

"How is it you don't give up that nasty habit?" said he.

Elisha waved his hand. "The evil habit is stronger than I," he said.

Presently they got up and went on. After walking for nearly another eight miles, they came to a large village and passed right through it. It had now grown hot. Elisha was tired out and wanted to rest and have a drink, but Efim did not stop. Efim was the better walker of the two, and Elisha found it hard to keep up with him.

"If I could only have a drink," said he.

"Well, have a drink," said Efim. "I don't want any."

Elisha stopped.

"You go on," he said, "but I'll just run in to the little hut there. I will catch you up in a moment."

"All right," said Efim, and he went on along the high road alone, while Elisha turned back to the hut.

It was a small hut plastered with clay, the bottom a dark color, the top whitewashed; but the clay had crumbled away. Evidently it was long since it had been re-plastered, and the thatch was off the roof on one side. The entrance to the hut was through the yard. Elisha entered the yard, and saw, lying close to a bank of earth that ran round the hut, a gaunt, beardless man with his shirt tucked into his trousers, as is the custom in Little Russia. The man must have lain down in the shade, but the sun had come round and now shone full on him. Though not asleep, he still lay there. Elisha called to him, and asked for a drink, but the man gave no answer.

"He is either ill or unfriendly," thought Elisha; and going to the door he heard a child crying in the hut. He took hold of the ring that served as a door handle, and knocked with it.

"Hey, masters!" he called. No answer. He knocked again with his staff.

"Hey, Christians!" Nothing stirred.

"Hey, servants of God!" Still no reply.

Elisha was about to turn away, when he thought he heard a groan the other side of the door.

"Dear me, some misfortune must have happened to the people! I had better have a look."

And Elisha entered the hut.

IV

Elisha turned the ring; the door was not fastened. He opened it and went along up the narrow passage. The door into the dwelling room was open. To the left was a brick oven; in front against the wall was an icon stand and a table before it, by the table was a bench on which sat an old woman, bareheaded and wearing only a single garment. There she sat with her head resting on the table, and near her was a thin, wax-colored boy, with a protruding stomach. He was asking for something, pulling at her sleeve, and crying bitterly. Elisha entered. The air in the hut was very foul. He looked round, and saw a woman lying on the floor behind the oven: she lay flat on the ground with her eyes closed and her throat rattling, now stretching out a leg, now dragging it in, tossing from side to side; and the foul smell came from her. Evidently she could do nothing for herself and no one had been attending to her needs. The old woman lifted her head, and saw the stranger.

"What do you want?" said she." What do you want man? We have nothing."

Elisha understood her, though she spoke in the Little-Russian dialect.

"I came in for a drink of water, servant of God," he said.

"There's no one – no one – we have nothing to fetch it in. Go your way."

Then Elisha asked:

"Is there no one among you, then, well enough to attend to that woman?"

"No, we have no one. My son is dying outside, and we are dying in here."

The little boy had ceased crying when he saw the stranger, but when the old woman began to speak, he began again, and clutching hold of her sleeve cried:

"Bread, Granny, bread."

Elisha was about to question the old woman, when the man staggered into the hut. He came along the passage, clinging to the wall, but as he was entering the dwelling room he fell in the corner near the threshold, and without trying to get up again to reach the bench, he began to speak in broken words. He brought out a word at a time, stopping to draw breath, and gasping.

"Illness has seized us…" said he, "and famine. He is dying… of hunger."

And he motioned towards the boy, and began to sob.

Elisha jerked up the sack behind his shoulder and pulling the straps off his arms, put it on the floor. Then he lifted it on to the bench, and untied the strings. Having opened the sack, he took out a loaf of bread, and, cutting off a piece with his knife, handed it to the man. The man would not take it, but pointed to the little boy and to a little girl crouching behind the oven, as if to say:

"Give it to them."

Elisha held it out to the boy. When the boy smelt bread, he stretched out his arms, and seizing the slice with both his little hands, bit into it so that his nose disappeared in the chunk. The little girl came out from behind the oven and fixed her eyes on the bread. Elisha gave her also a slice. Then he cut off another piece and gave it to the old woman, and she too began munching it.

"If only some water could be brought," she said, "their mouths are parched. I tried to fetch some water yesterday – or was it to-day – I can't remember, but I fell down and could go no further, and the pail has remained there, unless some one has taken it."

Elisha asked where the well was. The old woman told him. Elisha went out, found the pail, brought some water, and gave the people a drink. The children and the old woman ate some more bread with the water, but the man would not eat.

"I cannot eat," he said.

All this time the younger woman did not show any consciousness, but continued to toss from side to side. Presently Elisha went to the village shop and bought some millet, salt, flour, and oil. He found an axe, chopped some wood, and made a fire. The little girl came and helped him. Then he boiled some soup, and gave the starving people a meal.

V

The man ate a little, the old woman had some too, and the little girl and boy licked the bowl clean, and then curled up and fell fast asleep in one another's arms.

The man and the old woman then began telling Elisha how they had sunk to their present state.

"We were poor enough before," said they, "but when the crops failed, what we gathered hardly lasted us through the autumn. We had nothing left by the time winter came, and had to beg from the neighbors and from any one we could. At first they gave, then they began to refuse. Some would have been glad enough to help us, but had nothing to give. And we were ashamed of asking: we were in debt all round, and owed money, and flour, and bread."

"I went to look for work," the man said, "but could find none. Everywhere people were offering to work merely for their own keep. One day you'd get a short job, and then you might spend two days looking for work. Then the old woman and the girl went begging, further away. But they got very little; bread was so scarce. Still we scraped food together somehow, and hoped to struggle through till next harvest, but towards spring people ceased to give anything. And then this illness seized us. Things became worse and worse. One day we might have something to eat, and then nothing for two days. We began eating grass. Whether it was the grass, or what, made my wife ill, I don't know. She could not keep on her legs, and I had no strength left, and there was nothing to help us to recovery."

"I struggled on alone for a while," said the old woman, "but at last I broke down too for want of food, and grew quite weak. The girl also grew weak and timid. I told her to go to the neighbors – she would not leave the hut, but crept into a corner and sat there. The day before yesterday a neighbor looked in, but seeing that we were ill and hungry she turned away and left us. Her husband has had to go away, and she has nothing for her own little ones to eat. And so we lay, waiting for death."

Having heard their story, Elisha gave up the thought of overtaking his comrade that day, and remained with them all night.

In the morning he got up and began doing the housework, just as if it were his own home. He kneaded the bread with the old woman's help, and lit the fire. Then he went with the little girl to the neighbors to get the most necessary things, for there was nothing in the hut: everything had been sold for bread – cooking utensils, clothing, and all. So Elisha began replacing what was necessary, making some things himself, and buying some. He remained there one day, then another, and then a third. The little boy picked up strength and, whenever Elisha sat down, crept along the bench and nestled up to him. The little girl brightened up and helped in all the work, running after Elisha and calling,

"Daddy, daddy."

The old woman grew stronger, and managed to go out to see a neighbor. The man too improved, and was able to get about, holding on to the wall. Only the wife could not get up, but even she regained consciousness on the third day, and asked for food.

"Well," thought Elisha, "I never expected to waste so much time on the way. Now I must be getting on."

VI

The fourth day was the feast day after the summer fast, and Elisha thought:

"I will stay and break the fast with these people. I'll go and buy them something, and keep the feast with them, and tomorrow evening I will start."

So Elisha went into the village, bought milk, wheat flour and dripping, and helped the old woman to boil and bake for the morrow. On the feast day Elisha went to church, and then broke the fast with his friends at the hut. That day the wife got up, and managed to move about a bit. The husband had shaved and put on a clean shirt, which the old woman had washed for him; and he went to beg for mercy of a rich peasant in the village to whom his plowland and meadow were mortgaged. He went to beg the rich peasant to grant him the use of the meadow and field till after the harvest; but in the evening he came back very sad, and began to weep. The rich peasant had shown no mercy, but had said: "Bring me the money."

Elisha again grew thoughtful. "How are they to live now?" thought he to himself. "Other people will go haymaking, but there will be nothing for these to mow, their grass land is mortgaged. The rye will ripen. Others will reap (and what a fine crop mother earth is giving this year), but they have nothing to look forward to. Their three acres are pledged to the rich peasant. When I am gone, they'll drift back into the state I found them in."

Elisha was in two minds, but finally decided not to leave that evening, but to wait until the morrow. He went out into the yard to sleep. He said his prayers, and lay down; but he could not sleep. On the one hand he felt he ought to be going, for he had spent too much time and money as it was; on the other hand he felt sorry for the people.

"There seems to be no end to it," he said. "First I only meant to bring them a little water and give them each a slice of bread: and just see where it has landed me. It's a case of redeeming the meadow and the cornfield. And when I have done that, I shall have to buy a cow for them, and a horse for the man to cart his sheaves. A nice coil you've got yourself into, brother Elisha! You've slipped your cables and lost your reckoning!"

Elisha got up, lifted his coat which he had been using for a pillow, unfolded it, got out his snuffbox and took a pinch, thinking that it might perhaps clear his thoughts.

But no! He thought and thought, and came to no conclusion. He ought to be going; and yet pity held him back. He did not know what to do. He refolded his coat and put it under his head again. He lay thus for a long time, till the cocks had already crowed once: then he was quite drowsy. And suddenly it seemed as if some one had roused him. He saw that he was dressed for the journey, with the sack on his back and the staff in his hand, and the gate stood ajar so that he could just squeeze through. He was about to pass out, when his sack caught against the fence on one side: he tried to free it, but then his leg band caught on the other side and came undone. He pulled at the sack, and saw that it had not caught on the fence, but that the little girl was holding it and crying,

"Bread, daddy, bread!"

He looked at his foot, and there was the tiny boy holding him by the leg band, while the master of the hut and the old woman were looking at him through the window.

Elisha awoke, and said to himself in an audible voice:

"Tomorrow I will redeem their cornfield, and will buy them a horse, and flour to last till the harvest, and a cow for the little ones; or else while I go to seek the Lord beyond the sea, I may lose Him in myself."

Then Elisha fell asleep, and slept till morning. He awoke early, and going to the rich peasant, redeemed both the cornfield and the meadow land. He bought a scythe (for that also had been sold) and brought it back with him. Then he sent the man to mow, and himself went into the village. He heard that there was a horse and cart for sale at the public house, and he struck a bargain with the owner, and bought them. Then he bought a sack of flour, put it in the cart, and went to see about a cow. As he was going along he overtook two women talking as they went. Though they spoke the Little-Russian dialect, he understood what they were saying.

"At first, it seems, they did not know him; they thought he was just an ordinary man. He came in to ask for a drink of water, and then he remained. Just think of the things he has bought for them! Why they say he bought a horse and cart for them at the publican's, only this morning! There are not many such men in the world. It's worth while going to have a look at him."

Elisha heard and understood that he was being praised, and he did not go to buy the cow, but returned to the inn, paid for the horse, harnessed it, drove up to the hut, and got out. The people in the hut were astonished when they saw the horse. They thought it might be for them, but dared not ask. The man came out to open the gate.

"Where did you get a horse from, grandfather," he asked.

"Why, I bought it," said Elisha. "It was going cheap. Go and cut some grass and put it in the manger for it to eat during the night. And take in the sack."

The man unharnessed the horse, and carried the sack into the barn. Then he mowed some grass and put it in the manger. Everybody lay down to sleep. Elisha went outside and lay by the roadside. That evening he took his bag out with him. When everyone was asleep, he got up, packed and fastened his bag, wrapped the linen bands round his legs, put on his shoes and coat, and set off to follow Efim.

VII

When Elisha had walked rather more than three miles it began to grow light. He sat down under a tree, opened his bag, counted his money, and found he had only seventeen roubles and twenty kopeks left.

"Well," thought he, "it is no use trying to cross the sea with this. If I beg my way it may be worse than not going at all. Friend Efim will get to Jerusalem without me, and will place a candle at the shrines in my name. As for me, I'm afraid I shall never fulfil my vow in this life. I must be thankful it was made to a merciful Master, and to one who pardons sinners."

Elisha rose, jerked his bag well up on his shoulders, and turned back. Not wishing to be recognized by any one, he made a circuit to avoid the village, and walked briskly home-ward. Coming from home the way had seemed difficult to him, and he had found it hard to keep up with Efim, but now on his return journey, God helped him to get over the ground so that he hardly felt fatigue. Walking seemed like child's play. He went along swinging his staff, and did his forty to fifty miles a day.

When Elisha reached home the harvest was over. His family were delighted to see him again, and all wanted to know what had happened: Why and how he had been left behind? And why he had returned without reaching Jerusalem? But Elisha did not tell them.

"It was not God's will that I should get there," said he. "I lost my money on the way, and lagged behind my companion. Forgive me, for the Lord's sake!"

Elisha gave his old wife what money he had left. Then he questioned them about home affairs. Everything was going on well; all the work had been done, nothing neglected, and all were living in peace and concord.

Efim's family heard of his return the same day, and came for news of their old man; and to them Elisha gave the same answers.

"Efim is a fast walker. We parted three days before St. Peter's day, and I meant to catch him up again, but all sorts of things happened. I lost my money, and had no means to get any further, so I turned back."

The folks were astonished that so sensible a man should have acted so foolishly: should have started and not got to his destination, and should have squandered all his money. They wondered at it for a while, and then forgot all about it, and Elisha forgot it too. He set to work again on his homestead. With his son's help he cut wood for fuel for the winter. He and the women threshed the corn. Then he mended the thatch on the outhouses, put the bees under cover, and handed over to his neighbor the ten hives he had sold him in spring, and all the swarms that had come from them. His wife tried not to tell how many swarms there had been from these hives, but Elisha knew well enough from which there had been swarms and from which not. And instead of ten, he handed over seventeen swarms to his neighbor. Having got everything ready for the winter, Elisha sent his son away to find work, while he himself took to platting shoes of bark, and hollowing out logs for hives.

VIII

All that day while Elisha stopped behind in the hut with the sick people, Efim waited for him. He only went on a little way before he sat down. He waited and waited, had a nap, woke up again, and again sat waiting; but his comrade did not come. He gazed till his eyes ached. The sun was already sinking behind a tree, and still no Elisha was to be seen.

"Perhaps he has passed me," thought Efim, "or perhaps some one gave him a lift and he drove by while I slept, and did not see me. But how could he help seeing me? One can see so far here in the steppe. Shall I go back? Suppose he is on in front, we shall then miss each other completely and it will be still worse. I had better go on, and we shall be sure to meet where we put up for the night."

He came to a village, and told the watchman, if an old man of a certain description came along, to bring him to the hut where Efim stopped. But Elisha did not turn up that night. Efim went on, asking all he met whether they had not seen a little, bald-headed, old man? No one had seen such a traveller. Efim wondered, but went on alone, saying:

"We shall be sure to meet in Odessa, or on board the ship," and he did not trouble more about it.

On the way, he came across a pilgrim wearing a priest's coat, with long hair and a skullcap such as priests wear. This pilgrim had been to Mount Athos, and was now going to Jerusalem for the second time. They both stopped at the same place one night, and, having met, they travelled on together.

They got safely to Odessa, and there had to wait three days for a ship. Many pilgrims from many different parts were in the same case. Again Efim asked about Elisha, but no one had seen him.

Efim got himself a foreign passport, which cost him five roubles. He paid forty roubles for a return ticket to Jerusalem, and bought a supply of bread and herrings for the voyage.

The pilgrim began explaining to Efim how he might get on to the ship without paying his fare; but Efim would not listen. "No, I came prepared to pay, and I shall pay," said he.

The ship was freighted, and the pilgrims went on board, Efim and his new comrade among them. The anchors were weighed, and the ship put out to sea.

All day they sailed smoothly, but towards night a wind arose, rain came on, and the vessel tossed about and shipped water. The people were frightened: the women wailed and screamed, and some of the weaker men ran about the ship looking for shelter. Efim too was frightened, but he would not show it, and remained at the place on deck where he had settled down when first he came on board, beside some old men from Tambof. There they sat silent, all night and all next day, holding on to their sacks. On the third day it grew calm, and on the fifth day they anchored at Constantinople. Some of the pilgrims went on shore to visit the Church of St. Sophia, now held by the Turks. Efim remained on the ship, and only bought some white bread. They lay there for twenty-four hours, and then put to sea again. At Smyrna they stopped again; and at Alexandria; but at last they arrived safely at Jaffa, where all the pilgrims had to disembark. From there still it was more than forty miles by road to Jerusalem. When disembarking the people were again much frightened. The ship was high, and the people were dropped into boats, which rocked so much that it was easy to miss them and fall into the water. A couple of men did get a wetting, but at last all were safely landed.

They went on on foot, and at noon on the third day reached Jerusalem. They stopped outside the town, at the Russian inn, where their passports were endorsed. Then, after dinner, Efim visited the Holy Places with his companion, the pilgrim. It was not the time when they could be admitted to the Holy Sepulchre, but they went to the Patriarchate. All the pilgrims assembled there. The women were separated from the men, who were all told to sit in a circle, barefoot. Then a monk came in with a towel to wash their feet. He washed, wiped, and then kissed their feet, and did this to every one in the circle. Efim's feet were washed and kissed, with the rest. He stood through vespers and matins, prayed, placed candles at the shrines, handed in booklets inscribed with his parents names, that they might be mentioned in the church prayers. Here at the Patriarchate food and wine were given them. Next morning they went to the cell of Mary of Egypt, where she had lived doing penance. Here too they placed candles and had prayers read. From there they went to Abraham's Monastery, and saw the place where Abraham intended to slay his son as an offering to God. Then they visited the spot where Christ appeared to Mary Magdalene, and the Church of James, the Lord's brother. The pilgrim showed Efim all these places, and told him how much money to give at each place. At midday they returned to the inn and had dinner. As they were preparing to lie down and rest, the pilgrim cried out, and began to search his clothes, feeling them all over.

"My purse has been stolen, there were twenty-three roubles in it," said he, "two ten-rouble notes and the rest in change."

He sighed and lamented a great deal, but as there was no help for it, they lay down to sleep.

IX

As Efim lay there, he was assailed by temptation.

"No one has stolen any money from this pilgrim," thought he, "I do not believe he had any. He gave none away anywhere, though he made me give, and even borrowed a rouble of me."

This thought had no sooner crossed his mind, than Efim rebuked himself, saying: "What right have I to judge a man? It is a sin. I will think no more about it." But as soon as his thoughts began to wander, they turned again to the pilgrim: how interested he seemed to be in money, and how unlikely it sounded when he declared that his purse had been stolen.

"He never had any money," thought Efim. "It's an invention."

Towards evening they got up, and went to midnight Mass at the great Church of the Resurrection, where the Lord's Sepulchre is. The pilgrim kept close to Efim and went with him everywhere. They came to the Church; a great many pilgrims were there; some Russians and some of other nationalities: Greeks, Armenians, Turks, and Syrians. Efim entered the Holy Gates with the crowd. A monk led them past the Turkish sentinels, to the place where the Savior was taken down from the cross and anointed, and where candles were burning in nine great candlesticks. The monk showed and explained everything. Efim offered a candle there. Then the monk led Efim to the right, up the steps to Golgotha, to the place where the cross had stood. Efim prayed there. Then they showed him the cleft where the ground had been rent asunder to its nethermost depths; then the place where Christ's hands and feet were nailed to the cross; then Adam's tomb, where the blood of Christ had dripped on to Adam's bones. Then they showed him the stone on which Christ sat when the crown of thorns was placed on His head; then the post to which Christ was bound when He was scourged. Then Efim saw the stone with two holes for Christ's feet. They were going to show him something else, but there was a stir in the crowd, and the people all hurried to the church of the Lord's Sepulchre itself. The Latin Mass had just finished there, and the Russian Mass was beginning. And Efim went with the crowd to the tomb cut in the rock.

He tried to get rid of the pilgrim, against whom he was still sinning in his mind, but the pilgrim would not leave him, but went with him to the Mass at the Holy Sepulchre. They tried to get to the front, but were too late. There was such a crowd that it was impossible to move either backwards or forwards. Efim stood looking in front of him, praying, and every now and then feeling for his purse. He was in two minds: sometimes he thought that the pilgrim was deceiving him, and then again he thought that if the pilgrim spoke the truth and his purse had really been stolen, the same thing might happen to himself.

X

Efim stood there gazing into the little chapel in which was the Holy Sepulchre itself with thirty-six lamps burning above it. As he stood looking over the people's heads, he saw something that surprised him. Just beneath the lamps in which the sacred fire burns and in front of every one, Efim saw an old man in a gray coat, whose bald, shining head was just like Elisha Bodrof.

"It is like him," thought Efim, "but it cannot be Elisha. He could not have got ahead of me. The ship before ours started a week sooner. He could not have caught that; and he was not on ours, for I saw every pilgrim on board."

Hardly had Efim thought this, when the little old man began to pray, and bowed three times: once forwards to God, then once on each side – to the brethren. And as he turned his head to the right, Efim recognized him. It was Elisha Bodrof himself with his dark, curly beard turning gray at the cheeks, with his brows, his eyes and nose, and his expression of face. Yes, it was he!

Efim was very pleased to have found his comrade again, and wondered how Elisha had got ahead of him.

"Well done, Elisha!" thought he. "See how he has pushed ahead. He must have come across someone who showed him the way. When we get out, I will find him, get rid of this fellow in the skullcap, and keep to Elisha. Perhaps he will show me how to get to the front also."

Efim kept looking out, so as not to lose sight of Elisha. But when the Mass was over, the crowd began to sway, pushing forward to kiss the tomb, and pushed Efim aside. He was again seized with fear lest his purse should be stolen. Pressing it with his hand, he began elbowing through the crowd, anxious only to get out. When he reached the open, he went about for a long time searching for Elisha both outside and in the Church itself. In the cells of the Church he saw many people of all kinds, eating, and drinking wine, and reading and sleeping there. But Elisha was nowhere to be seen. So Efim returned to the inn without having found his comrade. That evening the pilgrim in the skullcap did not turn up. He had gone off without repaying the rouble, and Efim was left alone.

The next day Efim went to the Holy Sepulchre again, with an old man from Tambof, whom he had met on the ship. He tried to get to the front, but was again pressed back; so he stood by a pillar and prayed. He looked before him, and there in the foremost place under the lamps, close to the very Sepulchre of the Lord, stood Elisha, with his arms spread out like a priest at the altar, and with his bald head all shining.

"Well, now," thought Efim, "I won't lose him!"

He pushed forward to the front, but when he got there, there was no Elisha: he had evidently gone away.

Again on the third day Efim looked, and saw at the Sepulchre, in the holiest place, Elisha standing in the sight of all men, his arms outspread, and his eyes gazing upwards as if he saw something above. And his bald head was all shining.

"Well, this time," thought Efim, "he shall not escape me! I will go and stand at the door, then we can't miss one another!"

Efim went out and stood by the door till past noon. Everyone had passed out, but still Elisha did not appear.

Efim remained six weeks in Jerusalem, and went everywhere: to Bethlehem, and to Bethany, and to the Jordan. He had a new shroud sealed at the Holy Sepulchre for his burial, and he took a bottle of water from the Jordan, and some holy earth, and bought candles that had been lit at the sacred flame. In eight places he inscribed names to be prayed for, and he spent all his money, except just enough to get home with. Then he started homeward. He walked to Jaffa, sailed thence to Odessa, and walked home from there on foot.

XI

Efim travelled the same road he had come by; and as he drew nearer home his former anxiety returned as to how affairs were getting on in his absence. "Much water flows away in a year," the proverb says. It takes a lifetime to build up a homestead, but not long to ruin it, thought he. And he wondered how his son had managed without him, what sort of spring they were having, how the cattle had wintered, and whether the cottage was well finished. When Efim came to the district where he had parted from Elisha the summer before, he could hardly believe that the people living there were the same. The year before they had been starving, but now they were living in comfort. The harvest had been good, and the people had recovered and had forgotten their former misery.

One evening Efim reached the very place where Elisha had remained behind; and as he entered the village, a little girl in a white smock ran out of a hut.

"Daddy, daddy, come to our house!"

Efim meant to pass on, but the little girl would not let him. She took hold of his coat, laughing, and pulled him towards the hut, where a woman with a small boy came out into the porch and beckoned to him.

"Come in, grandfather," she said. "Have supper and spend the night with us."

So Efim went in.

"I may as well ask about Elisha," he thought. "I fancy this is the very hut he went to for a drink of water."

The woman helped him off with the bag he carried, and gave him water to wash his face. Then she made him sit down to table, and set milk, curd cakes and porridge before him. Efim thanked her, and praised her for her kindness to a pilgrim. The woman shook her head.

"We have good reason to welcome pilgrims," she said. "It was a pilgrim who showed us what life is. We were living forgetful of God, and God punished us almost to death. We reached such a pass last summer, that we all lay ill and helpless with nothing to eat. And we should have died, but that God sent an old man to help us – just such a one as you. He came in one day to ask for a drink of water, saw the state we were in, took pity on us, and remained with us. He gave us food and drink, and set us on our feet again; and he redeemed our land, and bought a cart and horse and gave them to us."

Here the old woman entering the hut, interrupted the younger one and said:

"We don't know whether it was a man, or an angel from God. He loved us all, pitied us all, and went away without telling us his name, so that we don't even know whom to pray for. I can see it all before me now! There I lay waiting for death, when in comes a bald-headed old man. He was not anything much to look at, and he asked for a drink of water. I, sinner that I am, thought to myself: 'What does he come prowling about here for?' And just think what he did! As soon as he saw us, he let down his bag, on this very spot, and untied it."

Here the little girl joined in.

"No, Granny," said she, "first he put it down here in the middle of the hut, and then he lifted it on to the bench."

And they began discussing and recalling all he had said and done, where he sat and slept, and what he had said to each of them.

At night the peasant himself came home on his horse, and he too began to tell about Elisha and how he had lived with them.

"Had he not come we should all have died in our sins. We were dying in despair, murmuring against God and man. But he set us on our feet again; and through him we learned to know God, and to believe that there is good in man. May the Lord bless him! We used to live like animals; he made human beings of us."

After giving Efim food and drink, they showed him where he was to sleep; and lay down to sleep themselves.

But though Efim lay down, he could not sleep. He could not get Elisha out of his mind, but remembered how he had seen him three times at Jerusalem, standing in the foremost place.

"So that is how he got ahead of me," thought Efim. "God may or may not have accepted my pilgrimage but He has certainly accepted his!"

Next morning Efim bade farewell to the people, who put some patties in his sack before they went to their work, and he continued his journey.

XII

Efim had been away just a year, and it was spring again when he reached home one evening. His son was not at home, but had gone to the public house and when he came back, he had had a drop too much. Efim began questioning him. Everything showed that the young fellow had been unsteady during his father's absence. The money had all been wrongly spent, and the work had been neglected. The father began to upbraid the son; and the son answered rudely.

"Why didn't you stay and look after it yourself?" he said. "You go off, taking the money with you and now you demand it of me!"

The old man grew angry, and struck his son.

In the morning Efim went to the village Elder to complain of his son's conduct. As he was passing Elisha's house, his friend's wife greeted him from the porch.

"How do you do, neighbor?" she said. "How do you do, dear friend? Did you get to Jerusalem safely?"

Efim stopped.

"Yes, thank God," he said. "I have been there. I lost sight of your old man, but I hear he got home safely."

The old woman was fond of talking:

"Yes, neighbor, he has come back," said she. "He's been back a long time. Soon after Assumption, I think it was, he returned. And we were glad the Lord had sent him back to us! We were dull without him. We can't expect much work from him any more, his years for work are past; but still he is the head of the household and it's more cheerful when he's at home. And how glad our lad was! He said, 'It's like being without sunlight, when father's away!' It was dull without him, dear friend. We're fond of him, and take good care of him."

"Is he at home now?"

"He is, dear friend. He is with his bees. He is hiving the swarms. He says they are swarming well this year. The Lord has given such strength to the bees that my husband doesn't remember the like. 'The Lord is not rewarding us according to our sins,' he says. Come in, dear neighbor, he will be so glad to see you again."

Efim passed through the passage into the yard and to the apiary, to see Elisha. There was Elisha in his gray coat, without any face-net or gloves, standing, under the birch trees, looking upwards, his arms stretched out and his bald head shining, as Efim had seen him at the Holy Sepulchre in Jerusalem: and above him the sunlight shone through the birches as the flames of fire had done in the holy place, and the golden bees flew round his head like a halo, and did not sting him.

Efim stopped. The old woman called to her husband.

"Here's your friend come," she cried.

Elisha looked round with a pleased face, and came towards Efim, gently picking bees out of his own beard.

"Good day, neighbor, good day, dear friend. Did you get there safely?"

"My feet walked there, and I have brought you some water from the river Jordan. You must come to my house for it. But whether the Lord accepted my efforts..."

"Well the Lord be thanked! May Christ bless you!" said Elisha.

Efim was silent for a while, and then added:

"My feet have been there, but whether my soul, or another's, has been there more truly..."

"That's God's business, neighbor, God's business," interrupted Elisha.

"On my return journey I stopped at the hut where you remained behind..."

Elisha was alarmed, and said hurriedly:

"God's business, neighbor, God's business! Come into the cottage, I'll give you some of our honey." And Elisha changed the conversation, and talked of home affairs.

Efim sighed, and did not speak to Elisha of the people in the hut, nor of how he had seen him in Jerusalem. But he now understood that the best way to keep one's vows to God and to do His will, is for each man while he lives to show love and do good to others.

1885

7

Where Love Is, God Is

In a certain town there lived a cobbler, Martin Avdeitch by name. He had a tiny room in a basement, the one window of which looked out on to the street. Through it one could only see the feet of those who passed by, but Martin recognized the people by their boots. He had lived long in the place and had many acquaintances. There was hardly a pair of boots in the neighborhood that had not been once or twice through his hands, so he often saw his own handiwork through the window. Some he had resoled, some patched, some stitched up, and to some he had even put fresh uppers. He had plenty to do, for he worked well, used good material, did not charge too much, and could be relied on. If he could do a job by the day required, he undertook it; if not, he told the truth and gave no false promises; so he was well known and never short of work.

Martin had always been a good man; but in his old age he began to think more about his soul and to draw nearer to God. While he still worked for a master, before he set up on his own account, his wife had died, leaving him with a three-year-old son. None of his elder children had lived, they had all died in infancy. At first Martin thought of sending his little son to his sister's in the country, but then he felt sorry to part with the boy, thinking: "It would be hard for my little Kapiton to have to grow up in a strange family; I will keep him with me."

Martin left his master and went into lodgings with his little son. But he had no luck with his children. No sooner had the boy reached an age when he could help his father and be a support as well as a joy to him, than he fell ill and, after being laid up for a week with a burning fever, died. Martin buried his son, and gave way to despair so great and overwhelming that he murmured against God. In his sorrow he prayed again and again that he too might die, reproaching God for having taken the son he loved, his only son while he, old as he was, remained alive. After that Martin left off going to church.

One day an old man from Martin's native village who had been a pilgrim for the last eight years, called in on his way from Troitsa Monastery. Martin opened his heart to him, and told him of his sorrow.

"I no longer even wish to live, holy man," he said. "All I ask of God is that I soon may die. I am now quite without hope in the world."

The old man replied: "You have no right to say such things, Martin. We cannot judge God's ways. Not our reasoning, but God's will, decides. If God willed that your son should die and you should live, it must be best so. As to your despair – that comes because you wish to live for your own happiness."

"What else should one live for?" asked Martin.

"For God, Martin," said the old man. "He gives you life, and you must live for Him. When you have learnt to live for Him, you will grieve no more, and all will seem easy to you."

Martin was silent awhile, and then asked: "But how is one to live for God?"

The old man answered: "How one may live for God has been shown us by Christ. Can you read? Then buy the Gospels, and read them: there you will see how God would have you live. You have it all there."

These words sank deep into Martin's heart, and that same day he went and bought himself a Testament in large print, and began to read.

At first he meant only to read on holidays, but having once begun he found it made his heart so light that he read every day. Sometimes he was so absorbed in his reading that the oil in his lamp burnt out before he could tear himself away from the book.

He continued to read every night, and the more he read the more clearly he understood what God required of him, and how he might live for God. And his heart grew lighter and lighter. Before, when he went to bed he used to lie with a heavy heart, moaning as he thought of his little Kapiton; but now he only repeated again and again: "Glory to Thee, glory to Thee, O Lord! Thy will be done!"

From that time Martin's whole life changed. Formerly, on holidays he used to go and have tea at the public house, and did not even refuse a glass or two of vodka. Sometimes, after having had a drop with a friend, he left the public house not drunk, but rather merry, and would say foolish things: shout at a man, or abuse him. Now, all that sort of thing passed away from him. His life became peaceful and joyful. He sat down to his work in the morning, and when he had finished his day's work he took the lamp down from the wall, stood it on the table, fetched his book from the shelf, opened it, and sat down to read. The more he read the better he understood, and the clearer and happier he felt in his mind.

It happened once that Martin sat up late, absorbed in his book. He was reading Luke's Gospel; and in the sixth chapter he came upon the verses:

"To him that smiteth thee on the one cheek offer also the other; and from him that taketh away thy cloak withhold not thy coat also. Give to every man that asketh thee; and of him that taketh away thy goods ask them not again. And as ye would that men should do to you, do ye also to them likewise."

He also read the verses where our Lord says:

"And why call ye me, Lord, Lord, and do not the things which I say? Whosoever cometh to me, and heareth my sayings, and doeth them, I will shew you to whom he is like: He is like a man which built an house, and digged deep, and laid the foundation on a rock: and when the flood arose, the stream beat vehemently upon that house, and could not shake it: for it was founded upon a rock. But he that heareth and doeth not, is like a man that without a foundation built an house upon the earth, against which the stream did beat vehemently, and immediately it fell; and the ruin of that house was great."

When Martin read these words his soul was glad within him. He took off his spectacles and laid them on the book, and leaning his elbows on the table pondered over what he had read. He tried his own life by the standard of those words, asking himself:

"Is my house built on the rock, or on sand? If it stands on the rock, it is well. It seems easy enough while one sits here alone, and one thinks one has done all that God commands; but as soon as I cease to be on my guard, I sin again. Still I will persevere. It brings such joy. Help me, O Lord!"

He thought all this, and was about to go to bed, but was loth to leave his book. So he went on reading the seventh chapter – about the centurion, the widow's son, and the answer to John's disciples – and he came to the part where a rich Pharisee invited the Lord to his house; and he read how the woman who was a sinner, anointed his feet and washed them with her tears, and how he justified her. Coming to the forty-fourth verse, he read:

"And turning to the woman, he said unto Simon, Seest thou this woman? I entered into thine house, thou gavest me no water for my feet: but she hath wetted my feet with her tears, and wiped them with her hair. Thou gavest me no kiss; but she, since the time I came in, hath not ceased to kiss my feet. My head with oil thou didst not anoint: but she hath anointed my feet with ointment."

He read these verses and thought: "He gave no water for his feet, gave no kiss, his head with oil he did not anoint..." And Martin took off his spectacles once more, laid them on his book, and pondered.

"He must have been like me, that Pharisee. He too thought only of himself – how to get a cup of tea, how to keep warm and comfortable; never a thought of his guest. He took care of himself, but for his guest he cared nothing at all. Yet who was the guest? The Lord himself! If he came to me, should I behave like that?"

Then Martin laid his head upon both his arms and, before he was aware of it, he fell asleep.

"Martin!" he suddenly heard a voice, as if some one had breathed the word above his ear.

He started from his sleep. "Who's there?" he asked.

He turned round and looked at the door; no one was there. He called again. Then he heard quite distinctly: "Martin, Martin! Look out into the street tomorrow, for I shall come."

Martin roused himself, rose from his chair and rubbed his eyes, but did not know whether he had heard these words in a dream or awake. He put out the lamp and lay down to sleep.

Next morning he rose before daylight, and after saying his prayers he lit the fire and prepared his cabbage soup and buckwheat porridge. Then he lit the samovar, put on his apron, and sat down by the window to his work. As he sat working Martin thought over what had happened the night before. At times it seemed to him like a dream, and at times he thought that he had really heard the voice. "Such things have happened before now," thought he.

So he sat by the window, looking out into the street more than he worked, and whenever any one passed in unfamiliar boots he would stoop and look up, so as to see not the feet only but the face of the passerby as well. A house porter passed in new felt boots; then a water carrier. Presently an old soldier of Nicholas' reign came near the window, spade in hand. Martin knew him by his boots, which were shabby old felt ones, goloshed with leather. The old man was called Stepanitch: a neighboring tradesman kept him in his house for charity, and his duty was to help the house porter. He began to clear away the snow before Martin's window. Martin glanced at him and then went on with his work.

"I must be growing crazy with age," said Martin, laughing at his fancy. "Stepanitch comes to clear away the snow, and I must needs imagine it's Christ coming to visit me. Old dotard that I am!"

Yet after he had made a dozen stitches he felt drawn to look out of the window again. He saw that Stepanitch had leaned his spade against the wall, and was either resting himself or trying to get warm. The man was old and broken down, and had evidently not enough strength even to clear away the snow.

"What if I called him in and gave him some tea?" thought Martin. "The samovar is just on the boil."

He stuck his awl in its place, and rose; and putting the samovar on the table, made tea. Then he tapped the window with his fingers. Stepanitch turned and came to the window. Martin beckoned to him to come in, and went himself to open the door.

"Come in," he said, "and warm yourself a bit. I'm sure you must be cold."

"May God bless you!" Stepanitch answered. "My bones do ache to be sure." He came in, first shaking off the snow, and lest he should leave marks on the floor he began wiping his feet; but as he did so he tottered and nearly fell.

"Don't trouble to wipe your feet," said Martin "I'll wipe up the floor – it's all in the day's work. Come, friend, sit down and have some tea."

Filling two tumblers, he passed one to his visitor, and pouring his own out into the saucer, began to blow on it.

Stepanitch emptied his glass, and, turning it upside down, put the remains of his piece of sugar on the top. He began to express his thanks, but it was plain that he would be glad of some more.

"Have another glass," said Martin, refilling the visitor's tumbler and his own. But while he drank his tea Martin kept looking out into the street.

"Are you expecting any one?" asked the visitor.

"Am I expecting any one? Well, now, I'm ashamed to tell you. It isn't that I really expect any one; but I heard something last night which I can't get out of my mind. Whether it was a vision, or only a fancy, I can't tell. You see, friend, last night I was reading the Gospel, about Christ the Lord, how he suffered, and how he walked on earth. You have heard tell of it, I dare say."

"I have heard tell of it," answered Stepanitch; "but I'm an ignorant man and not able to read."

"Well, you see, I was reading of how he walked on earth. I came to that part, you know, where he went to a Pharisee who did not receive him well. Well, friend, as I read about it, I thought now that man did not receive Christ the Lord with proper honor. Suppose such a thing could happen to such a man as myself, I thought, what would I not do to receive him! But that man gave him no reception at all. Well, friend, as I was thinking of this, I began to doze, and as I dozed I heard some one call me by name. I got up, and thought I heard someone whispering, 'Expect me; I will come tomorrow.' This happened twice over. And to tell you the truth, it sank so into my mind that, though I am ashamed of it myself, I keep on expecting him, the dear Lord!"

Stepanitch shook his head in silence, finished his tumbler and laid it on its side; but Martin stood it up again and refilled it for him.

"Here drink another glass, bless you! And I was thinking too, how he walked on earth and despised no one, but went mostly among common folk. He went with plain people, and chose his disciples from among the likes of us, from workmen like us, sinners that we are. 'He who raises himself,' he said, 'shall be humbled and he who humbles himself shall be raised.' 'You call me Lord,' he said, 'and I will wash your feet.' 'He who would be first,' he said, 'let him be the servant of all; because,' he said, 'blessed are the poor, the humble, the meek, and the merciful.'"

Stepanitch forgot his tea. He was an old man easily moved to tears, and as he sat and listened the tears ran down his cheeks.

"Come, drink some more," said Martin. But Stepanitch crossed himself, thanked him, moved away his tumbler, and rose.

"Thank you, Martin Avdeitch," he said, "you have given me food and comfort both for soul and body."

"You're very welcome. Come again another time. I am glad to have a guest," said Martin.

Stepanitch went away; and Martin poured out the last of the tea and drank it up. Then he put away the tea things and sat down to his work, stitching the back seam of a boot. And as he stitched he kept looking out of the window, waiting for Christ, and thinking about him and his doings. And his head was full of Christ's sayings.

Two soldiers went by: one in Government boots the other in boots of his own; then the master of a neighboring house, in shining goloshes; then a baker carrying a basket. All these passed on. Then a woman came up in worsted stockings and peasant-made shoes. She passed the window, but stopped by the wall. Martin glanced up at her through the window, and saw that she was a stranger, poorly dressed, and with a baby in her arms. She stopped by the wall with her back to the wind, trying to wrap the baby up though she had hardly anything to wrap it in. The woman had only summer clothes on, and even they were shabby and worn. Through the window Martin heard the baby crying, and the woman trying to soothe it, but unable to do so. Martin rose and going out of the door and up the steps he called to her.

"My dear, I say, my dear!"

The woman heard, and turned round.

"Why do you stand out there with the baby in the cold? Come inside. You can wrap him up better in a warm place. Come this way!"

The woman was surprised to see an old man in an apron, with spectacles on his nose, calling to her, but she followed him in.

They went down the steps, entered the little room, and the old man led her to the bed.

"There, sit down, my dear, near the stove. Warm yourself, and feed the baby."

"Haven't any milk. I have eaten nothing myself since early morning," said the woman, but still she took the baby to her breast.

Martin shook his head. He brought out a basin and some bread. Then he opened the oven door and poured some cabbage soup into the basin. He took out the porridge pot also but the porridge was not yet ready, so he spread a cloth on the table and served only the soup and bread.

"Sit down and eat, my dear, and I'll mind the baby. Why, bless me, I've had children of my own; I know how to manage them."

The woman crossed herself, and sitting down at the table began to eat, while Martin put the baby on the bed and sat down by it. He chucked and chucked, but having no teeth he could not do it well and the baby continued to cry. Then Martin tried poking at him with his finger; he drove his finger straight at the baby's mouth and then quickly drew it back, and did this again and again. He did not let the baby take his finger in its mouth, because it was all black with cobbler's wax. But the baby first grew quiet watching the finger, and then began to laugh. And Martin felt quite pleased.

The woman sat eating and talking, and told him who she was, and where she had been.

"I'm a soldier's wife," said she. "They sent my husband somewhere, far away, eight months ago, and I have heard nothing of him since. I had a place as cook till my baby was born, but then they would not keep me with a child. For three months now I have been struggling, unable to find a place, and I've had to sell all I had for food. I tried to go as a wet-nurse, but no one would have me; they said I was too starved-looking and thin. Now I have just been to see a tradesman's wife (a woman from our village is in service with her) and she has promised to take me. I thought it was all settled at last, but she tells me not to come till next week. It is far to her place, and I am fagged out, and baby is quite starved, poor mite. Fortunately our landlady has pity on us, and lets us lodge free, else I don't know what we should do."

Martin sighed. "Haven't you any warmer clothing?" he asked.

"How could I get warm clothing?" said she. "Why I pawned my last shawl for sixpence yesterday."

Then the woman came and took the child, and Martin got up. He went and looked among some things that were hanging on the wall, and brought back an old cloak.

"Here," he said, "though it's a worn-out old thing, it will do to wrap him up in."

The woman looked at the cloak, then at the old man, and taking it, burst into tears. Martin turned away, and groping under the bed brought out a small trunk. He fumbled about in it, and again sat down opposite the woman. And the woman said:

"The Lord bless you, friend. Surely Christ must have sent me to your window, else the child would have frozen. It was mild when I started, but now see how cold it has turned. Surely it must have been Christ who made you look out of your window and take pity on me, poor wretch!"

Martin smiled and said, "It is quite true; it was he made me do it. It was no mere chance made me look out."

And he told the woman his dream, and how he had heard the Lord's voice promising to visit him that day.

"Who knows? All things are possible," said the woman. And she got up and threw the cloak over her shoulders, wrapping it round herself and round the baby. Then she bowed, and thanked Martin once more.

"Take this for Christ's sake," said Martin, and gave her sixpence to get her shawl out of pawn. The woman crossed herself, and Martin did the same, and then he saw her out.

After the woman had gone, Martin ate some cabbage soup, cleared the things away, and sat down to work again. He sat and worked, but did not forget the window, and every time a shadow fell on it he looked up at once to see who was passing. People he knew and strangers passed by, but no one remarkable.

After a while Martin saw an apple-woman stop just in front of his window. She had a large basket, but there did not seem to be many apples left in it; she had evidently sold most of her stock. On her back she had a sack full of chips, which she was taking home. No doubt she had gathered them at some place where building was going on. The sack evidently hurt her, and she wanted to shift it from one shoulder to the other, so she put it down on the footpath and, placing her basket on a post, began to shake down the chips in the sack. While she was doing this a boy in a tattered cap ran up, snatched an apple out of the basket, and tried to slip away; but the old woman noticed it, and turning, caught the boy by his sleeve. He began to struggle, trying to free himself, but the old woman held on with both hands, knocked his cap off his head, and seized hold of his hair. The boy screamed and the old woman scolded. Martin dropped his awl, not waiting to stick it in its place, and rushed out of the door. Stumbling up the steps, and dropping his spectacles in his hurry, he ran out into the street. The old woman was pulling the boy's hair and scolding him, and threatening to take him to the police. The lad was struggling and protesting, saying, "I did not take it. What are you beating me for? Let me go!"

Martin separated them. He took the boy by the hand and said, "Let him go, Granny. Forgive him for Christ's sake."

"I'll pay him out, so that he won't forget it for a year! I'll take the rascal to the police!"

Martin began entreating the old woman.

"Let him go, Granny. He won't do it again. Let him go for Christ's sake!"

The old woman let go, and the boy wished to run away, but Martin stopped him.

"Ask the Granny's forgiveness!" said he. "And don't do it another time. I saw you take the apple."

The boy began to cry and to beg pardon.

"That's right. And now here's an apple for you, and Martin took an apple from the basket and gave it to the boy, saying, "I will pay you, Granny."

"You will spoil them that way, the young rascals," said the old woman. "He ought to be whipped so that he should remember it for a week."

"Oh, Granny, Granny," said Martin, "that's our way – but it's not God's way. If he should be whipped for stealing an apple, what should be done to us for our sins?"

The old woman was silent.

And Martin told her the parable of the lord who forgave his servant a large debt, and how the servant went out and seized his debtor by the throat. The old woman listened to it all, and the boy, too, stood by and listened.

"God bids us forgive," said Martin, "or else we shall not be forgiven. Forgive every one; and a thoughtless youngster most of all."

The old woman wagged her head and sighed.

"It's true enough," said she, "but they are getting terribly spoilt."

"Then we old ones must show them better ways," Martin replied.

"That's just what I say," said the old woman. "I have had seven of them myself, and only one daughter is left." And the old woman began to tell how and where she was living with her daughter, and how many grandchildren she had. "There now," she said, "I have but little strength left, yet I work hard for the sake of my grandchildren; and nice children they are, too. No one comes out to meet me but the children. Little Annie, now, won't leave me for any one. 'It's grandmother, dear grandmother, darling grandmother.'" And the old woman completely softened at the thought.

"Of course, it was only his childishness, God help him," said she, referring to the boy.

As the old woman was about to hoist her sack on her back, the lad sprang forward to her, saying, "Let me carry it for you, Granny. I'm going that way."

The old woman nodded her head, and put the sack on the boy's back, and they went down the street together, the old woman quite forgetting to ask Martin to pay for the apple. Martin stood and watched them as they went along talking to each other.

When they were out of sight Martin went back to the house. Having found his spectacles unbroken on the steps, he picked up his awl and sat down again to work. He worked a little, but could soon not see to pass the bristle through the holes in the leather; and presently he noticed the lamplighter passing on his way to light the street lamps.

"Seems it's time to light up," thought he. So he trimmed his lamp, hung it up, and sat down again to work. He finished off one boot and, turning it about, examined it. It was all right. Then he gathered his tools together, swept up the cuttings, put away the bristles and the thread and the awls, and, taking down the lamp, placed it on the table. Then he took the Gospels from the shelf. He meant to open them at the place he had marked the day before with a bit of morocco, but the book opened at another place. As Martin opened it, his yesterday's dream came back to his mind, and no sooner had he thought of it than he seemed to hear footsteps, as though some one were moving behind him. Martin turned round, and it seemed to him as if people were standing in the dark corner, but he could not make out who they were. And a voice whispered in his ear: "Martin, Martin, don't you know me?"

"Who is it?" muttered Martin.

"It is I," said the voice. And out of the dark corner stepped Stepanitch, who smiled and vanishing like a cloud was seen no more.

"It is I," said the voice again. And out of the darkness stepped the woman with the baby in her arms and the woman smiled and the baby laughed, and they too vanished.

"It is I," said the voice once more. And the old woman and the boy with the apple stepped out and both smiled, and then they too vanished.

And Martin's soul grew glad. He crossed himself, put on his spectacles, and began reading the Gospel just where it had opened; and at the top of the page he read

"I was a hungered, and ye gave me meat: I was thirsty, and ye gave me drink: I was a stranger, and ye took me in."

And at the bottom of the page he read:

"Inasmuch as ye did it unto one of these my brethren even these least, ye did it unto me"

And Martin understood that his dream had come true; and that the Savior had really come to him that day, and he had welcomed him.

1885

PART III

A Fairy Tale

8

The Story of Ivan the Fool

I

ONCE UPON A TIME, in a certain province of a certain country, there lived a rich peasant, who had three sons: Simon the Soldier, Taras the Stout, and Ivan the Fool, besides an unmarried daughter, Martha, who was deaf and dumb. Simon the Soldier went to the wars to serve the king; Taras the Stout went to a merchant's in town to trade, and Ivan the Fool stayed at home with the lass, to till the ground till his back bent.

Simon the Soldier obtained high rank and an estate, and married a nobleman's daughter. His pay was large and his estate was large, but yet he could not make ends meet. What the husband earned his lady wife squandered, and they never had money enough.

So Simon the Soldier went to his estate to collect the income, but his steward said, "where is any income to come from? We have neither cattle, nor tools, nor horse, nor plow, nor harrow. We must first get all these, and then the money will come."

Then Simon the Soldier went to his father and said: "You, father, are rich, but have given me nothing. Divide what you have, and give me a third part, that I may improve my estate."

But the old man said: "You brought nothing into my house; why should I give you a third part? It would be unfair to Ivan and to the girl."

But Simon answered, "He is a fool; and she is an old maid, and deaf and dumb besides; what's the good of property to them?"

The old man said, "We will see what Ivan says about it."

And Ivan said, "Let him take what he wants."

So Simon the Soldier took his share of his father's goods and removed them to his estate, and went off again to serve the king.

Taras the Stout also gathered much money, and married into a merchant's family, but still he wanted more. So he, also, came to his father and said, "Give me my portion."

But the old man did not wish to give Taras a share either, and said, "You brought nothing here. Ivan has earned all we have in the house, and why should we wrong him and the girl?"

But Taras said, "What does he need? He is a fool! He cannot marry, no one would have him; and the dumb lass does not need anything either. Look here, Ivan!" said he, "give me half the corn; I don't want the tools, and of the live stock I will take only the gray stallion, which is of no use to you for the plow."

Ivan laughed and said, "Take what you want. I will work to earn some more."

So they gave a share to Taras also, and he carted the corn away to town, and took the gray stallion. And Ivan was left with one old mare, to lead his peasant life as before, and to support his father and mother.

II

Now the old Devil was vexed that the brothers had not quarrelled over the division, but had parted peacefully; and he summoned three imps.

"Look here," said he, "there are three brothers: Simon the Soldier, Taras the Stout, and Ivan the Fool. They should have quarrelled, but are living peaceably and meet on friendly terms. The fool Ivan has spoilt the whole business for me. Now you three go and tackle those three brothers, and worry them till they scratch each other's eyes out! Do you think you can do it?"

"Yes, we'll do it," said they.

"How will you set about it?"

"Why," said they, "first we'll ruin them. And when they haven't a crust to eat we'll tie them up together, and then they'll fight each other, sure enough!"

"That's capital; I see you understand your business. Go, and don't come back till you've set them by the ears, or I'll skin you alive!"

The imps went off into a swamp, and began to consider how they should set to work. They disputed and disputed, each wanting the lightest job; but at last they decided to cast lots which of the brothers each imp should tackle. If one imp finished his task before the others, he was to come and help them. So the imps cast lots, and appointed a time to meet again in the swamp to learn who had succeeded and who needed help.

The appointed time came round, and the imps met again in the swamp as agreed. And each began to tell how matters stood. The first, who had undertaken Simon the Soldier, began: "My business is going on well. Tomorrow Simon will return to his father's house."

His comrades asked, "How did you manage it?"

"First," says he, "I made Simon so bold that he offered to conquer the whole world for his king; and the king made him his general and sent him to fight the King of India. They met for battle, but the night before, I dampened all the powder in Simon's camp, and made more straw soldiers for the Indian King than you could count. And when Simon's soldiers saw the straw soldiers surrounding them, they grew frightened. Simon ordered them to fire; but their cannons and guns would not go off. Then Simon's soldiers were quite frightened, and ran like sheep, and the Indian King slaughtered them. Simon was disgraced. He has been deprived of his estate, and tomorrow they intend to execute him. There is only one day's work left for me to do; I have just to let him out of prison that he may escape home. Tomorrow I shall be ready to help whichever of you needs me."

Then the second imp, who had Taras in hand, began to tell how he had fared. "I don't want any help," said he, "my job is going all right. Taras can't hold out for more than a week. First I caused him to grow greedy and fat. His covetousness became so great that whatever he saw he wanted to buy. He has spent all his money in buying immense lots of goods, and still continues to buy. Already he has begun to use borrowed money. His debts hang like a weight round his neck, and he is so involved that he can never get clear. In a week his bills come due, and before then I will spoil all his stock. He will be unable to pay and will have to go home to his father."

Then they asked the third imp (Ivan's), "And how are you getting on?"

"Well," said he, "my affair goes badly. First I spat into his drink to make his stomach ache, and then I went into his field and hammered the ground hard as a stone that he should not be able to till it. I thought he wouldn't plow it, but like the fool that he is, he came with his plow and began to make a furrow. He groaned with the pain in his stomach, but went on plowing. I broke his plow for him, but he went home, got out another, and again started plowing. I crept under the earth and caught hold of the plowshares, but there was no holding them; he leant heavily upon the plow, and the plowshare was sharp and cut my hands. He has all but finished plowing the field, only one little strip is left. Come brothers, and help me; for if we don't get the better of him, all our labor is lost. If the fool holds out and keeps on working the land, his brothers will never know want, for he will feed them both."

Simon the Soldier's imp promised to come next day to help, and so they parted.

III

Ivan had plowed up the whole fallow, all but one little strip. He came to finish it. Though his stomach ached, the plowing must be done. He freed the harness ropes, turned the plow, and began to work. He drove one furrow, but coming back the plow began to drag as if it had caught in a root. It was the imp, who had twisted his legs round the plowshare and was holding it back.

"What a strange thing!" thought Ivan. "There were no roots here at all, and yet here's a root."

Ivan pushed his hand deep into the furrow, groped about, and, feeling something soft, seized hold of it and pulled it out. It was black like a root, but it wriggled. Why, it was a live imp!

"What a nasty thing!" said Ivan, and he lifted his hand to dash it against the plow, but the imp squealed out:

"Don't hurt me, and I'll do anything you tell me to."

"What can you do?"

"Anything you tell me to."

Ivan scratched his head.

"My stomach aches," said he; "can you cure that?"

"Certainly I can."

"Well then, do so."

The imp went down into the furrow, searched about, scratched with his claws, and pulled out a bunch of three little roots, which he handed to Ivan.

"Here," says he, "whoever swallows one of these will be cured of any illness."

Ivan took the roots, separated them, and swallowed one. The pain in his stomach was cured at once. The imp again begged to be let off; "I will jump right into the earth, and never come back," said he.

"All right," said Ivan; "begone, and God be with you!"

And as soon as Ivan mentioned God, the imp plunged into the earth like a stone thrown into the water. Only a hole was left.

Ivan put the other two pieces of root into his cap and went on with his plowing. He plowed the strip to the end, turned his plow over, and went home. He unharnessed the horse, entered the hut, and there he saw his elder brother, Simon the Soldier and his wife, sitting at supper. Simon's estate had been confiscated, he himself had barely managed to escape from prison, and he had come back to live in his father's house.

Simon saw Ivan, and said: "I have come to live with you. Feed me and my wife till I get another appointment."

"All right," said Ivan, "you can stay with us."

But when Ivan was about to sit down on the bench the lady disliked the smell, and said to her husband. "I cannot sup with a dirty peasant."

So Simon the Soldier said, "My lady says you don't smell nice. You'd better go and eat outside."

"All right," said Ivan; "anyway I must spend the night outside, for I have to pasture the mare."

So he took some bread, and his coat, and went with the mare into the fields.

IV

Having finished his work that night, Simon's imp came, as agreed, to find Ivan's imp and help him to subdue the fool. He came to the field and searched and searched; but instead of his comrade he found only a hole.

"Clearly," thought he, "some evil has befallen my comrade. I must take his place. The field is plowed up, so the fool must be tackled in the meadow."

So the imp went to the meadows and flooded Ivan's hayfield with water, which left the grass all covered with mud.

Ivan returned from the pasture at dawn, sharpened his scythe, and went to mow the hayfield. He began to mow but had only swung the scythe once or twice when the edge turned so that it would not cut at all, but needed resharpening. Ivan struggled on for awhile, and then said: "It's no good. I must go home and bring a tool to straighten the scythe, and I'll get a chunk of bread at the same time. If I have to spend a week here, I won't leave till the mowing's done."

The imp heard this and thought to himself, "This fool is a tough 'un; I can't get round him this way. I must try some other dodge."

Ivan returned, sharpened his scythe, and began to mow. The imp crept into the grass and began to catch the scythe by the heel, sending the point into the earth. Ivan found the work very hard, but he mowed the whole meadow, except one little bit which was in the swamp. The imp crept into the swamp and, thought he to himself, "Though I cut my paws I will not let him mow."

Ivan reached the swamp. The grass didn't seem thick, but yet it resisted the scythe. Ivan grew angry and began to swing the scythe with all his might. The imp had to give in; he could not keep up with the scythe, and, seeing it was a bad business, he scrambled into a bush. Ivan swung the scythe, caught the bush, and cut off half the imp's tail. Then he finished mowing the grass, told his sister to rake it up, and went himself to mow the rye. He went with the scythe, but the dock-tailed imp was there first, and entangled the rye so that the scythe was of no use. But Ivan went home and got his sickle, and began to reap with that and he reaped the whole of the rye.

"Now it's time," said he, "to start on the oats."

The dock-tailed imp heard this, and thought, "I couldn't get the better of him on the rye, but I shall on the oats. Only wait till the morning."

In the morning the imp hurried to the oat field, but the oats were already mowed down! Ivan had mowed them by night, in order that less grain should shake out. The imp grew angry.

"He has cut me all over and tired me out – the fool. It is worse than war. The accursed fool never sleeps; one can't keep up with him. I will get into his stacks now and rot them."

So the imp entered the rye, and crept among the sheaves, and they began to rot. He heated them, grew warm himself, and fell asleep.

Ivan harnessed the mare, and went with the lass to cart the rye. He came to the heaps, and began to pitch the rye into the cart. He tossed two sheaves and again thrust his fork – right into the imp's back. He lifts the fork and sees on the prongs a live imp; dock-tailed, struggling, wriggling, and trying to jump off.

"What, you nasty thing, are you here again?"

"I'm another," said the imp. "The first was my brother. I've been with your brother Simon."

"Well," said Ivan, "whoever you are, you've met the same fate!"

He was about to dash him against the cart, but the imp cried out: "Let me off, and I will not only let you alone, but I'll do anything you tell me to do."

"What can you do?"

"I can make soldiers out of anything you like."

"But what use are they?"

"You can turn them to any use; they can do anything you please."

"Can they sing?"

"Yes, if you want them to."

"All right; you may make me some."

And the imp said, "Here, take a sheaf of rye, then bump it upright on the ground, and simply say:

'O sheaf! my slave
This order gave:
Where a straw has been
Let a soldier be seen!'"

Ivan took the sheaf, struck it on the ground, and said what the imp had told him to. The sheaf fell asunder, and all the straws changed into soldiers, with a trumpeter and a drummer playing in front, so that there was a whole regiment.

Ivan laughed.

"How clever!" said he. "This is fine! How pleased the girls will be!"

"Now let me go," said the imp.

"No," said Ivan, "I must make my soldiers of thrashed straw, otherwise good grain will be wasted. Teach me how to change them back again into the sheaf. I want to thrash it."

And the imp said, "Repeat:

'Let each be a straw
Who was soldier before,
For my true slave
This order gave!'"

Ivan said this, and the sheaf reappeared.

Again the imp began to beg, "Now let me go!"

"All right." And Ivan pressed him against the side of the cart, held him down with his hand, and pulled him off the fork.

"God be with you," said he.

And as soon as he mentioned God, the imp plunged into the earth like a stone into water. Only a hole was left.

Ivan returned home, and there was his other brother, Taras with his wife, sitting at supper.

Taras the Stout had failed to pay his debts, had run away from his creditors, and had come home to his father's house. When he saw Ivan, "Look here," said he, "till I can start in business again, I want you to keep me and my wife."

"All right," said Ivan, "you can live here, if you like."

Ivan took off his coat and sat down to table, but the merchant's wife said: "I cannot sit at table with this clown, he smells of perspiration."

Then Taras the Stout said, "Ivan, you smell too strong. Go and eat outside."

"All right," said Ivan, taking some bread and going into the yard. "It is time, anyhow, for me to go and pasture the mare."

V

Taras's imp, being also free that night, came, as agreed, to help his comrades subdue Ivan the Fool. He came to the cornfield, looked and looked for his comrades – no one was there. He only found a hole. He went to the meadow, and there he found an imp's tail in the swamp, and another hole in the rye stubble.

"Evidently, some ill luck has befallen my comrades," thought he. "I must take their place and tackle the fool."

So the imp went to look for Ivan, who had already stacked the corn and was cutting trees in the wood. The two brothers had begun to feel crowded, living together, and had told Ivan to cut down trees to build new houses for them.

The imp ran to the wood, climbed among the branches, and began to hinder Ivan from felling the trees. Ivan undercut one tree so that it should fall clear, but in falling it turned askew and caught among some branches. Ivan cut a pole with which to lever it aside, and with difficulty contrived to bring it to the ground. He set to work to fell another tree – again the same thing occurred; and with all his efforts he could hardly get the tree clear. He began on a third tree, and again the same thing happened.

Ivan had hoped to cut down half a hundred small trees, but had not felled even half a score, and now the night was come and he was tired out. The steam from him spread like a mist through the wood, but still he stuck to his work. He undercut another tree, but his back began to ache so that he could not stand. He drove his axe into the tree and sat down to rest.

The imp, noticing that Ivan had stopped work, grew cheerful.

"At last," thought he, "he is tired out! He will give it up. Now I can take a rest myself."

He seated himself astride a branch and chuckled. But soon Ivan got up, pulled the axe out, swung it and smote the tree from the opposite side with such force that the tree gave way at once and came crashing down. The imp had not expected this, and had no time to get his feet clear, and the tree in breaking, gripped his paw. Ivan began to lop off the branches, when he noticed a live imp hanging in the tree! Ivan was surprised.

"What, you nasty thing," says he, "so you are here again!"

"I am another one," says the imp. "I have been with your brother Taras."

"Whoever you are you have met your fate," said Ivan, and swinging his axe he was about to strike him with the haft, but the imp begged for mercy: "Don't strike me," said he, "and I will do anything you tell me to."

"What can you do?"

"I can make money for you, as much as you want."

"All right, make some." So the imp showed him how to do it.

"Take," said he, "some leaves from this oak and rub them in your hands, and gold will fall out on the ground."

Ivan took some leaves and rubbed them, and gold ran down from his hands.

"This stuff will do fine," said he, "for the fellows to play with on their holidays."

"Now let me go," said the imp.

"All right," said Ivan, and taking a lever he set the imp free. "Now begone! And God be with you," says he.

And as soon as he mentioned God, the imp plunged into the earth, like a stone into water. Only a hole was left.

VI

So the brothers built houses, and began to live apart; and Ivan finished the harvest work, brewed beer, and invited his brothers to spend the next holiday with him. His brothers would not come.

"We don't care about peasant feasts," said they.

So Ivan entertained the peasants and their wives, and drank until he was rather tipsy. Then he went into the street to a ring of dancers; and going up to them he told the women to sing a song in his honor; "for," said he, "I will give you something you never saw in your lives before!"

The women laughed and sang his praises, and when they had finished they said, "Now let us have your gift."

"I will bring it directly," said he.

He took a seed basket and ran into the woods. The women laughed. "He is a fool!" said they, and they began to talk of something else.

But soon Ivan came running back, carrying the basket full of something heavy.

"Shall I give it you?"

"Yes! give it to us."

Ivan took a handful of gold and threw it to the women. You should have seen them throw themselves upon it to pick it up! And the men around scrambled for it, and snatched it from one another. One old woman was nearly crushed to death. Ivan laughed.

"Oh, you fools!" says he. "Why did you crush the old grandmother? Be quiet, and I will give you some more," and he threw them some more. The people all crowded round, and Ivan threw them all the gold he had. They asked for more, but Ivan said, "I have no more just now. Another time I'll give you some more. Now let us dance, and you can sing me your songs."

The women began to sing.

"Your songs are no good," says he.

"Where will you find better ones?" say they.

"I'll soon show you," says he.

He went to the barn, took a sheaf, thrashed it, stood it up, and bumped it on the ground.

"Now," said he:

'O sheaf! my slave
This order gave:

Where a straw has been
Let a soldier be seen!'"

And the sheaf fell asunder and became so many soldiers. The
drums and trumpets began to play. Ivan ordered the soldiers to
play and sing. He led them out into the street, and the people
were amazed. The soldiers played and sang, and then Ivan (for-
bidding any one to follow him) led them back to the thrashing
ground, changed them into a sheaf again, and threw it in its place.

He then went home and lay down in the stables to sleep.

VII

Simon the Soldier heard of all these things next morning, and
went to his brother.

"Tell me," says he, "where you got those soldiers from, and
where you have taken them to?"

"What does it matter to you?" said Ivan.

"What does it matter? Why, with soldiers one can do anything. One can win a kingdom."

Ivan wondered.

"Really!" said he; "Why didn't you say so before? I'll make you
as many as you like. It's well the lass and I have thrashed so much
straw."

Ivan took his brother to the barn and said:

"Look here; if I make you some soldiers, you must take them
away at once, for if we have to feed them, they will eat up the
whole village in a day."

Simon the Soldier promised to lead the soldiers away; and
Ivan began to make them. He bumped a sheaf on the thrashing
floor – a company appeared. He bumped another sheaf, and
there was a second company. He made so many that they covered the field.

"Will that do?" he asked.

Simon was overjoyed, and said: "That will do! Thank you, Ivan!"

"All right" said Ivan. "If you want more, come back, and I'll make them. There is plenty of straw this season."

Simon the Soldier at once took command of his army, collected and organized it, and went off to make war.

Hardly had Simon the Soldier gone, when Taras the Stout came along. He, too, had heard of yesterday's affair, and he said to his brother:

"Show me where you get gold money! If I only had some to start with, I could make it bring me in money from all over the world."

Ivan was astonished.

"Really!" said he. "You should have told me sooner. I will make you as much as you like."

His brother was delighted.

"Give me three baskets-full to begin with."

"All right," said Ivan. "Come into the forest; or better still, let us harness the mare, for you won't be able to carry it all."

They drove to the forest, and Ivan began to rub the oak leaves. He made a great heap of gold.

"Will that do?"

Taras was overjoyed.

"It will do for the present," said he. "Thank you, Ivan!"

"All right," says Ivan, "if you want more, come back for it. There are plenty of leaves left."

Taras the Stout gathered up a whole cartload of money, and went off to trade.

So the two brothers went away: Simon to fight and Taras to buy and sell. And Simon the Soldier conquered a kingdom for himself; and Taras the Stout made much money in trade.

When the two brothers met, each told the other: Simon how he got the soldiers, and Taras how he got the money. And

Simon the Soldier said to his brother, "I have conquered a kingdom and live in grand style but I have not money enough to keep my soldiers."

And Taras the Stout said, "And I have made much money, but the trouble is, I have no one to guard it."

Then said Simon the Soldier, "Let us go to our brother. I will tell him to make more soldiers, and will give them to you to guard your money, and you can tell him to make money for me to feed my men."

And they drove away to Ivan; and Simon said, "Dear brother, I have not enough soldiers; make me another couple of ricks or so."

Ivan shook his head.

"No!" says he, "I will not make any more soldiers."

"But you promised you would."

"I know I promised, but I won't make any more."

"But why not, fool?"

"Because your soldiers killed a man. I was plowing the other day near the road, and I saw a woman taking a coffin along in a cart, and crying. I asked her who was dead. She said, 'Simon's soldiers have killed my husband in the war.' I thought the soldiers would only play tunes, but they have killed a man. I won't give you any more."

And he stuck to it, and would not make any more soldiers.

Taras the Stout, too, began to beg Ivan to make him more gold money. But Ivan shook his head.

"No, I won't make any more," said he.

"Didn't you promise?"

"I did, but I'll make no more," said he.

"Why not, fool?"

"Because your gold coins took away the cow from Michael's daughter."

"How?"

"Simply took it away! Michael's daughter had a cow. Her children used to drink the milk. But the other day her children came to me to ask for milk. I said, 'Where's your cow?' They answered, 'The steward of Taras the Stout came and gave mother three bits of gold, and she gave him the cow, so we have nothing to drink.' I thought you were only going to play with the gold pieces, but you have taken the children's cow away. I will not give you any more."

And Ivan stuck to it and would not give him any more. So the brothers went away. And as they went they discussed how they could meet their difficulties. And Simon said:

"Look here, I tell you what to do. You give me money to feed my soldiers, and I will give you half my kingdom with soldiers enough to guard your money." Taras agreed. So the brothers divided what they possessed, and both became kings, and both were rich.

VIII

Ivan lived at home, supporting his father and mother and working in the fields with his dumb sister. Now it happened that Ivan's yard dog fell sick, grew mangy, and was near dying. Ivan, pitying it, got some bread from his sister, put it in his cap, carried it out, and threw it to the dog. But the cap was torn, and together with the bread one of the little roots fell to the ground. The old dog ate it up with the bread, and as soon as she had swallowed it she jumped up and began to play, bark, and wag her tail – in short became quite well again.

The father and mother saw it and were amazed.

"How did you cure the dog?" asked they.

Ivan answered: "I had two little roots to cure any pain, and she swallowed one."

Now about that time it happened that the King's daughter fell ill, and the King proclaimed in every town and village, that

he would reward any one who could heal her, and if any unmarried man could heal the King's daughter he should have her
for his wife. This was proclaimed in Ivan's village as well as everywhere else.

His father and mother called Ivan, and said to him: "Have
you heard what the King has proclaimed? You said you had a
root that would cure any sickness. Go and heal the King's daughter, and you will be made happy for life."

"All right," said he.

And Ivan prepared to go, and they dressed him in his best.
But as he went out of the door he met a beggar woman with a
crippled hand.

"I have heard," said she, "that you can heal people. I pray you
cure my arm, for I cannot even put on my boots myself."

"All right," said Ivan, and giving the little root to the beggar
woman he told her to swallow it. She swallowed it, and was
cured. She was at once able to move her arm freely.

His father and mother came out to accompany Ivan to the
King, but when they heard that he had given away the root, and
that he had nothing left to cure the King's daughter with, they
began to scold him.

"You pity a beggar woman, but are not sorry for the King's
daughter!" said they. But Ivan felt sorry for the King's daughter
also. So he harnessed the horse, put straw in the cart to sit on,
and sat down to drive away.

"Where are you going, fool?"

"To cure the King's daughter."

"But you've nothing left to cure her with?"

"Never mind," said he, and drove off.

He drove to the King's palace, and as soon as he stepped on
the threshold the King's daughter got well.

The King was delighted, and had Ivan brought to him, and
had him dressed in fine robes.

"Be my son-in-law," said he.

"All right," said Ivan.

And Ivan married the Princess. Her father died soon after, and Ivan became King. So all three brothers were now kings.

IX

The three brothers lived and reigned. The eldest brother, Simon the Soldier, prospered. With his straw soldiers he levied real soldiers. He ordered throughout his whole kingdom a levy of one soldier from every ten houses, and each soldier had to be tall, and clean in body and in face. He gathered many such soldiers and trained them; and when any one opposed him, he sent these soldiers at once, and got his own way, so that every one began to fear him, and his life was a comfortable one. Whatever he cast his eyes on and wished for, was his. He sent soldiers, and they brought him all he desired.

Taras the Stout also lived comfortably. He did not waste the money he got from Ivan, but increased it largely. He introduced law and order into his kingdom. He kept his money in coffers, and taxed the people. He instituted a poll tax, tolls for walking and driving, and a tax on shoes and stockings and dress trimmings. And whatever he wished for he got. For the sake of money, people brought him everything, and they offered to work for him – for every one wanted money.

Ivan the Fool, also, did not live badly. As soon as he had buried his father-in-law, he took off all his royal robes and gave them to his wife to put away in a chest; and he again donned his hempen shirt, his breeches and peasant shoes, and started again to work.

"It's dull for me," said he. "I'm getting fat and have lost my appetite and my sleep." So he brought his father and mother and his dumb sister to live with him, and worked as before.

People said, "But you are a king!"

"Yes," said he, "but even a king must eat."

One of his ministers came to him and said, "We have no money to pay salaries."

"All right," says he, "then don't pay them."

"Then no one will serve."

"All right; let them not serve. They will have more time to work; let them cart manure. There is plenty of scavenging to be done."

And people came to Ivan to be tried. One said. "He stole my money." And Ivan said, "All right, that shows that he wanted it."

And they all got to know that Ivan was a fool. And his wife said to him, "People say that you are a fool."

"All right," said Ivan.

His wife thought and thought about it, but she also was a fool.

"Shall I go against my husband? Where the needle goes the thread follows," said she.

So she took off her royal dress, put it away in a chest, and went to the dumb girl to learn to work. And she learned to work and began to help her husband.

And all the wise men left Ivan's kingdom; only the fools remained.

Nobody had money. They lived and worked. They fed themselves; and they fed others.

X

The old Devil waited and waited for news from the imps of their having ruined the three brothers. But no news came. So he went himself to inquire about it. He searched and searched, but instead of finding the three imps he found only the three holes.

"Evidently they have failed," thought he. "I shall have to tackle it myself."

So he went to look for the brothers, but they were no longer in their old places. He found them in three different kingdoms. All three were living and reigning. This annoyed the old Devil very much.

"Well," said he, "I must try my own hand at the job."

First he went to King Simon. He did not go to him in his own shape, but disguised himself as a general, and drove to Simon's palace.

"I hear, King Simon," said he, "that you are a great warrior, and as I know that business well, I desire to serve you."

King Simon questioned him, and seeing that he was a wise man, took him into his service.

The new commander began to teach King Simon how to form a strong army.

"First," said he, "we must levy more soldiers, for there are in your kingdom many people unemployed. We must recruit all the young men without exception. Then you will have five times as many soldiers as formerly. Secondly, we must get new rifles and cannons. I will introduce rifles that will fire a hundred balls at once; they will fly out like peas. And I will get cannons that will consume with fire either man, or horse, or wall. They will burn up everything!"

Simon the King listened to the new commander, ordered all young men without exception to be enrolled as soldiers, and had new factories built in which he manufactured large quantities of improved rifles and cannons. Then he made haste to declare war against a neighboring king. As soon as he met the other army, King Simon ordered his soldiers to rain balls against it and shoot fire from the cannons, and at one blow he burned and crippled half the enemy's army. The neighboring king was so thoroughly frightened that he gave way and surrendered his kingdom. King Simon was delighted.

"Now," said he, "I will conquer the King of India."

But the Indian King had heard about King Simon and had adopted all his inventions, and added more of his own. The Indian King enlisted not only all the young men, but all the single women also, and got together a greater army even than King Simon's. And he copied all King Simon's rifles and cannons, and invented a way of flying through the air to throw explosive bombs from above.

King Simon set out to fight the Indian King, expecting to beat him as he had beaten the other king; but the scythe that had cut so well had lost its edge. The King of India did not let Simon's army come within gunshot, but sent his women through the air to hurl down explosive bombs on to Simon's army. The women began to rain down bombs on to the army like borax upon cockroaches. The army ran away, and Simon the King was left alone. So the Indian King took Simon's kingdom, and Simon the Soldier fled as best he might.

Having finished with this brother, the old Devil went to King Taras. Changing himself into a merchant, he settled in Taras's kingdom, started a house of business, and began spending money. He paid high prices for everything, and everybody hurried to the new merchant's to get money. And so much money spread among the people that they began to pay all their taxes promptly, and paid up all their arrears, and King Taras rejoiced.

"Thanks to the new merchant," thought he, "I shall have more money than ever; and my life will be yet more comfortable."

And Taras the King began to form fresh plans, and began to build a new palace. He gave notice that people should bring him wood and stone and come to work, and he fixed high prices for everything. King Taras thought people would come in crowds to work as before, but to his surprise all the wood and stone was taken to the merchant's, and all the workmen went there too. King Taras increased his price, but the merchant bid yet more. King Taras had much money, but the merchant had still more, and outbid the King at every point.

The King's palace was at a standstill and the building did not get on.

King Taras planned a garden, and when autumn came he called for the people to come and plant the garden, but nobody came. All the people were engaged digging a pond for the merchant. Winter came, and King Taras wanted to buy sable furs for a new overcoat. He sent to buy them, but the messengers returned and said, "There are no sables left. The merchant has all the furs. He gave the best price, and made carpets of the skins."

King Taras wanted to buy some stallions. He sent to buy them, but the messengers returned saying, "The merchant has all the good stallions; they are carrying water to fill his pond."

All the King's affairs came to a standstill. Nobody would work for him, for every one was busy working for the merchant; and they only brought King Taras the merchant's money to pay their taxes.

And the King collected so much money that he had nowhere to store it, and his life became wretched. He ceased to form plans, and would have been glad enough simply to live, but he was hardly able even to do that. He ran short of everything. One after another his cooks, coachmen, and servants left him to go to the merchant. Soon he lacked even food. When he sent to the market to buy anything, there was nothing to be got – the merchant had bought up everything, and people only brought the King money to pay their taxes.

Taras the King got angry and banished the merchant from the country. But the merchant settled just across the frontier, and went on as before. For the sake of the merchant's money, people took everything to him instead of to the King.

Things went badly with King Taras. For days together he had nothing to eat, and a rumor even got about that the merchant was boasting that he would buy up the King himself! King Taras got frightened, and did not know what to do.

At this time Simon the Soldier came to him, saying, "Help me, for the King of India has conquered me."

But King Taras himself was over head and ears in difficulties. "I myself," said he, "have had nothing to eat for two days."

XI

Having done with the two brothers, the old Devil went to Ivan. He changed himself into a General, and coming to Ivan began to persuade him that he ought to have an army.

"It does not become a king," said he, "to be without an army. Only give me the order, and I will collect soldiers from among your people, and form one."

Ivan listened to him. "All right," said Ivan, "form an army, and teach them to sing songs well. I like to hear them do that."

So the old Devil went through Ivan's kingdom to enlist men. He told them to go and be entered as soldiers, and each should have a quart of spirits and a fine red cap.

The people laughed.

"We have plenty of spirits," said they. "We make it ourselves; and as for caps, the women make all kinds of them, even striped ones with tassels."

So nobody would enlist.

The old Devil came to Ivan and said: "Your fools won't enlist of their own free will. We shall have to make them."

"All right," said Ivan, "you can try."

So the old Devil gave notice that all the people were to enlist, and that Ivan would put to death any one who refused.

The people came to the General and said, "You say that if we do not go as soldiers the King will put us to death, but you don't say what will happen if we do enlist. We have heard say that soldiers get killed!"

"Yes, that happens sometimes."

When the people heard this they became obstinate.

"We won't go," said they. "Better meet death at home. Either way we must die."

"Fools! You are fools!" said the old Devil. "A soldier may be killed or he may not, but if you don't go, King Ivan will have you killed for certain."

The people were puzzled, and went to Ivan the Fool to consult him.

"A General has come," said they, "who says we must all become soldiers. 'If you go as soldiers,' says he 'you may be killed or you may not, but if you don't go, King Ivan will certainly kill you.' Is this true?"

Ivan laughed and said, "How can I, alone, put all you to death? If I were not a fool I would explain it to you but as it is, I don't understand it myself."

"Then" said they, "we will not serve."

"All right," says he, "don't."

So the people went to the General and refused to enlist. And the old Devil saw that this game was up, and he went off and ingratiated himself with the King of Tarakan.

"Let us make war," says he, "and conquer King Ivan's country. It is true there is no money, but there is plenty of corn and cattle and everything else."

So the King of Tarakan prepared to make war. He mustered a great army, provided rifles and cannons, marched to the frontier, and entered Ivan's kingdom.

And people came to Ivan and said, "The King of Tarakan is coming to make war on us."

"All right," said Ivan, "let him come."

Having crossed the frontier, the King of Tarakan sent scouts to look for Ivan's army. They looked and looked, but there was no army! They waited and waited for one to appear somewhere, but there were no signs of an army, and nobody to fight with.

The King of Tarakan then sent to seize the villages. The soldiers came to a village, and the people, both men and women, rushed out in astonishment to stare at the soldiers. The soldiers began to take their corn and cattle; the people let them have it, and did not resist. The soldiers went on to another village; the same thing happened again. The soldiers went on for one day, and for two days, and everywhere the same thing happened. The people let them have everything, and no one resisted, but only invited the soldiers to live with them.

"Poor fellows," said they, "if you have a hard life in your own land, why don't you come and stay with us altogether?"

The soldiers marched and marched: still no army, only people living and feeding themselves and others, and not resisting, but inviting the soldiers to stay and live with them. The soldiers found it dull work, and they came to the King of Tarakan and said, "We cannot fight here, lead us elsewhere. War is all right, but what is this? It is like cutting pea soup! We will not make war here any more."

The King of Tarakan grew angry, and ordered his soldiers to overrun the whole kingdom, to destroy the villages, to burn the grain and the houses, and to slaughter the cattle. "And if you do not obey my orders," said he, "I will execute you all."

The soldiers were frightened, and began to act according to the King's orders. They began to burn houses and corn, and to kill cattle. But the fools still offered no resistance, and only wept. The old men wept, and the old women wept, and the young people wept.

"Why do you harm us?" they said. "Why do you waste good things? If you need them, why don't you take them for yourselves?"

At last the soldiers could stand it no longer. They refused to go any further, and the army disbanded and fled.

XII

The old Devil had to give it up. He could not get the better of Ivan with soldiers. So he changed himself into a fine gentleman, and settled down in Ivan's kingdom. He meant to overcome him by means of money, as he had overcome Taras the Stout.

"I wish," says he, "to do you a good turn, to teach you sense and reason. I will build a house among you and organize a trade."

"All right," said Ivan, "come and live among us if you like."

Next morning the fine gentleman went out into the public square with a big sack of gold and a sheet of paper, and said, "You all live like swine. I wish to teach you how to live properly. Build me a house according to this plan. You shall work, I will tell you how, and I will pay you with gold coins." And he showed them the gold.

The fools were astonished; there was no money in use among them; they bartered their goods, and paid one another with labor. They looked at the gold coins with surprise.

"What nice little things they are!" said they.

And they began to exchange their goods and labor for the gentleman's gold pieces. And the old Devil began, as in Taras's kingdom, to be free with his gold, and the people began to exchange everything for gold and to do all sorts of work for it.

The old Devil was delighted, and thought he to himself, "Things are going right this time. Now I shall ruin the Fool as I did Taras, and I shall buy him up body and soul."

But as soon as the fools had provided themselves with gold pieces they gave them to the women for necklaces. The lasses plaited them into their tresses, and at last the children in the street began to play with the little pieces. Everybody had plenty of them, and they stopped taking them. But the fine gentleman's mansion was not yet half built, and the grain and cattle for the year were not yet provided. So he gave notice that he wished people to come and work for him, and that he wanted cattle and grain; for each thing, and for each service, he was ready to give many more pieces of gold.

But nobody came to work and nothing was brought. Only sometimes a boy or a little girl would run up to exchange an egg for a gold coin, but nobody else came, and he had nothing to eat. And being hungry, the fine gentleman went through the village to try and buy something for dinner. He tried at one house, and offered a gold piece for a fowl, but the housewife wouldn't take it.

"I have a lot already," said she.

He tried at a widow's house to buy a herring, and offered a gold piece.

"I don't want it, my good sir," said she. "I have no children to play with it, and I myself already have three coins as curiosities."

He tried at a peasant's house to get bread, but neither would the peasant take money.

"I don't need it," said he, "but if you are begging 'for Christ's sake,' wait a bit and I'll tell the housewife to cut you a piece of bread."

At that the Devil spat, and ran away. To hear Christ's name mentioned, let alone receiving anything for Christ's sake, hurt him more than sticking a knife into him.

And so he got no bread. Every one had gold, and no matter where the old Devil went, nobody would give anything for money, but every one said, "Either bring something else, or come and work, or receive what you want in charity for Christ's sake."

But the old Devil had nothing but money; for work he had no liking, and as for taking anything "for Christ's sake" he could not do that. The old Devil grew very angry.

"What more do you want, when I give you money?" said he. "You can buy everything with gold, and hire any kind of laborer." But the fools did not heed him.

"No, we do not want money," said they. "We have no payments to make, and no taxes, so what should we do with it?"

The old Devil lay down to sleep – supperless.

The affair was told to Ivan the Fool. People came and asked him, "What are we to do? A fine gentleman has turned up, who likes to eat and drink and dress well, but he does not like to work, does not beg in 'Christ's name,' but only offers gold pieces to every one. At first people gave him all he wanted until they had plenty of gold pieces, but now no one gives him anything. What's to be done with him? He will die of hunger before long."

Ivan listened.

"All right," says he, "we must feed him. Let him live by turn at each house as a shepherd does."

There was no help for it. The old Devil had to begin making the round.

In due course the turn came for him to go to Ivan's house. The old Devil came in to dinner, and the dumb girl was getting it ready.

She had often been deceived by lazy folk who came early to dinner – without having done their share of work – and ate up all the porridge, so it had occurred to her to find out the sluggards by their hands. Those who had horny hands, she put at the table, but the others got only the scraps that were left over.

The old Devil sat down at the table, but the dumb girl seized him by the hands and looked at them – there were no hard places there: the hands were clean and smooth, with long nails. The dumb girl gave a grunt and pulled the Devil away from the table. And Ivan's wife said to him, "Don't be offended, fine gentleman. My sister-in-law does not allow any one to come to table who hasn't horny hands. But wait awhile, after the folk have eaten you shall have what is left."

The old Devil was offended that in the King's house they wished him to feed like a pig. He said to Ivan, "It is a foolish law you have in your kingdom that every one must work with his hands. It's your stupidity that invented it. Do people work only with their hands? What do you think wise men work with?"

And Ivan said, "How are we fools to know? We do most of our work with our hands and our backs."

"That is because you are fools! But I will teach you how to work with the head. Then you will know that it is more profitable to work with the head than with the hands."

Ivan was surprised.

"If that is so" said he, "then there is some sense in calling us fools!"

And the old Devil went on. "Only it is not easy to work with one's head. You give me nothing to eat, because I have no hard places on my hands, but you do not know that it is a hundred times more difficult to work with the head. Sometimes one's head quite splits."

Ivan became thoughtful.

"Why, then, friend, do you torture yourself so? Is it pleasant when the head splits? Would it not be better to do easier work with your hands and your back?"

But the Devil said, "I do it all out of pity for you fools. If I didn't torture myself you would remain fools for ever. But, having worked with my head, I can now teach you."

Ivan was surprised.

"Do teach us!" said he, "so that when our hands get cramped we may use our heads for a change."

And the Devil promised to teach the people. So Ivan gave notice throughout the kingdom that a fine gentleman had come who would teach everybody how to work with their heads; that with the head more could be done than with the hands; and that the people ought all to come and learn.

Now there was in Ivan's kingdom a high tower, with many steps leading up to a lantern on the top. And Ivan took the gentleman up there that every one might see him.

So the gentleman took his place on the top of the tower and began to speak, and the people came together to see him. They thought the gentleman would really show them how to work with the head without using the hands. But the old Devil only taught them in many words how they might live without working. The people could make nothing of it. They looked and considered, and at last went off to attend to their affairs.

The old Devil stood on the tower a whole day, and after that a second day, talking all the time. But standing there so long he grew hungry, and the fools never thought of taking food to him up in the tower. They thought that if he could work with his head better than with his hands, he could at any rate easily provide himself with bread.

The old Devil stood on the top of the tower yet another day, talking away. People came near, looked on for awhile, and then went away.

And Ivan asked, "Well, has the gentleman begun to work with his head yet?"

"Not yet," said the people; "he's still spouting away."

The old Devil stood on the tower one day more, but he began to grow weak, so that he staggered and hit his head against one of the pillars of the lantern. One of the people noticed it and told Ivan's wife, and she ran to her husband, who was in the field.

"Come and look," said she. "They say the gentleman is beginning to work with his head."

Ivan was surprised.

"Really?" says he, and he turned his horse round, and went to the tower. And by the time he reached the tower the old Devil was quite exhausted with hunger, and was staggering and knocking his head against the pillars. And just as Ivan arrived at the tower, the Devil stumbled, fell, and came bump, bump, bump, straight down the stairs to the bottom, counting each step with a knock of his head!

"Well!" says Ivan, "the fine gentleman told the truth when he said that 'sometimes one's head quite splits.' This is worse than blisters; after such work there will be swellings on the head."

The old Devil tumbled out at the foot of the stairs, and struck his head against the ground. Ivan was about to go up to him to see how much work he had done – when suddenly the earth opened and the old Devil fell through. Only a hole was left.

Ivan scratched his head.

"What a nasty thing," says he. "It's one of those devils again! What a whopper! He must be the father of them all."

Ivan is still living, and people crowd to his kingdom. His own brothers have come to live with him, and he feeds them, too. To every one who comes and says "Give me food!" Ivan says, "All right. You can stay with us; we have plenty of everything."

Only there is one special custom in his kingdom; whoever has horny hands comes to table, but whoever has not, must eat what the others leave.

1885

PART IV

STORIES WRITTEN TO PICTURES

9

EVIL ALLURES, BUT GOOD ENDURES

THERE LIVED in olden times a good and kindly man. He had this world's goods in abundance, and many slaves to serve him. And the slaves prided themselves on their master, saying:

"There is no better lord than ours under the sun. He feeds and clothes us well, and gives us work suited to our strength. He bears no malice and never speaks a harsh word to any one. He is not like other masters, who treat their slaves worse than cattle: punishing them whether they deserve it or not, and never giving them a friendly word. He wishes us well, does good, and speaks kindly to us. We do not wish for a better life."

Thus the slaves praised their lord, and the Devil, seeing it, was vexed that slaves should live in such love and harmony with their master. So getting one of them, whose name was Aleb, into his power, the Devil ordered him to tempt the other slaves. And one day, when they were all sitting together resting and talking of their master's goodness, Aleb raised his voice, and said:

"It is stupid to make so much of our master's goodness. The Devil himself would be kind to you, if you did what he wanted. We serve our master well, and humor him in all things. As soon as he thinks of anything, we do it: foreseeing all his wishes. What can he do but be kind to us? Just try how it will be if, instead of humoring him, we do him some harm instead. He will act like any one else, and will repay evil for evil, as the worst of masters do."

The other slaves began denying what Aleb had said and at last bet with him. Aleb undertook to make their master angry. If he failed, he was to lose his holiday garment; but if he succeeded, the other slaves were to give him theirs. Moreover, they promised to defend him against the master, and to set him free if he should be put in chains or imprisoned. Having arranged this bet, Aleb agreed to make his master angry next morning.

Aleb was a shepherd, and had in his charge a number of valuable, purebred sheep, of which his master was very fond. Next morning, when the master brought some visitors into the enclosure to show them the valuable sheep, Aleb winked at his companions, as if to say:

"See, now, how angry I will make him."

All the other slaves assembled, looking in at the gates or over the fence, and the Devil climbed a tree near by to see how his servant would do his work. The master walked about the enclosure, showing his guests the ewes and lambs, and presently he wished to show them his finest ram.

"All the rams are valuable," said he, "but I have one with closely twisted horns, which is priceless. I prize him as the apple of my eye."

Startled by the strangers, the sheep rushed about the enclosure, so that the visitors could not get a good look at the ram. As soon as it stood still, Aleb startled the sheep as if by accident, and they all got mixed up again. The visitors could not make out which was the priceless ram. At last the master got tired of it.

"Aleb, dear friend," he said, "pray catch our best ram for me, the one with the tightly twisted horns. Catch him very carefully, and hold him still for a moment."

Scarcely had the master said this, when Aleb rushed in among the sheep like a lion, and clutched the priceless ram. Holding him fast by the wool, he seized the left hind leg with one hand, and, before his master's eyes, lifted it and jerked it so that it snapped like a dry branch. He had broken the ram's leg and it fell bleating on to its knees. Then Aleb seized the right hind leg, while the left twisted round and hung quite limp. The visitors and the slaves exclaimed in dismay, and the Devil, sitting up in the tree, rejoiced that Aleb had done his task so cleverly. The master looked as black as thunder, frowned, bent his head, and did not say a word. The visitors and the slaves were silent, too, waiting to see what would follow. After remaining silent for a while, the master shook himself as if to throw off some burden. Then he lifted his head, and raising his eyes heavenward, remained so for a short time. Presently the wrinkles passed from his face, and he looked down at Aleb with a smile saying:

"Oh, Aleb, Aleb! Your master bade you anger me; but my master is stronger than yours. I am not angry with you, but I will make your master angry. You are afraid that I shall punish you, and you have been wishing for your freedom. Know, then, Aleb, that I shall not punish you; but, as you wish to be free, here, before my guests, I set you free. Go where you like, and take your holiday garment with you!"

And the kind master returned with his guests to the house; but the Devil, grinding his teeth, fell down from the tree, and sank through the ground.

1885

LITTLE GIRLS WISER THAN MEN

IT WAS AN EARLY EASTER. Sledging was only just over; snow still lay in the yards; and water ran in streams down the village street.

Two little girls from different houses happened to meet in a lane between two homesteads, where the dirty water after running through the farmyards had formed a large puddle. One girl was very small, the other a little bigger. Their mothers had dressed them both in new frocks. The little one wore a blue frock the other a yellow print, and both had red kerchiefs on their heads. They had just come from church when they met, and first they showed each other their finery, and then they began to play. Soon the fancy took them to splash about in the water, and the smaller one was going to step into the puddle, shoes and all, when the elder checked her:

"Don't go in so, Malasha," said she, "your mother will scold you. I will take off my shoes and stockings, and you take off yours."

They did so, and then, picking up their skirts, began walking towards each other through the puddle. The water came up to Malasha's ankles, and she said:

"It is deep, Akoulya, I'm afraid!"

"Come on," replied the other. "Don't be frightened. It won't get any deeper."

When they got near one another, Akoulya said:

"Mind, Malasha, don't splash. Walk carefully!"

She had hardly said this, when Malasha plumped down her foot so that the water splashed right on to Akoulya's frock. The frock was splashed, and so were Akoulya's eyes and nose. When she saw the stains on her frock, she was angry and ran after

Malasha to strike her. Malasha was frightened, and seeing that she had got herself into trouble, she scrambled out of the puddle, and prepared to run home. Just then Akoulya's mother happened to be passing, and seeing that her daughter's skirt was splashed, and her sleeves dirty, she said:

"You naughty, dirty girl, what have you been doing?"

"Malasha did it on purpose," replied the girl.

At this Akoulya's mother seized Malasha, and struck her on the back of her neck. Malasha began to howl so that she could be heard all down the street. Her mother came out.

"What are you beating my girl for?" said she; and began scolding her neighbor. One word led to another and they had an angry quarrel. The men came out and a crowd collected in the street, every one shouting and no one listening. They all went on quarrelling, till one gave another a push, and the affair had very nearly come to blows, when Akoulya's old grandmother, stepping in among them, tried to calm them.

"What are you thinking of, friends? Is it right to behave so? On a day like this, too! It is a time for rejoicing, and not for such folly as this."

They would not listen to the old woman and nearly knocked her off her feet. And she would not have been able to quiet the crowd if it had not been for Akoulya and Malasha themselves. While the women were abusing each other, Akoulya had wiped the mud off her frock, and gone back to the puddle. She took a stone and began scraping away the earth in front of the puddle to make a channel through which the water could run out into the street. Presently Malasha joined her, and with a chip of wood helped her dig the channel. Just as the men were beginning to fight, the water from the little girls' channel ran streaming into the street towards the very place where the old woman was trying to pacify the men. The girls followed it; one running along each side of the little stream.

"Catch it, Malasha! Catch it!" shouted Akoulya; while Malasha could not speak for laughing.

Highly delighted, and watching the chip float along on their stream, the little girls ran straight into the group of men; and the old woman, seeing them, said to the men:

"Are you not ashamed of yourselves? To go fighting on account of these lassies, when they themselves have forgotten all about it, and are playing happily together. Dear little souls! They are wiser than you!"

The men looked at the little girls and were ashamed, and, laughing at themselves, went back each to his own home.

"Except ye turn, and become as little children, ye shall in no wise enter into the kingdom of heaven."

1885

11

ILYAS

THERE ONCE LIVED, in the Government of Oufa, a Bashkir named Ilyas. His father, who died a year after he had found his son a wife, did not leave him much property. Ilyas then had only seven mares, two cows, and about a score of sheep. He was a good manager, however, and soon began to acquire more. He and his wife worked from morn till night; rising earlier than others and going later to bed; and his possessions increased year by year. Living in this way, Ilyas little by little acquired great wealth. At the end of thirty-five years he had 200 horses, 150 head of cattle, and 1,200 sheep. Hired laborers tended his flocks and herds, and hired women milked his mares and cows, and made kumiss, butter and cheese. Ilyas had an abundance of everything, and every one in the district envied him. They said of him:

"Ilyas is a fortunate man: he has plenty of everything. This world must be a pleasant place for him."

People of position heard of Ilyas and sought his acquaintance. Visitors came to him from afar; and he welcomed every one, and gave them food and drink. Whoever might come, there was always kumiss, tea, sherbet, and mutton to set before them. Whenever visitors arrived a sheep would be killed, or sometimes two; and if many guests came he would even slaughter a mare for them.

Ilyas had three children: two sons and a daughter; and he married them all off. While he was poor, his sons worked with him, and looked after the flocks and herds themselves; but when he grew rich they got spoiled and one of them took to drink. The eldest was killed in a brawl; and the younger, who had married a self-willed woman, ceased to obey his father, and they could not live together any more.

So they parted, and Ilyas gave his son a house and some of the cattle; and this diminished his wealth. Soon after that, a disease broke out among Ilyas's sheep, and many died. Then followed a bad harvest, and the hay crop failed; and many cattle died that winter. Then the Kirghiz captured his best herd of horses; and Ilyas's property dwindled away. It became smaller and smaller, while at the same time his strength grew less; till, by the time he was seventy years old, he had begun to sell his furs, carpets, saddles, and tents. At last he had to part with his remaining cattle, and found himself face to face with want. Before he knew how it had happened, he had lost everything, and in their old age he and his wife had to go into service. Ilyas had nothing left, except the clothes on his back, a fur cloak, a cup, his indoor shoes and overshoes, and his wife, Sham-Shemagi, who also was old by this time. The son who had parted from him had gone into a far country, and his daughter was dead, so that there was no one to help the old couple.

Their neighbor, Muhammad-Shah, took pity on them. Muhammad-Shah was neither rich nor poor, but lived comfortably, and was a good man. He remembered Ilyas's hospitality, and pitying him, said:

"Come and live with me, Ilyas, you and your old woman. In summer you can work in my melon garden as much as your strength allows, and in winter feed my cattle; and Sham-Shemagi shall milk my mares and make kumiss. I will feed and clothe you both. When you need anything, tell me, and you shall have it."

Ilyas thanked his neighbor, and he and his wife took service with Muhammad-Shah as laborers. At first the position seemed hard to them, but they got used to it, and lived on, working as much as their strength allowed.

Muhammad-Shah found it was to his advantage to keep such people, because, having been masters themselves, they knew how to manage and were not lazy, but did all the work they could. Yet it grieved Muhammad-Shah to see people brought so low who had been of such high standing.

It happened once that some of Muhammad-Shah's relatives came from a great distance to visit him, and a Mullah came too. Muhammad-Shah told Ilyas to catch a sheep and kill it. Ilyas skinned the sheep, and boiled it, and sent it in to the guests. The guests ate the mutton, had some tea, and then began drinking kumiss. As they were sitting with their host on down cushions on a carpet, conversing and sipping kumiss from their cups, Ilyas, having finished his work passed by the open door. Muhammad-Shah, seeing him pass, said to one of the guests:

"Did you notice that old man who passed just now?"

"Yes," said the visitor, "what is there remarkable about him?"

"Only this – that he was once the richest man among us," replied the host. "His name is Ilyas. You may have heard of him."

"Of course I have heard of him," the guest answered "I never saw him before, but his fame has spread far and wide."

"Yes, and now he has nothing left," said Muhammad-Shah, "and he lives with me as my laborer, and his old woman is here too – she milks the mares."

The guest was astonished: he clicked with his tongue, shook his head, and said:

"Fortune turns like a wheel. One man it lifts, another it sets down! Does not the old man grieve over all he has lost?"

"Who can tell. He lives quietly and peacefully, and works well."

"May I speak to him?" asked the guest. "I should like to ask him about his life."

"Why not?" replied the master, and he called from the kibitka in which they were sitting:

"Babay;" (which in the Bashkir tongue means "Grandfather") "come in and have a cup of kumiss with us, and call your wife here also."

Ilyas entered with his wife; and after exchanging greetings with his master and the guests, he repeated a prayer, and seated himself near the door. His wife passed in behind the curtain and sat down with her mistress.

A cup of kumiss was handed to Ilyas; he wished the guests and his master good health, bowed, drank a little, and put down the cup.

"Well, Daddy," said the guest who had wished to speak to him, "I suppose you feel rather sad at the sight of us. It must remind you of your former prosperity, and of your present sorrows."

Ilyas smiled, and said:

"If I were to tell you what is happiness and what is misfortune, you would not believe me. You had better ask my wife. She is a woman, and what is in her heart is on her tongue. She will tell you the whole truth."

The guest turned towards the curtain.

"Well, Granny," he cried, "tell me how your former happiness compares with your present misfortune."

And Sham-Shemagi answered from behind the curtain:

"This is what I think about it: My old man and I lived for fifty years seeking happiness and not finding it; and it is only now, these last two years, since we had nothing left and have lived as laborers, that we have found real happiness, and we wish for nothing better than our present lot."

The guests were astonished, and so was the master; he even rose and drew the curtain back, so as to see the old woman's face. There she stood with her arms folded, looking at her old husband, and smiling; and he smiled back at her. The old woman went on:

"I speak the truth and do not jest. For half a century we sought for happiness, and as long as we were rich we never found it. Now that we have nothing left, and have taken service as laborers, we have found such happiness that we want nothing better."

"But in what does your happiness consist?" asked the guest.

"Why, in this," she replied, "when we were rich my husband and I had so many cares that we had no time to talk to one another, or to think of our souls, or to pray to God. Now we had visitors, and had to consider what food to set before them, and what presents to give them, lest they should speak ill of us. When they left, we had to look after our laborers who were always trying to shirk work and get the best food, while we wanted to get all we could out of them. So we sinned. Then we were in fear lest a wolf should kill a foal or a calf, or thieves steal our horses. We lay awake at night, worrying lest the ewes should overlie their lambs, and we got up again and again to see that all was well. One thing attended to, another care would spring up: how, for instance, to get enough fodder for the winter. And besides that, my old man and I used to disagree. He would say we must do so and so, and I would differ from him; and then we disputed – sinning again. So we passed from one trouble to another, from one sin to another, and found no happiness."

"Well, and now?"

"Now, when my husband and I wake in the morning, we always have a loving word for one another and we live peacefully, having nothing to quarrel about. We have no care but how best to serve our master. We work as much as our strength allows and do it with a will, that our master may not lose but profit by us. When we come in, dinner or supper is ready and there is kumiss to drink. We have fuel to burn when it is cold and we have our fur cloak. And we have time to talk, time to think of our souls, and time to pray. For fifty years we sought happiness, but only now at last have we found it."

The guests laughed.

But Ilyas said:

"Do not laugh, friends. It is not a matter for jesting – it is the truth of life. We also were foolish at first, and wept at the loss of our wealth; but now God has shown us the truth, and we tell it, not for our own consolation, but for your good."

And the Mullah said:

"That is a wise speech. Ilyas has spoken the exact truth. The same is said in Holy Writ."

And the guests ceased laughing and became thoughtful.

1885

PART V

FOLKTALES RETOLD

12

THE THREE HERMITS

An Old Legend Current in the Volga District

And in praying use not vain repetitions, as the Gentiles do:
for they think that they shall be heard for their much
speaking. Be not therefore like unto them: for your Father
knoweth what things ye have need of, before ye ask Him.

– Matt. vi. 7, 8

A BISHOP was sailing from Archangel to the Solovetsk Monastery; and on the same vessel were a number of pilgrims on their
way to visit the shrines at that place. The voyage was a smooth
one – the wind favorable, and the weather fair. The pilgrims lay
on deck, eating, or sat in groups talking to one another. The
Bishop, too, came on deck, and as he was pacing up and down,
he noticed a group of men standing near the prow and listening
to a fisherman who was pointing to the sea and telling them
something. The Bishop stopped, and looked in the direction in
which the man was pointing. He could see nothing however, but
the sea glistening in the sunshine. He drew nearer to listen, but
when the man saw him, he took off his cap and was silent. The
rest of the people also took off their caps, and bowed.

"Do not let me disturb you, friends," said the Bishop. "I came
to hear what this good man was saying."

"The fisherman was telling us about the hermits," replied one,
a tradesman, rather bolder than the rest.

"What hermits?" asked the Bishop, going to the side of the
vessel and seating himself on a box. "Tell me about them. I
should like to hear. What were you pointing at?"

"Why, that little island you can just see over there," answered
the man, pointing to a spot ahead and a little to the right. "That

is the island where the hermits live for the salvation of their souls."

"Where is the island?" asked the Bishop. "I see nothing."

"There, in the distance, if you will please look along my hand. Do you see that little cloud? Below it and a bit to the left, there is just a faint streak. That is the island."

The Bishop looked carefully, but his unaccustomed eyes could make out nothing but the water shimmering in the sun.

"I cannot see it," he said. "But who are the hermits that live there?"

"They are holy men," answered the fisherman. "I had long heard tell of them, but never chanced to see them myself till the year before last."

And the fisherman related how once, when he was out fishing, he had been stranded at night upon that island, not knowing where he was. In the morning, as he wandered about the island, he came across an earth hut, and met an old man standing near it. Presently two others came out, and after having fed him, and dried his things, they helped him mend his boat.

"And what are they like?" asked the Bishop.

"One is a small man and his back is bent. He wears a priest's cassock and is very old; he must be more than a hundred, I should say. He is so old that the white of his beard is taking a greenish tinge, but he is always smiling, and his face is as bright as an angel's from heaven. The second is taller, but he also is very old. He wears a tattered peasant coat. His beard is broad, and of a yellowish gray color. He is a strong man. Before I had time to help him, he turned my boat over as if it were only a pail. He too, is kindly and cheerful. The third is tall, and has a beard as white as snow and reaching to his knees. He is stern, with overhanging eyebrows; and he wears nothing but a mat tied round his waist."

"And did they speak to you?" asked the Bishop.

"For the most part they did everything in silence and spoke but little even to one another. One of them would just give a glance, and the others would understand him. I asked the tallest whether they had lived there long. He frowned, and muttered something as if he were angry; but the oldest one took his hand and smiled, and then the tall one was quiet. The oldest one only said: 'Have mercy upon us,' and smiled."

While the fisherman was talking, the ship had drawn nearer to the island.

"There, now you can see it plainly, if your Grace will please to look," said the tradesman, pointing with his hand.

The Bishop looked, and now he really saw a dark streak – which was the island. Having looked at it a while, he left the prow of the vessel, and going to the stern, asked the helmsman:

"What island is that?"

"That one," replied the man, "has no name. There are many such in this sea."

"Is it true that there are hermits who live there for the salvation of their souls?"

"So it is said, your Grace, but I don't know if it's true. Fishermen say they have seen them; but of course they may only be spinning yarns."

"I should like to land on the island and see these men," said the Bishop. "How could I manage it?"

"The ship cannot get close to the island," replied the helmsman, "but you might be rowed there in a boat. You had better speak to the captain."

The captain was sent for and came.

"I should like to see these hermits," said the Bishop. "Could I not be rowed ashore?"

The captain tried to dissuade him.

"Of course it could be done," said he, "but we should lose much time. And if I might venture to say so to your Grace, the old men are not worth your pains. I have heard say that they are foolish old fellows, who understand nothing, and never speak a word, any more than the fish in the sea."

"I wish to see them," said the Bishop, "and I will pay you for your trouble and loss of time. Please let me have a boat."

There was no help for it; so the order was given. The sailors trimmed the sails, the steersman put up the helm, and the ship's course was set for the island. A chair was placed at the prow for the Bishop, and he sat there, looking ahead. The passengers all collected at the prow, and gazed at the island. Those who had the sharpest eyes could presently make out the rocks on it, and then a mud hut was seen. At last one man saw the hermits themselves. The captain brought a telescope and, after looking through it, handed it to the Bishop.

"It's right enough. There are three men standing on the shore. There, a little to the right of that big rock."

The Bishop took the telescope, got it into position, and he saw the three men: a tall one, a shorter one, and one very small and bent, standing on the shore and holding each other by the hand.

The captain turned to the Bishop.

"The vessel can get no nearer in than this, your Grace. If you wish to go ashore, we must ask you to go in the boat, while we anchor here."

The cable was quickly let out, the anchor cast, and the sails furled. There was a jerk, and the vessel shook. Then a boat having been lowered, the oarsmen jumped in, and the Bishop descended the ladder and took his seat. The men pulled at their oars, and the boat moved rapidly towards the island. When they came within a stone's throw they saw three old men: a tall one with only a mat tied round his waist: a shorter one in a tattered peasant coat, and a very old one bent with age and wearing an old cassock – all three standing hand in hand.

The oarsmen pulled in to the shore, and held on with the boathook while the Bishop got out.

The old men bowed to him, and he gave them his benediction, at which they bowed still lower. Then the Bishop began to speak to them.

"I have heard," he said, "that you, godly men, live here saving your own souls, and praying to our Lord Christ for your fellow men. I, an unworthy servant of Christ, am called, by God's mercy, to keep and teach His flock. I wished to see you, servants of God, and to do what I can to teach you, also."

The old men looked at each other smiling, but remained silent.

"Tell me," said the Bishop, "what you are doing to save your souls, and how you serve God on this island."

The second hermit sighed, and looked at the oldest, the very ancient one. The latter smiled, and said:

"We do not know how to serve God. We only serve and support ourselves, servant of God."

"But how do you pray to God?" asked the Bishop.

"We pray in this way," replied the hermit. "Three are ye, three are we, have mercy upon us."

And when the old man said this, all three raised their eyes to heaven, and repeated:

"Three are ye, three are we, have mercy upon us!"

The Bishop smiled.

"You have evidently heard something about the Holy Trinity," said he. "But you do not pray aright. You have won my affection, godly men. I see you wish to please the Lord, but you do not know how to serve Him. That is not the way to pray; but listen to me, and I will teach you. I will teach you, not a way of my own, but the way in which God in the Holy Scriptures has commanded all men to pray to Him."

And the Bishop began explaining to the hermits how God had revealed Himself to men; telling them of God the Father, and God the Son, and God the Holy Ghost.

"God the Son came down on earth," said he, "to save men, and this is how He taught us all to pray. Listen and repeat after me: 'Our Father.'"

And the first old man repeated after him, "Our Father," and the second said, "Our Father," and the third said, "Our Father."

"Which art in heaven," continued the Bishop.

The first hermit repeated, "Which art in heaven," but the second blundered over the words, and the tall hermit could not say them properly. His hair had grown over his mouth so that he could not speak plainly. The very old hermit, having no teeth, also mumbled indistinctly.

The Bishop repeated the words again, and the old men repeated them after him. The Bishop sat down on a stone, and the old men stood before him, watching his mouth, and repeating the words as he uttered them. And all day long the Bishop labored, saying a word twenty, thirty, a hundred times over, and the old men repeated it after him. They blundered, and he corrected them, and made them begin again.

The Bishop did not leave off till he had taught them the whole of the Lord's prayer so that they could not only repeat it after him, but could say it by themselves. The middle one was the first to know it, and to repeat the whole of it alone. The Bishop made him say it again and again, and at last the others could say it too.

It was getting dark, and the moon was appearing over the water, before the Bishop rose to return to the vessel. When he took leave of the old men, they all bowed down to the ground before him. He raised them, and kissed each of them, telling them to pray as he had taught them. Then he got into the boat and returned to the ship.

And as he sat in the boat and was rowed to the ship he could hear the three voices of the hermits loudly repeating the Lord's prayer. As the boat drew near the vessel their voices could no longer be heard, but they could still be seen in the moonlight, standing as he had left them on the shore, the shortest in the middle, the tallest on the right, the middle one on the left. As soon as the Bishop had reached the vessel and got on board, the anchor was weighed and the sails unfurled. The wind filled them, and the ship sailed away, and the Bishop took a seat in the stern and watched the island they had left. For a time he could still see the hermits, but presently they disappeared from sight, though the island was still visible. At last it too vanished, and only the sea was to be seen, rippling in the moonlight.

The pilgrims lay down to sleep, and all was quiet on deck. The Bishop did not wish to sleep, but sat alone at the stern, gazing at the sea where the island was no longer visible, and thinking of the good old men. He thought how pleased they had been to learn the Lord's prayer; and he thanked God for having sent him to teach and help such godly men.

So the Bishop sat, thinking, and gazing at the sea where the island had disappeared. And the moonlight flickered before his eyes, sparkling, now here, now there, upon the waves. Suddenly he saw something white and shining, on the bright path which the moon cast across the sea. Was it a seagull, or the little gleaming sail of some small boat? The Bishop fixed his eyes on it, wondering.

"It must be a boat sailing after us," thought he, "but it is overtaking us very rapidly. It was far, far away a minute ago, but now it is much nearer. It cannot be a boat, for I can see no sail; but whatever it may be, it is following us, and catching us up."

And he could not make out what it was. Not a boat, nor a bird, nor a fish! It was too large for a man, and besides a man could not be out there in the midst of the sea. The Bishop rose, and said to the helmsman:

"Look there, what is that, my friend? What is it?" the Bishop repeated, though he could now see plainly what it was – the three hermits running upon the water, all gleaming white, their gray beards shining, and approaching the ship as quickly as though it were not moving.

The steersman looked and let go the helm in terror.

"Oh Lord! The hermits are running after us on the water as though it were dry land!"

The passengers hearing him, jumped up, and crowded to the stern. They saw the hermits coming along hand in hand, and the two outer ones beckoning the ship to stop. All three were gliding along upon the water without moving their feet. Before the ship could be stopped, the hermits had reached it, and raising their heads, all three as with one voice, began to say:

"We have forgotten your teaching, servant of God. As long as we kept repeating it we remembered, but when we stopped saying it for a time, a word dropped out, and now it has all gone to pieces. We can remember nothing of it. Teach us again."

The Bishop crossed himself, and leaning over the ship's side, said:

"Your own prayer will reach the Lord, men of God. It is not for me to teach you. Pray for us sinners.

And the Bishop bowed low before the old men; and they turned and went back across the sea. And a light shone until daybreak on the spot where they were lost to sight.

1886

13

The Imp and the Crust

A POOR PEASANT set out early one morning to plow, taking with him for his breakfast a crust of bread. He got his plow ready, wrapped the bread in his coat, put it under a bush, and set to work. After a while when his horse was tired and he was hungry, the peasant fixed the plow, let the horse loose to graze and went to get his coat and his breakfast

He lifted the coat, but the bread was gone! He looked and looked, turned the coat over, shook it out – but the bread was gone. The peasant could not make this out at all.

"That's strange," thought he; "I saw no one, but all the same some one has been here and has taken the bread!"

It was an imp who had stolen the bread while the peasant was plowing, and at that moment he was sitting behind the bush, waiting to hear the peasant swear and call on the Devil.

The peasant was sorry to lose his breakfast, but "It can't be helped," said he. "After all, I shan't die of hunger! No doubt whoever took the bread needed it. May it do him good!"

And he went to the well, had a drink of water, and rested a bit. Then he caught his horse, harnessed it, and began plowing again.

The imp was crestfallen at not having made the peasant sin, and he went to report what had happened to the Devil, his master.

He came to the Devil and told how he had taken the peasant's bread, and how the peasant instead of cursing had said, "May it do him good!"

The Devil was angry, and replied: "If the man got the better of you, it was your own fault – you don't understand your business! If the peasants, and their wives after them, take to that sort of thing, it will be all up with us. The matter can't be left like that! Go back at once," said he, "and put things right. If in three years you don't get the better of that peasant, I'll have you ducked in holy water!"

The imp was frightened. He scampered back to earth, thinking how he could redeem his fault. He thought and thought, and at last hit upon a good plan.

He turned himself into a laboring man, and went and took service with the poor peasant. The first year he advised the peasant to sow corn in a marshy place. The peasant took his advice, and sowed in the marsh. The year turned out a very dry one, and the crops of the other peasants were all scorched by the sun, but the poor peasant's corn grew thick and tall and full-eared. Not only had he grain enough to last him for the whole year, but he had much left over besides.

The next year the imp advised the peasant to sow on the hill; and it turned out a wet summer. Other people's corn was beaten down and rotted and the ears did not fill; but the peasant's crop, up on the hill, was a fine one. He had more grain left over than before, so that he did not know what to do with it all.

Then the imp showed the peasant how he could mash the grain and distill spirit from it; and the peasant made strong drink, and began to drink it himself and to give it to his friends.

So the imp went to the Devil, his master, and boasted that he had made up for his failure. The Devil said that he would come and see for himself how the case stood.

He came to the peasant's house, and saw that the peasant had invited his well-to-do neighbors and was treating them to drink. His wife was offering the drink to the guests, and as she handed it round she tumbled against the table and spilt a glassful.

The peasant was angry, and scolded his wife: "What do you mean, you slut? Do you think it's ditchwater, you cripple, that you must go pouring good stuff like that over the floor?"

The imp nudged the Devil, his master, with his elbow: "See," said he, "that's the man who did not grudge his last crust!"

The peasant, still railing at his wife, began to carry the drink round himself. Just then a poor peasant returning from work came in uninvited. He greeted the company, sat down, and saw that they were drinking. Tired with his day's work he felt that he too would like a drop. He sat and sat, and his mouth kept watering, but the host instead of offering him any only muttered: "I can't find drink for every one who comes along."

This pleased the Devil; but the imp chuckled and said, "Wait a bit, there's more to come yet!"

The rich peasants drank, and their host drank too. And they began to make false, oily speeches to one another.

The Devil listened and listened, and praised the imp.

"If," said he, "the drink makes them so foxy that they begin to cheat each other, they will soon all be in our hands."

"Wait for what's coming," said the imp. "Let them have another glass all round. Now they are like foxes, wagging their tails and trying to get round one another; but presently you will see them like savage wolves."

The peasants had another glass each, and their talk became wilder and rougher. Instead of oily speeches they began to abuse and snarl at one another. Soon they took to fighting, and punched one another's noses. And the host joined in the fight, and he too got well beaten.

The Devil looked on and was much pleased at all this.

"This is first-rate!" said he.

But the imp replied: "Wait a bit – the best is yet to come. Wait till they have had a third glass. Now they are raging like wolves, but let them have one more glass, and they will be like swine."

The peasants had their third glass, and became quite like brutes. They muttered and shouted, not knowing why, and not listening to one another.

Then the party began to break up. Some went alone, some in twos, and some in threes, all staggering down the street. The host went out to speed his guests, but he fell on his nose into a puddle, smeared himself from top to toe, and lay there grunting like a hog.

This pleased the Devil still more.

"Well," said he, "you have hit on a first-rate drink, and have quite made up for your blunder about the bread. But now tell me how this drink is made. You must first have put in fox's blood: that was what made the peasants sly as foxes. Then, I suppose, you added wolf's blood: that is what made them fierce like wolves. And you must have finished off with swine's blood, to make them behave like swine."

"No," said the imp, "that was not the way I did it. All I did was to see that the peasant had more corn than he needed. The blood of the beasts is always in man; but as long as he has only enough corn for his needs, it is kept in bounds. While that was the case, the peasant did not grudge his last crust. But when he had corn left over, he looked for ways of getting pleasure out of it. And I showed him a pleasure – drinking! And when he began to turn God's good gifts into spirits for his own pleasure – the fox's, wolf's and swine's blood in him all came out. If only he goes on drinking, he will always be a beast!"

The Devil praised the imp, forgave him for his former blunder, and advanced him to a post of high honor.

1886

How Much Land
Does a Man Need?

I

AN ELDER SISTER came to visit her younger sister in the country. The elder was married to a tradesman in town, the younger to a peasant in the village. As the sisters sat over their tea talking, the elder began to boast of the advantages of town life: saying how comfortably they lived there, how well they dressed, what fine clothes her children wore, what good things they ate and drank, and how she went to the theater, promenades, and entertainments.

The younger sister was piqued, and in turn disparaged the life of a tradesman, and stood up for that of a peasant.

"I would not change my way of life for yours," said she. "We may live roughly, but at least we are free from anxiety. You live in better style than we do but though you often earn more than you need, you are very likely to lose all you have. You know the proverb, 'Loss and gain are brothers twain.' It often happens that people who are wealthy one day are begging their bread the next. Our way is safer. Though a peasant's life is not a fat one, it is a long one. We shall never grow rich, but we shall always have enough to eat."

The elder sister said sneeringly:

"Enough? Yes, if you like to share with the pigs and the calves! What do you know of elegance or manners! However much your goodman may slave, you will die as you are living – on a dung heap – and your children the same."

"Well, what of that?" replied the younger. "Of course our work is rough and coarse. But, on the other hand, it is sure; and we need not bow to any one. But you, in your towns, are surrounded by temptations; today all may be right, but tomorrow the Evil One may tempt your husband with cards, wine, or women, and all will go to ruin. Don't such things happen often enough?"

Pahom, the master of the house, was lying on the top of the oven, and he listened to the women's chatter.

"It is perfectly true," thought he. "Busy as we are from childhood tilling mother earth, we peasants have no time to let any nonsense settle in our heads. Our only trouble is that we haven't land enough. If I had plenty of land, I shouldn't fear the Devil himself!"

The women finished their tea, chatted a while about dress, and then cleared away the tea-things and lay down to sleep.

But the Devil had been sitting behind the oven, and had heard all that was said. He was pleased that the peasant's wife had led her husband into boasting, and that he had said that if he had plenty of land he would not fear the Devil himself.

"All right," thought the Devil. "We will have a tussle. I'll give you land enough; and by means of that land I will get you into my power."

II

Close to the village there lived a lady, a small landowner, who had an estate of about three hundred acres. She had always lived on good terms with the peasants, until she engaged as her steward an old soldier, who took to burdening the people with fines. However careful Pahom tried to be, it happened again and again that now a horse of his got among the lady's oats, now a cow strayed into her garden, now his calves found their way into her meadows – and he always had to pay a fine.

Pahom paid up, but grumbled, and, going home in a temper, was rough with his family. All through that summer, Pahom had much trouble because of this steward; and he was even glad when winter came and the cattle had to be stabled. Though he grudged the fodder when they could no longer graze on the pastureland, at least he was free from anxiety about them.

In the winter the news got about that the lady was going to sell her land, and that the keeper of the inn on the high road was bargaining for it. When the peasants heard this they were very much alarmed.

"Well," thought they, "if the innkeeper gets the land, he will worry us with fines worse than the lady's steward. We all depend on that estate."

So the peasants went on behalf of their commune and asked the lady not to sell the land to the innkeeper, offering her a better price for it themselves. The lady agreed to let them have it. Then the peasants tried to arrange for the commune to buy the whole estate so that it might be held by them all in common. They met twice to discuss it, but could not settle the matter; the Evil One sowed discord among them, and they could not agree. So they decided to buy the land individually, each according to his means; and the lady agreed to this plan as she had to the other.

Presently Pahom heard that a neighbor of his was buying fifty acres, and that the lady had consented to accept one half in cash and to wait a year for the other half. Pahom felt envious.

"Look at that," thought he, "the land is all being sold, and I shall get none of it." So he spoke to his wife.

"Other people are buying," said he, "and we must also buy twenty acres or so. Life is becoming impossible. That steward is simply crushing us with his fines."

So they put their heads together and considered how they could manage to buy it. They had one hundred roubles laid by. They sold a colt, and one half of their bees; hired out one of their sons as a laborer, and took his wages in advance; borrowed the rest from a brother-in-law, and so scraped together half the purchase money.

Having done this, Pahom chose out a farm of forty acres, some of it wooded, and went to the lady to bargain for it. They came to an agreement, and he shook hands with her upon it, and paid her a deposit in advance. Then they went to town and signed the deeds; he paying half the price down, and undertaking to pay the remainder within two years.

So now Pahom had land of his own. He borrowed seed, and sowed it on the land he had bought. The harvest was a good one, and within a year he had managed to pay off his debts both to the lady and to his brother-in-law. So he became a landowner, plowing and sowing his own land, making hay on his own land, cutting his own trees, and feeding his cattle on his own pasture. When he went out to plow his fields, or to look at his growing corn, or at his grass-meadows, his heart would fill with joy. The grass that grew and the flowers that bloomed there, seemed to him unlike any that grew elsewhere. Formerly, when he had passed by that land it had appeared the same as any other land, but now it seemed quite different.

III

So Pahom was well-contented, and everything would have been right if the neighboring peasants would only not have trespassed on his cornfields and meadows. He appealed to them most civilly, but they still went on: now the communal herdsmen would let the village cows stray into his meadows; then horses from the night pasture would get among his corn. Pahom turned them out again and again, and forgave their owners, and for a long time he forbore from prosecuting any one. But at last he lost patience and complained to the District Court. He knew it was the peasants' want of land, and no evil intent on their part, that caused the trouble; but he thought:

"I cannot go on overlooking it, or they will destroy all I have. They must be taught a lesson."

So he had them up, gave them one lesson, and then another, and two or three of the peasants were fined. After a time Pahom's neighbors began to bear him a grudge for this, and would now and then let their cattle on to his land on purpose. One peasant even got into Pahom's wood at night and cut down five young lime trees for their bark. Pahom passing through the wood one day noticed something white. He came nearer, and saw the stripped trunks lying on the ground, and close by stood the stumps, where the trees had been. Pahom was furious.

"If he had only cut one here and there it would have been bad enough," thought Pahom, "but the rascal has actually cut down a whole clump. If I could only find out who did this, I would pay him out."

He racked his brains as to who it could be. Finally he decided: "It must be Simon – no one else could have done it." So he went to Simon's homestead to have a look round, but he found nothing, and only had an angry scene. However, he now felt more certain than ever that Simon had done it, and he lodged a complaint. Simon was summoned. The case was tried, and retried, and at the end of it all Simon was acquitted, there being no evidence against him. Pahom felt still more aggrieved, and let his anger loose upon the Elder and the Judges.

"You let thieves grease your palms," said he. "If you were honest folk yourselves, you would not let a thief go free."

So Pahom quarrelled with the Judges and with his neighbors. Threats to burn his building began to be uttered. So though Pahom had more land, his place in the commune was much worse than before.

About this time a rumor got about that many people were moving to new parts.

"There's no need for me to leave my land," thought Pahom. "But some of the others might leave our village and then there would be more room for us. I would take over their land myself, and make my estate a bit bigger. I could then live more at ease. As it is, I am still too cramped to be comfortable."

One day Pahom was sitting at home, when a peasant, passing through the village, happened to call in. He was allowed to stay the night, and supper was given him. Pahom had a talk with this peasant and asked him where he came from. The stranger answered that he came from beyond the Volga, where he had been working. One word led to another, and the man went on to say that many people were settling in those parts. He told how some people from his village had settled there. They had joined the commune, and had had twenty-five acres per man granted them. The land was so good, he said, that the rye sown on it grew as high as a horse, and so thick that five cuts of a sickle made a sheaf. One peasant, he said, had brought nothing with him but his bare hands, and now he had six horses and two cows of his own.

Pahom's heart kindled with desire. He thought:

"Why should I suffer in this narrow hole, if one can live so well elsewhere? I will sell my land and my homestead here, and with the money I will start afresh over there and get everything new. In this crowded place one is always having trouble. But I must first go and find out all about it myself."

Towards summer he got ready and started. He went down the Volga on a steamer to Samara, then walked another three hundred miles on foot, and at last reached the place. It was just as the stranger had said. The peasants had plenty of land: every man had twenty-five acres of communal land given him for his use, and any one who had money could buy, besides, at two shillings an acre as much good freehold land as he wanted.

Having found out all he wished to know, Pahom returned home as autumn came on, and began selling off his belongings. He sold his land at a profit, sold his homestead and all his cattle, and withdrew from membership of the commune. He only waited till the spring, and then started with his family for the new settlement.

IV

As soon as Pahom and his family arrived at their new abode, he applied for admission into the commune of a large village. He stood treat to the Elders, and obtained the necessary documents. Five shares of communal land were given him for his own and his sons' use: that is to say – 125 acres (not all together but in different fields) besides the use of the communal pasture. Pahom put up the buildings he needed, and bought cattle. Of the communal land alone he had three times as much as at his former home, and the land was good corn land. He was ten times better off than he had been. He had plenty of arable land and pasturage, and could keep as many head of cattle as he liked.

At first, in the bustle of building and settling down, Pahom was pleased with it all, but when he got used to it he began to think that even here he had not enough land. The first year, he sowed wheat on his share of the communal land, and had a good crop. He wanted to go on sowing wheat, but had not enough communal land for the purpose, and what he had already used was not available; for in those parts wheat is only sown on virgin soil or on fallow land. It is sown for one or two years, and then the land lies fallow till it is again overgrown with prairie grass. There were many who wanted such land, and there was not enough for all; so that people quarrelled about it. Those who were better off, wanted it for growing wheat, and those who were poor, wanted it to let to dealers, so that they might raise money to pay their taxes. Pahom wanted to sow more wheat; so he rented land from a dealer for a year. He sowed much wheat and had a fine crop, but the land was too far from the village – the wheat had to be carted more than ten miles. After a time Pahom noticed that some peasant dealers were living on separate farms, and were growing wealthy; and he thought:

"If I were to buy some freehold land, and have a homestead on it, it would be a different thing altogether. Then it would all be nice and compact."

The question of buying freehold land recurred to him again and again.

He went on in the same way for three years: renting land and sowing wheat. The seasons turned out well and the crops were good, so that he began to lay money by. He might have gone on living contentedly, but he grew tired of having to rent other people's land every year, and having to scramble for it. Wherever there was good land to be had, the peasants would rush for it and it was taken up at once, so that unless you were sharp about it you got none. It happened in the third year that he and a dealer together rented a piece of pasture land from some peasants; and they had already plowed it up, when there was some dispute, and the peasants went to law about it, and things fell out so that the labor was all lost.

"If it were my own land," thought Pahom, "I should be independent, and there would not be all this unpleasantness."

So Pahom began looking out for land which he could buy; and he came across a peasant who had bought thirteen hundred acres, but having got into difficulties was willing to sell again cheap. Pahom bargained and haggled with him, and at last they settled the price at 1,500 roubles, part in cash and part to be paid later. They had all but clinched the matter, when a passing dealer happened to stop at Pahom's one day to get a feed for his horses. He drank tea with Pahom, and they had a talk. The dealer said that he was just returning from the land of the Bashkirs, far away, where he had bought thirteen thousand acres of land, all for 1,000 roubles. Pahom questioned him further, and the tradesman said:

"All one need do is to make friends with the chiefs. I gave away about one hundred roubles worth of dressing gowns and carpets, besides a case of tea, and I gave wine to those who would drink it; and I got the land for less than twopence an acre." And he showed Pahom the title deeds, saying:

"The land lies near a river, and the whole prairie is virgin soil."

Pahom plied him with questions, and the tradesman said:

"There is more land there than you could cover if you walked a year, and it all belongs to the Bashkirs. They are as simple as sheep, and land can be got almost for nothing."

"There now," thought Pahom, "with my one thousand roubles, why should I get only thirteen hundred acres, and saddle myself with a debt besides. If I take it out there, I can get more than ten times as much for the money."

V

Pahom inquired how to get to the place, and as soon as the tradesman had left him, he prepared to go there himself. He left his wife to look after the homestead, and started on his journey taking his man with him. They stopped at a town on their way, and bought a case of tea, some wine, and other presents, as the tradesman had advised. On and on they went until they had gone more than three hundred miles, and on the seventh day they came to a place where the Bashkirs had pitched their tents. It was all just as the tradesman had said. The people lived on the steppes, by a river, in felt-covered tents. They neither tilled the ground, nor ate bread. Their cattle and horses grazed in herds on the steppe. The colts were tethered behind the tents, and the mares were driven to them twice a day. The mares were milked, and from the milk kumiss was made. It was the women who prepared kumiss, and they also made cheese. As far as the men were concerned, drinking kumiss and tea, eating mutton, and playing on their pipes, was all they cared about. They were all stout and merry, and all the summer long they never thought of doing any work. They were quite ignorant, and knew no Russian, but were good-natured enough.

As soon as they saw Pahom, they came out of their tents and gathered round their visitor. An interpreter was found, and Pahom told them he had come about some land. The Bashkirs seemed very glad; they took Pahom and led him into one of the best tents, where they made him sit on some down cushions placed on a carpet, while they sat round him. They gave him tea and kumiss, and had a sheep killed, and gave him mutton to eat. Pahom took presents out of his cart and distributed them among the Bashkirs, and divided amongst them the tea. The Bashkirs were delighted. They talked a great deal among themselves, and then told the interpreter to translate.

"They wish to tell you," said the interpreter, "that they like you, and that it is our custom to do all we can to please a guest and to repay him for his gifts. You have given us presents, now tell us which of the things we possess please you best, that we may present them to you."

"What pleases me best here," answered Pahom "is your land. Our land is crowded, and the soil is exhausted; but you have plenty of land and it is good land. I never saw the like of it."

The interpreter translated. The Bashkirs talked among themselves for a while. Pahom could not understand what they were saying, but saw that they were much amused, and that they shouted and laughed. Then they were silent and looked at Pahom while the interpreter said:

"They wish me to tell you that in return for your presents they will gladly give you as much land as you want. You have only to point it out with your hand and it is yours."

The Bashkirs talked again for a while and began to dispute. Pahom asked what they were disputing about, and the interpreter told him that some of them thought they ought to ask their Chief about the land and not act in his absence, while others thought there was no need to wait for his return.

VI

While the Bashkirs were disputing, a man in a large fox-fur cap appeared on the scene. They all became silent and rose to their feet. The interpreter said, "This is our Chief himself."

Pahom immediately fetched the best dressing gown and five pounds of tea, and offered these to the Chief. The Chief accepted them, and seated himself in the place of honor. The Bashkirs at once began telling him something. The Chief listened for a while, then made a sign with his head for them to be silent, and addressing himself to Pahom, said in Russian:

"Well, let it be so. Choose whatever piece of land you like; we have plenty of it."

"How can I take as much as I like?" thought Pahom. "I must get a deed to make it secure, or else they may say, 'It is yours,' and afterwards may take it away again."

"Thank you for your kind words," he said aloud. "You have much land, and I only want a little. But I should like to be sure which bit is mine. Could it not be measured and made over to me? Life and death are in God's hands. You good people give it to me, but your children might wish to take it away again."

"You are quite right," said the Chief. "We will make it over to you."

"I heard that a dealer had been here," continued Pahom, "and that you gave him a little land, too, and signed title deeds to that effect. I should like to have it done in the same way."

The Chief understood.

"Yes," replied he, "that can be done quite easily. We have a scribe, and we will go to town with you and have the deed properly sealed."

"And what will be the price?" asked Pahom.

"Our price is always the same: one thousand roubles a day."

Pahom did not understand.

"A day? What measure is that? How many acres would that be?"

"We do not know how to reckon it out," said the Chief. "We sell it by the day. As much as you can go round on your feet in a day is yours, and the price is one thousand roubles a day."

Pahom was surprised.

"But in a day you can get round a large tract of land," he said.

The Chief laughed.

"It will all be yours!" said he. "But there is one condition: If you don't return on the same day to the spot whence you started, your money is lost."

"But how am I to mark the way that I have gone?"

"Why, we shall go to any spot you like, and stay there. You must start from that spot and make your round, taking a spade with you. Wherever you think necessary, make a mark. At every turning, dig a hole and pile up the turf; then afterwards we will go round with a plow from hole to hole. You may make as large a circuit as you please, but before the sun sets you must return to the place you started from. All the land you cover will be yours."

Pahom was delighted. It was decided to start early next morning. They talked a while, and after drinking some more kumiss and eating some more mutton, they had tea again, and then the night came on. They gave Pahom a feather bed to sleep on, and the Bashkirs dispersed for the night, promising to assemble the next morning at daybreak and ride out before sunrise to the appointed spot.

VII

Pahom lay on the feather bed, but could not sleep. He kept thinking about the land.

"What a large tract I will mark off!" thought he. "I can easily do thirty-five miles in a day. The days are long now, and within a circuit of thirty-five miles what a lot of land there will be! I will sell the poorer land, or let it to peasants, but I'll pick out the best and farm it. I will buy two ox teams, and hire two more labor-ers. About a hundred and fifty acres shall be plow land, and I will pasture cattle on the rest."

Pahom lay awake all night, and dozed off only just before dawn. Hardly were his eyes closed when he had a dream. He thought he was lying in that same tent, and heard somebody chuckling outside. He wondered who it could be, and rose and went out and he saw the Bashkir Chief sitting in front of the tent holding his sides and rolling about with laughter. Going nearer to the Chief, Pahom asked: "What are you laughing at?" But he saw that it was no longer the Chief, but the dealer who had recently stopped at his house and had told him about the land. Just as Pahom was going to ask, "Have you been here long?" he saw that it was not the dealer, but the peasant who had come up from the Volga, long ago, to Pahom's old home. Then he saw that it was not the peasant either, but the Devil himself with hoofs and horns sitting there and chuckling, and before him lay a man barefoot, prostrate on the ground, with only trousers and a shirt on. And Pahom dreamt that he looked more attentively to see what sort of a man it was that was lying there, and he saw that the man was dead and that it was himself! He awoke horror-struck.

"What things one does dream," thought he.

Looking round he saw through the open door that the dawn was breaking.

"It's time to wake them up," thought he. "We ought to be starting."

He got up, roused his man (who was sleeping in his cart), bade him harness; and went to call the Bashkirs.

"It's time to go to the steppe to measure the land," he said.

The Bashkirs rose and assembled, and the Chief came too. Then they began drinking kumiss again, and offered Pahom some tea, but he would not wait.

"If we are to go, let us go. It is high time," said he.

VIII

The Bashkirs got ready and they all started: some mounted on horses, and some in carts. Pahom drove in his own small cart with his servant, and took a spade with him. When they reached the steppe, the morning red was beginning to kindle. They ascended a hillock (called by the Bashkirs a shikhan) and dismounting from their carts and their horses, gathered in one spot. The Chief came up to Pahom and stretching out his arm towards the plain:

"See," said he, "all this, as far as your eye can reach, is ours. You may have any part of it you like."

Pahom's eyes glistened: it was all virgin soil, as flat as the palm of your hand, as black as the seed of a poppy, and in the hollows different kinds of grasses grew breast high.

The Chief took off his fox-fur cap, placed it on the ground and said:

"This will be the mark. Start from here, and return here again. All the land you go round shall be yours."

Pahom took out his money and put it on the cap. Then he took off his outer coat, remaining in his sleeveless undercoat. He unfastened his girdle and tied it tight below his stomach, put a little bag of bread into the breast of his coat, and tying a flask of water to his girdle, he drew up the tops of his boots, took the spade from his man, and stood ready to start. He considered for some moments which way he had better go – it was tempting everywhere.

"No matter," he concluded, "I will go towards the rising sun."

He turned his face to the east, stretched himself and waited for the sun to appear above the rim.

"I must lose no time," he thought, "and it is easier walking while it is still cool."

The sun's rays had hardly flashed above the horizon, before Pahom, carrying the spade over his shoulder went down into the steppe.

Pahom started walking neither slowly nor quickly. After having gone a thousand yards he stopped, dug a hole, and placed pieces of turf one on another to make it more visible. Then he went on; and now that he had walked off his stiffness he quickened his pace. After a while he dug another hole.

Pahom looked back. The hillock could be distinctly seen in the sunlight, with the people on it, and the glittering tires of the cart-wheels. At a rough guess Pahom concluded that he had walked three miles. It was growing warmer; he took off his undercoat, flung it across his shoulder, and went on again. It had grown quite warm now; he looked at the sun, it was time to think of breakfast.

"The first shift is done, but there are four in a day, and it is too soon yet to turn. But I will just take off my boots," said he to himself.

He sat down, took off his boots, stuck them into his girdle, and went on. It was easy walking now.

"I will go on for another three miles," thought he, "and then turn to the left. This spot is so fine, that it would be a pity to lose it. The further one goes, the better the land seems."

He went straight on for a while, and when he looked round, the hillock was scarcely visible and the people on it looked like black ants, and he could just see something glistening there in the sun.

"Ah," thought Pahom, "I have gone far enough in this direction, it is time to turn. Besides I am in a regular sweat, and very thirsty."

He stopped, dug a large hole, and heaped up pieces of turf. Next he untied his flask, had a drink, and then turned sharply to the left. He went on and on; the grass was high, and it was very hot.

Pahom began to grow tired: he looked at the sun and saw that it was noon.

"Well," he thought, "I must have a rest."

He sat down, and ate some bread and drank some water; but he did not lie down, thinking that if he did he might fall asleep. After sitting a little while, he went on again. At first he walked easily: the food had strengthened him; but it had become terribly hot, and he felt sleepy; still he went on, thinking: "An hour to suffer, a lifetime to live."

He went a long way in this direction also, and was about to turn to the left again, when he perceived a damp hollow: "It would be a pity to leave that out," he thought. "Flax would do well there." So he went on past the hollow, and dug a hole on the other side of it before he turned the corner. Pahom looked towards the hillock. The heat made the air hazy: it seemed to be quivering, and through the haze the people on the hillock could scarcely be seen.

"Ah!" thought Pahom, "I have made the sides too long; I must make this one shorter." And he went along the third side stepping faster. He looked at the sun: it was nearly half way to the horizon, and he had not yet done two miles of the third side of the square. He was still ten miles from the goal.

"No," he thought, "though it will make my land lopsided, I must hurry back in a straight line now. I might go too far, and as it is I have a great deal of land."

So Pahom hurriedly dug a hole, and turned straight towards the hillock.

IX

Pahom went straight towards the hillock, but he now walked with difficulty. He was done up with the heat, his bare feet were cut and bruised, and his legs began to fail. He longed to rest, but it was impossible if he meant to get back before sunset. The sun waits for no man, and it was sinking lower and lower.

"Oh dear," he thought, "if only I have not blundered trying for too much! What if I am too late?"

He looked towards the hillock and at the sun. He was still far from his goal, and the sun was already near the rim.

Pahom walked on and on; it was very hard walking, but he went quicker and quicker. He pressed on, but was still far from the place. He began running, threw away his coat, his boots, his flask, and his cap, and kept only the spade which he used as a support.

"What shall I do," he thought again, "I have grasped too much, and ruined the whole affair. I can't get there before the sun sets."

And this fear made him still more breathless. Pahom went on running, his soaking shirt and trousers stuck to him, and his mouth was parched. His breast was working like a blacksmith's bellows, his heart was beating like a hammer, and his legs were giving way as if they did not belong to him. Pahom was seized with terror lest he should die of the strain.

Though afraid of death, he could not stop. "After having run all that way they will call me a fool if I stop now," thought he. And he ran on and on, and drew near and heard the Bashkirs yelling and shouting to him, and their cries inflamed his heart still more. He gathered his last strength and ran on.

The sun was close to the rim, and cloaked in mist looked large, and red as blood. Now, yes now, it was about to set! The sun was quite low, but he was also quite near his aim. Pahom could already see the people on the hillock waving their arms to hurry him up. He could see the fox-fur cap on the ground, and the money on it, and the Chief sitting on the ground holding his sides. And Pahom remembered his dream.

"There is plenty of land," thought he, "but will God let me live on it? I have lost my life, I have lost my life! I shall never reach that spot!"

Pahom looked at the sun, which had reached the earth: one side of it had already disappeared. With all his remaining strength he rushed on, bending his body forward so that his legs could hardly follow fast enough to keep him from falling. Just as he reached the hillock it suddenly grew dark. He looked up – the sun had already set! He gave a cry: "All my labor has been in vain," thought he, and was about to stop, but he heard the Bashkirs still shouting, and remembered that though to him, from below, the sun seemed to have set, they on the hillock could still see it. He took a long breath and ran up the hillock. It was still light there. He reached the top and saw the cap. Before it sat the Chief laughing and holding his sides. Again Pahom remembered his dream, and he uttered a cry: his legs gave way beneath him, he fell forward and reached the cap with his hands.

"Ah, that's a fine fellow!" exclaimed the Chief. "He has gained much land!"

Pahom's servant came running up and tried to raise him, but he saw that blood was flowing from his mouth. Pahom was dead!

The Bashkirs clicked their tongues to show their pity.

His servant picked up the spade and dug a grave long enough for Pahom to lie in, and buried him in it. Six feet from his head to his heels was all he needed.

1886

15

A Grain as Big as a Hen's Egg

ONE DAY some children found, in a ravine, a thing shaped like a grain of corn, with a groove down the middle, but as large as a hen's egg. A traveller passing by saw the thing, bought it from the children for a penny, and taking it to town sold it to the King as a curiosity.

The King called together his wise men, and told them to find out what the thing was. The wise men pondered and pondered and could not make head or tail of it, till one day, when the thing was lying on a windowsill, a hen flew in and pecked at it till she made a hole in it, and then every one saw that it was a grain of corn. The wise men went to the King and said:

"It is a grain of corn."

At this the King was much surprised; and he ordered the learned men to find out when and where such corn had grown. The learned men pondered again, and searched in their books, but could find nothing about it. So they returned to the King and said:

"We can give you no answer. There is nothing about it in our books. You will have to ask the peasants; perhaps some of them may have heard from their fathers when and where grain grew to such a size."

So the King gave orders that some very old peasant should be brought before him; and his servants found such a man and brought him to the King. Old and bent, ashy pale and toothless, he just managed with the help of two crutches to totter into the King's presence.

The King showed him the grain, but the old man could hardly see it; he took it, however, and felt it with his hands. The King questioned him, saying:

"Can you tell us, old man, where such grain as this grew? Have you ever bought such corn, or sown such in your fields?"

The old man was so deaf that he could hardly hear what the King said, and only understood with great difficulty.

"No!" he answered at last, "I never sowed nor reaped any like it in my fields, nor did I ever buy any such. When we bought corn, the grains were always as small as they are now. But you might ask my father. He may have heard where such grain grew."

So the King sent for the old man's father, and he was found and brought before the King. He came walking with one crutch. The King showed him the grain, and the old peasant, who was still able to see, took a good look at it. And the King asked him:

"Can you not tell us, old man, where corn like this used to grow? Have you ever bought any like it, or sown any in your fields?"

Though the old man was rather hard of hearing, he still heard better than his son had done.

"No," he said, "I never sowed nor reaped any grain like this in my field. As to buying, I never bought any, for in my time money was not yet in use. Every one grew his own corn, and when there was any need we shared with one another. I do not know where corn like this grew. Ours was larger and yielded more flour than present-day grain, but I never saw any like this. I have, however, heard my father say that in his time the grain grew larger and yielded more flour than ours. You had better ask him."

So the King sent for this old man's father, and they found him too, and brought him before the King. He entered walking easily and without crutches: his eye was clear, his hearing good, and he spoke distinctly. The King showed him the grain, and the old grandfather looked at it, and turned it about in his hand.

"It is long since I saw such a fine grain," said he, and he bit a piece off and tasted it.

"It's the very same kind," he added.

"Tell me, grandfather," said the King, "when and where was such corn grown? Have you ever bought any like it, or sown any in your fields?"

And the old man replied:

"Corn like this used to grow everywhere in my time. I lived on corn like this in my young days, and fed others on it. It was grain like this that we used to sow and reap and thresh."

And the King asked:

"Tell me, grandfather, did you buy it anywhere, or did you grow it all yourself?"

The old man smiled.

"In my time," he answered, "no one ever thought of such a sin as buying or selling bread; and we knew nothing of money. Each man had corn enough of his own."

"Then tell me, grandfather," asked the King, "where was your field, where did you grow corn like this?"

And the grandfather answered:

"My field was God's earth. Wherever I ploughed, there was my field. Land was free. It was a thing no man called his own. Labor was the only thing men called their own."

"Answer me two more questions," said the King. "The first is, Why did the earth bear such grain then and has ceased to do so now? And the second is, Why your grandson walks with two crutches, your son with one, and you yourself with none? Your eyes are bright, your teeth sound, and your speech clear and pleasant to the ear. How have these things come about?"

And the old man answered:

"These things are so, because men have ceased to live by their own labor, and have taken to depending on the labor of others. In the old time, men lived according to God's law. They had what was their own, and coveted not what others had produced."

1886

16

The Godson

Ye have heard that it was said, An eye for an eye, and a tooth
for a tooth, but I say unto you, Resist not him that is evil.
—Matt. v. 38, 39

Vengeance is mine; I will repay.   *—Rom. xii. 19*

I

A SON WAS BORN to a poor peasant. He was glad and went to his
neighbor to ask him to stand godfather to the boy. The neighbor
refused – he did not like standing godfather to a poor man's child.
The peasant asked another neighbor, but he too refused, and after
that the poor father went to every house in the village, but found
no one willing to be godfather to his son. So he set off to another
village, and on the way he met a man who stopped and said:

"Good day, my good man; where are you off to?"

"God has given me a child," said the peasant, "to rejoice my
eyes in youth, to comfort my old age, and to pray for my soul
after death. But I am poor, and no one in our village will stand
godfather to him, so I am now on my way to seek a godfather
for him elsewhere."

"Let me be godfather," said the stranger.

The peasant was glad, and thanked him, but added:

"And whom shall I ask to be godmother?"

"Go to the town," replied the stranger, "and, in the square,
you will see a stone house with shop windows in the front. At the
entrance you will find the tradesman to whom it belongs. Ask
him to let his daughter stand godmother to your child."

The peasant hesitated.

"How can I ask a rich tradesman?" said he. "He will despise
me, and will not let his daughter come."

"Don't trouble about that. Go and ask. Get everything ready by tomorrow morning, and I will come to the christening."

The poor peasant returned home, and then drove to the town to find the tradesman. He had hardly taken his horse into the yard, when the tradesman himself came out.

"What do you want?" said he.

"Why, sir," said the peasant, "you see God has given me a son to rejoice my eyes in youth, to comfort my old age, and to pray for my soul after death. Be so kind as to let your daughter stand godmother to him."

"And when is the christening?" said the tradesman.

"Tomorrow morning."

"Very well. Go in peace. She shall be with you at Mass tomorrow morning."

The next day the godmother came, and the godfather also, and the infant was baptized. Immediately after the christening the godfather went away. They did not know who he was, and never saw him again.

II

The child grew up to be a joy to his parents. He was strong, willing to work, clever and obedient. When he was ten years old his parents sent him to school to learn to read and write. What others learnt in five years, he learnt in one, and soon there was nothing more they could teach him.

Easter came round, and the boy went to see his godmother, to give her his Easter greeting.

"Father and mother," said he when he got home again, "where does my godfather live? I should like to give him my Easter greeting, too."

And his father answered:

"We know nothing about your godfather, dear son. We often regret it ourselves. Since the day you were christened we have never seen him, nor had any news of him. We do not know where he lives, or even whether he is still alive."

The son bowed to his parents.

"Father and mother," said he, "let me go and look for my godfather. I must find him and give him my Easter greeting."

So his father and mother let him go, and the boy set off to find his godfather.

III

The boy left the house and set out along the road. He had been walking for several hours when he met a stranger who stopped him and said:

"Good day to you, my boy. Where are you going?"

And the boy answered:

"I went to see my godmother and to give her my Easter greeting, and when I got home I asked my parents where my godfather lives, that I might go and greet him also. They told me they did not know. They said he went away as soon as I was christened, and they know nothing about him, not even if he be still alive. But I wished to see my godfather, and so I have set out to look for him."

Then the stranger said: "I am your godfather."

The boy was glad to hear this. After kissing his godfather three times for an Easter greeting, he asked him:

"Which way are you going now, godfather? If you are coming our way, please come to our house; but if you are going home, I will go with you."

"I have no time now," replied his godfather, "to come to your house. I have business in several villages; but I shall return home again tomorrow. Come and see me then."

"But how shall I find you, godfather?"

"When you leave home, go straight towards the rising sun, and you will come to a forest; going through the forest you will come to a glade. When you reach this glade sit down and rest awhile, and look around you and see what happens. On the further side of the forest you will find a garden, and in it a house with a golden roof. That is my home. Go up to the gate, and I will myself be there to meet you."

And having said this the godfather disappeared from his godson's sight.

IV

The boy did as his godfather had told him. He walked eastward until he reached a forest, and there he came to a glade, and in the midst of the glade he saw a pine tree to a branch of which was tied a rope supporting a heavy log of oak. Close under this log stood a wooden trough filled with honey. Hardly had the boy had time to wonder why the honey was placed there, and why the log hung above it, when he heard a crackling in the wood, and saw some bears approaching; a she-bear, followed by a yearling and three tiny cubs. The she-bear, sniffing the air, went straight to the trough, the cubs following her. She thrust her muzzle into the honey, and called the cubs to do the same. They scampered up and began to eat. As they did so, the log, which the she-bear had moved aside with her head, swung away a little and, returning, gave the cubs a push. Seeing this the she-bear shoved the log away with her paw. It swung further out and returned more forcibly, striking one cub on the back and another on the head. The cubs ran away howling with pain, and the mother, with a growl, caught the log in her fore paws and, raising it above her head flung it away. The log flew high in the air and the yearling, rushing to the trough, pushed his muzzle into the honey and began to suck noisily. The others also drew near, but they had not reached the trough when the log, flying back, struck the yearling on the head and killed him. The mother growled louder than before and, seizing the log, flung it from her with all her might. It flew higher than the branch it was tied to; so high that the rope slackened; and the she-bear returned to the trough, and the little cubs after her. The log flew higher and higher, then stopped, and began to fall. The nearer it came the faster it swung, and at last, at full speed, it crashed down on her head. The she-bear rolled over, her legs jerked and she died! The cubs ran away into the forest.

V

The boy watched all this in surprise, and then continued his way. Leaving the forest, he came upon a large garden in the midst of which stood a lofty palace with a golden roof. At the gate stood his godfather, smiling. He welcomed his godson, and led him through the gateway into the garden. The boy had never dreamed of such beauty and delight as surrounded him in that place.

Then his godfather led him into the palace, which was even more beautiful inside than outside. The godfather showed the boy through all the rooms: each brighter and finer than the other, but at last they came to one door that was sealed up.

"You see this door," said he. "It is not locked, but only sealed. It can be opened, but I forbid you to open it. You may live here, and go where you please and enjoy all the delights of the place. My only command is – do not open that door! But should you ever do so, remember what you saw in the forest."

Having said this the godfather went away. The godson remained in the palace, and life there was so bright and joyful that he thought he had only been there three hours, when he had really lived there thirty years. When thirty years had gone by, the godson happened to be passing the sealed door one day, and he wondered why his godfather had forbidden him to enter that room.

"I'll just look in and see what is there," thought he, and he gave the door a push. The seals gave way, the door opened, and the godson entering saw a hall more lofty and beautiful than all the others, and in the midst of it a throne. He wandered about the hall for a while, and then mounted the steps and seated himself upon the throne. As he sat there he noticed a sceptre leaning against the throne, and took it in his hand. Hardly had he done so when the four walls of the hall suddenly disappeared. The godson looked around, and saw the whole world, and all that men were doing in it. He looked in front, and saw the sea with ships sailing on it. He looked to the right, and saw where strange heathen people lived. He looked to the left, and saw where men who were Christians, but not Russians, lived. He looked round, and on the fourth side, he saw Russian people, like himself.

"I will look," said he, "and see what is happening at home, and whether the harvest is good."

He looked towards his father's fields and saw the sheaves standing in stooks. He began counting them to see whether there was much corn, when he noticed a peasant driving in a cart. It was night, and the godson thought it was his father coming to cart the corn by night. But as he looked he recognized Vasily Koudryashof, the thief, driving into the field and beginning to load the sheaves on to his cart. This made the godson angry, and he called out:

"Father, the sheaves are being stolen from our field!"

His father, who was out with the horses in the night-pasture, woke up.

"I dreamt the sheaves were being stolen," said he. "I will just ride down and see."

So he got on a horse and rode out to the field. Finding Vasily there, he called together other peasants to help him, and Vasily was beaten, bound, and taken to prison.

Then the godson looked at the town, where his godmother lived. He saw that she was now married to a tradesman. She lay asleep, and her husband rose and went to his mistress. The godson shouted to her:

"Get up, get up, your husband has taken to evil ways."

The godmother jumped up and dressed, and finding out where her husband was, she shamed and beat his mistress, and drove him away.

Then the godson looked for his mother, and saw her lying asleep in her cottage. And a thief crept into the cottage and began to break open the chest in which she kept her things. The mother awoke and screamed, and the robber seizing an axe, swung it over his head to kill her.

The godson could not refrain from hurling the sceptre at the robber. It struck him upon the temple, and killed him on the spot.

VI

As soon as the godson had killed the robber, the walls closed and the hall became just as it had been before.

Then the door opened and the godfather entered, and coming up to his godson he took him by the hand and led him down from the throne.

"You have not obeyed my command," said he. "You did one wrong thing, when you opened the forbidden door; another, when you mounted the throne and took my sceptre into your hands; and you have now done a third wrong, which has much increased the evil in the world. Had you sat here an hour longer, you would have ruined half mankind."

Then the godfather led his godson back to the throne, and took the sceptre in his hand; and again the walls fell asunder and all things became visible. And the godfather said:

"See what you have done to your father. Vasily has now been a year in prison, and has come out having learnt every kind of wickedness, and has become quite incorrigible. See, he has stolen two of your father's horses, and he is now setting fire to his barn. All this you have brought upon your father."

The godson saw his father's barn breaking into flames, but his godfather shut off the sight from him, and told him to look another way.

"Here is your godmother's husband," he said. "It is a year since he left his wife, and now he goes after other women. His former mistress has sunk to still lower depths. Sorrow has driven his wife to drink. That's what you have done to your godmother."

The godfather shut off this also, and showed the godson his father's house. There he saw his mother weeping for her sins, repenting, and saying:

"It would have been better had the robber killed me that night. I should not have sinned so heavily."

"That," said the godfather, "is what you have done to your mother."

He shut this off also, and pointed downwards; and the godson saw two warders holding the robber in front of a prison-house.

And the godfather said:

"This man had murdered ten men. He should have expiated his sins himself, but by killing him you have taken his sins on yourself. Now you must answer for all his sins. That is what you have done to yourself. The she-bear pushed the log aside once, and disturbed her cubs; she pushed it again, and killed her yearling; she pushed it a third time, and was killed herself. You have done the same. Now I give you thirty years to go into the world and atone for the robber's sins. If you do not atone for them, you will have to take his place."

"How am I to atone for his sins?" asked the godson.

And the godfather answered:

"When you have rid the world of as much evil as you have brought into it, you will have atoned both for your own sins and for those of the robber."

"How can I destroy evil in the world?" the godson asked.

"Go out," replied the godfather, "and walk straight towards the rising sun. After a time you will come to a field with some men in it. Notice what they are doing, and teach them what you know. Then go on and note what you see. On the fourth day you will come to a forest. In the midst of the forest is a cell and in the cell lives a hermit. Tell him all that has happened. He will teach you what to do. When you have done all he tells you, you will have atoned for your own and the robber's sins."

And, having said this, the godfather led his godson out of the gate.

VII

The godson went his way, and as he went he thought:

"How am I to destroy evil in the world? Evil is destroyed by banishing evil men, keeping them in prison, or putting them to death. How then am I to destroy evil without taking the sins of others upon myself?"

The godson pondered over it for a long time, but could come to no conclusion. He went on until he came to a field where corn was growing thick and good and ready for the reapers. The godson saw that a little calf had got in among the corn. Some men who were at hand saw it, and mounting their horses they chased it backwards and forwards through the corn. Each time the calf was about to come out of the corn some one rode up and the calf got frightened and turned back again, and they all galloped after it, trampling down the corn. On the road stood a woman crying.

"They will chase my calf to death," she said.

And the godson said to the peasants:

"What are you doing? Come out of the cornfield all of you, and let the woman call her calf."

The men did so; and the woman came to the edge of the cornfield and called to the calf. "Come along, Browney, come along," said she. The calf pricked up its ears, listened a while, and then ran towards the woman of its own accord, and hid its head in her skirts, almost knocking her over. The men were glad, the woman was glad, and so was the little calf.

The godson went on, and he thought:

"Now I see that evil spreads evil. The more people try to drive away evil, the more the evil grows. Evil, it seems, cannot be destroyed by evil; but in what way it can be destroyed, I do not know. The calf obeyed its mistress and so all went well; but if it had not obeyed her, how could we have got it out of the field?"

The godson pondered again, but came to no conclusion, and continued his way.

VIII

He went on until he came to a village. At the furthest end he stopped and asked leave to stay the night. The woman of the house was there alone, housecleaning, and she let him in. The godson entered, and taking his seat upon the brick oven he watched what the woman was doing. He saw her finish scrubbing the room and begin scrubbing the table. Having done this, she began wiping the table with a dirty cloth. She wiped it from side to side – but it did not come clean. The soiled cloth left streaks of dirt. Then she wiped it the other way. The first streaks disappeared, but others came in their place. Then she wiped it from one end to the other, but again the same thing happened. The soiled cloth messed the table; when one streak was wiped off another was left on. The godson watched for awhile in silence, and then said:

"What are you doing, mistress?"

"Don't you see I'm cleaning up for the holiday. Only I can't manage this table, it won't come clean. I'm quite tired out."

"You should rinse your cloth," said the godson, "before you wipe the table with it."

The woman did so, and soon had the table clean.

"Thank you for telling me," said she.

In the morning he took leave of the woman and went on his way. After walking a good while, he came to the edge of a forest. There he saw some peasants who were making wheel-rims of bent wood. Coming nearer, the godson saw that the men were going round and round, but could not bend the wood.

He stood and looked on, and noticed that the block, to which the piece of wood was fastened, was not fixed, but as the men moved round it went round too. Then the godson said:

"What are you doing, friends?"

"Why, don't you see, we are making wheel rims. We have twice steamed the wood, and are quite tired out, but the wood will not bend."

"You should fix the block, friends," said the godson, "or else it goes round when you do."

The peasants took his advice and fixed the block, and then the work went on merrily.

The godson spent the night with them, and then went on. He walked all day and all night, and just before dawn he came upon some drovers encamped for the night, and lay down beside them. He saw that they had got all their cattle settled, and were trying to light a fire. They had taken dry twigs and lighted them, but before the twigs had time to burn up, they smothered them with damp brushwood. The brushwood hissed and the fire smouldered and went out. Then the drovers brought more dry wood, lit it, and again put on the brushwood – and again the fire went out. They struggled with it for a long time, but could not get the fire to burn. Then the godson said:

"Do not be in such a hurry to put on the brushwood. Let the dry wood burn up properly before you put any on. When the fire is well alight you can put on as much as you please."

The drovers followed his advice. They let the fire burn up fiercely before adding the brushwood, which then flared up so that they soon had a roaring fire.

The godson remained with them for a while, and then continued his way. He went on, wondering what the three things he had seen might mean; but he could not fathom them.

IX

The godson walked the whole of that day, and in the evening came to another forest. There he found a hermit's cell, at which he knocked.

"Who is there?" asked a voice from within.

"A great sinner," replied the godson. "I must atone for another's sins as well as for my own."

The hermit hearing this came out.

"What sins are those that you have to bear for another?"

The godson told him everything: about his godfather; about the she-bear with the cubs; about the throne in the sealed room; about the commands his godfather had given him, as well as about the peasants he had seen trampling down the corn, and the calf that ran out when its mistress called it.

"I have seen that one cannot destroy evil by evil," said he, "but I cannot understand how it is to be destroyed. Teach me how it can be done."

"Tell me," replied the hermit, "what else you have seen on your way."

The godson told him about the woman washing the table, and the men making cart-wheels, and the drovers fighting their fire.

The hermit listened to it all, and then went back to his cell and brought out an old jagged axe.

"Come with me," said he.

When they had gone some way, the hermit pointed to a tree.

"Cut it down," he said.

The godson felled the tree.

"Now chop it into three," said the hermit.

The godson chopped the tree into three pieces. Then the hermit went back to his cell, and brought out some blazing sticks.

"Burn those three logs," said he.

So the godson made a fire, and burnt the three logs till only three charred stumps remained.

"Now plant them half in the ground, like this."

The godson did so.

"You see that river at the foot of the hill. Bring water from there in your mouth, and water these stumps. Water this stump, as you taught the woman: this one as you taught the wheelwrights: and this one, as you taught the drovers. When all three have taken root and from these charred stumps apple trees have sprung you will know how to destroy evil in men, and will have atoned for all your sins."

Having said this, the hermit returned to his cell. The godson pondered for a long time, but could not understand what the hermit meant. Nevertheless he set to work to do as he had been told.

X

The godson went down to the river, filled his mouth with water, and returning, emptied it on to one of the charred stumps. This he did again and again, and watered all three stumps. When he was hungry and quite tired out, he went to the cell to ask the old hermit for some food. He opened the door, and there upon a bench he saw the old man lying dead. The godson looked round for food, and he found some dried bread and ate a little of it. Then he took a spade and set to work to dig the hermit's grave. During the night he carried water and watered the stumps, and in the day he dug the grave. He had hardly finished the grave and was about to bury the corpse, when some people from the village came, bringing food for the old man.

The people heard that the old hermit was dead, and that he had given the godson his blessing, and left him in his place. So they buried the old man, gave the bread they had brought to the godson, and promising to bring him some more, they went away.

The godson remained in the old man's place. There he lived, eating the food people brought him, and doing as he had been told: carrying water from the river in his mouth and watering the charred stumps.

He lived thus for a year, and many people visited him. His fame spread abroad, as a holy man who lived in the forest and brought water from the bottom of a hill in his mouth to water charred stumps for the salvation of his soul. People flocked to see him. Rich merchants drove up bringing him presents, but he kept only the barest necessaries for himself, and gave the rest away to the poor.

And so the godson lived: carrying water in his mouth and watering the stumps half the day, and resting and receiving people the other half. And he began to think that this was the way he had been told to live, in order to destroy evil and atone for his sins.

He spent two years in this manner, not omitting for a single day to water the stumps. But still not one of them sprouted.

One day, as he sat in his cell, he heard a man ride past, singing as he went. The godson came out to see what sort of a man it was. He saw a strong young fellow, well dressed, and mounted on a handsome, well-saddled horse.

The godson stopped him, and asked him who he was, and where he was going.

"I am a robber," the man answered, drawing rein. "I ride about the highways killing people; and the more I kill, the merrier are the songs I sing."

The godson was horror-struck, and thought:

"How can the evil be destroyed in such a man as this? It is easy to speak to those who come to me of their own accord and confess their sins. But this one boasts of the evil he does."

So he said nothing, and turned away, thinking: "What am I to do now? This robber may take to riding about here, and he will frighten away the people. They will leave off coming to me. It will be a loss to them, and I shall not know how to live."

So the godson turned back, and said to the robber:

"People come to me here, not to boast of their sins, but to repent, and to pray for forgiveness. Repent of your sins, if you fear God; but if there is no repentance in your heart, then go away and never come here again. Do not trouble me, and do not frighten people away from me. If you do not hearken, God will punish you."

The robber laughed:

"I am not afraid of God, and I will not listen to you. You are not my master," said he. "You live by your piety, and I by my robbery. We all must live. You may teach the old women who come to you, but you have nothing to teach me. And because you have reminded me of God, I will kill two more men tomorrow. I would kill you, but I do not want to soil my hands just now. See that in future you keep out of my way!"

Having uttered this threat, the robber rode away. He did not come again, and the godson lived in peace, as before, for eight more years.

XI

One night the godson watered his stumps, and, after returning to his cell, he sat down to rest, and watched the footpath, wondering if some one would soon come. But no one came at all that day. He sat alone till evening, feeling lonely and dull, and he thought about his past life. He remembered how the robber had reproached him for living by his piety; and he reflected on his way of life. "I am not living as the hermit commanded me to," thought he. "The hermit laid a penance upon me, and I have made both a living and fame out of it; and have been so tempted by it, that now I feel dull when people do not come to me; and when they do come, I only rejoice because they praise my holiness. That is not how one should live. I have been led astray by love of praise. I have not atoned for my past sins, but have added fresh ones. I will go to another part of the forest where people will not find me; and I will live so as to atone for my old sins and commit no fresh ones."

Having come to this conclusion the godson filled a bag with dried bread and, taking a spade, left the cell and started for a ravine he knew of in a lonely spot, where he could dig himself a cave and hide from the people.

As he was going along with his bag and his spade he saw the robber riding towards him. The godson was frightened, and started to run away, but the robber overtook him.

"Where are you going?" asked the robber.

The godson told him he wished to get away from the people and live somewhere where no one would come to him. This surprised the robber.

"What will you live on, if people do not come to see you?" asked he.

The godson had not even thought of this, but the robber's question reminded him that food would be necessary.

"On what God pleases to give me," he replied.

The robber said nothing, and rode away.

"Why did I not say anything to him about his way of life?" thought the godson. "He might repent now. Today he seems in a gentler mood, and has not threatened to kill me." And he shouted to the robber:

"You have still to repent of your sins. You cannot escape from God."

The robber turned his horse, and drawing a knife from his girdle threatened the hermit with it. The latter was alarmed, and ran away further into the forest.

The robber did not follow him, but only shouted:

"Twice I have let you off, old man, but next time you come in my way I will kill you!"

Having said this, he rode away. In the evening when the godson went to water his stumps – one of them was sprouting! A little apple tree was growing out of it.

XII

After hiding himself from everybody, the godson lived all alone. When his supply of bread was exhausted, he thought: "Now I must go and look for some roots to eat." He had not gone far, however, before he saw a bag of dried bread hanging on a branch. He took it down, and as long as it lasted he lived upon that.

When he had eaten it all, he found another bagful on the same branch. So he lived on, his only trouble being his fear of the robber. Whenever he heard the robber passing he hid thinking:

"He may kill me before I have had time to atone for my sins."

In this way he lived for ten more years. The one apple tree continued to grow, but the other two stumps remained exactly as they were.

One morning the godson rose early and went to his work. By the time he had thoroughly moistened the ground round the stumps, he was tired out and sat down to rest. As he sat there he thought to himself:

"I have sinned, and have become afraid of death. It may be God's will that I should redeem my sins by death."

Hardly had this thought crossed his mind when he heard the robber riding up, swearing at something. When the godson heard this, he thought:

"No evil and no good can befall me from anyone but from God."

And he went to meet the robber. He saw the robber was not alone, but behind him on the saddle sat another man, gagged, and bound hand and foot. The man was doing nothing, but the robber was abusing him violently. The godson went up and stood in front of the horse.

"Where are you taking this man?" he asked.

"Into the forest," replied the robber. "He is a merchant's son, and will not tell me where his father's money is hidden. I am going to flog him till he tells me."

And the robber spurred on his horse, but the godson caught hold of his bridle, and would not let him pass.

"Let this man go!" he said.

The robber grew angry, and raised his arm to strike.

"Would you like a taste of what I am going to give this man? Have I not promised to kill you? Let go!"

The godson was not afraid.

"You shall not go," said he. "I do not fear you. I fear no one but God, and He wills that I should not let you pass. Set this man free!"

The robber frowned, and snatching out his knife, cut the ropes with which the merchant's son was bound, and set him free.

"Get away both of you," he said, "and beware the hour you cross my path again."

The merchant's son jumped down and ran away. The robber was about to ride on, but the godson stopped him again, and again spoke to him about giving up his evil life. The robber heard him to the end in silence, and then rode away without a word.

The next morning the godson went to water his stumps and lo! the second stump was sprouting. A second young apple tree had begun to grow.

XIII

Another ten years had gone by. The godson was sitting quietly one day, desiring nothing, fearing nothing, and with a heart full of joy.

"What blessings God showers on men!" thought he. "Yet how needlessly they torment themselves. What prevents them from living happily?"

And remembering all the evil in men, and the troubles they bring upon themselves, his heart filled with pity.

"It is wrong of me to live as I do," he said to himself. "I must go and teach others what I have myself learnt."

Hardly had he thought this, when he heard the robber approaching. He let him pass, thinking:

"It is no good talking to him, he will not understand."

That was his first thought, but he changed his mind and went out into the road. He saw that the robber was gloomy, and was riding with downcast eyes. The godson looked at him, pitied him, and running up to him laid his hand upon his knee.

"Brother, dear," said he, "have some pity on your own soul! In you lives the spirit of God. You suffer, and torment others, and lay up more and more suffering for the future. Yet God loves you, and has prepared such blessings for you. Do not ruin yourself utterly. Change your life!"

The robber frowned and turned away.

"Leave me alone!" said he.

But the godson held the robber still faster, and began to weep.

Then the robber lifted his eyes and looked at the godson. He looked at him for a long time, and alighting from his horse, fell on his knees at the godson's feet.

"You have overcome me, old man," said he. "For twenty years I have resisted you, but now you have conquered me. Do what you will with me, for I have no more power over myself. When you first tried to persuade me, it only angered me more. Only when you hid yourself from men did I begin to consider your words: for I saw then that you asked nothing of them for yourself. Since that day I have brought food for you, hanging it upon the tree."

Then the godson remembered that the woman got her table clean only after she had rinsed her cloth. In the same way, it was only when he ceased caring about himself, and cleansed his own heart, that he was able to cleanse the hearts of others.

The robber went on.

"When I saw that you did not fear death, my heart turned."

Then the godson remembered that the wheelwrights could not bend the rims until they had fixed their block. So, not till he had cast away the fear of death and made his life fast in God, could he subdue this man's unruly heart.

"But my heart did not quite melt," continued the robber, "until you pitied me and wept for me."

The godson, full of joy, led the robber to the place where the stumps were. And when they got there, they saw that from the third stump an apple tree had begun to sprout. And the godson remembered that the drovers had not been able to light the damp wood until the fire had burnt up well. So it was only when his own heart burnt warmly, that another's heart had been kindled by it.

And the godson was full of joy that he had at last atoned for his sins.

He told all this to the robber, and died. The robber buried him, and lived as the godson had commanded him, teaching to others what the godson had taught him.

1886

17

The Repentant Sinner

And he said unto Jesus, Lord, remember me when thou com-
est into thy Kingdom. And Jesus said unto him, Verily I say
unto thee, today shalt thou be with me in paradise.

– Luke xxiii. 42, 43

THERE WAS ONCE a man who lived for seventy years in the
world, and lived in sin all that time. He fell ill but even then did
not repent. Only at the last moment, as he was dying, he wept
and said:

"Lord! forgive me, as Thou forgavest the thief upon the cross."

And as he said these words, his soul left his body. And the soul
of the sinner, feeling love towards God and faith in His mercy,
went to the gates of heaven and knocked, praying to be let into
the heavenly kingdom.

Then a voice spoke from within the gate:

"What man is it that knocks at the gates of Paradise and what
deeds did he do during his life?"

And the voice of the Accuser replied, recounting all the man's
evil deeds, and not a single good one.

And the voice from within the gates answered:

"Sinners cannot enter into the kingdom of heaven. Go hence!"

Then the man said:

"Lord, I hear thy voice, but cannot see thy face, nor do I know
thy name."

The voice answered:

"I am Peter, the Apostle."

And the sinner replied:

"Have pity on me, Apostle Peter! Remember man's weakness,
and God's mercy. Wert not thou a disciple of Christ? Didst not

thou hear his teaching from his own lips, and hadst thou not his example before thee? Remember then how, when he sorrowed and was grieved in spirit, and three times asked thee to keep awake and pray, thou didst sleep, because thine eyes were heavy, and three times he found thee sleeping. So it was with me. Remember, also, how thou didst promise to be faithful unto death, and yet didst thrice deny him, when he was taken before Caiaphas. So it was with me. And remember, too, how when the cock crowed thou didst go out and didst weep bitterly. So it is with me. Thou canst not refuse to let me in."

And the voice behind the gates was silent.

Then the sinner stood a little while, and again began to knock, and to ask to be let into the kingdom of heaven.

And he heard another voice behind the gates, which said:

"Who is this man, and how did he live on earth?"

And the voice of the Accuser again repeated all the sinner's evil deeds, and not a single good one.

And the voice from behind the gates replied:

"Go hence! Such sinners cannot live with us in Paradise." Then the sinner said:

"Lord, I hear thy voice, but I see thee not, nor do I know thy name."

And the voice answered:

"I am David: king and prophet."

The sinner did not despair, nor did he leave the gates of Paradise, but said:

"Have pity on me, King David! Remember man's weakness, and God's mercy. God loved thee and exalted thee among men. Thou hadst all: a kingdom, and honor, and riches, and wives, and children; but thou sawest from thy housetop the wife of a poor man, and sin entered into thee, and thou tookest the wife of Uriah, and didst slay him with the sword of the Ammonites. Thou, a rich man, didst take from the poor man his one ewe lamb, and didst kill him. I have done likewise. Remember, then, how thou didst repent, and how thou saidst, 'I acknowledge my transgressions: my sin is ever before me.' I have done the same. Thou canst not refuse to let me in."

And the voice from within the gates was silent.

The sinner having stood a little while, began knocking again, and asking to be let into the kingdom of heaven. And a third voice was heard within the gates, saying:

"Who is this man, and how has he spent his life on earth?"

And the voice of the Accuser replied for the third time, recounting the sinner's evil deeds, and not mentioning one good deed.

And the voice within the gates said:

"Depart hence! Sinners cannot enter into the kingdom of heaven."

And the sinner said:

"Thy voice I hear, but thy face I see not, neither do I know thy name."

Then the voice replied:

"I am John the Divine, the beloved disciple of Christ."

And the sinner rejoiced and said:

"Now surely I shall be allowed to enter. Peter and David must let me in, because they know man's weakness and God's mercy; and thou wilt let me in, because thou lovest much. Was it not thou, John the Divine who wrote that God is Love, and that he who loves not, knows not God? And in thine old age didst thou not say unto men: 'Brethren, love one another.' How, then, canst thou look on me with hatred, and drive me away? Either thou must renounce what thou hast said, or loving me, must let me enter the kingdom of heaven."

And the gates of Paradise opened, and John embraced the repentant sinner and took him into the kingdom of heaven.

1886

18

THE EMPTY DRUM

A Folktale Long Current in the Region of the Volga

EMELYAN WAS A LABORER and worked for a master. Crossing the meadows one day on his way to work, he nearly trod on a frog that jumped right in front of him, but he just managed to avoid it. Suddenly he heard some one calling to him from behind.

Emelyan looked round and saw a lovely lassie, who said to him: "Why don't you get married, Emelyan?"

"How can I marry, my lass?" said he. "I have but the clothes I stand up in, nothing more, and no one would have me for a husband."

"Take me for a wife," said she.

Emelyan liked the maid. "I should be glad to," said he, "but where and how could we live?"

"Why trouble about that?" said the girl. "One only has to work more and sleep less, and one can clothe and feed oneself anywhere."

"Very well then, let us marry," said Emelyan. "Where shall we go to?"

"Let us go to town."

So Emelyan and the lass went to town, and she took him to a small hut on the very edge of the town, and they married and began housekeeping.

One day the King, driving through the town, passed by Emelyan's hut. Emelyan's wife came out to see the King. The King noticed her and was quite surprised.

"Where did such a beauty come from?" said he and stopping his carriage he called Emelyan's wife and asked her: "Who are you?"

"The peasant Emelyan's wife," said she.

"Why did you, who are such a beauty, marry a peasant?" said the King. "You ought to be a queen!"

"Thank you for your kind words," said she, "but a peasant husband is good enough for me."

The King talked to her awhile and then drove on. He returned to the palace, but could not get Emelyan's wife out of his head. All night he did not sleep, but kept thinking how to get her for himself. He could think of no way of doing it, so he called his servants and told them they must find a way.

The King's servants said: "Command Emelyan to come to the palace to work, and we will work him so hard that he will die. His wife will be left a widow, and then you can take her for yourself."

The King followed their advice. He sent an order that Emelyan should come to the palace as a workman and that he should live at the palace, and his wife with him.

The messengers came to Emelyan and gave him the King's message. His wife said, "Go, Emelyan; work all day, but come back home at night."

So Emelyan went, and when he got to the palace the King's steward asked him, "Why have you come alone, without your wife?"

"Why should I drag her about?" said Emelyan. "She has a house to live in."

At the King's palace they gave Emelyan work enough for two. He began the job not hoping to finish it; but when evening came, lo and behold! it was all done. The steward saw that it was finished, and set him four times as much for next day.

Emelyan went home. Everything there was swept and tidy; the oven was heated, his supper was cooked and ready, and his wife sat by the table sewing and waiting for his return. She greeted him, laid the table, gave him to eat and drink, and then began to ask him about his work.

"Ah!" said he, "it's a bad business: they give me tasks beyond my strength, and want to kill me with work."

"Don't fret about the work," said she, "don't look either before or behind to see how much you have done or how much there is left to do; only keep on working and all will be right."

So Emelyan lay down and slept. Next morning he went to work again and worked without once looking round. And, lo and behold! by the evening it was all done, and before dark he came home for the night.

Again and again they increased Emelyan's work, but he always got through it in good time and went back to his hut to sleep. A week passed, and the King's servants saw they could not crush him with rough work so they tried giving him work that required skill. But this, also, was of no avail. Carpentering, and masonry, and roofing, whatever they set him to do, Emelyan had it ready in time, and went home to his wife at night. So a second week passed.

Then the King called his servants and said: "Am I to feed you for nothing? Two weeks have gone, and I don't see that you have done anything. You were going to tire Emelyan out with work, but I see from my windows how he goes home every evening – singing cheerfully! Do you mean to make a fool of me?"

The King's servants began to excuse themselves. "We tried our best to wear him out with rough work," they said, "but nothing was too hard for him; he cleared it all off as though he had swept it away with a broom. There was no tiring him out. Then we set him to tasks needing skill, which we did not think he was clever enough to do, but he managed them all. No matter what one sets him, he does it all, no one knows how. Either he or his wife must know some spell that helps them. We ourselves are sick of him, and wish to find a task he cannot master. We have now thought of setting him to build a cathedral in a single day. Send for Emelyan, and order him to build a cathedral in front of the palace in a single day. Then, if he does not do it, let his head be cut off for disobedience."

The King sent for Emelyan. "Listen to my command," said he: "build me a new cathedral on the square in front of my palace, and have it ready by tomorrow evening. If you have it ready I will reward you, but if not I will have your head cut off."

When Emelyan heard the King's command he turned away and went home. "My end is near," thought he. And coming to his wife, he said: "Get ready, wife we must fly from here, or I shall be lost by no fault of my own."

"What has frightened you so?" said she, "and why should we run away?"

"How can I help being frightened? The King has ordered me, tomorrow, in a single day, to build him a cathedral. If I fail he will cut my head off. There is only one thing to be done: we must fly while there is yet time."

But his wife would not hear of it. "The King has many soldiers," said she. "They would catch us anywhere. We cannot escape from him, but must obey him as long as strength holds out."

"How can I obey him when the task is beyond my strength?"

"Eh, goodman, don't be downhearted. Eat your supper now, and go to sleep. Rise early in the morning and all will get done."

So Emelyan lay down and slept. His wife roused him early next day. "Go quickly," said she, "and finish the cathedral. Here are nails and a hammer; there is still enough work there for a day."

Emelyan went into the town, reached the palace square, and there stood a large cathedral not quite finished. Emelyan set to work to do what was needed, and by the evening all was ready.

When the King awoke he looked out from his palace, and saw the cathedral, and Emelyan going about driving in nails here and there. And the King was not pleased to have the cathedral – he was annoyed at not being able to condemn Emelyan and take his wife. Again he called his servants. "Emelyan has done this task also," said the King, "and there is no excuse for putting him to death. Even this work was not too hard for him. You must find a more cunning plan, or I will cut off your heads as well as his."

So his servants planned that Emelyan should be ordered to make a river round the palace, with ships sailing on it. And the King sent for Emelyan and set him this new task.

"If," said he, "you could build a cathedral in one night, you can also do this. Tomorrow all must be ready. If not, I will have your head off."

Emelyan was more downcast than before, and returned to his wife sad at heart.

"Why are you so sad?" said his wife. "Has the King set you a fresh task?"

Emelyan told her about it. "We must fly," said he.

But his wife replied: "There is no escaping the soldiers; they will catch us wherever we go. There is nothing for it but to obey."

"How can I do it?" groaned Emelyan.

"Eh! eh! goodman," said she, "don't be downhearted. Eat your supper now, and go to sleep. Rise early, and all will get done in good time."

So Emelyan lay down and slept. In the morning his wife woke him. "Go," said she "to the palace – all is ready. Only, near the wharf in front of the palace, there is a mound left; take a spade and level it."

When the King awoke he saw a river where there had not been one; ships were sailing up and down, and Emelyan was levelling a mound with a spade. The King wondered, but was pleased neither with the river nor with the ships, so vexed was he at not being able to condemn Emelyan. "There is no task," thought he, "that he cannot manage. What is to be done?" And he called his servants and again asked their advice.

"Find some task," said he, "which Emelyan cannot compass. For whatever we plan he fulfills, and I cannot take his wife from him."

The King's servants thought and thought, and at last devised a plan. They came to the King and said: "Send for Emelyan and say to him: 'Go to there, don't know where,' and bring back 'that, don't know what.' Then he will not be able to escape you. No matter where he goes, you can say that he has not gone to the right place, and no matter what he brings, you can say it is not the right thing. Then you can have him beheaded and can take his wife."

The King was pleased. "That is well thought of," said he. So the King sent for Emelyan and said to him: "Go to 'there, don't know where,' and bring back 'that, don't know what.' If you fail to bring it, I will have you beheaded."

Emelyan returned to his wife and told her what the King had said. His wife became thoughtful.

"Well," said she, "they have taught the King how to catch you. Now we must act warily." So she sat and thought, and at last said to her husband: "You must go far, to our Grandam – the old peasant woman, the mother of soldiers – and you must ask her aid. If she helps you to anything, go straight to the palace with it, I shall be there: I cannot escape them now. They will take me by force, but it will not be for long. If you do everything as Grandam directs, you will soon save me."

So the wife got her husband ready for the journey. She gave him a wallet, and also a spindle. "Give her this," said she. "By this token she will know that you are my husband." And his wife showed him his road.

Emelyan set off. He left the town behind, and came to where some soldiers were being drilled. Emelyan stood and watched them. After drill the soldiers sat down to rest. Then Emelyan went up to them and asked: "Do you know, brothers, the way to 'there, don't know where,' and how I can get 'that, don't know what'?"

The soldiers listened to him with surprise. "Who sent you on this errand?" said they

"The King," said he.

"From the day we became soldiers," said they, "we go 'don't know where,' and never yet have we got there; and we seek 'don't know what,' and cannot find it. We cannot help you."

Emelyan sat a while with the soldiers and then went on again. He trudged many a mile, and at last came to a wood. In the wood was a hut, and in the hut sat an old, old woman, the mother of peasant soldiers, spinning flax and weeping. And as she spun she did not put her fingers to her mouth to wet them with spittle, but to her eyes to wet them with tears. When the old woman saw Emelyan she cried out at him: "Why have you come here?" Then Emelyan gave her the spindle, and said his wife had sent it.

The old woman softened at once, and began to question him. And Emelyan told her his whole life: how he married the lass; how they went to live in the town; how he had worked, and what he had done at the palace; how he built the cathedral, and made a river with ships on it, and how the King had now told him to go to "there, don't know where," and bring back "that, don't know what."

The Grandam listened to the end, and ceased weeping. She muttered to herself: "The time has surely come," and said to him: "All right, my lad. Sit down now, and I will give you something to eat."

Emelyan ate, and then the Grandam told him what to do. "Here," said she, "is a ball of thread; roll it before you, and follow where it goes. You must go far till you come right to the sea. When you get there you will see a great city. Enter the city and ask for a night's lodging at the furthest house. There look out for what you are seeking."

"How shall I know it when I see it, Granny?" said he.

"When you see something men obey more than father or mother, that is it. Seize that, and take it to the King. When you bring it to the King, he will say it is not right, and you must answer: 'If it is not the right thing it must be smashed,' and you must beat it, and carry it to the river, break it in pieces, and throw it into the water. Then you will get your wife back and my tears will be dried."

Emelyan bade farewell to the Grandam and began rolling his ball before him. It rolled and rolled until at last it reached the sea. By the sea stood a great city, and at the further end of the city was a big house. There Emelyan begged for a night's lodging, and was granted it. He lay down to sleep, and in the morning awoke and heard a father rousing his son to go and cut wood for the fire. But the son did not obey. "It is too early," said he, "there is time enough." Then Emelyan heard the mother say, "Go, my son, your father's bones ache; would you have him go himself? It is time to be up!"

But the son only murmured some words and fell asleep again. Hardly was he asleep when something thundered and rattled in the street. Up jumped the son and quickly putting on his clothes ran out into the street. Up jumped Emelyan, too, and ran after him to see what it was that a son obeys more than father or mother. What he saw was a man walking along the street carrying, tied to his stomach, a thing which he beat with sticks, and that it was that rattled and thundered so, and that the son had obeyed. Emelyan ran up and had a look at it. He saw it was round, like a small tub, with a skin stretched over both ends, and he asked what it was called.

He was told, "A drum."

"And is it empty?"

"Yes, it is empty."

Emelyan was surprised. He asked them to give the thing to him, but they would not. So Emelyan left off asking, and followed the drummer. All day he followed, and when the drummer at last lay down to sleep, Emelyan snatched the drum from him and ran away with it.

He ran and ran, till at last he got back to his own town. He went to see his wife, but she was not at home. The day after he went away, the King had taken her. So Emelyan went to the palace, and sent in a message to the King: "He has returned who went to 'there, don't know where,' and he has brought with him 'that, don't know what.'"

They told the King, and the King said he was to come again next day.

But Emelyan said, "Tell the King I am here today, and have brought what the King wanted. Let him come out to me, or I will go in to him!"

The King came out. "Where have you been?" said he.

Emelyan told him.

"That's not the right place," said the King. "What have you brought?"

Emelyan pointed to the drum, but the King did not look at it. "That is not it."

"If it is not the right thing," said Emelyan, "it must be smashed, and may the devil take it!"

And Emelyan left the palace, carrying the drum and beating it. And as he beat it all the King's army ran out to follow Emelyan, and they saluted him and waited his commands.

The King, from his window, began to shout at his army telling them not to follow Emelyan. They did not listen to what he said, but all followed Emelyan.

When the King saw that, he gave orders that Emelyan's wife should be taken back to him, and he sent to ask Emelyan to give him the drum.

"It can't be done," said Emelyan. "I was told to smash it and to throw the splinters into the river."

So Emelyan went down to the river carrying the drum, and the soldiers followed him. When he reached the river bank Emelyan smashed the drum to splinters, and threw the splinters into the stream. And then all the soldiers ran away.

Emelyan took his wife and went home with her. And after that the King ceased to trouble him; and so they lived happily ever after.

1891

PART VI

ADAPTATIONS FROM THE FRENCH

THE COFFEEHOUSE OF SURAT

After Bernardin De Saint-Pierre

IN THE TOWN OF SURAT, in India, was a coffeehouse where many travellers and foreigners from all parts of the world met and conversed.

One day a learned Persian theologian visited this coffeehouse. He was a man who had spent his life studying the nature of the Deity, and reading and writing books upon the subject. He had thought, read, and written so much about God, that eventually he lost his wits, became quite confused, and ceased even to believe in the existence of a God. The Shah, hearing of this, had banished him from Persia.

After having argued all his life about the First Cause, this unfortunate theologian had ended by quite perplexing himself, and instead of understanding that he had lost his own reason, he began to think that there was no higher Reason controlling the universe.

This man had an African slave who followed him everywhere. When the theologian entered the coffeehouse, the slave remained outside, near the door sitting on a stone in the glare of the sun, and driving away the flies that buzzed around him. The Persian having settled down on a divan in the coffeehouse, ordered himself a cup of opium. When he had drunk it and the opium had begun to quicken the workings of his brain, he addressed his slave through the open door:

"Tell me, wretched slave," said he, "do you think there is a God, or not?"

"Of course there is," said the slave, and immediately drew from under his girdle a small idol of wood.

"There," said he, "that is the God who has guarded me from the day of my birth. Every one in our country worships the fetish tree, from the wood of which this God was made."

This conversation between the theologian and his slave was listened to with surprise by the other guests in the coffeehouse. They were astonished at the master's question, and yet more so at the slave's reply.

One of them, a Brahmin, on hearing the words spoken by the slave, turned to him and said:

"Miserable fool! Is it possible you believe that God can be carried under a man's girdle? There is one God – Brahma, and he is greater than the whole world, for he created it. Brahma is the One, the mighty God, and in His honor are built the temples on the Ganges' banks, where his true priests, the Brahmins, worship him. They know the true God, and none but they. A thousand score of years have passed, and yet through revolution after revolution these priests have held their sway, because Brahma, the one true God, has protected them."

So spoke the Brahmin, thinking to convince every one; but a Jewish broker who was present replied to him, and said:

"No! the temple of the true God is not in India. Neither does God protect the Brahmin caste. The true God is not the God of the Brahmins, but of Abraham, Isaac, and Jacob. None does He protect but His chosen people, the Israelites. From the commencement of the world, our nation has been beloved of Him, and ours alone. If we are now scattered over the whole earth it is but to try us; for God has promised that He will one day gather His people together in Jerusalem. Then, with the Temple of Jerusalem – the wonder of the ancient world – restored to its splendor, shall Israel be established a ruler over all nations."

So spoke the Jew, and burst into tears. He wished to say more, but an Italian missionary who was there interrupted him.

"What you are saying is untrue," said he to the Jew. "You attribute injustice to God. He cannot love your nation above the rest. Nay rather, even if it be true that of old He favored the Israelites, it is now nineteen hundred years since they angered Him, and caused Him to destroy their nation and scatter them over the earth, so that their faith makes no converts and has died out except here and there. God shows preference to no nation, but calls all who wish to be saved to the bosom of the Catholic Church of Rome, the one outside whose borders no salvation can be found."

So spoke the Italian. But a Protestant minister who happened to be present, growing pale, turned to the Catholic missionary and exclaimed:

"How can you say that salvation belongs to your religion? Those only will be saved, who serve God according to the Gospel, in spirit and in truth, as bidden by the word of Christ."

Then a Turk, an officeholder in the customhouse at Surat, who was sitting in the coffeehouse smoking a pipe, turned with an air of superiority to both the Christians.

"Your belief in your Roman religion is vain," said he. "It was superseded twelve hundred years ago by the true faith: that of Mohammed! You cannot but observe how the true Mohammedan faith continues to spread both in Europe and Asia, and even in the enlightened country of China. You say yourselves that God has rejected the Jews; and, as a proof, you quote the fact that the Jews are humiliated and their faith does not spread. Confess then the truth of Mohammedanism, for it is triumphant and spreads far and wide. None will be saved but the followers of Mohammed, God's latest prophet; and of them, only the followers of Omar, and not of Ali, for the latter are false to the faith."

To this the Persian theologian, who was of the sect of Ali, wished to reply; but by this time a great dispute had arisen among all the strangers of different faiths and creeds present. There were Abyssinian Christians, Lamas from Tibet, Ismailians and Fire-worshippers. They all argued about the nature of God, and how He should be worshipped. Each of them asserted that in his country alone was the true God known and rightly worshipped.

Every one argued and shouted, except a Chinaman, a student of Confucius, who sat quietly in one corner of the coffeehouse, not joining in the dispute. He sat there drinking tea and listening to what the others said, but did not speak himself.

The Turk noticed him sitting there, and appealed to him, saying:

"You can confirm what I say, my good Chinaman. You hold your peace, but if you spoke I know you would uphold my opinion. Traders from your country, who come to me for assistance, tell me that though many religions have been introduced into China, you Chinese consider Mohammedanism the best of all, and adopt it willingly. Confirm, then, my words, and tell us your opinion of the true God and of His prophet."

"Yes, yes," said the rest, turning to the Chinaman, "let us hear what you think on the subject."

The Chinaman, the student of Confucius, closed his eyes, and thought a while. Then he opened them again, and drawing his hands out of the wide sleeves of his garment, and folding them on his breast, he spoke as follows, in a calm and quiet voice.

Sirs, it seems to me that it is chiefly pride that prevents men agreeing with one another on matters of faith. If you care to listen to me, I will tell you a story which will explain this by an example.

I came here from China on an English steamer which had been round the world. We stopped for fresh water, and landed on the east coast of the island of Sumatra. It was midday, and some of us, having landed, sat in the shade of some coconut palms by the seashore, not far from a native village. We were a party of men of different nationalities.

As we sat there, a blind man approached us. We learnt afterwards that he had gone blind from gazing too long and too persistently at the sun, trying to find out what it is, in order to seize its light.

He strove a long time to accomplish this, constantly looking at the sun; but the only result was that his eyes were in-
jured by its brightness, and he became blind.

Then he said to himself:

"The light of the sun is not a liquid; for if it were a liquid
it would be possible to pour it from one vessel into another,
and it would be moved, like water, by the wind. Neither is it
fire; for if it were fire, water would extinguish it. Neither is
light a spirit, for it is seen by the eye, nor is it matter, for it
cannot be moved. Therefore, as the light of the sun is neither
liquid, nor fire, nor spirit, nor matter, it is – nothing!"

So he argued, and, as a result of always looking at the sun
and always thinking about it, he lost both his sight and his
reason. And when he went quite blind, he became fully convinced that the sun did not exist.

With this blind man came a slave, who after placing his
master in the shade of a coconut tree, picked up a coconut
from the ground, and began making it into a night-light. He
twisted a wick from the fibre of the coconut: squeezed oil
from the nut into the shell, and soaked the wick in it.

As the slave sat doing this, the blind man sighed and said
to him:

"Well, slave, was I not right when I told you there is no
sun? Do you not see how dark it is? Yet people say there is a
sun...But if so, what is it?"

"I do not know what the sun is," said the slave "That is no
business of mine. But I know what light is. Here, I have made
a night-light, by the help of which I can serve you and find
anything I want in the hut."

And the slave picked up the coconut shell, saying:

"This is my sun."

A lame man with crutches, who was sitting near by heard
these words, and laughed:

"You have evidently been blind all your life," said he to the
blind man, "not to know what the sun is, I will tell you what
it is. The sun is a ball of fire, which rises every morning out of

the sea and goes down again among the mountains of our island each evening. We have all seen this, and if you had had
your eyesight you too would have seen it."

A fisherman, who had been listening to the conversation,
said:

"It is plain enough that you have never been beyond your
own island. If you were not lame, and if you had been out as
I have in a fishing boat, you would know that the sun does
not set among the mountains of our island, but as it rises from
the ocean every morning so it sets again in the sea every night.
What I am telling you is true, for I see it every day with my
own eyes."

Then an Indian who was of our party, interrupted him by
saying:

"I am astonished that a reasonable man should talk such
nonsense. How can a ball of fire possibly descend into the
water and not be extinguished? The sun is not a ball of fire at
all, it is the Deity named Deva who rides for ever in a chariot
round the golden mountain, Meru. Sometimes the evil ser-
pents Ragu and Ketu attack Deva and swallow him: and then
the earth is dark. But our priests pray that the Deity may be
released, and then he is set free. Only such ignorant men as
you, who have never been beyond their own island, can imagine that the sun shines for their country alone."

Then the master of an Egyptian vessel, who was present,
spoke in his turn.

"No," said he, "you also are wrong. The sun is not a Deity,
and does not move only round India and its golden mountain. I have sailed much on the Black Sea, and along the coasts
of Arabia, and have been to Madagascar and to the Philippines. The sun lights the whole earth, and not India alone. It
does not circle round one mountain, but rises far in the east,
beyond the Isles of Japan, and sets far, far away in the west,
beyond the islands of England. That is why the Japanese call
their country 'Nippon,' that is 'the birth of the sun.' I know

this well, for I have myself seen much, and heard more from my grandfather, who sailed to the very ends of the sea."

He would have gone on, but an English sailor from our ship interrupted him.

"There is no country," he said, "where people know so much about the sun's movements as in England. The sun, as every one in England knows, rises nowhere and sets nowhere. It is always moving round the earth. We can be sure of this for we have just been round the world ourselves, and nowhere knocked up against the sun. Wherever we went, the sun showed itself in the morning and hid itself at night, just as it does here."

And the Englishman took a stick and, drawing circles on the sand, tried to explain how the sun moves in the heavens and goes round the world. But he was unable to explain it clearly, and pointing to the ship's pilot said:

"This man knows more about it than I do. He can explain it properly."

The pilot, who was an intelligent man, had listened in silence to the talk till he was asked to speak. Now every one turned to him, and he said:

"You are all misleading one another, and are yourselves deceived. The sun does not go round the earth, but the earth goes round the sun, revolving as it goes and turning towards the sun in the course of each twenty-four hours, not only Japan, and the Philippines and Sumatra where we now are, but Africa, and Europe and America, and many lands besides. The sun does not shine for some one mountain, or for some one island, or for some one sea, nor even for one earth alone, but for other planets as well as our earth. If you would only look up at the heavens, instead of at the ground beneath your own feet, you might all understand this, and would then no longer suppose that the sun shines for you, or for your country alone."

Thus spoke the wise pilot, who had voyaged much about the world, and had gazed much upon the heavens above.

"So on matters of faith," continued the Chinaman, the student of Confucius, "it is pride that causes error and discord among men. As with the sun, so it is with God. Each man wants to have a special God of his own, or at least a special God for his native land. Each nation wishes to confine in its own temples Him, whom the world cannot contain.

"Can any temple compare with that which God Himself has built to unite all men in one faith and one religion?

"All human temples are built on the model of this temple, which is God's own world. Every temple has its fonts, its vaulted roof, its lamps, its pictures or sculptures, its inscriptions, its books of the law, its offerings, its altars and its priests. But in what temple is there such a font as the ocean; such a vault as that of the heavens; such lamps as the sun, moon, and stars; or any figures to be compared with living, loving, mutually helpful men? Where are there any records of God's goodness so easy to understand as the blessings which God has strewn abroad for man's happiness? Where is there any book of the law so clear to each man as that written in his heart? What sacrifices equal the self-denials which loving men and women make for one another? And what altar can be compared with the heart of a good man, on which God Himself accepts the sacrifice?

"The higher a man's conception of God, the better will he know Him. And the better he knows God, the nearer will he draw to Him, imitating His goodness, His mercy, and His love of man.

"Therefore, let him who sees the sun's whole light filling the world, refrain from blaming or despising the superstitious man, who in his own idol sees one ray of that same light. Let him not despise even the unbeliever who is blind and cannot see the sun at all."

So spoke the Chinaman, the student of Confucius; and all who were present in the coffeehouse were silent, and disputed no more as to whose faith was the best.

1893

20

TOO DEAR!

Tolstoy's Adaptation of a Story by Guy de Maupassant

NEAR THE BORDERS of France and Italy, on the shore of the Mediterranean Sea, lies a tiny little kingdom called Monaco. Many a small country town can boast more inhabitants than this kingdom, for there are only about seven thousand of them all told, and if all the land in the kingdom were divided there would not be an acre for each inhabitant. But in this toy kingdom there is a real king; and he has a palace, and courtiers, and ministers, and a bishop, and generals, and an army.

It is not a large army, only sixty men in all, but still it is an army. There are also taxes in this kingdom as elsewhere: a tax on tobacco, and on wine and spirits, and a poll tax. But though the people there drink and smoke as people do in other countries, there are so few of them that the king would have been hard put to it to feed his courtiers and officials and to keep himself, if he had not found a new and special source of revenue. This special revenue comes from a gaming house, where people play roulette. People play, and whether they win or lose the keeper always gets a percentage on the turnover; and out of his profits he pays a large sum to the king. The reason he pays so much is that it is the only such gambling establishment left in Europe. Some of the little German Sovereigns used to keep gaming houses of the same kind, but some years ago they were forbidden to do so. The reason they were stopped was because these gaming houses did so much harm. A man would come and try his luck, then he would risk all he had and lose it, then he would even risk money that did not belong to him and lose that too, and then, in despair, he would drown or shoot himself. So the Germans forbade their rulers to make money in this way; but there was no one to stop the King of Monaco, and he remained with a monopoly of the business.

So now every one who wants to gamble goes to Monaco. Whether they win or lose, the king gains by it. "You can't earn stone palaces by honest labor," as the proverb says; and the King of Monaco knows it is a dirty business, but what is he to do? He has to live; and to draw a revenue from drink and from tobacco is also not a nice thing. So he lives and reigns, and rakes in the money, and holds his court with all the ceremony of a real king.

He has his coronation, his levees; he rewards, sentences, and pardons, and he also has his reviews, councils, laws, and courts of justice: just like other kings, only all on a smaller scale.

Now it happened a few years ago that a murder was committed in this toy king's domains. The people of that kingdom are peaceable, and such a thing had not happened before. The judges assembled with much ceremony and tried the case in the most judicial manner. There were judges, and prosecutors, and jurymen, and barristers. They argued and judged, and at last they condemned the criminal to have his head cut off as the law directs. So far so good. Next they submitted the sentence to the king. The king read the sentence and confirmed it. "If the fellow must be executed, execute him."

There was only one hitch in the matter; and that was that they had neither a guillotine for cutting heads off, nor an executioner. The Ministers considered the matter, and decided to address an inquiry to the French Government, asking whether the French could not lend them a machine and an expert to cut off the criminal's head; and if so, would the French kindly inform them what the cost would be. The letter was sent. A week later the reply came: a machine and an expert could be supplied, and the cost would be 16,000 francs. This was laid before the king. He thought it over. Sixteen thousand francs! "The wretch is not worth the money," said he. "Can't it be done, somehow, cheaper?

Why, 16,000 francs is more than two francs a head on the whole population. The people won't stand it, and it may cause a riot!"

So a Council was called to consider what could be done; and it was decided to send a similar inquiry to the King of Italy. The French Government is republican, and has no proper respect for kings; but the King of Italy was a brother monarch, and might be induced to do the thing cheaper. So the letter was written, and a prompt reply was received.

The Italian Government wrote that they would have pleasure in supplying both a machine and an expert; and the whole cost would be 12,000 francs, including travelling expenses. This was cheaper, but still it seemed too much. The rascal was really not worth the money. It would still mean nearly two francs more per head on the taxes. Another Council was called. They discussed and considered how it could be done with less expense. Could not one of the soldiers perhaps be got to do it in a rough and homely fashion? The General was called and was asked: "Can't you find us a soldier who would cut the man's head off? In war they don't mind killing people. In fact, that is what they are trained for." So the General talked it over with the soldiers to see whether one of them would not undertake the job. But none of the soldiers would do it. "No," they said, "we don't know how to do it; it is not a thing we have been taught."

What was to be done? Again the Ministers considered and re-considered. They assembled a commission, and a committee, and a subcommittee, and at last they decided that the best thing would be to alter the death sentence to one of imprisonment for life. This would enable the king to show his mercy, and it would come cheaper.

The king agreed to this, and so the matter was arranged. The only hitch now was that there was no suitable prison for a man sentenced for life. There was a small lockup where people were sometimes kept temporarily, but there was no strong prison fit for permanent use. However, they managed to find a place that would do, and they put the young fellow there and placed a guard over him. The guard had to watch the criminal, and had also to fetch his food from the palace kitchen.

The prisoner remained there month after month till a year had passed. But when a year had passed, the king, looking over the account of his income and expenditure one day, noticed a new item of expenditure. This was for the keep of the criminal; nor was it a small item either. There was a special guard, and there was also the man's food. It came to more than 600 francs a year. And the worst of it was that the fellow was still young and healthy, and might live for fifty years. When one came to reckon it up, the matter was serious. It would never do. So the king summoned his Ministers and said to them:

"You must find some cheaper way of dealing with this rascal. The present plan is too expensive." And the Ministers met and considered and reconsidered, till one of them said: "Gentlemen, in my opinion we must dismiss the guard." "But then," rejoined another Minister, "the fellow will run away." "Well," said the first speaker, "let him run away, and be hanged to him!" So they reported the result of their deliberations to the king, and he agreed with them. The guard was dismissed, and they waited to see what would happen. All that happened was that at dinnertime the criminal came out, and, not finding his guard, he went to the king's kitchen to fetch his own dinner. He took what was given him, returned to the prison, shut the door on himself, and stayed inside. Next day the same thing occurred. He went for his food at the proper time; but as for running away, he did not show the least sign of it! What was to be done? They considered the matter again.

"We shall have to tell him straight out," said they "that we do not want to keep him." So the Minister of Justice had him brought before him.

"Why do you not run away?" said the Minister. "There is no guard to keep you. You can go where you like, and the king will not mind."

"I daresay the king would not mind," replied the man, "but I have nowhere to go. What can I do? You have ruined my character by your sentence, and people will turn their backs on me. Besides, I have got out of the way of working. You have treated me badly. It is not fair. In the first place, when once you sentenced me to death you ought to have executed me; but you did not do it. That is one thing. I did not complain about that. Then you sentenced me to imprisonment for life and put a guard to bring me my food; but after a time you took him away again and I had to fetch my own food. Again I did not complain. But now you actually want me to go away! I can't agree to that. You may do as you like, but I won't go away!"

What was to be done? Once more the Council was summoned. What course could they adopt? The man would not go. They reflected and considered. The only way to get rid of him was to offer him a pension. And so they reported to the king. "There is nothing else for it," said they; "we must get rid of him somehow." The sum fixed was 600 francs, and this was announced to the prisoner.

"Well," said he, "I don't mind, so long as you undertake to pay it regularly. On that condition I am willing to go."

So the matter was settled. He received one-third of his annuity in advance, and left the king's dominions. It was only a quarter of an hour by rail; and he emigrated, and settled just across the frontier, where he bought a bit of land, started market-gardening, and now lives comfortably. He always goes at the proper time to draw his pension. Having received it, he goes to the gaming tables, stakes two or three francs, sometimes wins and sometimes loses, and then returns home. He lives peaceably and well.

It is a good thing that he did not commit his crime in a country where they do not grudge expense to cut a man's head off, or to keeping him in prison for life.

1897

PART VII

STORIES GIVEN TO AID
THE PERSECUTED JEWS

21

ESARHADDON, KING OF ASSYRIA

THE ASSYRIAN KING, Esarhaddon, had conquered the kingdom of King Lailie, had destroyed and burnt the towns, taken all the inhabitants captive to his own country, slaughtered the warriors, beheaded some chieftains and impaled or flayed others, and had confined King Lailie himself in a cage.

As he lay on his bed one night, King Esarhaddon was thinking how he should execute Lailie, when suddenly he heard a rustling near his bed, and opening his eyes saw an old man with a long gray beard and mild eyes.

"You wish to execute Lailie?" asked the old man.

"Yes," answered the King. "But I cannot make up my mind how to do it."

"But you are Lailie," said the old man.

"That's not true," replied the King. "Lailie is Lailie, and I am I."

"You and Lailie are one," said the old man. "You only imagine you are not Lailie, and that Lailie is not you."

"What do you mean by that?" said the King. "Here am I, lying on a soft bed; around me are obedient men slaves and women slaves, and tomorrow I shall feast with my friends as I did today; whereas Lailie is sitting like a bird in a cage, and tomorrow he will be impaled, and with his tongue hanging out will struggle till he dies, and his body will be torn in pieces by dogs."

"You cannot destroy his life," said the old man.

"And how about the fourteen thousand warriors I killed, with whose bodies I built a mound?" said the King. "I am alive, but they no longer exist. Does not that prove that I can destroy life?"

"How do you know they no longer exist?"

"Because I no longer see them. And, above all, they were tormented, but I was not. It was ill for them, but well for me."

"That, also, only seems so to you. You tortured yourself, but not them."

"I do not understand," said the King.

"Do you wish to understand?"

"Yes, I do."

"Then come here," said the old man, pointing to a large font full of water.

The King rose and approached the font.

"Strip, and enter the font."

Esarhaddon did as the old man bade him.

"As soon as I begin to pour this water over you," said the old man, filling a pitcher with the water, "dip down your head."

The old man tilted the pitcher over the King's head and the King bent his head till it was under water.

And as soon as King Esarhaddon was under the water he felt that he was no longer Esarhaddon, but some one else. And, feeling himself to be that other man, he saw himself lying on a rich bed, beside a beautiful woman. He had never seen her before, but he knew she was his wife. The woman raised herself and said to him:

"Dear husband, Lailie! You were wearied by yesterday's work and have slept longer than usual, and I have guarded your rest, and have not roused you. But now the Princes await you in the Great Hall. Dress and go out to them."

And Esarhaddon – understanding from these words that he was Lailie, and not feeling at all surprised at this, but only wondering that he did not know it before – rose, dressed, and went into the Great Hall where the Princes awaited him.

The Princes greeted Lailie, their King, bowing to the ground, and then they rose, and at his word sat down before him; and the eldest of the Princes began to speak, saying that it was impossible longer to endure the insults of the wicked King Esarhaddon, and that they must make war on him. But Lailie disagreed, and gave

orders that envoys shall be sent to remonstrate with King Esarhaddon; and he dismissed the Princes from the audience. Afterwards he appointed men of note to act as ambassadors, and
impressed on them what they were to say to King Esarhaddon.
Having finished this business, Esarhaddon – feeling himself to
be Lailie – rode out to hunt wild asses. The hunt was successful.
He killed two wild asses himself, and having returned home,
feasted with his friends, and witnessed a dance of slave girls. The
next day he went to the Court, where he was awaited by petition-
ers, suitors, and prisoners brought for trial; and there as usual he
decided the cases submitted to him. Having finished this business, he again rode out to his favourite amusement: the hunt.
And again he was successful: this time killing with his own hand
an old lioness, and capturing her two cubs. After the hunt he
again feasted with his friends, and was entertained with music
and dances, and the night he spent with the wife whom he loved.

So, dividing his time between kingly duties and pleasures, he
lived for days and weeks, awaiting the return of the ambassadors
he had sent to that King Esarhaddon who used to be himself.
Not till a month had passed did the ambassadors return, and
they returned with their noses and ears cut off.

King Esarhaddon had ordered them to tell Lailie that what
had been done to them – the ambassadors – would be done to
King Lailie himself also, unless he sent immediately a tribute of
silver, gold, and cypress wood, and came himself to pay homage
to King Esarhaddon.

Lailie, formerly Esarhaddon, again assembled the Princes, and
took counsel with them as to what he should do. They all with
one accord said that war must be made against Esarhaddon,
without waiting for him to attack them. The King agreed; and
taking his place at the head of the army, started on the campaign.
The campaign lasted seven days. Each day the King rode round
the army to rouse the courage of his warriors. On the eighth day

his army met that of Esarhaddon in a broad valley through which a river flowed. Lailie's army fought bravely, but Lailie, formerly Esarhaddon, saw the enemy swarming down from the mountains like ants, overrunning the valley and overwhelming his army; and, in his chariot, he flung himself into the midst of the battle, hewing and felling the enemy. But the warriors of Lailie were but as hundreds, while those of Esarhaddon were as thousands; and Lailie felt himself wounded and taken prisoner. Nine days he journeyed with other captives, bound, and guarded by the warriors of Esarhaddon. On the tenth day he reached Nineveh, and was placed in a cage. Lailie suffered not so much from hunger and from his wound as from shame and impotent rage. He felt how powerless he was to avenge himself on his enemy for all he was suffering. All he could do was to deprive his enemies of the pleasure of seeing his sufferings; and he firmly resolved to endure courageously, without a murmur, all they could do to him. For twenty days he sat in his cage, awaiting execution. He saw his relatives and friends led out to death; he heard the groans of those who were executed: some had their hands and feet cut off, others were flayed alive, but he showed neither disquietude, nor pity, nor fear. He saw the wife he loved, bound, and led by two black eunuchs. He knew she was being taken as a slave to Esarhaddon. That, too, he bore without a murmur. But one of the guards placed to watch him said, "I pity you, Lailie; you were a king, but what are you now?" And hearing these words, Lailie remembered all he had lost. He clutched the bars of his cage, and, wishing to kill himself, beat his head against them. But he had not the strength to do so and, groaning in despair, he fell upon the floor of his cage.

At last two executioners opened his cage door, and having strapped his arms tight behind him, led him to the place of execution, which was soaked with blood. Lailie saw a sharp stake dripping with blood, from which the corpse of one of his friends had just been torn, and he understood that this had been done that the stake might serve for his own execution. They stripped Lailie of his clothes. He was startled at the leanness of his once strong, handsome body. The two executioners seized that body by its lean thighs; they lifted him up and were about to let him fall upon the stake.

"This is death, destruction!" thought Lailie, and, forgetful of his resolve to remain bravely calm to the end, he sobbed and prayed for mercy. But no one listened to him.

"But this cannot be," thought he. "Surely I am asleep. It is a dream." And he made an effort to rouse himself, and did indeed awake, to find himself neither Esarhaddon nor Lailie – but some kind of an animal. He was astonished that he was an animal, and astonished, also, at not having known this before.

He was grazing in a valley, tearing the tender grass with his teeth, and brushing away flies with his long tail. Around him was frolicking a long-legged, dark gray ass-colt, striped down its back. Kicking up its hind legs, the colt galloped full speed to Esarhaddon, and poking him under the stomach with its smooth little muzzle, searched for the teat, and, finding it, quieted down, swallowing regularly. Esarhaddon understood that he was a she-ass, the colt's mother, and this neither surprised nor grieved him, but rather gave him pleasure. He experienced a glad feeling of simultaneous life in himself and in his offspring.

But suddenly something flew near with a whistling sound and hit him in the side, and with its sharp point entered his skin and flesh. Feeling a burning pain, Esarhaddon – who was at the same time the ass – tore the udder from the colt's teeth, and laying back his ears galloped to the herd from which he had strayed. The colt kept up with him, galloping by his side. They had already nearly reached the herd, which had started off, when another arrow in full flight struck the colt's neck. It pierced the skin and quivered in its flesh. The colt sobbed piteously and fell upon its knees. Esarhaddon could not abandon it, and remained standing over it. The colt rose, tottered on its long, thin legs, and again fell. A fearful two-legged being – a man – ran up and cut its throat.

"This cannot be; it is still a dream!" thought Esarhaddon, and made a last effort to awake. "Surely I am not Lailie, nor the ass, but Esarhaddon!"

He cried out, and at the same instant lifted his head out of the font…The old man was standing by him, pouring over his head the last drops from the pitcher.

"Oh, how terribly I have suffered! And for how long!" said Esarhaddon.

"Long?" replied the old man, "you have only dipped your head under water and lifted it again; see, the water is not yet all out of the pitcher. Do you now understand?"

Esarhaddon did not reply, but only looked at the old man with terror.

"Do you now understand," continued the old man, "that Lailie is you, and the warriors you put to death were you also? And not the warriors only, but the animals which you slew when hunting and ate at your feasts were also you. You thought life dwelt in you alone but I have drawn aside the veil of delusion, and have let you see that by doing evil to others you have done it to yourself also. Life is one in them all, and yours is but a portion of this same common life. And only in that one part of life that is yours, can you make life better or worse – increasing or decreasing it. You can only improve life in yourself by destroying the barriers that divide your life from that of others, and by considering others as yourself, and loving them. By so doing you increase your share of life. You injure your life when you think of it as the only life, and try to add to its welfare at the expense of other lives. By so doing you only lessen it. To destroy the life that dwells in others is beyond your power. The life of those you have slain has vanished from your eyes, but is not destroyed. You thought to lengthen your own life and to shorten theirs, but you cannot do this. Life knows neither time nor space. The life of a moment, and the life of a thousand years: your life and the life of all the visible and invisible beings in the world, are equal. To destroy life, or to alter it, is impossible; for life is the one thing that exists. All else, but seems to us to be."

Having said this the old man vanished.

Next morning King Esarhaddon gave orders that Lailie and all the prisoners should be set at liberty and that the executions should cease.

On the third day he called his son Assur-bani-pal, and gave the kingdom over into his hands; and he himself went into the desert to think over all he had learnt. Afterwards he went about as a wanderer through the towns and villages, preaching to the people that all life is one, and that when men wish to harm others, they really do evil to themselves.

1903

22

WORK, DEATH, AND SICKNESS:
A LEGEND

A legend from the South American Indians

GOD, SAY THEY, at first made men so that they had no need to work: they needed neither houses, nor clothes, nor food, and they all lived till they were a hundred, and did not know what illness was.

When, after some time, God looked to see how people were living, he saw that instead of being happy in their life, they had quarrelled with one another, and, each caring for himself, had brought matters to such a pass that far from enjoying life, they cursed it.

Then God said to himself: "This comes of their living separately, each for himself." And to change this state of things, God so arranged matters that it became impossible for people to live without working. To avoid suffering from cold and hunger, they were now obliged to build dwellings, and to dig the ground, and to grow and gather fruits and grain.

"Work will bring them together," thought God. "They cannot make their tools, prepare and transport their timber, build their houses, sow and gather their harvests, spin and weave, and make their clothes, each one alone by himself."

"It will make them understand that the more heartily they work together, the more they will have and the better they will live; and this will unite them."

Time passed on, and again God came to see how men were living, and whether they were now happy.

But he found them living worse than before. They worked together (that they could not help doing), but not all together, being broken up into little groups. And each group tried to snatch work from other groups, and they hindered one another, wasting time and strength in their struggles, so that things went ill with them all.

Having seen that this, too, was not well, God decided so as to arrange things that man should not know the time of his death, but might die at any moment; and he announced this to them.

"Knowing that each of them may die at any moment," thought God, "they will not, by grasping at gains that may last so short a time, spoil the hours of life allotted to them."

But it turned out otherwise. When God returned to see how people were living, he saw that their life was as bad as ever.

Those who were strongest, availing themselves of the fact that men might die at any time, subdued those who were weaker, killing some and threatening others with death. And it came about that the strongest and their descendants did no work, and suffered from the weariness of idleness, while those who were weaker had to work beyond their strength, and suffered from lack of rest. Each set of men feared and hated the other. And the life of man became yet more unhappy.

Having seen all this, God, to mend matters, decided to make use of one last means; he sent all kinds of sickness among men. God thought that when all men were exposed to sickness they would understand that those who are well should have pity on those who are sick, and should help them, that when they themselves fall ill those who are well might in turn help them.

And again God went away, but when He came back to see how men lived now that they were subject to sicknesses, he saw that their life was worse even than before. The very sickness that in God's purpose should have united men, had divided them more than ever. Those men who were strong enough to make others work, forced them also to wait on them in times of sickness; but they did not, in their turn, look after others who were ill. And those who were forced to work for others and to look after them when sick, were so worn with work that they had no time to look after their own sick, but left them without attendance. That the sight of sick folk might not disturb the pleasures of the wealthy, houses were arranged in which these poor people suffered and died, far from those whose sympathy might have cheered them, and in the arms of hired people who nursed them without compassion, or even with disgust. Moreover, people considered many of the illnesses infectious, and, fearing to catch them, not only avoided the sick, but even separated themselves from those who attended the sick.

Then God said to Himself: "If even this means will not bring men to understand wherein their happiness lies, let them be taught by suffering." And God left men to themselves.

And, left to themselves, men lived long before they understood that they all ought to be, and might be, happy. Only in the very latest times have a few of them begun to understand that work ought not to be a bugbear to some and like galley slavery for others, but should be a common and happy occupation, uniting all men. They have begun to understand that with death constantly threatening each of us, the only reasonable business of every man is to spend the years, months, hours, and minutes, allotted him – in unity and love. They have begun to understand that sickness, far from dividing men, should, on the contrary, give opportunity for loving union with one another.

1903

23

THREE QUESTIONS

IT ONCE OCCURRED to a certain king, that if he always knew the right time to begin everything; if he knew who were the right people to listen to, and whom to avoid, and, above all, if he always knew what was the most important thing to do, he would never fail in anything he might undertake.

And this thought having occurred to him, he had it proclaimed throughout his kingdom that he would give a great reward to any one who would teach him what was the right time for every action, and who were the most necessary people, and how he might know what was the most important thing to do.

And learned men came to the King, but they all answered his questions differently.

In reply to the first question, some said that to know the right time for every action, one must draw up in advance, a table of days, months and years, and must live strictly according to it. Only thus, said they, could everything be done at its proper time. Others declared that it was impossible to decide beforehand the right time for every action; but that, not letting oneself be absorbed in idle pastimes, one should always attend to all that was going on, and then do what was most needful. Others, again, said that however attentive the King might be to what was going on, it was impossible for one man to decide correctly the right time for every action, but that he should have a Council of wise men, who would help him to fix the proper time for everything.

But then again others said there were some things which could not wait to be laid before a Council, but about which one had at once to decide whether to undertake them or not. But in order to decide that, one must know beforehand what was going to happen. It is only magicians who know that; and, therefore, in order to know the right time for every action, one must consult magicians.

Equally various were the answers to the second question. Some said, the people the King most needed were his councillors; others, the priests; others, the doctors; while some said the warriors were the most necessary.

To the third question, as to what was the most important occupation: some replied that the most important thing in the world was science. Others said it was skill in warfare; and others, again, that it was religious worship.

All the answers being different, the King agreed with none of them, and gave the reward to none. But still wishing to find the right answers to his questions, he decided to consult a hermit, widely renowned for his wisdom.

The hermit lived in a wood which he never quitted, and he received none but common folk. So the King put on simple clothes, and before reaching the hermit's cell dismounted from his horse, and, leaving his bodyguard behind, went on alone.

When the King approached, the hermit was digging the ground in front of his hut. Seeing the King, he greeted him and went on digging. The hermit was frail and weak, and each time he stuck his spade into the ground and turned a little earth, he breathed heavily.

The King went up to him and said: "I have come to you, wise hermit, to ask you to answer three questions: How can I learn to do the right thing at the right time? Who are the people I most need, and to whom should I, therefore, pay more attention than to the rest? And, what affairs are the most important and need my first attention?"

The hermit listened to the King, but answered nothing. He just spat on his hand and recommenced digging.

"You are tired," said the King, "let me take the spade and work awhile for you."

"Thanks!" said the hermit, and, giving the spade to the King, he sat down on the ground.

When he had dug two beds, the King stopped and repeated his questions. The hermit again gave no answer, but rose, stretched out his hand for the spade, and said:

"Now rest awhile – and let me work a bit."

But the King did not give him the spade, and continued to dig. One hour passed, and another. The sun began to sink behind the trees, and the King at last stuck the spade into the ground, and said:

"I came to you, wise man, for an answer to my questions. If you can give me none, tell me so, and I will return home."

"Here comes some one running," said the hermit, "let us see who it is."

The King turned round, and saw a bearded man come running out of the wood. The man held his hands pressed against his stomach, and blood was flowing from under them. When he reached the King, he fell fainting on the ground moaning feebly. The King and the hermit unfastened the man's clothing. There was a large wound in his stomach. The King washed it as best he could, and bandaged it with his handkerchief and with a towel the hermit had. But the blood would not stop flowing, and the King again and again removed the bandage soaked with warm blood, and washed and rebandaged the wound. When at last the blood ceased flowing, the man revived and asked for something to drink. The King brought fresh water and gave it to him. Meanwhile the sun had set, and it had become cool. So the King, with the hermit's help, carried the wounded man into the hut and laid him on the bed. Lying on the bed the man closed his eyes and was quiet; but the King was so tired with his walk and with the work he had done, that he crouched down on the threshold, and also fell asleep – so soundly that he slept all through the short summer night. When he awoke in the morning, it was long before he could remember where he was, or who was the strange bearded man lying on the bed and gazing intently at him with shining eyes.

"Forgive me!" said the bearded man in a weak voice, when he saw that the King was awake and was looking at him.

"I do not know you, and have nothing to forgive you for," said the King.

"You do not know me, but I know you. I am that enemy of yours who swore to revenge himself on you, because you executed his brother and seized his property. I knew you had gone alone to see the hermit, and I resolved to kill you on your way back. But the day passed and you did not return. So I came out from my ambush to find you, and I came upon your bodyguard, and they recognized me, and wounded me. I escaped from them, but should have bled to death had you not dressed my wound. I wished to kill you, and you have saved my life. Now, if I live, and if you wish it, I will serve you as your most faithful slave, and will bid my sons do the same. Forgive me!"

The King was very glad to have made peace with his enemy so easily, and to have gained him for a friend, and he not only forgave him, but said he would send his servants and his own physician to attend him, and promised to restore his property.

Having taken leave of the wounded man, the King went out into the porch and looked around for the hermit. Before going away he wished once more to beg an answer to the questions he had put. The hermit was outside, on his knees, sowing seeds in the beds that had been dug the day before.

The King approached him, and said:

"For the last time, I pray you to answer my questions, wise man."

"You have already been answered!" said the hermit still crouching on his thin legs, and looking up at the King, who stood before him.

"How answered? What do you mean?" asked the King.

"Do you not see?" replied the hermit. "If you had not pitied my weakness yesterday, and had not dug these beds for me, but had gone your way, that man would have attacked you, and you would have repented of not having stayed with me. So the most important time was when you were digging the beds; and I was the most important man; and to do me good was your most important business. Afterwards, when that man ran to us, the most important time was when you were attending to him, for if you had not bound up his wounds he would have died without having made peace with you. So he was the most important man, and what you did for him was your most important business. Remember then: there is only one time that is important – Now! It is the most important time because it is the only time when we have any power. The most necessary man is he with whom you are, for no man knows whether he will ever have dealings with any one else: and the most important affair is, to do him good, because for that purpose alone was man sent into this life!"

1903

OTHER TITLES FROM PLOUGH

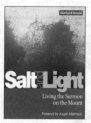

SALT AND LIGHT
Living the Sermon on the Mount
Eberhard Arnold

Talks and writings on the transformative power of a life lived by Jesus' revolutionary teachings in the Sermon on the Mount.

GOD'S REVOLUTION
Justice, Community, and the Coming Kingdom
Eberhard Arnold

Topically arranged excerpts from the author's talks and writings on the church, community, marriage and family issues, government, and world suffering.

WHY WE LIVE IN COMMUNITY
with two interpretive talks by Thomas Merton
Eberhard Arnold

A time-honored manifesto that adds a fresh, engaging voice to the vital discussion of the basis, meaning, and purpose of community.

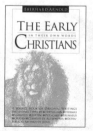

THE EARLY CHRISTIANS
In Their Own Words
Edited by Eberhard Arnold

A topically arranged collection of primary sources that provides a guide and yardstick for Christians today. This is a book that all students, priests, librarians, and history lovers will want on their shelves.

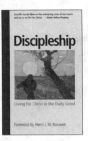

DISCIPLESHIP
Living for Christ in the Daily Grind
J. Heinrich Arnold

A collection of thoughts on following Christ in the nitty-gritty of daily life. Includes sections on love, humility, forgiveness, leadership, community, suffering, salvation, and the kingdom of God.

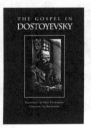

THE GOSPEL IN DOSTOYEVSKY
Edited by the Bruderhof

An introduction to the "great, God-haunted Russian" comprised of passages from *The Brothers Karamazov, Crime and Punishment,* and *The Idiot.*

THE VIOLENCE OF LOVE
Oscar Romero
Comp. and transl. by J. R. Brockman, S.J.

In Romero's words we encounter a man of God humbly and confidently calling us to conversion and action. Those who let his message touch them will never see life in the same way again.

ACTION IN WAITING
Christoph Blumhardt
Afterword by Karl Barth

Grasp the joy of losing yourself in service to God and others. Blumhardt, in his quest to get to the essentials of faith, burns away the religious trappings of modern piety like so much chaff.

F

SEEKING PEACE
Notes and Conversations Along the Way
J. Christoph Arnold

Seeking Peace explores many facets of humankind's ageless search for peace. It plumbs a wealth of spiritual traditions and draws on the wisdom of some exceptional (and some very ordinary) people who have found peace in surprising places.

WHY FORGIVE?
J. Christoph Arnold

Stories of real people scarred by crime, betrayal, abuse, and bigotry, who have earned the right to tell you that forgiveness is the only way to whole-